Descent Into Paradise

P. Sinclair

"The path to paradise begins in hell." ~ *Dante Alighieri*

Published by Clink Street Publishing 2015

Copyright © P. Sinclair 2015

*The author asserts the moral right under the Copyright, Designs and Patents Act 1988
to be identified as the author of this work.*

*All rights reserved. No part of this publication may be reproduced, stored in a retrieval system
or transmitted, in any form or by any means without the prior consent of the author, nor be
otherwise circulated in any form of binding or cover other than that which it is published and
without a similar condition being imposed on the subsequent purchaser.*

*ISBN: 978-1-909477-99-5
Ebook: 978-1-910782-00-2*

CHAPTER 1

JUNE 5, 1967
ISRAEL TEL NOF AIR FORCE BASE
OPERATION MOKED

Having completed their final briefing, the pilots of the 105th Squadron boarded their aircraft. Six minutes later, the lead French built Dassault Mirage 111C roared off the runway, its destination 240 nautical miles southwest; estimated flight time to target, 38 minutes. As the bluish green waters of the Mediterranean raced a mere 100 feet beneath the belly of his supersonic aircraft, the Squadron leader listened intently as sixteen clicks came over his headset. Satisfied the entire Squadron was now safely in the air, his attention shifted to the mission ahead. Operating under strict radio silence, there would be no further communication before reaching their target.

Twenty feet beneath the bustling streets of Tel Aviv, the acrid smell of smoke and body odor permeated the underground bunker as tensions began to mount. Peering intently at the operations map, the Israeli Defense Minister watched in silence as 48 black magnets, each representing an Israeli warplane, moved across the Mediterranean towards the Egyptian coast.

In stark contrast to the thousands of Israeli commuters innocently going about their daily existence just above, the men and women of the Israeli Defense Force General Command fully appreciated the gravity of their current situation. Of the 200 planes available for combat, the Israeli Air Force had just committed 188 to this first strike, leaving only twelve fighters to defend the skies over Israel against enemy attack. Operation Moked, as the Defense Minister was keenly aware, was the ultimate gamble of a desperate nation. The final decision to launch a preemptive airstrike, made the previous evening, had been his alone, and now he bore the weight of that decision as the very fate of Israel depended upon its outcome.

JUNE 4, 1967
JERUSALEM

Lieutenant Jacob Datre awoke to the calls for morning prayer, a daily ritual for Muslim inhabitants living in the old Jewish Quarter. Having unexpectedly been given the weekend off by his General, he had invited his wife, Eileen, to meet him at the King David Hotel. Despite the fact their flat was only a short distance away, Jacob, having always dreamed of staying at Israel's most prestigious hotel, decided he would do so in case he never got another chance. Ensconced in one of the hotel's luxurious top floor suites, the young couple enjoyed a wild weekend of parties, expensive dinners, and intense lovemaking, hoping beyond hope a new addition to the family might be the blessed outcome.

Sunday morning found them lying in bed happily exhausted, at least until the phone rang rudely intruding upon their private paradise.

"That was General Argov."

By the look on her husband's face, Eileen knew their romantic weekend had come to its conclusion.

"I must go. I want you to drive up to Ben Ami today. You can stay with my parents until this is over. It will be safer up there."

Eileen, looking into his eyes, then asked the question all Israelis wanted an answer to:

"What's going to happen, Jacob?"

"We will attack Egypt first with everything we've got. If we are able to defeat them quickly and decisively, then we stand a chance. If not, then we will all be in God's hands."

"The Sinai?"

Jacob, knowing the enemy would love to discover where Israel's elite Commando Unit was heading, knew he was breaching security when he answered simply, "Yes."

Eileen knew better than to ask any more questions, or to tell him to be careful. Their generation of young Sabras would rather die fighting than submit to the degradation suffered by their forefathers. Her faith in him, and all the soldiers like him, gave her the strength to face whatever fate had in store for them. As he finished getting ready, she told him once more how much she loved him. Having lost her own parents, she knew she could best support him by being there for his.

"Don't worry about us, I will take care of your parents until you get back."

JUNE 5, 1967

At 07h30, approximately twelve miles off the Egyptian coast, the Israeli pilots came out of hiding. Igniting their afterburners, they went supersonic as they climbed to 6,000 feet to commence their bombing runs. Caught completely unaware, Egyptian air control suddenly picked up all 48 planes as they gained altitude. This was the moment the Israeli Generals feared. If the Egyptian fighters were aloft, the Mirage, burdened by its heavy armament, was no match for the advanced MIG 21 fighters supplied to the Egyptians by the Russians. Fortunately for the Israelis, the Egyptian pilots were creatures of habit, and, as predicted, were all enjoying their morning breakfast when 48 fighter bombers, two to a runway, screamed straight over their unprotected airfields, each releasing two 500 kilogram high explosive bombs approximately 300 yards apart. The attack plan called for the initial strike force to utilize these 'bunker busters', to render the Egyptian airfields inoperable. Minutes later, now unable to take off, some 290 aircraft, virtually the entire Egyptian Air Force, helplessly awaited the next wave of Israeli aircraft already en route.

JUNE 6, 1967
TEL AVIV

Reports continued to pour into the War Room depicting one victory after another. An exhausted Defense Minister couldn't believe his good fortune. Having ordered complete radio silence on all news coming from the front, only he and his top command knew of the incredible destruction inflicted upon both the Egyptian Air Force and their armored divisions in the Sinai. Not only was the Egyptian Air Force destroyed, the Israelis had managed to knock out both the Jordanian and Syrian Air Forces as well. On only the second full day of operations, the Israelis were now in complete control of the skies. Without air cover, the Egyptian Army was suffering debilitating losses as they beat a hasty retreat. Long lines of burned out vehicles now stretched across the desert in their wake, the napalm bombs causing untold damage on the helpless convoys below.

As the Israelis celebrated this wholesale slaughter, their one area of concern remained Jerusalem. Despite an Israeli offer of peace, the Jordanians, whose army had been placed under the direct control of the Egyptians, chose instead to launch an assault on Jerusalem. Unwilling to use their air force in the Holy City, the task of taking Jerusalem fell into the hands of Israel's elite paratroopers.

General Argov, commander of the famed Special Forces Unit, Sayeret Matkin, looked forward to a good night's rest. Having routed the Egyptian armored divisions in the Sinai with a furious all night attack, it was clear to him their forces were now in full retreat, heading back towards the Suez Canal in total disarray. Central Command, having reached the same conclusion, now ordered his troops back to Jerusalem.

The General waited until dinner to deliver the news. Hot and exhausted after 24 hours of continuous combat, he had decided to spend the night in the desert and move out in the morning. His men needed the rest, and he supposed the Jordanians wouldn't mind living one more day.

Lieutenant Jacob Datre and his men were only too glad to leave the blazing heat of the Sinai. For Jacob, Jerusalem was not only home but the holiest city in the world, one deserving of being liberated from the clutches of the Jordanian Muslims. Apparently, he was not the only one who shared that belief. His General may be agnostic, but the elite troops he commanded were clearly not.

JUNE 8, 1967
WEST BANK – ABU DIS

The Egyptian General in charge of the Jordanian Legion had set up headquarters in the small village of Abu Dis just east of the Old City of Jerusalem. Trained by the British during the Second World War, the General knew the caliber of the troops under his command. They were well-disciplined and well-armed. The problem was, they were not well motivated. Despite the alliance formed between King Hussein and the Egyptians, that piece of paper had not translated into any loyalty as both sides continued to distrust the other. The Jordanians had fought hard up to this point, but now, with both their air forces effectively grounded, the General knew, as did his Jordanian counterparts, that the end result of this conflict had already been determined. With the Israeli paratroopers edging their way towards his position just east of Jerusalem, his instinct for survival gradually overcame his military training. After all, he reasoned, the bulk of the inhabitants in Abu Dis were Palestinians so no Egyptian blood would be spilled. As fate would have it, his orders to retreat were timely. Using the cover of darkness to pull out his troops, the only ones left to counter the Israeli Special Forces attack were the poor souls who lived there.

Emir Nabile, whose family had been forced out of their home in Palestine during the fighting in 1948, had no intention of repeating that exercise. He, and his fellow Palestinian fighters, watched in dismay as the Jordanians prepared to leave. In a heated discussion with the Egyptian General, Emir tried to convince him to stay and fight . His only response was to advise the Palestinians to leave as well, the sooner the better. In a war council convened shortly thereafter, it was decided amongst the men of the village that they would rather die fighting the hated Jews than be uprooted once again; the only concession agreed to by some being the evacuation of their women and children. The rest simply refused to leave their homes. Abu Nabile, aged twelve, begged his father to allow him to remain and fight.

"My son, you have the heart of a lion, and your request makes your father proud indeed. If it were not for the wellbeing of your beloved mother, I might be persuaded to say yes. For her sake, I must ask that you do as I say." Holding up his hand to fend off the furious protest he knew was coming, he went on. "Son, you are young to carry the mantle of head of the family, but sometimes life is not fair. Take your mother to Beirut, there we have friends who will assist you. If I survive, I will find you. If not, I have no doubt you will grow up to become a fierce warrior. Then, you shall avenge my death and all those who died fighting to defend their homeland. Now go. May Allah protect you and grant you eternal peace." Those were the last words the young boy heard his father speak.

The first artillery shells exploded into the center of Abu Dis just before dawn. Thousands of tiny metal shards ripped through paper-thin walls, killing all those still asleep in their beds. Screams of terror pierced the night as fires erupted throughout the village. Crackling flames, fueled by dry thatched roofs, leapt into the air, consuming everything in their path.

General Argov ordered his men to move out as the artillery fire subsided. They were greeted by the familiar sound of AK-47s on full automatic. Today, the Israelis would pay for this real estate in blood. A brief, but intense, firefight ensued ending only when the last Palestinian fighter died, a single bullet to the head ending his misery. Six Israeli commandos died in the skirmish, twelve were wounded, two seriously, a heavy toll for a unit of 45 elite soldiers.

The firefight over, they cautiously made their final approach towards the village square. The eerie wailing of distraught women mourning their dead pierced the early morning air. Entering the square, they were greeted by three elderly women shaking their fists in the air and shouting obscenities. The response was one short burst of gunfire, followed by silence. As the sun finally made an appearance, Jacob, who had suffered a slight wound to his upper left arm, saw her first. The young girl sat motionless atop the ruins of what had once been her home. Jacob heard a click. Acting purely on instinct, he thrust his rifle barrel up to deflect the soldier's aim. The bullet sailed harmlessly into the air.

"Hold your fire," he shouted.

As they came closer, the little girl turned to run, but the mound of rubble beneath her gave way. Tumbling to the ground, she rolled over several times before ending up in a tangle of limbs, blood oozing down her face from a deep cut over her left eye. Jacob knelt down to check her pulse as a medic came running up beside him.

"Let me take care of her, Lieutenant," he said in a brusque tone.

The stench of human excrement mixed with burning corpses assailed his nostrils as Jacob surveyed the village. Charred bodies, large and small, lay smoldering near the ruins of burning homes. All that remained of Abu Dis was death and destruction. When he finally realized the fight was over, Jacob allowed himself a smile; Jews from all over the world would rejoice tonight. Jerusalem was now part of Israel.

The young Palestinian girl opened her eyes to see the medic sitting beside her. Raising her head slightly, she felt a throbbing pain shoot through her eyes, forcing a tiny yelp. Terrified and unsure of the soldier's intentions, she watched as he handed over his canteen. Sensing he meant no harm, she accepted. Then in fluent Arabic, he asked her name.

"Shasa," came the squeaky reply.

"Shasa, what a pretty name," he smiled. "How are you feeling?"

"My head hurts." Reaching up to show him, she felt the large gauze bandage covering her forehead.

Walking back, Jacob could see the girl was now sitting up.

"How's the patient, doctor?"

"She has a nasty cut, but she will be fine, if left alone."

The past 72 hours had witnessed many atrocities on both sides. In four days of bloody fighting, the commandos had not taken a single prisoner, having neither the facilities to deal with them nor any desire to take any. The young medic was certainly within his right to be disgusted, thought Jacob as countless women and children had died as a result. Choosing to ignore the rebuke and simply rejoice in the liberation of Jerusalem, Jacob motioned for the young man to follow. "The men are setting up camp. We are standing down until further orders."

CHAPTER 2

SEPTEMBER 1981

The Boeing 747 Jumbo jet first encountered the storm flying at 37,000 feet some 220 miles west of Ben Gurion Airport. The pilot, alerted to heavy turbulence by air traffic control, clicked on his microphone requesting all passengers be seated with their seatbelts securely fastened.

Both General George Bradley and Major Pete Watson glanced out the window as the sky darkened on the horizon. "Looks a bit menacing," Pete remarked.

"Sure does," replied the General. "This part of the world can be just that."

For the Major, this was his first trip to Israel. The youthful-looking son of a Maine lobsterman had the US Armed Forces to thank for expanding his horizon past the cold Atlantic waters of the Penobscot Bay. Boston University offered him a full scholarship through the Army's Reserve Officers Training Corps program, better known as ROTC. Initially seeing the army strictly as a means to a quality education, he surprised himself by remaining on after his initial mandatory tour of duty expired. Now, years later, a veteran of numerous special ops missions, this quiet soft-spoken soldier exuded confidence and a dry sense of humor infectious to all those around him. His tough yet friendly demeanor had earned him the respect of his peers as well as that of his superior officers. This trip was the result of his most recent promotion: command of the Army's elite anti-terrorist group, a highly secretive black operations team made up of Army Rangers and some of his fellow Delta Force commandos. General Bradley had recently been tasked by the incoming President to put together a rapid response team for the sole purpose of directly combating what the President, and many others, viewed as a growing threat to American security both at home and abroad, namely international terrorism. Bradley's first move was to bring Watson on board and his next was to schedule this trip to Israel.

During the long flight over the Atlantic, Pete heard firsthand what his new commanding officer had in mind.

"The truth is, we're not yet equipped to fight these terrorist organizations effectively, and our intelligence community has its finger so far up its ass they can't even find that.

Hell, if it were left up to me, I would shit-can all those overpaid bureaucrats at Langley, and use that money to pay the Israelis to tell us what they know."

Pete, smiling inwardly, was beginning to enjoy his new commander.

"You want to know what I want out of this trip, Major? It's real simple. I want to establish a direct link with the Israeli military as well as their intelligence service. Nobody knows more about combating terrorism than Mossad and the Israeli Special Forces. Son, you are about to meet the best-trained, best-informed counter terrorist outfit in the world today. We are going to school, soldier. You're going to learn every trick these Israelis ever thought of. Then you're going to come up with a few of your own. In the end, we're going to field the best goddamned counter-terrorist force in the world, understood?"

"Yes, sir," Pete answered emphatically. "But—"

The General, clearly not accustomed to anything beyond 'Yes, sir', nodded reluctantly.

"Why would the Israelis be willing to share their intelligence with us?"

The General gave him a big smile as he leaned back in his seat, looking out the window. "You just leave that with me."

Descent Into Paradise

General Yuri Argov sat staring out his office window. Rain pelted against the glass, driven by an angry northeast wind howling down from the Golan Heights. A wicked bolt of lightning heralded yet another thunderous roar from the heavens. He watched curiously as the weathered window frame, warped and peeling from years of abuse, fought bravely to resist yet another onslaught of water fighting to get inside. The 54-year old army general slumped back against his worn leather chair.

A knock on the door interrupted his thoughts, "Excuse me, General, I've just received word that our guests will be delayed at least one hour. Apparently, no flights are being allowed to land due to weather." With that pronouncement, his striking female assistant turned to leave.

"Thank you Shasa, please let me know when they arrive."

As he watched her gently close the door, he was once again struck by the transformation of this very accomplished young woman from the frightened little girl he had first seen sitting atop the ruins of what had been her home. He once again thanked God, and his young lieutenant, for persuading him to bring this young child back to Israel. Lord knows she had repaid him many times over for that simple act of mercy. The irony of an Israeli Defense Minister employing a full-blooded Palestinian as a staff assistant was certainly not lost upon him, but the fact was, while not Jewish, she had grown up in Israel, her adopted parents were both Israelis, and, quite frankly, that was good enough for him.

Satisfied by his own straightforward reasoning, the General's mind returned to the present. Israel found herself facing yet another threat. Equally menacing as either the Six Day War or the Yom Kippur War, this conflict would not be decided on the battlefield. This time, bombs wouldn't be delivered by planes or armored divisions but rather by civilians who appeared perfectly harmless. Reminiscent of the World War II kamikazes of Japan, these human sacrificial lambs were willing to die for their cause and take as many innocent lives as they could with them. To make matters worse, in the past month alone, Israeli intelligence had detected more than two dozen new Iranian operatives in southern Lebanon. Sent in by the new Islamic regime in Iran, whose recent rise to power had been fueled by their pledge of the total destruction of the Jewish state, their presence had further exacerbated an already disturbing increase in terrorist raids launched into northern Israel.

Funded and trained by the Iranians and Syrians, the Hezbollah terrorist group, as they called themselves, was proving to be far more militant and dangerous than Arafat's Palestinian Liberation Organization. The General knew something must be done, and soon.

"General, your guests have arrived," announced Shasa. A few moments later, General Argov embraced General Bradley as Shasa and Major Watson looked on.

"George, it has been much too long. How nice to see you."

"Yuri, it seems like only yesterday we were roasting in those bloody tanks of yours treading through the desert."

"Oh, those were the days, old friend. We surely taught those damned Egyptians a lesson in armored warfare."

The two generals then lost themselves in old war stories. Pete looked up, noticing Shasa's reaction with some amusement. Apparently, this was not the first time the General's assistant had been subjected to these stories. While listening politely, Pete found himself paying more attention to the long legs perched in the chair directly opposite him. The conversation eventually turned serious as Argov gave his guests a quick overview of the region's politics.

"The Iranians have made it clear that they intend to replace Arafat and his PLO with their own organization, Hezbollah as they call themselves, to wage war on us from southern Lebanon. And the Syrians are pouring money and materials into Lebanon as if they had already annexed it."

"What will Israel do?" questioned Bradley. Pausing, General Argov looked around the room before he answered calmly.

"George, we have no option other to invade Lebanon and clear our border of these vermin."

"Yuri, that is a rather bold move. Are you suggesting your government has already made that decision?"

"Yes," came the simple reply.

"We realize the furor this will create in the international community, but, quite frankly, at this point we simply have no choice."

The conversation then turned to the purpose of the Americans' visit.

"George, I have spoken with the commander of our Sayeret Matkin commando unit, and he is looking forward to this joint exercise. What else can I do to assist?"

"Yuri, as you know, my boys will be flying directly into Palmachim Air Force Base tomorrow, but I first wanted you to meet their commander, Major Peter Watson. Peering over the top of his half-rimmed glasses directly at the young American, the Israeli Defense Minister's voice betrayed some emotion as he spoke.

"Major, your General has been a devoted friend of Israel for many years. As you just heard, we fought the Egyptians together in the Sinai desert in '73 and have remained close friends ever since. I have arranged for you to train with my old outfit, one of the most revered units of the Israeli Defense Force. Simply put, Sayeret Matkin is the tip of the Israeli spear. I trust you will both learn something useful from each other to our mutual benefit."

As he looked straight into the General's dark gray eyes, Pete responded, "General, we hold your special forces in the highest regard and look forward to working together."

Descent Into Paradise

Bradley then added, "Watson here is a fine soldier, one of the best we've got. But quite honestly, Yuri, while our boys are solid, they're inexperienced in your type of warfare. What I really want to find out is can our troops operate with yours so, if necessary, we'll be ready to go into action and work seamlessly together? Hell, everyone knows you have the best counter-terrorist units in the world, and we are here to learn from the best."

"That is most kind of you to say," responded General Argov. "The fact is most of our weapons are manufactured in the States; so that shouldn't be an issue, and nearly all our commandos speak some English. I honestly don't believe the problem will be a military one. It's the politics I worry about."

Bradley nodded, adding, "As to politics, I recently had the pleasure of meeting our newly elected President. Let me assure you Yuri, this is one tough son of a bitch who is not a bit confused about where he stands on terrorism, or those damned drug cartels for that matter. The truth is, he views both as a direct threat to the security of the United States and has charged me with the task of assembling a rapid response force to deal with these people wherever they choose to hide. Believe me when I tell you we are in this together, old friend, you have my personal assurance of that."

The meeting ended with General Argov apologizing for not being able to join them for dinner.

Alone in his office once again, Argov contemplated what he had just heard. Would the Americans finally be willing to commit their combat troops to the war against these terrorists? His thoughts drifted back to 1955 when, as a raw recruit, he remembered the words of the great David Ben Gurion. "Never forget," the old man had said of the Arab leaders, "from their point of view, we stole their land. They do not care if God bequeathed this land to us, for their God is not our God. They do not care about Hitler and Nazi Germany; that has nothing to do with them." He had ended by reminding his audience that the only thing standing between survival and the ultimate Armageddon was the Israeli Defense Force. Looking skyward, Argov whispered to the great man's spirit, "And, by the grace of God, the American army."

CHAPTER 3

BEIRUT
SHATILA CAMP

The heat shimmering off the corrugated metal roofs obscured the squalid scene of camp life at midday. The shouting of angry mothers, overwrought by their inability to care for their young, mixed with the crying of babies and shrieking youngsters. This incessant noise was the background for the men at Nouri's Café, as they sat and pondered their next move.

Three plastic tables, the entire seating capacity of the café, were brought together for the nine men in attendance. The young skinny blond boy waiting on tables hurried back and forth from the kitchen, bringing the men first their ouzos and then their lunch. Old Nouri had given him a white shirt, several sizes too large and not exactly spotless. His faded red apron fell just above his black sneakers. Very proud of his new uniform, the boy desperately tried to play the part.

Back in the kitchen, Mr. Nouri, who was busily placing small glasses of ouzo on a tray, whispered, "Moussa, I want you to listen very carefully to everything these men say. After they leave, you must tell me all that you heard." With that, he shuffled off to his antiquated grill and began cooking lunch.

Outside, the dark haired stranger suddenly pounded his fist on the table as he spoke. "The Israelis are going to invade, and they're not going to stop before they kill all of you!"

At the head of the table sitting quietly sat the undisputed leader of Shatila, the very popular Abu Nabile., Abu had invited Colonel Mir to lunch so that his key lieutenants could hear what the Iranian had to say. Mir had arrived in Beirut several months ago from Tehran, tasked with the assignment of building an alternative military organization to Arafat's PLO. His argument, which had proven quite persuasive, was simply that Arafat, unable to muster any significant support from within the Arab world, now found himself isolated and unable to fight the Israelis with any meaningful results. Mir had contacted Abu several weeks earlier hoping to persuade him to join forces with Hezbollah, thereby giving the young upstart group greater credibility amongst the young Palestinian fighters. Up to this point, Abu had not been inclined to do so. Now, he questioned the Iranian's assumption that Israel planned to attack the Palestinian refugee camps located on the very outskirts of Beirut.

"Do you really believe the Israelis would dare attack Beirut itself? I can't believe the Americans would sit back and allow that to happen."

"Forget the Americans. I'm telling you that's exactly what those bastards are preparing to do. Sharon intends to eliminate the PLO as an effective fighting force once and for all, and to do that he must come here."

Moussa listened as best he could while appearing not to.

After lunch, Mr. Nouri always closed the café for his midday nap. Today, however, he put two dishes of food on the table and motioned to Moussa.

"Sit down, boy, and help yourself, but first tell me everything you heard." Mr. Nouri, anxious to hear what had been discussed between Abu and this stranger, sat down quietly stroking his long white beard. Moussa then relayed all he remembered, including what the Colonel had said about the Israelis attacking Shatila. The old man listened intently then, without any acknowledgement, got up from the table. "Please clean up when you are finished and be sure to lock the door when you leave."

Taking pity on the emaciated youngster, he added, "There is some leftover pita bread on the stove. Take it home if you want, it won't be any good tomorrow. Please be back early in the morning." Then, he slowly made his way out the door.

Moussa wasted no time stuffing food into his mouth, afraid someone might take it before he finished. Leaning back in his chair with a satisfied grin, he realized that this was the first time since he left the orphanage that he had been given a meal. Everything came at a price; that much he had learned. Pita bread safely tucked under his shirt, he locked the door and went home.

Home was a short walk away tucked in the northeastern corner of the camp. Moussa had discovered this hideaway, hidden from view by a dirt embankment, when playing hide and seek with friends. He could clearly remember climbing the dirt hill, tripping over the top and hitting his head on something hard. It turned out to be an old abandoned concrete sewer pipe. Vines had grown all around it, hiding the opening from view. Having used it to elude his playmates more than once, he came to the conclusion his hiding place would make the perfect home. Too old to stay in the camp orphanage, he had slept outside during the summer, but the winter months proved to be too cold. Now he had his own place, private and secluded, where he could stay warm and block out the human misery surrounding him. One of many orphans living in the camp, he had literally grown up alone. He had learned the hard way how to survive. Fortunately, he was very good at it. Just barely a teenager, Moussa had his own home, a job, food to eat, and clothes to wear. He was certainly well off, at least by Shatila standards.

CHAPTER 4

The huge Lockheed C-5 Galaxy touched down, dwarfing the two Israeli fighter jets escorting it into Israel's largest air force base.

As 110 American commandos descended onto Israeli soil, curious onlookers watched as the nose cone of the massive cargo plane opened to disgorge the latest hardware developed for the US Army's elite Rangers and Delta Force. Jet-black Sikorsky-built Black Hawk helicopters descended slowly to the ground followed by the smaller but lethal dark green Apache 64 gunships. With their rotor blades neatly folded, they looked rather harmless exiting their imposing fixed-wing transport. Soon, however, with rotors fully extended, their thumping would strike fear into the souls of any poor bastards unlucky enough to confront the Special Forces currently assembling.

The eagerly awaited joint exercises began with a short briefing by General Argov. "First, let me welcome our American friends to Israel. As everyone here knows, we are currently faced with an unprecedented rise in incidents of terrorism worldwide. Today, in this room, are assembled some of the most capable soldiers our two countries have ever produced. Together, we will stamp out this evil wherever we find it."

Pausing briefly, Argov continued, "Over the next several days, General Bradley and I hope to integrate our respective forces into one operational unit capable of striking the enemy wherever he may choose to hide. We Israelis respect the proud history and the indisputable prowess of the American armed forces and stand ready to learn from the best combat soldiers the world has ever witnessed. Now, I am honored to present my good friend, General George Bradley of the United States Army."

General Bradley rose and made his way to the podium.

"Gentlemen, the President of the United States recently charged me with the task of developing a combat force ready and able to defend the security of the United States against any terrorist force, regardless of where they may choose to base their operations." Looking slowly around the auditorium, "I believe you gentlemen present are all that stand between maintaining our democracies as we know them and the chaos our enemies would hope to inflict upon us. Our respective governments are elected to make policies, but it is up to us in the military to enforce those policies. From this day forward, our enemies will soon learn that acts of terrorism will come at a very heavy price. You, gentlemen, are that price."

After the Generals' introductory remarks concluded, Pete sensed someone approaching from behind. He turned as a tall, dark-complexioned Israeli officer extended his hand and laughingly joked, "Major Watson, allow me to introduce myself and welcome you personally. I am Major Zev Megrid, the unfortunate commander of these Army rejects."

Pete rose and the two men silently sized each other up like two boxers entering the ring. Facing Pete was a very handsome and charming young Sabra whose warm smile belied the steely gaze which transfixed his American counterpart.

For the next hour, the two majors discussed their upcoming schedule and logistics. To their mutual surprise, what began as a purely professional discussion soon flowed into more of a personal one.

The following day, soldiers from both countries stood side-by-side, comparing weaponry and combat equipment. Both

Descent Into Paradise

Special Forces used the American-made Apache 64 gunship for fire support and the Black Hawk helicopter for troop insertions. The standard assault rifle of choice for both was the Colt CAR. As for heavier firepower, the Israelis favored the Israeli made Uzi submachine gun.

All in all, their heavy equipment, most of which was indeed manufactured in the US, was virtually identical. As to tactics, both favored lightning-quick raids, coming in by helicopter below the enemy's radar, always at night. Again, American technology was favored using advanced fire-control systems enabling pilots to light up their targets regardless of visibility. Fast roping down was an art both Special Forces were adept at, each preferring it to inherent risks of disembarking on the ground.

That evening, after a full day of strategic exercises, the two squadrons ate dinner together. In the Delta Force, soldiers, officers, and other related military personnel ate at the same table. There were no Officer Clubs, just pure respect, and it showed.

Most of the Israeli soldiers spoke some English, and all were quite interested in learning more about life in America.

The following morning at dawn, the Americans began the exercises role-playing as 'terrorists'. Three hours later, the neutral military advisors ruled all the 'terrorists' officially killed. Clearly, General Bradley's view of the Israelis' prowess had not been an exaggeration. That evening, the Americans held a special meeting without their hosts, directed by one very irate commanding officer. The following day saw quite a different outcome. This time, the number of Israeli 'terrorist casualties' far exceeded those of their American counterparts. That evening at dinner more than a few heated conversations were conducted, solely in Hebrew.

Descent Into Paradise

As both Special Forces concluded their joint exercises at Palmachim, a black Citroen glided to a stop opposite a small, unobtrusive red brick building. Located in a quiet residential suburb of Tel Aviv, the dwelling appeared to be just another private residence. Shasa, sitting quietly in the back seat, knew better. As she waited patiently for General Argov to appear, she knew something important was in the making. She had only seen this building once before; it was the only time she had witnessed her boss truly irate. He never shared with her why, but she knew he didn't have much use for whatever transpired inside. Argov interrupted her thoughts by opening the rear door. As General Bradley climbed in the front seat, Argov instructed his driver to take them to the Air Base.

"Damn good meeting!" Bradley exclaimed as they pulled away.

"George, let me just caution you, the Director and I go back a long way," Argov replied with little enthusiasm. "All I will say is that you never know if that man is telling the whole truth or just his version of what he wants you to believe."

Bradley knew Argov and the Director didn't get along, but, since he needed both, he kept his comments neutral.

"Despite all our high-tech gadgets, Yuri, your Director has forgotten more about these terrorist cells than all the intelligence our CIA has compiled in its database. We just need to persuade that little son of a bitch to share some of his dirty little secrets with us. Then, you and I can have the pleasure of sending those Islamic zealots straight to Allah's Paradise so they can screw all those damned virgins they keep bragging about. Martyrs, my ass. Why those stupid bastards think they're going anywhere other than hell when they blow themselves to smithereens is beyond me."

"George," said Argov with a sigh, "many of these young men have simply given up on life. They have grown up in squalid camps with no hope for the future and, as such, become prime recruits for these religious fanatics whose hatred of us consumes their daily existence. We Jews find ourselves living in a cauldron of hatred, and I'm afraid it is just a matter of time before it boils over."

Shasa listened to the conversation intently, for she had become increasingly curious as to exactly how the Israeli Intelligence Service operated. She could remember many dinner conversations at home when her father spoke of Mossad in almost reverential terms. To him, they were Israel's first line of defense. She could hear him lecture, "We may not match them in numbers, but Mossad will always outwit them."

The car began to slow as it approached the massive gates leading into Palmachim Air Force Base.

The troops were enjoying their final dinner together as the two Generals preceded Shasa into the mess hall. Even dressed in standard-issue combat fatigues, Shasa always commanded men's attention. Looking over in Pete's direction, a radiant smile lit her face as she headed towards his table. Somewhat embarrassed but very flattered, Pete stood up to greet her. To his surprise, she ran right past him and straight into the waiting arms of Major Megrid.

"Zev," she cried, "I hoped you would be here. Did you get my letters? You never responded."

Holding up his hand in mock surrender, he put his finger softly over her mouth.

"Hold on, little one," he laughed as he gave her a big hug, lifting her effortlessly off the floor.

Hand-in-hand, they passed tables of admiring and envious men, leaving Pete standing there quite alone.

Once outside, Zev looked for somewhere private where they could sit down and talk.

Descent Into Paradise

"Zev, are you alright? You seem distracted."

"That I am." He laughed. "I must admit, I always picture you as the little girl I left behind in Ben Ami, not the beautiful woman who walked into the mess hall this evening."

Blushing slightly, she laughed as she held his hand a bit tighter.

"Why Major, I never thought you noticed."

"If that were true, I'd have been the only male in that room who didn't."

Shasa had been innocently captivated with this handsome warrior since the first day they had met as children. Other than her adopted Israeli mother, Eileen, Zev was the only person who spoke to her in Arabic. To him, she was always the 'little one'. Shasa had just turned twelve when Zev was forced to leave their kibbutz due to his unruly behavior. Over the past ten years, they had only seen each other on three occasions, most recently two years ago when Zev had come back to visit her family. His stories about the army had intrigued her to the point that she begged her adopted father, Jacob, a former Lieutenant himself in Sayeret Matkin, to allow her to enlist in the Israeli army. After finally relenting, he had brought her to see General Argov, who not only arranged for her to enlist, but also assigned her directly to his personal staff. After they caught each other up on all their news, Zev saw his men begin to exit the mess hall.

"Little one, I need to go. What are you doing tomorrow evening?"

"I have no plans."

"Well, now you do, because you are having dinner with me."

"I would love to." Then, after a momentary hesitation, she asked if they should invite Major Watson to join them.

Zev stopped in his tracks. A thin smile crossed his dark face, exposing bright white teeth.

"That's fine with me, but how do you two even know each other?"

"The truth is I have only met Pete once in General Argov's office before they came to the base," she said defensively.

"Pete, is it? Well, I see the formalities have been dispensed with already."

"Oh Zev, stop it. If you think it best not to include him, that's fine with me. It's you I really want to see anyway."

The next evening, having given their respective troops the night off, the three of them drove to the Barn, a rustic little restaurant set in a small village some ten miles outside of Tel Aviv. The proprietor was an elderly woman who waddled out of the kitchen.

"Come along children, I have a nice table by the fire, very romantic." Noticing Pete's uniform, she asked with a heavy accent, "Where are you from, young man?"

"I was born and raised in a small fishing village on the coast of Maine."

"I have relatives in New York. They always are telling me to come live in America, but I think I am content to die right here."

"Where are you from originally?" Pete asked politely.

"Poland." Pulling up her sleeve, she showed him her wrinkled arm. "Via Auschwitz." She then turned to go back to the kitchen as the waiter arrived with a pitcher of water. After they had ordered drinks, Pete looked across the table.

"I hope I didn't upset her?"

"No, don't worry. She showed you those numbers because she does not want anyone to forget what happened there. In this country, she is regarded as one of God's special children, delivered out of hell for a higher purpose. Israel is that purpose, and she would gladly die defending it."

Descent Into Paradise

As their drinks arrived, Pete offered a toast thanking them for inviting him and toasting everyone's health. He then asked how they knew each other.

Zev proceeded to relate Shasa's celebrated arrival into his small kibbutz directly from the war zone, complete with an armored escort by members of the Israeli military.

"Hell, you would have thought the Queen of Sheba was arriving."

"No, actually, it was someone far more important," Shasa interjected playfully.

"Actually, it was this royal little pain-in-the-ass who thought she was important."

The banter went back and forth until finally the real story came out. Zev described a pixy little seven year old, escorted by Lieutenant Datre, showing up at their one room school, not speaking a word of Hebrew. Confused, Pete asked where she had come from.

"My village was shelled by the Israelis. The soldiers killed everyone else, but, for some reason, they brought me back to Israel. That's how I ended up in Ben Ami."

"When was that?" asked Pete.

"In 1967, during what everyone calls the Six Day War, as it only lasted that short amount of time."

"So you're not Israeli?" Pete asked, mystified.

"My natural parents were Palestinian Muslims, if that is your question."

Zev then turned the conversation to the menu. "Pete, I don't know if you like it, but they are known for their lamb stew and their local wines. This valley produces some of the best grapes in Israel. And while we are on the subject of grapes, I would like to propose a toast to our esteemed guest, Major Pete Watson of the United States Army. I must confess that the troops of Sayeret Matkin have finally met their match."

Pete raised his glass. "Here's to the day we fight together against real terrorists."

Soon large bowls of lamb stew arrived, their rich aroma warming the table.

The conversation then turned to Pete's upbringing and decision to join the Army. Finally, the old lady had to ask them to leave, as she needed to get some sleep.

The next morning, it was with fond farewells that the U.S. and Israeli Special Forces parted company with promises of getting together again to fight real terrorists. As Pete finished packing, an orderly approached him. "There's a car standing by sir, we can leave whenever you are ready."

"I'll be ready in ten minutes, thank you."

Later that day in Tel Aviv, Pete and Zev met with their respective generals for lunch at the Officers Club, briefing them on the results of their combat exercises. In response to the most critical question posed, Pete responded, "Yes, I believe the two forces can interface seamlessly in a combat environment. The basic equipment packages we both use can be easily interchanged; language is the only issue. None of our boys is fluent in Hebrew so we would require English to be the sole language spoken on any future missions."

"I concur," added Zev. "Since most of us speak passable English, I don't see that as an issue."

General Bradley took Pete aside when the meeting concluded. "I need to be at the Pentagon in the morning so I am moving up my departure to this afternoon. I want to congratulate you on a job well done. This Major Megrid fellow speaks very highly of you and your team. According to Argov, his soldiers have enthusiastically endorsed the notion of joint missions in the future."

"Thank you, sir. I feel we held our own out there. And you were right, they're the most competent outfit I've ever trained with."

"I won't need you back until next Wednesday so take a few days off son, you've earned it."

CHAPTER 5

CHILE

The pungent aroma of Havana cigars filled the den of the Rios' Chilean compound as waiters finished serving drinks.

A handsome young man in his late twenties sat patiently behind a large mahogany desk, waiting until the room was quiet, a ploy his late father often used.

"Make them wait and wonder, never rush the discussion, bring all the attention on yourself; that, my boy, has the aroma of power." Juan could hear his father's voice as if he were sitting in the room.

"Gentleman," said Juan Rios finally, "I invited you here tonight to assure you that the family business will continue and hopefully prosper. As is the custom when there is a change of leadership, I will ask you tonight to take a new oath of loyalty to me. But before I ask you to make any commitment, I think it fair to inform you as to what I plan to do. Should any of you then wish to leave, you are welcome to do so. As long as you do nothing to harm our future operations, you will be excused of all your former obligations and may go with my blessing."

Looking slowly around the room, he saw he had everyone's full attention.

"The business model crafted by my father will be maintained, but it is my intention to expand our business internationally. The premature death of my parents, God rest their souls, has served to hasten this decision, for while my father generally approved of what I intend to do, he told me he was simply too old to take it on.

"Tonight marks the beginning of this journey. Gentlemen, now is the time to decide. You are all invited to join me, or to leave and go your own way." He paused for a moment to allow anyone who wished to speak to have the opportunity. To his surprise, not a sound was uttered. "Very well gentlemen, may I ask all of you to raise your glass and swear your oath of loyalty to me as the new head of the Rios family. The oath is as follows so please repeat after me. I swear my loyalty to you, Juan Rios, and agree to be punished by death if I break this oath. I swear this on the head of our blessed Virgin Mary."

They all chorused.

"Gentlemen, I thank you. We will meet here at the house tomorrow morning at 10h30."

Last to leave the meeting was Miguel, head of the family's security force. For the past several years, Miguel had been his father's most trusted lieutenant. As he approached the front door to leave, Juan spoke. "Would you grant me the honor of a moment of your time at this late hour before you leave?"

"Of course Juan, whatever you wish."

The two men walked back to the library where Juan motioned him to sit down.

"Miguel, I wish only to ask you one question. Why did you do it?"

A frown crossed the old man's forehead as he replied, "Do what, Juan? What are you referring to?"

Juan snapped, "Don't play me for the innocent fool, my friend! I know all about your relationships, both financial and amorous. You see, I took the liberty of doing some independent investigative work after the 'accidental' death of my parents. What I have found is really quite troubling. It would seem you are a very wealthy man, Miguel. Either you are extremely frugal, or you have a source of income outside our family business, eh?"

"I swear to you Juan, any monies I have been able to put away have nothing to do with any disloyalty to you or your family. I swear to the Holy Mother on my Bible."

"How about my little Madonna, who would appear to occupy both our beds from time to time. What have you to say about that?"

Juan stared coldly at the older man waiting patiently for his reply as Miguel turned a very pale color.

Miguel bowed his head in shame. "I can not refute that. It is true. I can only offer you my apology and my resignation. She is a most beautiful woman and very difficult to refuse. I am afraid my passion for beautiful women overcame my sense of common decency."

"It is not your resignation I ask for, Miguel, it is your head."

Pulling out a small 9-millimeter pistol, Juan handed it over to his security chief and told him if he were loyal to his oath of tonight, he would know what to do. Asking only for forgiveness, he placed the pistol to his temple and pulled the trigger. It simply clicked on the hammer. Handing him a glass of water, Juan explained. "A guilty man would have turned that gun on me. I'm sorry, my friend, to have put you through this ordeal, but I must know who is truly on our side before we move forward. Someone close to me swore it was you who had set them up. Though it breaks my heart, I think I now know whom our problem is. Go home now, Señor, we will meet tomorrow at ten. Please though, no more evenings with my little pet. You know how jealous I can get."

The next morning, all seven of Juan's lieutenants arrived at the compound amidst very tight security. He began the meeting with his vision for the future.

"The drug cartels of the 1970s failed for several reasons," he began. "They would not, or could not, operate as businesses and they lacked the necessary enforcement mechanism to deal with their competition. My goal is very straightforward. The Rios family is going to run our business in the same manner as any multinational corporation. Our product is desired worldwide; therefore I intend to establish an international distribution network supplied by manufacturing facilities here in South America, as well as the Middle East. Furthermore, I will upgrade our accounting and cash management systems to effectively manage our growth in sales. Finally, I plan to establish an effective private military force to safeguard us from the authorities as well as our competition. If anything can still amaze me, it is the fact that considering the enormous amount of wealth that has been accumulated over the past decade by the various cartels, not one family in South or Central America has put together a first rate security force. Not even our brethren in Colombia have had the foresight to understand the implications of that error."

Juan then went to stand by the fireplace as he continued, "Gentlemen, we intend to begin this audacious plan with a trip to Tel Aviv. There, we have set up a meeting with a member of the Jewish Intelligence Agency and representatives of the South African government. My proposal to them has been to purchase state-of-the-art Israeli arms, which will be paid for using American dollars. These arms will then be shipped out of Haifa in Chilean freighters under the cover of medical supplies. In Valparaiso, where the appropriate harbormasters will be persuaded to look the other way, we will offload those items necessary to arm ourselves. Again, under the guise of medical supplies, we will ship the balance to Cape Town paid for in Swiss francs deposited directly into secure numbered accounts in Switzerland."

Juan paused for effect. "The Israelis sell their excess arms for hard currency, which they desperately need. We arm ourselves and launder large quantities of cash. And the South Africans get around their arms embargo. In other words, everyone benefits."

There were murmurs of assent and admiration from the men sitting around the table. It was indeed an audacious scheme but the way Juan described it, not an impossible one.

Miguel was the first to speak. "Juan, have you approached the interested parties about this already or are you simply conjecturing at this point?"

"My dear Miguel, I am well beyond conjecture. We in fact have a meeting scheduled with the South African ambassador and a representative from Mossad at the South African embassy in Tel Aviv."

Rios's chief henchman, Estoban, then spoke up. "Juan, I thought our President already had some Israeli advisors working for his secret police. How are we going to deal with that?" There was a murmur of voices all discussing this point when Juan casually replied.

"Simple, I have already mentioned this concern to my contacts at Mossad. This entire operation will be kept completely confidential. Pinochet will never know of their involvement. In fact, it is my understanding that the very same ship we will be using to transport our goods will also carry a shipment to our esteemed President as well."

This brought a hearty laugh from everyone.

"Wouldn't that be the ultimate joke on that little prick," said a voice in the background. "We should bury that bastard and all his cronies with his own weapons."

All of a sudden, the laughter died down as all eyes were fixed on the door into the library. Juan turned to see his luscious Madonna enter the room, carrying a large tray full of sandwiches and fruits. Watching with amusement her parading in front of his lieutenants, Juan could not help but admire the sexuality of this extraordinary blonde creature who appeared wearing a black skintight one-piece pants suit, leaving very little to the imagination.

"My dear, since when have you gone to work in the kitchen? I will have to make sure that you are put on the payroll."

Smiling that alluring sexy smile, she demurely replied, "Oh darling, I thought you knew. I have been on the payroll for years."

This brought another round of nervous guffaws from the group. Even Juan had to laugh at her audacity. Of the entire household, only Madonna dared talk back to Juan. Everyone else would have feared for their lives to openly joust with the young new head of the family.

"Well my dear, since you have been duly employed, would you mind bringing us our drinks as well?" Juan asked, as Madonna put the tray down on the big sofa table.

Pushing a strand of her long blonde hair off her face, she sidled up to Juan and cooed, "Certainly, Señor, is that all you desire?"

"That one is nothing but trouble, eh Miguel?"

Miguel squirmed in his seat as he absorbed the jibe. It is well deserved, he thought miserably. How he had ever allowed himself to be taken in by that wild filly, he would never know. Then, thinking of her sculptured body and outrageous behavior, he needed only remember her in bed to know the reason why.

"Now back to business," smiled Juan.

"Ricardo, would you please share with us your plans for structuring the Family finances."

"Certainly, Juan," answered the elegant and brilliant Ricardo Menez. After completing his college education with Juan in the United States, Ricardo had stayed on to attend the

Wharton Business School in Philadelphia. Having grown up together as best friends all their lives, they provided each other the combination of friendship and advice that benefitted both personally as well as the business.

"I would like to begin by stating the main thrust of our financial plan will be to launder our cash income from drug operations into legitimate businesses across the global financial markets. As Juan has just mentioned, we will be using the Israeli/South African connection to convert large sums of cash into Swiss francs through conventional European sources. We will then ask several Swiss banks to invest and manage our portfolios. We also intend to purchase our own bank holding company, most likely in Florida, in order to receive cash deposits through its branches. The bank holding company will be purchased through a friendly takeover using stock purchases made by American nominees. These stock purchases will be totally legitimate and will be funded directly from our Swiss accounts. Innocent American executives who will have no clue as to our involvement will manage the bank. We, in turn, will control the whole operation through the Board of Directors, a majority of whom will of course be beholden directly to us."

He quickly glanced at Juan, who gave him a nod of approval.

"As to the more personal aspects of our plan. Juan has authorized me to set up a personal retirement fund for each of you present today. These individual accounts will be established in various banks throughout Europe and Japan. They will be funded annually based upon a formula tied to the amount of profit generated during that year. It is our hope that each of you will feel that if, for any reason, you desire to retire into a more peaceful existence, you will be able to do so in comfort for both you and your loved ones."

Descent Into Paradise

Of course what Ricardo did not verbalize was his strong feeling that this mechanism would vastly reduce the temptation on the part of these men to sell out the Family for any personal gain.

CHAPTER 6

The village of Ben Ami was nestled in a lush green valley, at the foot of the Golan Heights in the northern part of Israel. Once Shasa learned General Bradley had given Pete the option of remaining in Israel for an extended weekend, she had quickly offered to show him her adopted country.

"Israel is really quite small, so we can see most of it before you have to leave," she had explained, "but I must ask if you would mind terribly if we spent tonight at my parents' house? I promised them I would see them this weekend."

Pete did not hesitate in his acceptance. His curiosity in seeing more of Israel and his delight in spending more time with Shasa made it an easy decision.

When they pulled up to a tiny stone house, a booming voice from inside yelled, "Mama, Mama, Shasa is home, hurry!"

As her father came running out to embrace his daughter, his joy knew no bounds.

After an extended embrace, she shyly introduced him to Pete.

"Papa, I would like you to meet my new American friend, Major Peter Watson."

"Major," said Jacob, "it is my pleasure to welcome you to our home. Please come in. Shasa's mother is just washing up."

"Thank you, sir, I was just telling your daughter how much your village reminds me of where I grew up."

"Please call me Jacob, sir makes me feel like I'm back in the army."

At that moment, Shasa's mother, Eileen, came rushing out of the house. After brief introductions, mother and daughter disappeared, arm in arm, into the house as if the two men didn't exist. Jacob then turned to Pete. "Please forgive us, Major. My wife has not seen Shasa in several months. This is a joyous moment for us, you'll have to excuse our poor manners."

"Please go join them, I know how excited she is to see you both!"

Alone, Pete settled into a very inviting lounge chair to enjoy his first meaningful quiet moment since his arrival. Taking a deep breath, his senses were rewarded by a multitude of subtle fragrances. Purple and red wisteria hung in profusion from the elegant arbors above. Lemons and oranges adorned the small fruit trees, which formed a natural screen from the dirt road winding downhill just beyond. The sound of water trickling from the worn stone fountain partially hidden in the corner completed a setting so serene that Pete, who hadn't slept well in over a week, closed his eyes for a restful moment. When Shasa finally returned, she found him fast asleep.

Eileen, following right behind her with a tray full of assorted appetizers, quietly whispered to let him sleep. Observing Shasa just staring at the American soldier, she needed no feminine intuition to know her child's thoughts or feelings. She simply asked, "How long have you both known each other?"

"We met last week in General Argov's office. Pete came over with the American Special Forces to train with Zev's unit, and the three of us had dinner. We all had such a good time that I offered to show Pete around Israel before he returns back to the States."

"Well, dinner with two handsome devils. Aren't you the lucky girl? How is Zev? Your father and I miss seeing that little rascal."

Pete rose to his feet, still groggy as he heard them talking.

"Please sit down, Major. We didn't mean to wake you."

Descent Into Paradise

As Eileen headed to the kitchen to prepare dinner, Shasa offered to show him around. Pete couldn't help noticing the curious stares directed their way as they wandered down towards a small tributary, which circled the village. Shasa whispered in his ear, "They don't know what to think. They can't believe I am dressed in an Israeli uniform walking beside an American soldier."

Finding a bit of privacy under a big willow tree, they sat quietly, the only sound coming from the water rustling down over its rocky bottom. It was several moments before he turned to Shasa and saw the tears running down her cheeks.

"I'm sorry!" After a short pause, she whispered, "I used to sit here all day by myself. Nobody could make fun of me if they couldn't find me. The only person who ever looked after me was Zev, and he left when I was only twelve."

"What about your family? Any brothers or sisters?"

"No, only me. My grandparents both died shortly after I arrived, and my parents couldn't have children so it was just the three of us. I think that may be one reason I was brought back to Israel."

Dinner that night couldn't have been more enjoyable. She loved being with her parents, and, by the end of dessert, it was apparent a bond was quickly forming between both men. Shasa watched with fascination as they carried on as though they had known each other for years.

"I think Papa likes your young American soldier," remarked Eileen as they washed up after dinner.

"I think so too. Do you like him, Mama?"

"Very much. But I do worry for you. I realize he is only over here for a short time and that obviously puts some pressure on both of you, so please be careful. That's all I'll say."

When Pete came in to thank the ladies for dinner, he announced he was going to turn in early. Shasa and he were leaving in the morning, and Pete wanted her parents to have some time alone with their daughter.

It was almost midnight when Shasa wearily climbed into bed with her parents, something she had not done since she was a little girl. Jacob, who was not one for expressing his feelings readily, volunteered how much he enjoyed talking to her new friend.

"Quite a handsome boy as well."

"Papa," Shasa leaned over to kiss him, "No man could ever compete with you."

Hugging her to his chest, she never saw the tears running down his cheek.

They stayed up for hours talking. Finally, Eileen fell asleep, leaving the two of them to discuss politics. In soft whispers, Shasa recounted her dinner with Pete and Zev. She shared with him her mentioning to Pete that her birth parents were Palestinian Muslims and the look of shock on Pete's face.

"Tell me, Shasa, how would you feel if you were made to choose sides?"

"I don't really know, Papa. I still don't understand why you forced my people off their land? What did they do to you?" It was, of course, the ultimate question at the very core of all this violence and hatred.

Jacob held her hand as he struggled for a reply. "You first must understand one sacred point. For centuries, we Jews have suffered various forms of persecution. Finally, we have come home as ordained by God in the Torah. We will never give this up because it is all we have. There is nowhere else for us to go. Can you understand that, Shasa?"

"I understand Papa, but doesn't this land also belong to those who grew up here? Why can't we just live together and stop fighting?"

"I'm not sure this land will ever be big enough for everyone, my dear. The two cultures are just so different, I question if we could ever co-exist in harmony."

Feeling an anxiety deep within her, Shasa looked up at Jacob. "Then what will happen to all the poor Palestinians who no longer have a home? Will they all be killed?"

"I really can't answer that. What I do know is a solution must be found, otherwise I'm afraid very few of us will die a natural death."

After a long pause, she whispered back, "Do you fear death, Papa?"

Staring across the room, he couldn't help but wonder how many cruel memories haunted this poor child. Here she lay in bed beside him, innocently trusting him as her own father. Yet he had been directly responsible for the artillery attack that had killed her entire family. What cruel irony, he thought morosely. How many parents had to carry that burden through life? How many children innocently lay in bed beside the murderers of their own flesh and blood and called them Papa?

"I think I am afraid of death, Shasa. God knows I've seen enough of it, but somehow I never can get used to the idea. And you? Does death frighten you?"

"I don't really know. I do think life can be so cruel that, for some people, death may actually be a relief."

Jacob pondered that observation. "Shasa, we live in turbulent times. There is suffering all around us. There has been much suffering right here in this room. I suppose we all have to make a choice. Do we wish to carry on, or do we simply give up? I think either notion is acceptable, yet there are many of us who go through life having already given up. If you are going to choose to carry on, Shasa, then live life to the fullest. Enjoy the good times as well as the bad, for life is full of both. Life is for the living. We will all die sooner or later; some of us will choose the moment and go quickly. Some poor souls will waste a lifetime in fear. I only hope God will look kindly upon you in the future."

As they both lay there in silence, Shasa let out a big yawn. The magic of the evening had left the room, leaving only question marks behind. As she got up, she kissed her father good night, adding, "I hope God will look kindly upon all of us."

The next morning at breakfast, Shasa informed her parents of their imminent departure. Surprisingly, it seemed to both Pete and Shasa that her parents were very much in favor of the idea.

The drive to the coast took several hours. For most of the trip, neither was in a talkative mood. On a deeper level, a bond was quickly forming between them, which required few words.

Pete let Shasa drive, as she knew the way and seemed quite relaxed about handling the endless stream of traffic that roared by in both directions. My God, he thought to himself, how does anyone survive on these roads?

"Do people always drive like this?" Pete shouted over the din of the big diesel truck roaring past them. Shasa just laughed, telling him to relax. The helplessness he had found in many young women was certainly not the case here. She seemed quite capable of taking complete charge of any situation, leaving him to follow or not.

Lost in these thoughts, Pete was surprised when her Jeep slowed down to turn into a driveway hidden from the road by tall sculptured hedges. Down this narrow road they drove past an array of bushes and plants of all varieties, each offering a wonderful aroma thankfully replacing the lingering smell of diesel fumes. As the pale blue ocean finally came into view, the smell of salt water, familiar since birth, replaced all others. Stopping the car, Shasa, a huge smile lighting up her whole face, looked over at him, laughing, "This is absolutely my favorite spot in the whole world. My Grandparents brought me here as a young girl, and I fell in love with it. Just wait until you see the hotel."

Perched up on a great cliff overlooking the beautiful waters of the Mediterranean sat a magnificent stone structure. The grounds were lush with tropical plants, the smell of freshly cut grass wafting through the air. This is heaven, he thought.

There were not many military Jeeps parked in the circular driveway as they drove up, but no one seemed to notice that fact as Shasa came to a stop. The bellboys all rushed to see who could help her out first. Pete felt as if he didn't exist as they whistled around her. It was becoming quite obvious that she just attracted men to her naturally. As he approached the front desk, the thought crossed his mind: should he ask for one room or two?

Shasa saved him when she said, "Good afternoon, we have reservations for Major Watson and Private Datre, please."

"Yes ma'am, if you would just sign here and give us your addresses. We have adjoining Oceanside rooms ready, as per your request. Your rooms are located on the third floor to your right as you come off the elevator. Would you like someone to escort you up?"

"No thank you," smiled Shasa.

"Very good, please enjoy your stay and if we can be of assistance, do not hesitate to let us know."

Opening the door, Pete was treated to a spectacular view of the coast below. After a leisurely lunch served on the terrace, they decided to head down to the beach. As Pete had not anticipated the need for any beachwear, he first headed down to the small shop adjacent to the lobby to find a suitable bathing suit. When he caught up with Shasa, who had gone down ahead to lay claim to one of the cabanas, he wasn't sure who sported the least amount of clothing, he in his clinging black Speedo or Shasa in her revealing yellow bikini. Feeling a bit self-conscious, Pete took her hand and headed straight for the sanctuary of the pale blue Mediterranean. The water was delightfully warm for the former lobsterman used to the freezing waters off the coast of Maine. Pete reveled in the freedom he now felt and, without a word, headed out to sea.

Unable to keep up, Shasa soon stopped and just watched him glide through the water with long, effortless strokes. Standing 6'2" and weighing just over 195 pounds, mostly pure muscle, Pete tended to be much larger than most of his Israeli counterparts. The fact that he moved with such a casual grace only served to enhance his physical appeal.

Pete found himself well offshore when he finally took a breather. Treading water, he looked back at the hotel and beach, thinking what a lovely spot it was. Somehow, he had always pictured the Middle East as large expanses of desert with huge lakes of oil buried below. He swam slowly back to shore, realizing Shasa must have already gone back to the room.

That evening, they sat on their balcony watching the sun slowly slide into the ocean. It reminded him of many an evening in Maine. The smell of saltwater, the sea gulls floating carelessly through the air, the crashing of the waves as they relentlessly pounded the shore, all added up to a scene very reminiscent of home. As he sat there lost in thought, the sky began to turn a shade of pink as the sea swallowed the last glimpse of the setting sun.

Taking Shasa by the hand, Pete asked if she would mind having an early dinner. The evening was warm, so they chose to sit outside on the terrace.

Over dinner, Shasa found herself unusually talkative, openly sharing her innermost dreams: "I want a house full of children and to live somewhere free of this constant violence and fear of death."

Pete could only respond, "I can't imagine what it must be like living here. Being a soldier, violence and death come with the territory, but here you live with it every minute of every day."

"Pete, here violence is part of our everyday existence. We're taught to accept it. "

Pete got up and went over to her chair. "Come on, let's go upstairs and think of something more positive."

They got up early Sunday morning, not wanting to waste a moment of their short time together. After breakfast on their patio, they went for a long walk down the beach. Having left all the hotel guests far behind, they soon discovered a beautiful little cove where the water was very shallow. Warmed by the sun, it was if they had their own giant natural bathtub. Cuddling up beside him, Shasa asked Pete what it was like growing up in Maine. He shared some of his favorite memories, including helping his dad pull up lobster traps.

"Are you close to your parents?"

"Yes, as close as most children I suppose. We really didn't talk that much about emotions. It was taken for granted that we all loved each other, so we really were never that affectionate."

"Do you love them?" Shasa asked while rubbing some sun lotion on his back.

"Oh yes, very much. I don't get back home very often, but we talk on the phone once every couple of weeks."

"Is the coast of Maine like this?"

"Yes, it is just as beautiful but in a different way. The Maine coast is rugged, much rockier than this. There are no great sandy beaches, and if you and I had been sitting in the water this long, we would have turned blue long ago." He laughed when she asked him how cold the water was.

"When I first started helping my father haul in his lobster traps, my mother insisted I wear a life preserver. Once we were away from the dock, my father would tell me to take the silly thing off. He would say, 'Son, if you're in that water more than fifteen minutes, you're a dead man, so unless that life preserver has a heater attached to it, it isn't going to do much good'."

Shasa smiled, picturing this rugged soldier as a little boy.

"Why did you decide to become a soldier?"

He told her about the Army's program to pay for college tuition in exchange for two years of active service and six years of reserve duty.

"I never thought I would make a career as a soldier, but here I am lying in a pool of warm water with a beautiful woman in Israel."

"Well, soldier, I know the world is a safer place with you guarding it." She leaned over and kissed him.

They spent their last full day together absorbed in their own private paradise, imagining a life together without consideration of a world they temporarily chose to ignore.

It wasn't until they entered her room after dinner that reality took over.

"Pete," she whispered as she embraced him. "Thank you for giving me the best time of my life. I can't believe you are leaving tomorrow. Just as we were getting to know each other, you will be halfway across the world."

Finding it difficult to express his own intense feelings, he just held her close, stroking her thick black hair. Finally, he just whispered, "I will come back soon, I promise."

Finally, Shasa pulled away. Taking his hand in hers, she led him over to the bed, turning off the lights as she went. Without another word, she slipped off her shoes and began to unbutton her blouse.

The El Al flight taxied towards the runway as the pilot asked the flight attendants to prepare for takeoff. Gathering speed,

Descent Into Paradise

the huge Boeing jetliner gracefully lifted off the runway, heading due west. Pete sat back and closed his eyes, reliving their last moments together. Sparkling pale green eyes looked into his as if to ask 'will we ever see each other again?' As he pushed her hair off her face to give her one last kiss, he could clearly picture that long thin white scar over her left eyebrow, standing out against her brown skin, the only imperfection on an otherwise perfect face. Her perfume still lingered on his collar where she had buried her head.

Shasa watched helplessly as the huge 747 lifted off the runway. When it was no longer in sight, she climbed into her Jeep and wept.

CHAPTER 7

The rendezvous in the isolated mountain village of Sohmor was scheduled for 21h00. Abu checked his watch, one hour to go. The ever-present bazooka strapped to his back looked more like a giant toy than a weapon capable of dismantling a heavy tank. Considered quiet and reserved by most who knew him, Abu's hatred of the Jews exposed a darker side of his complex personality. Driven by the need to avenge the death of his father, his reputation amongst his men was that of a cold-blooded killer. Anyone who had accompanied him on a mission into Israel soon realized that no amount of Jewish blood could satiate his thirst.

Tonight, he carefully surveyed the village square of Sohmor. Most people were in their homes preparing for bed. No guards were posted that he could see. He made a mental note to correct that upon his return.

They had left Beirut early that morning, driving south in two ancient Mercedes-Benz sedans. The plan called for them to spend the night in Sohmor, then leave at dawn in the back of the two village trucks transporting the week's produce to market. From there, they would proceed on foot to their target.

By 20h30, his men were deployed to cover all possible angles of approach. Abu knew of too many instances of treachery by Israeli spies to take any chances.

Thirty-five minutes later, a tall lanky teenager rode his dilapidated bicycle up to the rendezvous.

Abu watched as the teenager leaned his bike against the building. He appeared to be alone as he gave the pre-arranged calling sign.

Descent Into Paradise

Abu signaled for his men to come out of hiding. The young boy then took them over to the two trucks loaded with melons.

"Three men to a truck. The boy will come with me," whispered Abu. The next morning the trucks were heavier than normal, but the drivers seemed not to notice.

The marketplace was only two miles north of the Israeli border. From there, numerous mountain trails crisscrossed the Golan Heights, Israeli territory since the Six Day War. While the mountains offered obvious advantages to the Israelis as a defensive border against invading armies, the many crevices also offered avenues through which the border could easily be penetrated.

As the men disembarked, another young boy was making his way up to the 'nest' as the Palestinians aptly named it. From there, he could use army binoculars to track the crossing and warn them by radio if any Israeli patrols were in the area.

It was just before noon when he picked up the bobbing head of Abu Nabile, quickly followed by six more closely behind. Satisfied there was no sign of dust or movement on the horizon, he sent the all-clear sign to the squad.

The sun had descended behind the mountains before Abu called his first halt. Now safely across the border, he estimated it should only take them another 45 minutes to navigate the dense overgrown mountain path they had chosen to access the target. Ten minutes later, his muscles screaming in protest, he strapped on his bazooka.

Baba, Abu's faithful friend and self-proclaimed bodyguard, was second in command. Posted as the rear guard, he was the last man to access the ridge. Abu lay there on his elbows, using the last rays of twilight to get a fix on the target. The plan was to fire their mortars into the Israeli settlement, then make it back across the border before daybreak.

Descent Into Paradise

Baba carefully lined up the five mortar shells gratefully unloaded by those poor souls assigned to carry them. The Stinger missile, his specialty, remained tightly strapped to his back.

Finally satisfied with his calculations, Abu motioned for his friend to join him. "Baba, get ready, the lights are starting to go out."

Before he climbed to the observation perch he had already selected, Abu briefed the squad one more time on his hand signals so they could relay any adjustments needed once the first shells exploded. All was in place when the residents of Ben Ami began to settle down for the night.

Jacob Datre's head came off his pillow when he first heard the familiar shriek of the incoming mortar round. Grabbing Eileen, he pulled her out the back door. "Hurry, we need to get down to the stream!" They had just started to run when the first shell landed. Exploding harmlessly short of the village, Jacob prayed they could make it down to the protection of the gulley in time, but just as they started down the path, Eileen tripped, falling headfirst into the olive tree on the edge of their property. Jacob hurriedly grabbed her hand to help her down the narrow path, but she had lost consciousness when her head slammed into the trunk. Slowed by the weight of her limp body, he knew, as he heard the next round come screaming overhead, that they weren't going to make it. His last thought before the shell exploded was of his beloved daughter.

Abu swore at himself. He had miscalculated the distance, not taking into account the height from which they were firing. The first shell had fallen just short of the settlement. Making the necessary adjustment, he could now see the explosions falling amongst the scattered cottages below.

Descent Into Paradise

Once the last round was fired, he motioned for his men to follow. Picking up his bazooka, he set off due north towards the safety of the Lebanese border, leaving Ben Ami to tend to its dead and wounded.

Mildred Goldberg was having the time of her life. Widowed the previous year, she had decided to pack her bags and leave New York to spend her remaining years in Israel. A youthful grandmother, she had no intention of wasting away on Social Security and memories. She was determined to go back to her religious roots, living out the remainder of her time in a productive and meaningful way.

Through a friend, she had ended up in a small kibbutz nestled into the mountains of Israel's northern border with Lebanon. She loved the sense of community and especially all the young children who made her feel a part of their lives.

This morning she had volunteered to drive the children to one of their favorite events, an all-day fair held once a year by a wealthy family who lived on a beautiful farm in the lush valley below. No matter how many times she traveled this lonely mountain road, she could never take for granted just how beautiful it was. She thanked the good Lord once again for giving her the courage to leave New York and all that was familiar to her.

Her only sadness was that Hyman could not be with her. Her beloved husband of 40 years had slaved his whole life in the family grocery store. Seldom taking a vacation, he had worked hard and put enough money away for the kids to go to college. Then, just when it looked like they might finally be able to retire and enjoy some time together, he went to bed one night and never woke up. His heart apparently decided to retire first.

Tears began to well in her eyes as she thought of how life could be so cruel to such a fine man. "Well, Hyman," she whispered, "I hope you can hear me. I loved you then, I love you now, and I'll one day be by your side."

"Who are you talking to, Mrs. Goldberg?" one of the young girls seated in the front row asked. Several of the children began giggling and some of the boys made the cuckoo sign around their heads setting off more giggles.

Mildred just chuckled as she downshifted; the bus backfired, sending the kids into new fits of laughter and pantomimes.

Abu, not sure what had made the noise, motioned his men to halt. Baba then pointed down at the road to the yellow school bus, still backfiring as it made its way down the winding mountain road. Baba looked over at Abu, a wide grin across his broad face as he told his old friend, "You carried that ugly monster all this way, you might as well see if it still works."

Pausing for a moment, Abu just smiled. He knew they should continue, yet something inside him made him stop. Motioning for the rest of the squad to go on without him, he took a long deep breath and turned back.

"Oh no, you're not getting all the credit. I'm going with you, just in case you miss." Taking a handful of grenades out of his pack, Baba followed him back up the track as the rest of the squad continued due north for the border.

Moments later, as Mildred rounded a sharp bend in the road, she saw two Arab men kneeling down not 50 yards away, one of whom held something very large staring right at her. Before a scream could exit her throat, her husband's face flashed vividly in her mind, and she knew she was going to him.

The entire bus exploded in a huge ball of fire. None of the children could have known what hit them, as they all died instantly. Abu stood there a moment, admiring the black cloud of smoke now rising up from the wreckage. He knew from experience what would come next, but he couldn't help himself. Smiling, he knelt down, tracing his personal killing sign in the soft sand beside the road.

JERUSALEM

"How many casualties?" asked the Israeli Prime Minister.

"In Ben Ami, over 30 confirmed dead, eight of them children. The school bus carried two adults and 22 children. There were no survivors," came the response.

"My God, a school bus! What kind of men would deliberately kill innocent children?"

"Blood thirsty terrorist bastards! We should annihilate them all," came back a quick reply.

"Recommendations?" asked the Prime Minister to his cabinet.

"Kill ten Arabs for every Jewish casualty." The room acknowledged the suggestion with loud applause.

The Prime Minister turned to General Argov. "General, I will leave the details to you, but I want blood, and apparently I am not alone."

That evening, Yuri Argov sat absorbed by the images filling his TV screen. A long procession of small caskets, each carried by a team of military pallbearers, crossed the screen past weeping mothers and distraught fathers all dressed in black. A simmering fury began to build inside him like a slow burning fuse. Having already determined his response, he reached for the green operations phone beside him.

Hours later, a sleek Phantom fighter jet taxied onto an active runway as two black Sikorsky helicopters rose into the night sky. Armed with Hellcat air-to-ground missiles, each helicopter also carried a squad of twelve Israeli paratroopers. The night suddenly erupted into flames as the Phantom streaked westward out over the Mediterranean, its afterburners propelling it skyward.

The flight plan called for the pilot to approach the target from the sea, dropping his payload of high incendiary bombs with no advance warning.

The village of Sohmor in southern Lebanon was a small enclave of Palestinians whom had settled there some twenty years earlier, eking out a meager living from the rocky soil. Tonight, as the villagers slept, the Israeli pilots activated their fire control systems. Three miles ahead, the attack helicopters witnessed a huge orange ball of flame reach skywards as Sohmor erupted in flames. Minutes later, both choppers went to hover, unleashing their own Hellfire missiles at any structure left standing.

The plan was to land the troops just outside the village on the southern perimeter. The troops were charged with killing anyone left alive.

The evening news led with its top story. "Israeli defense forces wasted no time retaliating for the bombing of Ben Ami and the brutal murder of 22 school children riding their school bus on Tuesday morning."

The screen then showed the charred ruins of a small village still smoldering.

"Military sources have informed us that the Lebanese village of Sohmor was the launching point for the terrorists responsible for Tuesday's bloody massacre. Israeli forces attacked Sohmor just past midnight in a daring night raid. Preliminary estimates report over 500 Palestinian casualties. So far, we have received no word of any survivors. Please stay tuned. We will bring you any further reports as they become available."

Descent Into Paradise

Argov turned off the TV. The top military officer in the Israeli Army slumped back in his chair, picturing his elite troops gunning down women and children as they fled from their burning homes in the middle of the night.

CHAPTER 8

Shasa, having just hung up the phone with Pete, hurried to get ready for dinner. Putting on her makeup, she wondered why she was going to all this effort to look nice for her girlfriends. The fact was she didn't have many friends and their Friday night get together was something she looked forward to. Fortunately for her, she was out with her two friends when the news of Ben Ami was first televised. When she finally arrived back at her apartment later that night, a very concerned Zev Megrid was there waiting for her. After hearing the news, images of Abu Dis flashed through her head; soldiers shouting, dead bodies sprawled on the ground, and women wailing over their dead until they too lay lifeless. Once more, she felt alone and isolated. Her fleeting joy at seeing Zev now turned into despair at the thought of never seeing Eileen and Jacob again. Looking sadly at Zev, she asked a question neither could possibly answer.

"Is this our fate? To have everyone we love and care for be killed; to live a life without family or loved ones?"

It was after midnight when Zev finally left her alone lying in bed. Unable to sleep, she could feel this dark cloud gradually overwhelm her. Those sparkling eyes, always so full of life, now simply reflected the emptiness within.

The next morning, Zev woke her with the news of General Argov's offer to fly them both up to Ben Ami for the state funeral.

"Apparently, even the Prime Minister will be there. We need to be at Palmachim by noon."

The funeral was a communal affair with all the surviving residents dressed in black. The Prime Minister gave the eulogy from a stage full of dignitaries, including the Director of Mossad, who afterwards came over to pay his respect.

"You must be Shasa. Your father was a man for whom I had great admiration and respect, a great soldier of Israel. I know his loss saddens all those who knew him."

"Thank you. He was a wonderful father who always spoke highly of you and the work your Agency does in protecting Israel."

"That's most kind of you to say. I only wish we had done a better job protecting him and all the poor souls who perished here in Ben Ami."

Just then, General Argov appeared and, taking Shasa by the arm, announced their imminent departure. As they walked over to where the helicopters were parked, Shasa pretended to listen to the kind words of her boss, but her real attention was on the conversation taking place several steps behind.

The helicopter carrying the Israeli Defense Minister and his two guests landed back at the Israeli Air Base just before dinner. Once inside Zev's car, Shasa wanted to hear everything the Director had said. Zev, grateful to see a spark of life flash into those beautiful green eyes, informed her he would tell her everything, but only upon the condition she would join him for dinner. Upon her acceptance, he headed directly for a place he knew would provide fun memories.

THE BARN

Seated at the very same table by the fire where they had sat with Pete, Zev shared with her the conversation initiated by the Director of Mossad.

"Intelligence believes the man who led the raid on Ben Ami also is responsible for killing all the schoolchildren as well.

Descent Into Paradise

They also believe he is the same man responsible for numerous other raids into Israel involving hundreds of casualties. It was clear the Director wants this guy very badly."

"How do they know it's the same person?"

"According to the Director, he always leaves his personal sign sketched into the dirt. It would appear he is taunting us by letting us know he is the one responsible. Pretty stupid if you ask me."

"Do they have a name?"

"Indeed they do. Abu Nabile, a Palestinian who is based in Beirut."

"And what did he want?"

"You."

Looking back at him with a perplexed look, she slowly began to realize why he had come over to introduce himself.

"Does he know I am Palestinian?"

"He had heard rumors, but I think he wanted to see for himself. By the way, he thought you were quite beautiful."

"And?"

"And he asked if I thought you might be willing to help him."

Shasa sat back, remaining silent for a moment as she pondered that request. The anger which had threatened to consume her the past 24 hours had now found an outlet.

CHAPTER 9

MIAMI BEACH

Upon checking into his hotel room, Pete once again tried to reach Shasa by phone. Again, he only got her answering machine. Zev had warned him the death of her Israeli parents had sent her deep within a protective shell, one from which she had yet to exit. His advice had been to give her some time and not push to see her. For Pete, that was easier said than done. Several times already he had gone out to Dulles Airport prepared to just fly over and take his chances, but each time he thought better of it and returned home. Finally, he decided to move on with his life and scheduling this trip to Florida was the first step.

He had enjoyed his free day on the beach immensely although, as he showered and dressed for dinner, he knew there would be a price to pay for spending all day in the sun. As Pete strolled into the bar downstairs, he surmised his dinner partner had already arrived. Although a bit shorter than he would have guessed from the pictures in his dossier, those blazing blue eyes, so out of place on his otherwise dark Latin features, gave him away immediately. The sole reason he had flown down to Miami stood casually at the bar, seemingly oblivious to the world around him.

"Good evening Major, a pleasure to meet you."

"And you as well. Apparently, we have both been reviewing dossiers."

"I must admit, Major, yours makes for far more interesting reading. Of course your face is a bit redder than the one in your photograph, but I assume that's from enjoying our lovely tropical paradise. Please sit, may I buy you a drink?"

Descent Into Paradise

As he ordered a draft beer, Pete took a moment to study the features of the man, who, at a relatively young age, had already earned a reputation in the drug enforcement world. Handsome and calm were his first two impressions. Pete fully expected a cocky street urchin full of hype and street slang. Instead, he quickly discovered he was in the company of an educated well-spoken gentleman. Fluent in both English and Spanish, the young Mexican proved to be quite well read and completely up to speed with the policies being initiated by the new administration. Even more impressive, Pete discovered the Mexican knew a great deal about what he and General Bradley were planning.

"Major, I applaud your efforts and that of your boss. It's about time someone in Washington got serious about this whole war on drugs slogan they have been hyping. I can't tell you how many good agents we have lost over the past several years."

"Lost in terms of lives or just giving up and leaving the Agency?"

"Both, Major. Lives lost come with the territory, but the revolving door comes from a combination of poor policies, lack of any serious follow through, and most disturbingly, corruption at the highest levels."

"That's quite a serious assertion. To make a public statement such as that, I assume you must have some personal knowledge or proof of some kind."

"Oh, believe me Major, I don't go around making such statements without solid backup."

"Please, call me Pete. Major works well in the service, but to be honest, I prefer Pete."

"OK Pete, what do you say we go eat? Do you like Cuban food?"

"To be honest, I have never tried it. There aren't many Cubans living where I come from. Way too cold, I guess."

"Well, if you're up for something new, I have made us reservations at a wonderful spot which I think serves the best Cuban food in the city."

"It's your city, so I will follow your lead with pleasure."

Dinner was delicious and quite entertaining as both men formed a genuine liking for the other. It wasn't until dessert arrived that they finally got down to the business at hand.

"Before we get into the real reason for this little visit," started Pete, "I have to ask you about your street name, do your friends call you La Bota?"

"No, most of my friends just call me Bota, so you are welcome to use that. Otherwise, I simply go by my full name, La Bota," he added, smiling.

"And do you mind if I ask how you came by it?"

"As a young boy in Mexico, my grandfather used to have me shake out his boots every morning to make sure no insects or small animals had decided to spend the night inside. One day, a scorpion came tumbling out and my two sisters started screaming. Since I was too young and stupid to realize what it was, I killed it with my grandfather's boot. He was so impressed; he started calling me La Bota. In English, it means 'the boot'. In Spanish, it means more like the enforcer. Somehow, it has just stuck with me."

"And your real name, that seems to be quite a well-kept secret."

"Yes, and quite frankly, I prefer to keep it that way."

"Anything to do with the 'corruption in high places' you referred to earlier, or just the type of people you find yourself exposed to?"

"To be honest, both. And you would be well served, my friend, not trusting anyone either. I am sorry to say ours is a dirty business, one where betrayal and death go hand in hand. I welcome your help and that of the Armed Forces, as I hope and trust it will bring a level of professionalism and competency we have yet to enjoy."

"I certainly hope so, my friend. Now, here is what I'm looking for."

CHAPTER 10

TEL AVIV

Graduation was approaching quickly. Shasa's native tongue had come back to her quite naturally. The hardest part of the training had been psychological. It was one thing to learn the physical art of hand-to-hand combat. It was quite another to stick a knife into another human being and watch them die inches from your face.

People who were experts at killing had carefully indoctrinated her. She had been shown numerous videos emphasizing the carnage to innocent Israelis at Ben Ami, complete with close-ups of the school children whose dismembered bodies lay sprawled on the ground. Her trainers had made sure she understood how evil the men were whom she now planned to kill.

Soon after graduation, she was given her first assignment: search out and terminate with extreme prejudice the Palestinian terrorist known as Abu Nabile.

Outfitted in a torn peasant dress with sandals, a scarf tied around her head, and exuding none of the elegance that had once transfixed Major Watson, Shasa resembled a young Palestinian woman seeking refuge from the violence that had killed her entire family. Having been inserted into Lebanon by sea on a lonely stretch of beach some twenty miles south of Beirut, she slowly made her way north along a well-traveled dirt road.

On her first day of travel, she had the good fortune of meeting a kind elderly man, who introduced himself only as Omar. When Shasa asked innocently where he lived, she received a more serious answer than she had expected.

Descent Into Paradise

"Ever since the Jews burned down my home many years ago, I've chosen not to settle down anywhere. My home will always be in Palestine, even if it's only a memory." They talked throughout the evening as he cooked a simple meal over the fire. She told him that she was traveling to Beirut.

"You need to be very careful, young lady, there is nothing but trouble up there for us Palestinians."

"Why do you say that? I was told many of our people have settled there."

Stroking his beard, he replied, "That is true. Those Palestinian refugee camps are overflowing with human misery. Inside, you have a number of ways to die. The lucky ones get killed in battle. For the rest, it is either disease or, for many my age, quite simply, a broken heart. Why would you want to go there, my child? Do you wish to die?"

"No, I do not, at least not yet. But I am alone. I was told I have relatives there."

Nodding, the old man looked back into the fire.

"I see, then I will help you get there." That was all he said before pulling his blanket up to his chin and falling asleep.

The two of them spent the next several days walking north along the coast. For Shasa, the exercise and fresh salt air were a tonic for her tortured soul. The stress of the past months gradually melted away in the warm sun tempered by the cool ocean breeze. Omar turned out to be a wonderful companion, full of interesting stories about his exodus out of Palestine and his years in exile wandering throughout southern Lebanon. One evening, they decided to camp on the beach. They were nearing Beirut, and her clothes were filthy, so as Omar made a fire, she decided to take a swim. As the sun lowered itself below the horizon, she waded into the warm water wearing only her underwear. As she let the salt water wash away the accumulated dirt and dust of the day's journey, her mind couldn't help but travel south along this very coast to the last time she had gone for an evening swim. That night, she went to bed thinking of Pete for the first time in months.

The following afternoon, they reached the quaint coastal town of Damour. That evening, Omar pointed out the lights of Beirut in the distance. "I will miss you, Shasa. For these past few days I have felt young again, and for that, I thank you."

Shasa leaned over to kiss him on the forehead saying, "And you, my friend, have given me back my smile. For that, I will always be thankful."

"You remind me of my youngest daughter, competent and strong, yet full of sadness. I only pray you will find happiness and learn to enjoy all the wonderful things life has to offer."

Shasa hesitated but finally asked, "Where is your daughter now?"

She knew the answer before he spoke.

"She died several years ago. Having watched as her husband was dragged out of bed and summarily executed by Israeli soldiers, she then had to endure watching their eighteen month old baby daughter die of pneumonia because the makeshift clinic didn't have the proper medication."

He paused as if reliving the horror of it. "That was three years ago. Until the day she died, I never saw her smile again. In the end, I believe she just wanted to be with her husband and daughter. I do miss her terribly."

He looked over at Shasa, feeling a few tears run silently down his cheek. "I don't know why Allah allowed me to live to see my children and grandchildren die. I have lost my family, my home, my friends, and my country. I told Him there is nothing left to take, you have it all."

Then a small smile creased his jagged mouth. "At least He gave me you on this blessed trip."

The next morning, Shasa awoke first. Blowing gently into the dying embers of the night fire, she resurrected a flame to heat their morning tea. Omar was still sound asleep when she poured her second cup. He had still not moved when she finished. Reaching over to touch him, he still did not stir. Alarmed, she shook him gently. "Omar, it's Shasa, it is time to get up, we must leave." Still no response. Putting her forefinger on his neck, she felt for a pulse. Nothing.

Slowly, she stood up. Gazing down at him, she could clearly see the slight smile on his wrinkled face.

"I will miss you, my friend. Please say hello to your daughter for me, and may Allah grant you eternal peace."

Shasa stared at the faded red letters inscribed along the arch. SHATILA proclaimed the end of her long journey. Entering the Palestinian refugee camp, Shasa's first order of business was to sell her mule. The proceeds enabled her to rent a sixth of a tent occupied by five single women, all of who were widows with no family. She quickly learned that single young women were not very popular. The men tended to view them as prostitutes, and married women viewed them as potential threats. The only jobs available were menial ones, such as cleaning or cooking for those no longer able to look after themselves. Shasa was fortunate. She found a nice elderly lady whose husband had suffered a stroke. Unable to care for him by herself, she was willing to pay Shasa a small but adequate sum, to assist her. Not only did Shasa now have a steady source of income, she had an invaluable source of information.

The old woman had been a refugee in Shatila for over fifteen years. Forced to flee their village during the 1967 war, she and her husband had arrived before many of the current residents and, as a result, they had a tent all to themselves, a rare luxury in such an overcrowded environment. Upon learning that Shasa was born in the neighboring village of Abu Dis, the woman immediately invited her to move in and live with them, working for food and shelter. "How absolutely incredible you're alive, my child, we were told everyone perished that horrible day. What a small world. My husband and I knew your parents, wonderful people. Thanks be to Allah my husband was traveling that day or I'm sure he would have perished as well." Soon thereafter, Shasa was introduced to another long-term resident of Shatila, Ramira Nabile. Sasha soon discovered Ramira and her son Abu were from her own village of Abu Dis. As fate would have it, Abu's parents were also friends of her own mother and father. Having spent the past thirteen years in Israel, memories of her childhood in Abu Dis had faded over time. Now that she was back amongst her own people, however, she found herself remembering more and more details about her own family. Listening to the stories told by her parents' friends, she found herself missing them more and more.

So absorbed was she in learning about her early childhood, she was taken aback when, one sunny morning, shouting erupted throughout the camp and gunshots filled the air. When she rushed outside to see what was wrong, the old lady came out explaining, "They are most likely celebrating the return of Ramira's boy. He went into Israel last week."

Realizing she was about to see the man whom she had agreed to kill, the son of her parents' good friends the Nabiles, she joined the crowd gathering at the main gate. Several minutes later, a group of six men, two clearly wounded, exited two Jeeps to wild cheering and guns firing. The men acknowledged the cheers by holding their weapons above their heads in some sort of victory sign.

The cheering soon turned into songs of praise for Allah, interspersed with random firing of AK-47s into the air. Shasa remained in the background, calmly observing the man Israeli intelligence identified responsible for the death of her beloved Israeli parents in addition to hundreds of innocent civilians.

That night, a huge celebration was organized to honor the returning heroes. Shasa asked permission to go, which the old lady graciously gave her. For the first time in weeks, Shasa washed her hair and instead of tying it up in a ponytail, she let it fall down past her shoulders. Unpacking her one colorful dress, she spent several minutes in front of the mirror. Judging from the stares she received, the transformation was readily apparent.

Shatila was in a festive mood. Women scurried from one tent to the next, excitedly chatting away about the killing of twelve Israeli soldiers. Large campfires were set in the middle of the celebratory square where people gathered for occasions such as this. Even the children were caught up in the excitement, brandishing their toy rifles in imitation of their elders. Shasa could only imagine the excitement the destruction of Ben Ami had caused.

Abu and his five comrades appeared after everyone had sat down. Shasa seated herself near the front so she could get an unobstructed view of the men as they came in. The applause and shouting was deafening. Songs were sung depicting the bravery of the soldiers, as men and women joined with their children jumping up and down. Even the meal was delicious until she discovered her mule had been one of the main ingredients.

Despite several unsolicited male invitations, Shasa remained alone, her attention focused on the homecoming hero. He sat completely still, as if he were just a passive observer. When it came time for the men to speak, he simply nodded to the boy seated next to him. The teenager, clearly overwhelmed with emotion as the crowd shouted encouragement, began hesitantly to describe their mission. Leaving out not a single detail, he described their ambush of the Israeli patrol. When he ended by describing Abu pulling out his killing knife to slit the throat of the only soldier left alive, the crowd went wild. Still, not a muscle moved in his face as he just listened impassively. In fact, the only time she witnessed any emotion cross his stern features was when he glanced over at her, something that occurred more than once.

It was a week before Shasa saw him again. He was walking past her as she swept the area in front of her tent. Their eyes met for only a moment, then he was gone. Some minutes later, however, he came back, walking very slowly. This time he stopped.

"You must be the woman from Abu Dis my mother told me about. Welcome," he said somewhat awkwardly.

"Thank you," she replied, equally shyly.

"What is your name?"

"Shasa." She kept her eyes down, pretending to look embarrassed.

"I am Abu."

"I know, I saw you at the celebration."

"Ah yes, I thought so."

Shasa knew by instinct she must go slowly with this man, so, without responding, she turned to go back into the tent, waving goodbye to him as she turned.

Abu walked on without looking back, but the bait had been swallowed. He would return.

CHAPTER 11

Pete received the emergency message from General Bradley while conducting training exercises at Fort Bragg.

'Major,' it read, 'We have a Code One situation developing in Beirut. You are to leave for Tel Aviv tonight. A military plane has been put at your disposal for the flight to Palmachim Air Force Base where you will receive further instructions. Good luck.' It was signed, 'General George Bradley.' Utterly confounded as to what had transpired, he landed the next morning to an effusive greeting from none other than Zev Megrid.

"My God Zev, what's going on?"

"Pete, I'm afraid we're both in the dark on this one. All I know is I got pulled out of a field exercise last night and brought here to meet you. Something serious must be going down, but I have no idea what it is."

The answer arrived shortly in the form of a black Lincoln Town Car.

"Good afternoon, gentlemen. Allow me to introduce myself. I work for the Israeli Intelligence Agency. You may call me Simon."

Pete immediately wondered how Mossad figured into this equation. Settling back into the plush seat, he listened carefully as Zev turned to Simon. "I trust you have an explanation for why we are here."

"I do indeed, Major. I have been asked to give you both a ride to Ben Gurion Airport as time is of the essence."

Pete sat quietly as he absorbed the news.

"Someone has just kidnapped Mary Riordan, the wife of the American CIA Station Chief in Beirut.

Descent Into Paradise

"The information we currently possess," Simon continued, "would suggest the Palestinians are holding her here."

Pete watched closely as the Israeli agent touched his finger to an aerial photograph of the Shatila Camp on the outskirts of Beirut.

"We're further led to believe her ultimate fate awaits the arrival of a certain individual known as Abu Nabile. We believe he is the very same one who led the raid against Ben Ami and killed those poor schoolchildren as well. We also believe he may be responsible for a recent ambush of an Israeli army patrol, killing all eight soldiers and wounding nine civilians in the process. Since that took place several days ago, he should be nearing Beirut as we speak."

Upon landing in Beirut, they were driven immediately to a safe house Mossad kept for just such a purpose. Located near the airport, it also happened to be near the Camp. While Pete got some much needed sleep during the short flight up to Beirut, as it didn't appear either were going to get much rest during the next 24 hours, Zev contemplated what he just heard. The plan, clearly masterminded by the Intelligence Service, called for them to be inserted into the camp that night with the help of a Mossad operative. They were then to meet another agent inside the camp who would direct them to where the American hostage was being kept. What was lacking, however, was a viable way to exit the camp once the hostage had been secured. Knowing full well that these refugee camps were extremely crowded, Zev was less than optimistic about the odds of their escaping without some sort of outside help. Uncomfortable with the overall planning, he made a mental note to call General Argov upon their arrival.

That evening, having slept again for several hours, Pete showered, and then came down for a light dinner and final

Descent Into Paradise

briefing. When Zev finished giving Pete his thoughts, the only question on Pete's mind was the extraction.

"As to that little problem, I was just assured help would be made available if needed." He then explained what General Argov had arranged.

As Zev lay down to get some rest himself, he couldn't help but wonder if this mission was even feasible. He knew from his conversation with Argov that the army was very skeptical of this entire exercise but was getting pressured by the politicians to help the Americans. According to Argov, Mossad had some complicity in the whole affair and were anxious the Americans not discover exactly what. He also learned Shasa was now in the camp but unlikely to be of any help. Ultimately, despite Pete's repeated inquiries as to her whereabouts, Zev had decided not to share this information with Pete, as he didn't want his American friend distracted from the task at hand. Unable to sleep, he lay there quietly, that familiar gnawing in his gut unabated.

He just closed his eyes, trying to picture what lay ahead. He believed they could enter the camp undetected and, with a bit of good fortune, discover where the American hostage was being held. But how realistic was it to believe the three of them could simply exit a crowded refugee camp without anyone noticing?

It was 22h00 when the two Special Forces Officers left the house dressed as Muslim women, their faces covered by traditional Shirkas, leaving only their eyes exposed to public view. Their assigned driver was already waiting outside to take them to where another agent awaited their arrival. As they approached the water tower on the edge of the camp, the driver pulled over to the curb.

"I will wait here," was all he said as the two got out of the car.

Descent Into Paradise

Anxious to get back to his paper, he did not notice what happened next.

A young Palestinian boy with long curly hair strode up to the two women, started shouting at them and jerked them towards the barbed wire fence separating the refugee camp from the outside world. As the threesome approached the fence underneath the water tower, the boy whispered, "Here, there is a small opening in the fence. Mark it well from the other side as I will wait for you here. Also, I have been instructed to give you this." As he handed over a small black box he added, "Only use it in an emergency, but if necessary, simply press this button, then get down on the ground. The transmitter will identify you to the pilots."

With that, the two black robed figures disappeared through the small opening and found themselves inside a living hell.

Mossad had spent years and many thousands of dollars recruiting informants in all the major Palestinian camps. Their initial contact was with one of those agents. Zev had been skeptical of relying on anyone associated with the Israeli Intelligence Agency as General Argov had informed him that Mossad's preference was to eliminate the hostage, effectively severing any potential ties to their own complicity. In the end, however, he felt he had no other viable option. Despite his misgivings, none of which he had shared with Pete, they found the tent, described in their briefing, with little difficulty. There were only a few black tents in Shatila and only one with a bronze rooster perched above. They had just approached the front entrance when a voice greeted them. "Welcome to my home. I have been expecting you. I trust you have already met my nephew by the water tower."

"The young man with long hair?"

"That would be him."

Descent Into Paradise

After the obligatory pleasantries, Zev asked their host where they were keeping the hostage.

"Right across the way. I saw her only yesterday. You are just in time. Abu returned to the camp just last evening, and that can only mean trouble."

Reaching into the folds of their garments, they each pulled out a slender dagger. Tonight would be knives only unless they got in trouble.

Zev then handed their host a small smoke bomb. "Give us five minutes, then pull the pin. Place it just outside the back of your tent, then start yelling 'fire'."

In a tent city like this, fire was a dreaded nightmare for sparks could ignite canvas tents very quickly. Added to that, the crowded conditions would make escape very difficult. Hopefully, the ensuing panic would provide the distraction they needed. As they edged over to the tent where Mary was supposedly being detained, they were surprised by the absence of any guards. Surmising that resistance would be found inside, they silently used their knives to cut a small peephole in the canvas.

Inside the smoky tent, they could make out four sleeping bodies but none appeared to be female. With rising despair, they knew they only had several minutes left before the smoke bomb ignited. Inching their way to the other side, they looked in to see an empty floor. Fighting back a rising tide of panic, they retraced their steps to the black tent, stopping abruptly when they heard voices inside.

"Who were they and what did they want? Cut him a little lower next time, but don't kill him until he talks."

A piercing scream was the only response.

"Fehid, let me explain something to you. You are a traitor, and you are going to die. Tell me what I want to know and you'll die quickly. Refuse me, and you will die a slow painful death along with all your family. That I promise you."

"Abu, please, not my family. They are not involved," groaned an agonized voice.

"Go get his daughter. We'll start with her."

As a struggling young woman was pulled into the main room, Abu reached out and pulled her to him. Taking a long curved knife from its sheath, he slowly began to cut away her nightclothes. When she was standing in front of her father totally naked, shaking with fear, Abu motioned to one of his men to undress. Grinning a toothless smile, the man began to take down his pants. Aroused by the lovely girl standing in front of him, the huge man moved with startling quickness. Grabbing her from Abu, he literally threw her to the floor. As she began to scream, he reached back then hit her with the back of his hand. She continued to whimper as the man penetrated her and began to drive himself deeper and deeper until he let out a great howl of triumph. Her father sat silently in the corner, his head in his hands unable to watch. Still, he refused to talk.

Abu, surprised that this little performance failed to yield results, decided to raise the level of pain.

"Bring in the boy," he ordered. "This old goat obviously doesn't care about his daughter."

Into the room came a very proud teenager with a defiant look on his face. As he stood looking straight at Abu, he could not help but admire the boy's courage.

"Strip him," he barked out, glaring at the youth.

"I can undress myself," snorted the boy. "Abu, our great hero raping young girls. You make us all very proud!"

Abu, taken aback by this unexpected criticism, momentarily flinched, then spat out, "We'll see if your bravery extends beyond your mouth, young man." Turning to face Fehid, Abu snarled, "I am going to kill your son, and I am going to do it slowly right here in front of you. When I am through with him, I am going to feed him and your daughter, or what's left of her, to the dogs. This I promise if you don't tell me what I want to know."

After ten seconds of silence, Abu shrugged his shoulders and walked over to the proud boy.

"What's your name?"

Receiving no response, Abu instructed his two men to hold the boy still. Then with a lightening quick stroke, he took his dagger and drew it across the boy's cheek opening up a large gash that bled profusely. As Fehid watched in horror, his son lost an ear without making a sound. Then Abu reached for the boy's penis.

"You're a brave lad who deserves more than this pig for a father."

Abu was about to use his dagger once again when Fehid groaned, "No, stop it, please, enough. I will tell you what you want to know."

Outside, Zev and Pete knew they had run out of time. The decision was made without a word being spoken. Pete unzipped a smoke bomb from his pack and rolled it between several tents. With smoke now billowing out, the word fire became a shrieking chorus. Panic quickly ensued, causing the interrogation inside to cease momentarily.

Pete and Zev began to edge away from the crowd, heading back in the direction of the large water tower. Prudence dictated a slow exit, but fear seemed to prompt a quicker step than befitted two elderly ladies.

Without any warning, Zev felt the muzzle of a handgun stuck in the small of his back. A voice then whispered, "Don't make a sound; just follow me."

Descent Into Paradise

Hoping this was Shasa, Zev motioned for Pete to follow. The woman, her face covered in traditional Muslim fashion, led them into a large tent. Propped up against the far wall was a frail figure with filthy blonde hair covering most of her face. Pete and Zev deduced instantly this must be the American hostage, but the gun in Zev's back was still very much present. Having heard the commotion outside, Shasa had witnessed two rather large ladies walking, not running, and deduced these were the men sent to rescue Mary.

"Please, we don't have much time. Who are you and why are you here?"

Zev pointed at the woman in the corner without saying a word.

"What's her name?"

Zev gave her Mary's name saying they were here to bring her home. Surprised to hear Zev's voice, she took a quick glance at the other 'woman' wondering if they had sent Pete as well. Keeping her voice to a whisper, she told them what needed to be done.

By this time, Abu began to suspect that the smoke bomb was no innocent prank. Instead, he was fast reaching the conclusion that someone was trying to rescue the American hostage.

That notion was soon confirmed when one of his men came rushing back with the grim news that there were two dead bodies lying in the tent where the hostage had been kept. Abu had heard enough. Rushing out of the tent, he headed straight for the main entrance to the camp, shouting to all who could hear that the Israelis were trying to rescue the American hostage. With plumes of smoke distracting everyone's attention, Shasa led them through a maze of tents towards the water tower, Pete and Zev keeping Mary Riordan between them. Just as they were approached the last tent, a mere twenty yards away from freedom, a lady suddenly appeared around the corner. There, blocking their path, stood Abu's mother, Ramira Nabile. Calmly pointing her pistol directly at Sasha, she began speaking in a low voice that belied the intensity of the hatred her eyes betrayed.

"So, it is you. Something about you never felt quite right, just showing up here after all these years out of the blue. Then, I remembered hearing a story about the Israelis taking a little girl with them. Now, here you are helping your friends remove our hostage. I should shoot you right here for the traitor you are, but I want my son to see this for himself. You may be pretty, but he will never forgive you for this."

But, before she could shout for help, Shasa heard the distinctive sound of a small caliber handgun. Directly in front of her, Ramira looked at her with a blank expression, blood oozing from a small hole in the middle of her forehead. "Let's move," said Zev calmly, his gun once again hidden under his robes. Stepping out from the cover provided by the crowded tents, they saw a small group of curious onlookers had gathered in the small play area between them and the water tower, amongst whom were the nice elderly couple Shasa worked for. Walking very slowly with their heads down, they tried to inch their way towards the exit without raising any suspicion, but they had only made it halfway across the yard when the elderly lady recognized her.

"Shasa, what on earth are you doing?"

At that point, Zev realized, even though the water tower was now just yards away, they weren't going to make it. As he reached into his pocket, people all around him were beginning to realize these were indeed the culprits being sought.

"Stop them!" someone nearby shouted, "they are trying to escape with the American girl!"

Descent Into Paradise

"Shasa!" another voice yelled, "are you OK? What are you doing?"

Shasa now faced a dilemma. If she left with Zev and Pete, she may never get another chance to kill Abu. If she didn't, she was going to face some interesting questions. Before she could decide, her thoughts were interrupted by the very loud thumping sounds of a helicopter approaching the camp. Pete, momentarily stunned by hearing Shasa's name, reached out, pulling her to the ground. Seconds later, bright searchlights lit up the area around them as machine gun fire decimated those poor souls unlucky enough to be close by. Ropes suddenly dropped down on them as both Pete and Zev knew what to expect next. It was a classic Special Forces hot evacuation. Zev grabbed the rope with a leather harness, placed it around Mary's waist, and then clipped it snugly under her armpits, as they were both lifted straight into the air. As Pete turned to place the other harness around Shasa, she made up her mind. Grabbing his Colt, which he had holstered under his belt to free up both hands, she whispered into his ear that she loved him. She pulled him close as she shot him in his side just before securing the evacuation harness under his arms. He, not her, then shot upward in the air. The pilot, hearing the rattle of small arms hammering into his armored underbelly, decided he could not chance a bullet hitting one of his rotors so, as soon as Pete was off the ground, he went dark, flying sideways over the neighboring buildings with Pete still dangling below. By the time they were able to bring him into the hold, the medical team had already gone to work on Mary. Miraculously, she made it unscathed. Other than several scrapes and bruises, it was quickly determined that she was not seriously wounded. Pete, on the other hand, had not been so lucky. Besides the wound to his side, which was not life threatening, he had taken another bullet in his upper torso as he was being pulled up that was far more serious. Unable to do more, the medical staff gave him a shot of morphine and kept him immobile so that no further damage could occur. Zev had also taken a bullet through his right leg. Despite the pain, he had been fully conscious as they brought him in.

"How is he?" he asked anxiously looking over at where Pete was now hooked up to multiple bags of various fluids.

"Not sure," was the only reply he got. Ominously, as he looked over at the medical team, nobody gave him thumbs up, so he just lay down gradually losing consciousness as the morphine numbed his body and mind.

Pete woke up somewhat disoriented. Seeing what appeared to be a navy nurse hovering over him, he haltingly asked her where he was.

"Major, you are safe and sound on board the USS Forestall."

"How did I get here?" he croaked.

"By helicopter last night. You and your young lady friend caused quite the commotion, you did!"

"Shasa is here? Where is she? Is she alright?" Pete tried to sit up.

The nurse, muscular for her size, easily put a restraining hand on his shoulder.

"No sir, you are not going anywhere until these wounds heal. I thought the young lady's name was Mary, I didn't hear anything about any Shasa. Now please lie down and let me look at these dressings."

Pain surged through his body as the nurse undid the multiple bandages that seemed to cover his entire body. He never saw the small hypodermic needle that put him back to sleep.

"Doctor, our patient has come back to life, but he was in so much pain I gave him another shot of morphine."

Descent Into Paradise

"That's fine, there will be plenty of time to debrief him on the cruise home. Let him get some rest. God only knows what he's been through."

Mary woke up with her husband sound asleep on the couch facing her bed. She had no idea where she was, but she knew it wasn't their home and she knew she would never sleep in that house again. Exhausted, she lay back down, her mind wandering over the last tumultuous days. Closing her eyes, she could still hear the ominous sounds of the helicopter's giant rotors thumping in the night, its machine guns blasting innocent bystanders whose bodies were ripped apart as they stood there helplessly. The images were so vivid and so horrible that she opened her eyes hoping they might stop, knowing full well she could never erase what happened last night nor any other night of her ordeal. Placing a hand on her tummy, she dreaded seeing her doctor, for she already knew her baby had died along with all those other innocent women and children who had the misfortune of being near her.

Zev was badly bruised and shaken as he awoke in an Israeli military hospital. Feeling numbness down his right side, he realized his right leg was heavily bandaged. More worrisome, however, was the fact he had no feeling in his right foot.

"Good afternoon, Major. How are you?" asked a cheery voice.

"Nurse, please tell me the truth. How bad is it?"

"Major, your legs are just fine. It is your right hip that's the problem. The doctor was able to remove the bullet and bone fragments, but the damage was so severe that he had to insert a metal plate when he reset the bone. Until that takes and the hip heals, I am afraid you will need to remain here. The good news is that, according to the surgeon, you should be as good as new in a couple of months."

Relieved, he asked if she had any news of the other wounded soldier.

"I heard was he was alive when they landed on the American ship. That's all I know at the moment."

CHAPTER 12

Abu looked down at Shasa as she sat on the ground, Pete's gun still in her hand.

"Shasa! Praise Allah, I thought they killed you."

Reaching down to help her up, they embraced to great cheering from everyone around them.

"What incredible bravery, taking that man's gun and shooting him. You are truly an inspiration to our people."

"Abu, I am so relieved to see you alive. I feared you might be amongst the dead! I could not let them just take away our hostage. I only fear I failed."

"Never! You must not think that way, you are an inspiration to everyone here. Now we must get you to a doctor." Looking around at all the dead and wounded, she pushed him away.

"I am fine, these poor souls need a doctor, not me."

The next morning, Abu awoke in a dreadful mood. The news of his mother's death had only increased his fury. That familiar cold look of death was etched across his face as he stormed outside with several of his men. He headed straight to the big black tent, pulling the entire family out into the open. Determined to finish what he started the night before, he asked Fehid why he assisted the Israelis.

"I swear to you, I did not tell them anything. Please believe me, that information did not come from me."

"Liar! I have had enough of your deceit. I now pronounce the sentence of death upon you and your family for your treacherous activities against all the people in this camp. Shoot them where they stand like the pigs they are."

"No, please listen to me. Spare my family, and I will tell you who the real traitor is."

As Abu turned away in disgust, he saw Shasa cover her mouth. Mistaking her look of fear for anguish, he took her by the arm. "Come with me. You don't need to witness any more killing." As they walked away arm in arm, they heard Fehid yelling, "It's her who's the traitor."

Then the familiar rattling sound of AK-47s drowned out any further protests. Abu never saw the finger pointing in their direction as they walked away. Later that day, Shasa carefully examined the row of dead bodies lined up to be buried in one mass grave. Stooping over to put a flower on each body, she carefully noted with relief that all those who were privy to her involvement with the hostage rescue would be taking that information with them wherever they were heading next. May it be a happier place, she whispered to herself.

CHAPTER 13

Pete had asked that his wheelchair be placed on the starboard side of the ship so he could see the Boston skyline as it appeared on the horizon. The destroyer had made a smooth run across the Atlantic, and the fresh salt air had certainly done nothing to impede his recovery. As they approached the harbor, he could feel the ship's giant turbines begin to reduce power. After debriefing him, Captain Lewis had personally given him his orders and handed him a letter from General Bradley. He was to meet his parents at the dock and take a medical leave. The personal note from General Bradley also suggested that the General would come visit him up in Maine.

The USS Forestall docked at the naval shipyard where Pete's mother and father were anxiously awaiting. Their patience was rewarded as, at long last, they saw their son waving affectionately at them from his wheelchair as he was escorted off the ship by the Captain himself and the entire medical staff.

Pale and emaciated from his ordeal, Pete looked up into the concerned face of his mother as she burst into tears. His father, visibly uncomfortable with this unexpected show of emotion, shook his son's hand and then graciously turned to thank the Captain. He, in turn, addressed both parents by informing them that he and his entire crew were proud to have been given the honor of bringing their son home.

They drove home in relative silence with Pete lying down on a mattress his parents had put into the back of their Chevy station wagon.

Descent Into Paradise

Camden is a beautiful fishing village just north of Rockland, Maine. Nestled at the foot of a small mountain range, it boasts a picturesque harbor filled with a flotilla of local fishing boats mixed in with some elegant yachts awaiting their owners from Boston and beyond to sail through the lovely islands dotting the Penobscot Bay.

Although Pete had last been home four years ago, his bedroom had not been touched since he had left for college. Lying down on his four-poster bed, he stared straight into the blue eyes of Julie Christie, whose framed poster was still strategically hung so she looked right at him when he awoke.

His desk was still adorned with high school pictures. He smiled when he saw one in particular. There he was, as an innocent young boy in his dirty football uniform, hugging the homecoming queen. He remembered those simpler times and youthful joys with fondness. He wondered what had become of Susan Lear. Did she still look as beautiful as he remembered her that cold, autumn day? They had amorously celebrated the football team's final game, the victory capping a perfect undefeated season. Pete had been the victorious captain and Susan the undisputed queen of the campus. It was his first sexual encounter, and he remembered every detail as if it were yesterday.

His sexual journey into the past ended abruptly as his mother knocked on the door to announce she was bringing him a tray of homemade cookies with his afternoon tea.

"We need to put some flesh back on those bones, you are way too skinny, young man."

"I'll leave that up to you, mom."

Pete had just come downstairs when the doorbell rang. A courier in military uniform handed him a folder marked 'Confidential', got his signature, saluted, then turned and left.

Descent Into Paradise

He quickly opened the letter that read, 'Dear Pete, I trust you have recuperated sufficiently to entertain guests. I am scheduled to arrive tomorrow at noon. I hope you can spare me the afternoon. There is much to discuss,' signed, General George Bradley.

The General arrived in a yellow and red Down East Taxi cab. The driver, overwhelmed by driving a real life general, refused to accept any money. In fact, he insisted upon walking the General to the door, saluting him as he reluctantly went back to his cab.

The General greeted Pete's mom at the door.

"Good afternoon Ma'am, you must be Mrs. Watson. I am George Bradley,"

"Of course, we were expecting you, General. Please come in. The truth is, we don't get to entertain many generals in our little town, so please forgive the poor taxi driver."

"Oh, I am quite flattered by the attention, Ma'am. Believe me, we are not treated with nearly as much respect in the nation's capital."

He smiled as he took off his coat and walked in to the living room to see Pete on the sofa.

Pete immediately tried to stand up, saying in a rather weak voice, "Good afternoon, General, and welcome to Maine."

"Thank you, how are you feeling? I will say that you look far better than those first few reports I received."

Mrs. Watson wanted to leave the two men alone, so as she walked out of the living room she said, "I am going to do the grocery shopping. Please, General, help yourself to the cookie jar. Also, can you join us for dinner tonight?"

"Thank you for asking, but, unfortunately, I can only stay a short time. I will, however, gladly partake of the cookie jar."

"Please do. Pete, remember you are not fully recovered, so don't overdo," she admonished sternly.

The two men shared a conspiratorial smile as Mrs. Watson walked briskly towards the garage.

Smiling, the General asked, "How do you feel, my boy?"

"Oh, I am recovering slowly. I still feel weak, but luckily the pain has subsided, so I am off everything except aspirin."

"Good, so you are alright to talk awhile?"

"Absolutely, sir."

The General reached over to the table by the sofa and took two tollhouse cookies out of the jar. Then he started to brief Pete.

"First, Mary Riordan is fully recovered physically. Emotionally, I think she will need more time. Apparently, she very much wants to thank you in person and wishes you a speedy and full recovery. She also asked to have her thanks conveyed to Major Megrid, who apparently is still in the hospital recovering from a broken hip. I am informed he will be up and around in the next several weeks and is expected to make a full recovery. He also sends you his regards, as they both have been very concerned about you."

"And Shasa. Did she make it out?"

"That I don't know. Mossad is very tight lipped about their agents, especially when they're in the field."

"What is the situation in Beirut? Has anyone discovered who was really behind this?"

"No, not yet, and the two of us have to keep very quiet about that whole episode. You were entrusted with very confidential information, as I am sure you realize, which needs to be kept between the two of us. We never could have obtained Mary's whereabouts without the Israelis' help, so we cannot betray their trust. Agreed?"

"Completely sir, I think the whole thing stinks, although I do agree that, without their help, none of us would have made it out of there alive."

"Pete, you and I are simple soldiers. We obey orders and do the best we can. Let the politicians worry about who shot whom over there. We need to keep our communication lines open if we want access to good intelligence."

"General, I hope you didn't travel all this way just to make sure I would keep this confidential. You know me better than that."

"I know, Pete, but I couldn't take any chances. I needed to hear it from you directly. I also wanted to see how my best officer was doing and to give you an update on Mrs. Riordan and Zev. Hurry up and get well. I have an uneasy feeling the Israelis are getting ready to launch that full scale invasion into Lebanon that Argov spoke of."

They both got up, Pete more slowly than normal.

"Let me help you up to bed son, you look pale. I can see my way out just fine."

The General helped him into bed. Pete now realized why he had been brought home in the secure confines of a Navy Destroyer.

CHAPTER 14

Guns fired into the air, while the more religious raised their hands to Allah asking him to guide his warriors to victory. Tomorrow morning, six chosen Fedayeen would leave Shatila on their way north into Israel. The PLO commanders in Damour were still deciding the mission's details, but to the men and women of Shatila, the details didn't concern them. The fact that a blow would be struck against the hated Jews was all that mattered.

Tonight, the women would prepare a feast to honor the young men who would soon risk their lives to avenge the wrongs done to their people. Shasa sat peeling onions and chopping mushrooms. A large black pot hung on a hinge over the wood fire filled with a lamb stew. Shasa and four other women were responsible for the evening feast. They all participated with great joy and anticipation of the celebration to come.

"Shasa, when are you leaving tonight? Are you eating with us?" asked the youngest of the four.

"No, I will be in Damour tonight, although I can't bear the thought of missing this stew. It smells so good." Shasa poured the chopped vegetables into the bubbling pot, stirring the ingredients to enjoy the tangy aroma. "I want a full report tomorrow when I return, don't forget one detail."

"I promise, Shasa. I'm so excited; I just hope Mohammed will speak to me. He is so shy, he just looks at the ground every time I go near him."

Poor girl, thought Shasa, she is at that age where the world revolves around young boys, who had been taught from birth not to lust after women until they married. Islam is certainly not an easy religion to follow. Shasa began to wonder if Abu would come to her. He clearly had something in mind, or he would not have invited her to share his bedroom. The problem, as she well understood, was that Abu Nabile was a strict Muslim. Now that his strict mother was no longer around to chaperone them, would he finally succumb to earthly temptations or simply continue to beg her to marry him? What an irony, she laughed to herself, here I am luring this man into bed, and he is still resisting me.

A green Land Rover pulled up in front of the entrance gate at 18h00. A man, heavily armed, got out to fetch Shasa from her tent. He grabbed her overnight bag and, without a word, led her back to the car. Once inside, they headed west, passing a young boy with long curly hair sitting outside the gates playing his guitar. Shasa waved as he looked up. Ten minutes later, the signal went out to an Israeli fishing vessel anchored off the coast that the Leopard was loose.

Not a word was uttered during the drive down the coast to Damour. Shasa arrived with the distinct feeling that she was an unwelcome addition to the night's festivities.

The temperature began to drop with the setting sun. The fog bank, which had sat offshore all afternoon, now began to creep in, carried by the evening breeze. As the harbor slowly disappeared from view, the only evidence of its existence was the clanging of the navigational buoys marking the main channel.

Shrouded by mist, the last supplies were loaded aboard the Israeli gunboat docked at Pier 4. Like a great black cat, she lay there tethered to the dock, sleek and silent. Captain Rosen, having just received his final instructions from Admiral Nurov, climbed on deck.

Descent Into Paradise

"Everyone onboard?" he barked as he came up the ramp.

"Aye, aye sir."

At 18h40, the two GE twin-engine diesels roared to life, growling and gurgling in their anticipation to be unleashed. Minutes later, Captain Rosen set his course due north and went to full throttle. The gunboat cut through the gentle Mediterranean swells at 35 knots, leaving a long rooster tail bubbling up in its wake.

At 21h15, the Captain reduced speed, altering his course northeastward towards a spit of land twelve miles south of Beirut. Turning over the helm to his First Lieutenant, Rosen went down to confer with his passengers. Lt. Commander Betz and his five-man squad felt the gunboat reduce speed as they lay on their narrow bunks.

"OK men, let's get ready," Betz said as he bounced to the floor. The squad, affectionately known in the Israeli Navy as the Bat Men, was one of the groups comprising Sayeret 13. Comparable to the Navy Seals in America, the Bat Men were amongst the most elite soldiers in the Israeli Defense Force. As such, they were accorded great respect by the rest of their comrades, including Captain Rosen.

"Lt. Commander, we are approximately fifteen minutes from our drop off, which will put us exactly one half mile offshore of Damour."

"Thank you, Captain," acknowledged Betz. Checking his watch, he saw they were right on schedule.

Fifteen minutes later, the six commandoes dropped over the stern, heading for the secluded beach just south of the cliffs.

Lt. Commander Betz surfaced just off shore. Quickly surveying the scene, he confirmed the beach was deserted. The house was constructed at the far end of the beach where the sand gave way to a rocky promontory. A large porch stood on wooden pilings extending the house over the rocks below, offering exceptional views of the whole coastline. It was the rear of the house upon which he now focused his attention. It was there the extraction would take place. He observed four windows on the second floor. All four opened up onto the beach where a determined agent could leap to safety. Pulling his mask back on, he readjusted his heading, stopping as the water shoaled to four feet.

Able to stand now, the men removed their tanks and other equipment, retaining only their Uzis strapped to their backs.

The plan was for Seaman Makov to remain in the water with the equipment. This would ensure that no strangers could detect the gear from the beach, and, if necessary, enable them to make a quick exit straight into the sea. An extra tank and facemask had been brought along for the return swim.

The five men going ashore now split into two groups. Lt. Commander Betz and Lieutenant Eison would approach the house from the water, swimming in as close as possible without being detected. The other three would set up a firewall to take out any pursuers if necessary. Intelligence had informed them that the Leopard would make her escape any time after 22h00. The operative would decide when and how, based on how the circumstances presented themselves. The great unknown was how many Arabs would be alerted to her escape. That uncertainty was the reason Betz had detailed the three-man firewall.

At 22h10, the squad was in place. Fifteen minutes went by before any movement was detected. A guard leaned over the porch railing, surveying the beach. He lit a cigarette, then turned his back to face towards the house, completely unaware of the three night scopes focused on the back of his head.

Lieutenant Eison was the first to see her. Tapping Betz on the shoulder, he pointed to an open window on the second floor. They both got ready, but she only stared out the window for a moment, as if checking to make sure they were there, and then she disappeared.

Whispering into his mic, Betz made sure the squad now had the location of the room. All answered in the affirmative.

Her bedroom was filled with beautiful furnishings, the centerpiece being a very large four-poster bed. She had not eaten since breakfast, but she got the distinct feeling there would be no room service tonight. Abu had instructed her to remain upstairs, so, since she was apparently confined to her room, she decided to take a hot bath, a luxury she had sorely missed.

Abu finally came upstairs, entering a room illuminated only by candlelight. His eyes went directly to the breathtaking woman lying on the bed reading a magazine.

"I am sorry, Abu, I was so tired I had to lie down," Shasa purred.

Abu just stood there staring. She prayed his carnal desire would overcome his Muslim upbringing. Breaking the silence she said, "How was your dinner?"

"It was interesting, the usual planning before a mission. I just let everyone have their say, then I do whatever I think best," he smiled. "Now enough about war, what am I going to do with you?"

"Well, if you are looking for suggestions, I vote you take a shower, then climb in here next to me."

He looked longingly at her, conflicting emotions clearly playing across his face. He then turned slowly, locked the door and walked silently into the bathroom.

Abu lingered in the shower, letting the hot water beat down upon his aching muscles, taut with tension. His instincts warned him of danger, but his body craved the woman waiting for him in the next room.

A loud knocking on the door interrupted Shasa's preparations. "What do you want?" she asked in an annoyed voice. It was Baba, Abu's self-appointed bodyguard who had never appreciated having to share his best friend with such a pretty distraction.

"I have an urgent message for Abu. I need to speak with him now!"

"He's taking a shower. I will have him come downstairs when he gets out."

Knowing the time had finally come, she went over to the window. Opening it wide, she looked down to the sandy beach, hoping to spot her rescuers below. Instead, all she saw were endless waves breaking upon the shore, the entire coast illuminated by a huge full moon making its debut just above the far horizon.

Taking a deep breath, she reached behind her back, unsheathing the long slender stiletto, which had been waiting patiently all these months. Despite the doubts that had crept into her mind the past few months, she walked over to the bathroom, relieved Abu was still in the shower. Steam poured out as she opened the door a crack.

"Abu, I have a message for you from Baba."

Abu sighed as he turned off the shower. "What now?" he sighed.

Holding up a large white bath-towel, she coyly offered it to him. He stepped out, embarrassed by his nakedness in her presence, quickly taking the towel from her outstretched hands to cover him. The bathroom was so small that the two of them could barely fit. As he wrapped the towel around his waist, he noticed she was now fully dressed.

Descent Into Paradise

His mouth formed the question he never got to ask. A shocked expression and an agonizing moan was all he could manage as the razor sharp stiletto sliced through flesh and muscle on its way from his kidneys to his lungs. Shasa held him firmly as he sank slowly to his knees. His facial expression was a mixture of pain and surprise as he slumped to the floor. Staring up into those beautiful eyes, his own filled with bewilderment.

Without a word, she slowly removed her knife, wiped his blood from the blade on the bath towel, and left him on the bathroom floor to die in a pool of his own blood. Walking swiftly over to the open window, she first checked to see if there was any movement below. All was silent as she let herself fall to the ground.

Baba, having come back upstairs, knocked again, his patience at an end. He had never trusted this girl since the first day they met. Something about her just didn't sit right with him. When she still didn't respond, he made up his mind. Taking a step back, he thrust his giant shoulder through the pine door, unhinging it as he crashed into the bedroom.

The room was empty as he called Abu's name, the only movement the curtains blowing in from the ocean breeze. He immediately moved to the open window, praying he would not see Abu's body lying in the sand. Then he heard a soft moan coming from the bathroom. In an instant, he found Abu crumpled on the floor, blood oozing out of the knife wound in his back.

He immediately lifted him up like a small child in his arms and carried him down to the makeshift hospital in the basement. There, a doctor examined the wound with his fingers as the nurse quickly took his blood pressure. The doctor beckoned the giant bodyguard into the room. "How long ago did this happen?"

Descent Into Paradise

"Ten minutes at the most. I was waiting outside his bedroom…" Baba abruptly stopped as he realized two things: the doctor didn't need to know those details, and every minute he wasted here was a minute Shasa had to get further away.

The doctor paid him no further attention as he barked orders to his nurse. Yelling for help as he ran upstairs, Baba grabbed his guns, then headed straight for the beach. He moved incredibly quickly for such a huge man.

Betz saw her climb out the window just before he heard the awkward thump as she hit the ground.

"Come on," he whispered as she got to her feet. Shasa tried to walk, but fell back down as the pain shot up her right ankle.

"Can you walk or should we carry you?" Betz asked anxiously as he bent over her.

Shasa, looking somewhat dazed as these two blackened creatures spoke to her in Hebrew, announced that she thought she could walk. "It's my ankle, I must have twisted it when I landed."

Both men had their attention fixed on the house, which was still quiet. Whispering into his mic, Betz alerted his men that the extraction was now code green.

Seaman Makov, who had stayed behind with the equipment, now began to make his way towards the house towing the equipment behind him.

Shasa got up, took one step, and fell again. "Damn," she winced as she bent over to feel it, "I think it's broken."

Betz looked at Eison. "Pick her up." Whispering into his mic, he alerted the squad. "The Leopard is hurt, we're going wet. Provide cover as planned."

The three men constituting the firewall immediately began to move back towards the rendezvous, keeping the house under constant supervision as they went. They had almost reached it when the first shouts were heard.

Descent Into Paradise

Betz quickly shot a glance over his shoulder to see a dozen men hurl themselves onto the beach from behind the house. Up on the porch, several more appeared carrying AK-47s.

"We need cover fire," he yelled into his mic. He barely finished speaking when one of the men on the porch fell onto the rocks behind them. The second man, however, opened fire, spraying bullets all around them.

As Betz feared, he and Eison were drawing all the fire, and they were still a good 30 yards from the safety of the ocean. Just then, he heard the Uzis engage. Without looking back, he urged Eison to go on as he positioned himself behind his struggling lieutenant to give them some cover. Paying no attention to the firefight now raging behind him, Eison hit the water on a dead run, telling Shasa to take deep breaths. All three went headfirst underwater just as Eison felt a sharp pain in his left thigh. When Betz saw blood in the water, he took Shasa under his own power. Using his free hand, he pointed for Eison to swim on to the rendezvous.

Betz, with Shasa in tow, then surfaced briefly to let them both get a lungful of air. He could hear the battle raging, yet thankfully relatively few bullets were landing near them. Most of the Arabs had focused their attention on the three commandos now approaching the water's edge. Having allowed himself and Shasa a few quick breaths, he took them both back underwater following the trail of blood from his wounded comrade. Back on the beach, one of the Israelis was down, a bullet having broken his right arm. The other two were desperately trying to drag him into the water as they both used their free hand to return fire.

Seaman Makov was in a panic. He did not know if he should swim towards his Commander or try to help the wounded man on the beach.

Descent Into Paradise

Captain Rosen, who had brought his gunboat closer to shore to facilitate an easier extraction, could now clearly see the fight taking place on the beach. As he ordered the helmsman to take them in even closer, he turned to his gunner.

"I want two rounds on that porch now!"

Seconds later, the gunboat opened fire with devastating effect. The first shell was a direct hit. The porch literally exploded upon impact and began to crumble onto the rocks below. Bodies could be seen plummeting down onto the rocky shore. The next round succeeded in silencing any further gunfire from the front of the house.

Only one man was still firing from the beach. Yelling obscenities at the black figures entering the water, he aimed his final rounds at the one white face in the group. Then, just as he was about to pull the trigger, he was spun around by the impact of a bullet piercing his left side. Slumping to the ground, he reached for his fallen rifle. The searing pain brought tears to his eyes, but his desire to kill commanded his body to try once more.

"Gunner, put a round on the beach. There's still one gun firing off to the right. Do you see it?"

"Aye, aye Captain, I see it."

Baba fought to steady his aim. His whole body was shaking as he tried to position the gun against his shoulder. Several heads had now gone underwater, but the one he wanted was still trying to put on her diving mask. She now appeared in the V of his notch. Letting out a long breath, he slowly squeezed the trigger.

Betz was still trying desperately to fit the mask over Shasa's head, but for some reason she could not get it to stay on. Staying on the surface this long could only invite trouble. Rechecking the shoreline, there, under the light of a full moon, he saw an Arab kneeling on the sand taking direct aim at them.

Descent Into Paradise

Without warning, he pulled Shasa back underwater just as the muzzle flashed. He watched the bullet enter the water just above them as Shasa fought to go back to the surface. Knowing the gunman had marked their location; he pulled her ten yards to their right before allowing her to surface. When they did, the gunman had disappeared. In his place was a large smoking crater.

With three wounded, the Commander now faced a difficult decision. He knew neither Shasa nor the two wounded men could swim back to the gunship underwater. He wasn't even sure they could make it on the surface. He also knew that Captain Rosen was operating under orders from the Admiral not to leave any physical evidence of their involvement in tonight's extraction. On the other hand, going back ashore was not a viable option as he could see armed soldiers milling about behind the house. His dilemma was further exacerbated by the fact that blood in the water now brought the added danger of sharks into the equation.

Captain Rosen waited anxiously for the squad to surface. He had already breached his clear instructions from the Admiral to keep his ship completely out of sight from shore. He had clearly seen the danger the Bat Men were in and had acted accordingly. Now, he was becoming convinced there must have been casualties on shore as there was still no contact at the rendezvous point. Having alerted the shore of his presence already, he realized there was no further harm sending in his high-speed zodiac. Minutes later, a grateful Lt. Commander Betz heard the whine of an outboard motor, his dilemma no longer a worry.

CHAPTER 15

TEL AVIV

Shasa's medical leave lasted barely two weeks before she was summoned to a meeting at Mossad's headquarters. Still on crutches, the Director had kindly sent a car to her apartment.

An elderly lady came to get her. She looked like someone's kind old grandmother who had come by to serve cookies and tea. As they made their way up a circular staircase to the second floor, it was difficult to decide who was having a harder time, Shasa on crutches or her aged guide. The Director, a small balding man with thick glasses, stared at her as she entered his office. Seated behind an old desk covered with papers strewn every which way, he simply acknowledged her entrance by asking her to sit down.

"Welcome home Shasa, I am anxious to hear all about your time in Shatila."

She spent the next half hour responding to a variety of detailed questions. Describing the refugees who lived there, the demeanor of the Palestinians in general, and Abu in particular. She explained how she had set him up and killed him at the Yellow House. Then she finished her story with a brief account of her extraction.

"You are to be highly commended for your efforts."

Shasa smiled at the compliment but was totally stunned a moment later when the Director added, "Unfortunately, Abu survived. We have an excellent source who confirms he is badly injured but is now in Beirut at the Barbir Hospital."

"Are you sure, sir? I put that knife through his kidneys straight into his lung."

"I'm sure you did, my dear, but the fact is, he somehow survived. However, I did not bring you here to chastise you over that. You have done admirable work, and now I have a special assignment I wish you to undertake."

The South African Ambassador's home was located in a fashionable suburb of Tel Aviv. Tucked away in a predominantly residential neighborhood, the three-story stone house did not look like an official diplomatic residence. There were no flags flying out front, in fact, the only identification was a brass plaque on the front door with 'S.A. Ambassador' in block letters.

Ambassador Hunsmeyer was a career diplomat. Having risen slowly through the bureaucracy, he had spent most of his career posted in Europe.

In an unusual telex, the Ambassador had received an urgent message direct from the South African President instructing him to consummate a transaction between a Miss Datre and a Mr. Rios, both of whom were scheduled to arrive at his private residence later this morning. He had been instructed to agree to whatever terms were offered, the only non-negotiable item being the delivery schedule.

A very large black man whose bald head was the size of a bowling ball greeted Juan and Ricardo at the front door. As they entered the front hall, the butler announced in a very cultured English accent that the Ambassador would receive them in the garden. Walking behind the giant, Juan smiled, thinking he could use a butler as impressive as this huge South African.

The garden was a lovely setting for a meeting. The neatly trimmed hedge formed a backdrop to a lush perennial bed of multicolored roses and flowers bordering a stone terrace. Behind the hedge, on either side, was a row of orange trees whose sensual aroma wafted gently in the air. An ornate fountain was set in the brick wall separating the Embassy from its neighbor, its cascading waterfall providing just enough sound to mask any conversation being carried on within.

The Ambassador rose to greet them as Juan and Ricardo appeared. "A pleasure to meet you, Mr. Ambassador. What a lovely setting," commented Juan as they shook hands. Juan's eye then shifted to the fountain, by which stood one of the most stunning women he had ever seen. The Ambassador, noticing Juan's gaze, went on to introduce Miss Datre of the Israeli Intelligence Service to his South American guests.

"May I offer you all a drink? Coffee, tea or maybe something a bit stronger?"

Juan couldn't help but notice the red jowls of the Ambassador, and thought he might have company if he accepted the latter. His guests all requested coffee, much to the Ambassador's chagrin.

Once their coffee had arrived, Shasa raised her cup for a toast. "Mr. Ambassador, if I may, I would like to welcome our distinguished guests from Chile and thank you for hosting all of us this morning."

Her toast was echoed by Juan before she continued, "If you will allow me, I think it might be useful for me to outline our proposal to make sure we are all in accord." The three men nodded in agreement. Shasa then continued, "Israel is committed to assist the South African government in defending itself against the growing threat of a communist takeover. The misguided attempt by the West to impose their moral values on the government of South Africa is not acceptable to Israel, and therefore we have refused to abide by the trade sanctions now in place. Having said that, it does not pay to antagonize one's allies. Therefore, we would like to find a way to circumvent those sanctions without drawing any undue attention to our activities."

Descent Into Paradise

Pausing for a moment to drink her coffee, Shasa smiled at Juan as she continued,

"That is where our guests from Chile enter the picture. It is my understanding, Señor Rios, that your group is interested in purchasing certain trade goods from us, utilizing American currency for payment. In return for Israel processing those payments, you will resell those same goods to South Africa, arranging the necessary manifest to go through your customs without, shall I say, undue inspection."

She continued to look over at Juan for his acknowledgement. As she waited for his reply, she studied him more closely. He was a very handsome gentleman, well dressed and mannerly, but there was something cold about him, which gave her a sense of unease.

"Yes," Juan replied, "You are quite correct. We will agree to purchase the goods you are now storing in Haifa, ship them directly to a port in Chile, then on to South Africa. We only ask two things in return. First, that you process our cash payments without alerting the United States authorities. Second, you agree to supply my group with similar goods to the ones being shipped on to South Africa."

"I assume, Señor, that you are willing to pay for whatever goods are delivered directly to you on a similar basis?"

"Absolutely, we agree to the same cost structure as our South African friends, but we would insist upon paying cash on delivery in Haifa for the entire shipment."

Ambassador Hunsmeyer then asked how they would like to be paid upon delivery in Cape Town.

Ricardo answered, "We would request that you wire one half of the agreed upon price into an account in Geneva upon acknowledgement of our payment to Miss Datre. This will take place just prior to the scheduled departure from Israel. The balance would be expected upon delivery in Cape Town."

Descent Into Paradise

The Ambassador then asked, "Just to make it clear, we will pay you the same amount the Israelis charge you plus the shipping costs from Chile, is that correct?"

"No," replied Ricardo, "it is my understanding that you will reimburse us for your portion of the Israeli goods plus all transportation costs from Israel to Chile, then from there on to Cape Town. I trust that will not present a problem, Mr. Ambassador?"

"I would agree that since our goods will make up the vast majority of the shipment, it is only fair that we pick up the transportation costs. The only unusual part is paying you in Swiss francs while you will be paying in US dollars. Would it be acceptable to you to use the official exchange rate published in London the day of the wire transfer?"

"Perfectly acceptable, sir."

"Then, gentlemen, as that is settled, we have only to agree on the price and decide whose ships will carry the cargo," said Shasa.

"Miss Datre," Juan suggested, "I believe it will make my job much easier if the ship in question is known to our harbor officials."

Both Shasa and Ambassador Hunsmeyer readily agreed to let Juan choose the shipping company, leaving only the final price of the goods in question to be determined.

"The inventory list I sent both of you is the official export list we use worldwide. Those prices may be eligible for a discount up to 10% depending upon the volume ordered in any one year. Those calculations can be found at the bottom of the last page.

Are there any issues there?" asked Shasa.

"Mr. Ambassador, since you are paying for the vast majority of the shipment," said Juan, "I will defer to you. I am agreeable to those amounts for my goods."

Descent Into Paradise

"My government has authorized me to accept the prices as listed, taking into account we will likely qualify for the volume discount as outlined."

"Very good then, I will prepare the contract for your signatures later today or first thing tomorrow. Señor, are you both staying at the Royal Blue Hotel?"

"Yes, we are. It was an excellent suggestion."

"Fine, if it would be acceptable, I will have a courier bring you the documents as soon as they are prepared."

"As long as we can leave by tomorrow evening, that will be fine."

The Ambassador then announced, "Excellent. Now will you all please join me for lunch? Señor Rios and Señor Menez, with all due respect for the quality wines of your country, if you have not yet been introduced to our South African wines, you are in for a pleasant surprise."

Juan and Ricardo, having consumed way too much food and wine for lunch, decided it prudent to take a stroll through the beautifully landscaped grounds of Tel Aviv's newest premier hotel.

"Well, Ricardo, what do you think?"

"Juan, this little arrangement will not only make us rich, but we will soon be the most powerful entity in all of South America."

Juan smiled, thinking of what they had pulled off. "Just think of it, Ricardo. Nobody on the entire South American continent will possess the sophisticated weapons we will soon have access to." Suddenly he paused. "Ricardo, I just realized we're missing one very important piece of this whole scheme."

Ricardo, looking puzzled, asked, "And what might that be?"

"Someone who knows how to use all this expensive hardware," replied Juan.

Descent Into Paradise

"I think we may need to pay another visit to our new friend Miss Datre before we go."

With a very sly smile Ricardo nodded his agreement, wondering silently if this was the only reason his good friend wanted to schedule another visit.

The headquarters of the Israeli Intelligence Service was not what either man expected as the cab pulled up to the nondescript building. The two South Americans exiting the taxi were duly filmed as they walked up to the entrance. The door opened without a knock and the men were ushered into a sparsely furnished room on the second floor.

"Not quite the level of hospitality as at our luncheon," smirked Juan.

"Gentlemen, I did not expect to see you quite so soon. I trust nothing has happened to change your minds?" Shasa asked as she walked in, her elegant outfit rather incongruous in this bleak surrounding.

"No, actually, we were hoping you might expand our little arrangement, Miss Datre. It just occurred to us that we have nobody in Chile who would be qualified to use or service the goods we plan to purchase."

"Is that so? Well, I can see where that might present a problem, Señor. As I'm sure you can appreciate, however, we are already pushing our normal boundaries by agreeing to launder what we all know to be dirty money and providing sophisticated military arms to a private entity. Should this arrangement ever become public, it could prove quite detrimental for us. Actually, for both of us."

Neither Juan nor Ricardo missed the implied threat of that last sentence.

"Training a paramilitary force in Chile may be a bit much for my superiors."

Descent Into Paradise

To which Juan replied, "Miss Datre, if you are insinuating that your Agency does not train foreign military forces, as well as those of a more personal nature, nor, for that matter, launder what you refer to as dirty money on a daily basis, I'm afraid you are either very ignorant or a liar. I can take you to my country tomorrow and show you the Secret Police, alias the President's Palace Guard, half of whom speak Hebrew! Please include at least one military adviser in your contracts, Miss Datre, or don't bother to bring them." Juan and Ricardo were both on their feet in a flash and without another word left the building.

"Bastards," swore Shasa after they left. "Nothing but a bunch of arrogant, petty crooks with too much money," she fumed as she made her way over to the Director's office.

The Director looked up as she stormed into his office. "Problems?"

"Those two South American drug dealers just came in here demanding that we now include a military adviser to train their damned peasants how to use and service all the weapons they are about to buy!"

"Sit and calm down." The Director motioned to a chair.

"Actually, this may just be the opportunity we have been looking for. We have been searching for a way to infiltrate these people for years. I'm quite confident many of these terrorist cells are selling drugs to finance their operations. Hell, half the damned Beqaa Valley is now growing hashish as its primary export crop."

Shasa knew he had a point and reluctantly agreed.

The next morning a courier arrived at the Royal Blue Hotel with documents for a Mr. Juan Rios.

"I told you they would fold. Look at this, one military advisor with the rank of Major will be provided from the Israeli Special

Forces, provided he is compensated for his work at a salary of $100,000 per year, payable monthly to our friends here in Tel Aviv. I bet this poor Major won't see a nickel of that. Well, we will fix that, eh, amigo."

Juan looked at Ricardo with a big grin.

CHAPTER 16

ARLINGTON, VIRGINIA
THE PENTAGON

"General Bradley, I have General Argov on the phone from Israel."

"Thank you Mattie, is the line secure?"

"Yes sir, it is on automatic scrambler, shall I put him through?"

"Please."

"Hello Yuri, it is late for you."

"Good afternoon, George, yes, it is rather late for an old man like myself. Unfortunately, there is much chaos over here that knows no time limits. How are things with you?"

"Fine, a bit calmer over here I expect."

"Good, I am glad of that. George, I am calling to ask a personal favor of you. I believe you met my assistant, Shasa Datre when you were last here."

"Yes, I remember her well. I believe she is the one who helped get Watson and Megrid out of that nasty situation with the Riordan kidnapping."

"Of course, she was up there on a mission for our intelligence people at the time. George, as you may have heard, terrorists killed her parents in a raid on her village recently. You see, her father and I served in the Army together and became good friends. As she no longer has any family, I feel a sense of responsibility for her well-being. Right now, Mossad has her in its clutches and no good will come of that. It would give me much relief if…"

"Just tell me what I can do to help."

"I want her back under my control. The easiest way for me to accomplish that is to send her over to your conference next week in Boston. Mossad feels obligated to send someone over, and, if you request it, I can put that request straight through to the Director. He can hardly deny both of us."

"Of course she can come. Just have your secretary fax over her personal information; we will take care of her accommodations. I will place a call to the Director and make the request personally."

"Thank you, George, I truly appreciate the help."

Shasa was summoned back in to the Director's office. Having successfully completed the arrangements between the Rios group in Chile and the South Africans, she assumed it had something to do with that. To her surprise, however, the Director had other plans.

"I want you to go to America on a special assignment. Several months ago, you apparently met a certain American General. George Bradley is his name. Do you remember?"

Shasa was not thinking of the General when she answered somewhat blankly, "Yes, I remember."

"Good, he has personally requested that we send you to America to attend a special briefing on antiterrorism that he is conducting. According to my information, Bradley has recently created a joint task force, at the direct request of the White House, to combat terrorism across the globe. It would appear that the Americans are also interested in finally getting serious about their so-called 'war on drugs'. I would venture a guess Bradley finally has a Commander-in-Chief who understands how the real world operates. Stunning that it has taken them this long to comprehend that these terrorists and the drug cartels are thick as thieves. A rather obvious conclusion I would have thought, but I suppose we should be grateful that they reached it at all! At any rate, the General knows you work for us and has made a direct request for you to be involved. For what exact reason, I'm not sure, but I suspect your former boss has something to do with it."

"What role am I to play?"

"You will do whatever General Bradley requests. He is the best friend this country has in the US Armed Forces, so, within reason, we will give him whatever he asks for. Understood?"

Shasa, seeing the intensity in the Director's eyes for the first time, was reminded of his reputation. This was an order, not a request, so she simply replied, "Yes, sir. When do I leave?"

"You will receive your orders directly from General Argov. Until further notice, you will report to him."

As Shasa got up to leave, the Director had one last message, "Shasa, remember, whatever Bradley wants, please do your very best to give it to him. But any intelligence information he requests from us must be vetted through me, and me alone. On this, you will report directly to me. Is that clear?"

"I understand fully, Director."

Nodding slightly, the Director turned back to the papers on his desk.

Spring was trying hard to reach Maine. The last two months had seen Pete at the gym every day. His stamina was finally built up to the point he could handle a full two-hour workout in the local YMCA. Only his heart had not fully healed.

Pete walked briskly down the street, greeting old friends as he passed the stores on Main Street. At the Post Office, they handed him his special delivery letter. He opened it, realizing immediately his leave was about to end. The letter read, "Dear Captain Watson, I am hosting a conference in Boston at the end of the month which I would like you present. Representatives from the DEA, FBI, and CIA will also be in attendance,

Descent Into Paradise

as well as two representatives from Mossad. Please get in touch with Mattie for the details."

For a brief moment, Pete thought about going back to lobstering with his dad. It was only a fleeting thought. The truth was, as wonderful as Camden had been to recuperate, the better he felt, the more restless he had become.

Shasa tried to sleep on the flight but could not. Her mind kept going over the same scenario. He surely would be there, spot her, and then come running into her arms. Then the picture ended. What would she say? Pete darling, you know the only reason I shot you was because I love you.

"Are you alright?" asked Simon.

"Yes, yes of course, just a bit airsick, I suppose," was all she could muster.

"Should I get you an airbag?"

"No thank you. I will be fine in a minute."

She had never spent any time around this man who would be her liaison throughout this assignment. Simon was the only name she knew him by. He was certainly an important figure within Mossad. Highly secretive, his role was never discussed openly. All she knew was the Director treated him with great respect, and there were precious few about whom she could make that statement. He seemed kindly enough as they sat together, so she decided to strike up a conversation.

"Have you been to America before?"

Turning towards her, he answered in a soft voice, "Actually, I was born there. I fought in Europe during World War II, then emigrated to Palestine after the war."

Smiling at her, he went on, "I guess that dates me, eh?"

Wanting him to continue, Shasa looked at him with obvious admiration. "You must have some wonderful stories to tell."

Descent Into Paradise

"Interesting maybe. Wonderful, I'm not sure I would use that description."

She sensed a bit of hesitation, but he must have decided she was safe as he then told her about his early days in Palestine. "It was an uncomfortable existence to be sure. Here we came over to settle down in a land, which clearly did not belong to us. But, having nowhere else to go, we felt we had no alternative other than to push forward. Clearly, the Arabs wanted no part of us, and the British treated us with equal contempt. It was a humble beginning, I can assure you."

Simon then continued after sipping his hot tea.

"The poor Palestinians. I have always felt great remorse that the price of our homeland had to come at their expense. The bitter irony is that we did to them what had just been done to us. We now call them terrorists. Are they?" he posed thoughtfully. "Or are they simply fighting to get their homes back? Is that terrorism? If it is, then I guess we have all been guilty of terrorism of one sort or another."

Shasa could see the pain reflected in those wistful eyes as he stared into the back of the seat in front of him.

Trying to keep him talking, she asked, "Where did you end up settling?"

Turning back towards her, he went on, "Actually, I joined a group of Germans, who planned on heading up towards the Golan Heights. I guess it was as close to the Alps as they were going to get. We ran into much resistance as the Palestinians began to realize we were planning to stay. After much bloodshed, those of us who survived settled down in a small village that became our new collective home."

Unfortunately for her, the pilot's voice came over the intercom announcing their descent into Boston. This must have brought Simon back into the present, for he seemed to lose his train of thought, instead opening a discussion on the upcoming conference with her and what he hoped to achieve.

CHAPTER 17

BOSTON

General Bradley stood at the podium to open the conference. "I would like to welcome all of you here today for the first in a series of vital strategic meetings designed to forge a comprehensive strategy to counter the growing threat of international terrorism around the globe. For some time now it has been my belief that the drug cartels and the international terrorist networks have formed an unholy alliance. As we sit here today, it is clear to me that they are acting in harmony across national boundaries, while we, the major law enforcement agencies of the world, are still working in isolated groups, reluctant to work together or even share our intelligence with each other. To make matters worse, this is occurring not just between nations, but between agencies within the same nation, ours being the most egregious example. Today, I have asked that representatives from all the major agencies around the globe be present. As some of you may be aware, the President of the United States recently appointed me to head a collective effort to put an end to the reckless and unlawful behavior of these criminals who seem bent upon the destruction of our most sacred institutions and beliefs. As of today, ladies and gentlemen, I can assure you that the full might of the United States Armed Forces will be brought to bear on any organization found guilty of either selling illegal drugs or committing any organized acts of violence against the United States or any of our allies anywhere around the globe. These are not idle words or idle threats. They are the direct orders of my Commander–In-Chief, and they will be carried out to the best of my ability. Now, before we get into our program for today, I would ask each of you to please introduce yourself as we go around the room."

At that moment, having had trouble getting a taxi, Shasa and Simon entered the room.

Pete just stared as she sat down, not daring to believe what his eyes assured him to be true. His thoughts were soon interrupted by the booming voice of General Bradley.

"Major Watson, would you please start by introducing yourself, so we can move on."

Shasa studiously avoided eye contact with anyone throughout the morning session. Lunch was served to all in their seats so it was not until near the end of the afternoon session that she finally dared look in his direction. When she did, his seat was empty. She barely heard Simon as he responded to a direct question from one of the CIA representatives.

"We learned of Mrs. Riordan's presence in Shatila through an operative stationed there. As soon as it became known, we immediately passed that information on directly to General Bradley, as he was our point of contact at the time."

This was the answer Argov and Bradley had decided upon before the conference began. The Riordan kidnapping and subsequent rescue operation had been a source of controversy ever since the operation had concluded. Suspecting that the question would arise, the General had made sure Pete would be absent when the meeting was opened up for general questions.

The conference proved useful if only to help achieve better coordination amongst the various entities. By the end of the day, it was agreed that all information gathered by any agency should be passed on to Bradley's office for immediate processing and general dissemination. The General, in turn, promised to keep the FBI, DEA, and the CIA completely up to speed on any developments, which might fall under their areas of jurisdiction. Security of all data transmitted would be the General's responsibility, with any leaks or suspected leaks being dealt with in military fashion. Translation: no fair trials need be observed. This point was not lost on any of the participants. It was an enthusiastic and excited group of military officers and government bureaucrats who reconvened for dinner that evening.

Pete set his alarm for 5:30pm, only allowing himself an hour's nap. Having still not fully regained his strength, he deemed it best to get some rest before his evening meetings. At 6:00pm sharp, there was a knock on his door.

"Bota, welcome. Come on in. It's great to see you."

"And you as well, my friend. How are you feeling? I just learned of your ordeal this morning."

"I'm better, thanks. No lasting damage, just feeling a bit weak. Please, have a seat. I ordered some drinks and food, which should be coming up shortly. I thought, given our last conversation in Miami, meeting here in the room might be better than letting on we know each other."

"Very wise indeed, my friend."

The DEA agent then gave his report.

"I believe the most promising lead we've come up with so far is a young lady in Valparaiso, Chile. I spent some time down there and it became apparent to me that this Juan Rios is a very dangerous character indeed. His parents were both murdered by a rival drug lord some months ago, and, from everything I could gather, he has big plans for expanding the family business, including replacing the old guard with a much more competent and ruthless team."

"Tell me about this young lady in Valparaiso. How does she play into this?"

"Her name is Marianna. She grew up on a small farm in the hills just above Valparaiso, which is a bustling port town just west of Santiago. Her family's farm also happens to be very close to where Rios has his family compound. The interesting part, besides her extraordinary beauty, is her sister Madonna is Juan Rios's mistress."

"Interesting. How did you find out about these two sisters?"

"I happen to have a friend who does business down that way. He met Marianna, who was working his hotel bar one night some months back. She commands $100 for an hour of her company and $500 for spending the night. Top of the line for down there, but she is truly a tigress in bed."

Pete decided not to inquire how his new friend was aware of such details.

Still smiling, he responded, "I assume your statement about being a 'promising lead' was business, not personal?"

"Let's just say that some informants are more interesting than others, and she ranks amongst the more interesting."

"Anything else?"

"No, just be careful. I just got quizzed by my boss as to why I had been invited."

"What did you tell him?"

"I played ignorant. Said I didn't know, and, for fun, told him I thought he had invited me."

"His name's Cabot, right?"

"That's right. Apparently, the name Cabot means something up here in Boston. Obviously, the guy's got more money than brains, but I suppose going to Harvard gives you a leg up on the rest of us."

Pete had only met Henry Cabot briefly that morning, but he knew his General was not a big fan of the Drug Enforcement Agency's boss.

"I'll let the General know to play dumb if Cabot gets nosy. For now, I suggest we keep our dealings strictly between the two of us."

"Works for me."

"Anything else?"

"No, not now. We have other operations going in Columbia which may prove useful, but, quite frankly, this Rios crowd scares me more than the others at this point."

After La Bota left, Pete digested what he had heard. Both he and General Bradley were convinced the only way to achieve any meaningful results in stopping the flow of illegal drugs into the US was to interdict them before they arrived on shore. Once inside, they were just too difficult to detect. The main problem, as they both knew, was the DEA had not been successful in penetrating the inner circles of any of the major cartels. Without any viable intelligence as to how those operations functioned, it was virtually impossible to come up with a viable strategy to counteract the ever-increasing amounts of illegal contraband flowing across the borders. As the picture became clearer, Pete thought, La Bota's contempt for his boss was becoming more understandable.

After a quick shave, he made his way to the private room the General had reserved for dinner.

Shasa came down halfway through the first course, as her stomach had fallen victim to a bad case of nerves. Pete noticed her immediately as she sat down next to Simon. He decided to approach her after dinner. Shortly after Shasa sat down, Simon, who had been briefed about the liaison between them, decided to bring the matter to the surface.

"I had an opportunity to speak to Major Watson on the elevator. He tells me he is well on his way towards a full recovery."

Descent Into Paradise

Shasa, realizing Simon probably knew the full story, merely replied, "I am very pleased to hear that. Shooting your enemy is one thing. Shooting a friend is quite another."

"I can sympathize completely, but think for a moment how it must be for the poor soul who gets shot."

Shasa, flashing a look of anger at her dinner partner, responded in a louder voice than necessary, "And you might think for a moment that had I not intervened, that poor American hostage would most likely not be alive today, although I realize that might not unduly upset some of you."

As a waiter appeared to clear the dessert plates, Simon chose not to respond. Coffee was offered to anyone who wished to stay. Most everyone did. Small groups of people gathered around the room discussing the day's affairs, among them the General, Shasa, and Simon. Pete decided the moment was right.

"Major," Simon said, as he spied him coming over, "Please come say hello to your erstwhile assailant and savior."

Shasa, obviously ill at ease, smiled at Pete as she held out her hand awkwardly, "I am relieved to hear that your wound has healed satisfactorily. I have suffered for you ever since that awful night."

Pete simply replied honestly, "According to the naval surgeon, your shot simply grazed my side. It was the slug from an AK-47 which apparently caused the real damage."

The General decided to put it more bluntly: "Pete told me directly that neither he, nor Major Megrid, would have made it out of that camp alive if this brave young lady had not acted as she did."

Shasa, ill at ease from all the attention, thanked them before excusing herself to go up to her room.

The conference ended at noon the following day with agreements in place as to how the various agencies would work together in the future. General Bradley was in great spirits as he spied Pete in the lobby.

"Watson, I believe it is time you got back to work. What do you say?"

"I'm ready, sir. Tell me where and when to report, and I will be there."

"Tuesday at 08h00 sharp in my office. That gives you the weekend to wrap up your affairs in Maine."

Pete watched as the General turned to shake hands with Bota's nemesis, Henry Cabot, the head of the DEA, leaving Pete to say, "Yes sir," to himself.

"Talking to yourself?" Simon queried as he approached him from behind. "Maybe you are in need of a bit more rest." He smiled.

Turning around, Pete grinned as he answered, "That decision was just made for me. I am to report back on Tuesday."

"Well then, I suggest you enjoy your last days of vacation," said Simon.

"I certainly will, thank you. What will you do now, are you back to Israel?"

"No, as a matter of fact, I am on my way to New Jersey to visit relatives. Our flight home is not until Tuesday evening. I just wanted to say goodbye and wish you all the best as you rejoin the fight."

"Thank you, Simon. I hope you have a good visit with your family."

Shasa observed Simon shaking hands with Pete. I have put this off long enough, she thought, walking towards them.

Pete had just turned around when he saw her approaching, causing an awkward moment before either spoke.

"Pete, I owe you a big apology, one which I am very late issuing," Shasa murmured.

Descent Into Paradise

"You mean about the shooting, or not returning any of my phone calls?"

She had hoped this might go smoothly but never really expected it to. Well aware of the pain she had inflicted, emotionally as well as physically, she could now only hope their relationship was not beyond repair.

"I was referring to your phone calls, as I believe I have already apologized for the other."

Somehow, they managed to survive the initial five minutes, after which his wounded pride and her raw nerves diminished to the point where meaningful communication was allowed to take place. They agreed to have lunch at the hotel where Shasa nervously found herself doing most of the talking. She explained why she had gone to Shatila in the first place, and why she had not exited with them. Having explained her motive for shooting him in the side, she finished by describing her own extraction by the Israeli Bat Men once she had concluded her mission. By the time she had finished, they were the last diners left. Realizing this was her attempt at reconciliation, he decided it was time he reciprocated. It wasn't very long before hurt and anger were replaced by the affection and admiration they had felt from their very first moment together. On their way to the elevator, Pete asked about her plans for the weekend.

"I am not sure. I thought I might take a tour so I could learn about how the original colonies were settled. What about you?"

"I am driving back home tonight. I was hoping you might join me."

Shasa looked him in the eye as she thought through that proposal. It was just what she had hoped, but could she handle her emotions? Her heart had been broken too many times already. Dare she risk it again? His beseeching look, however, pushed her to say yes.

Descent Into Paradise

"Wonderful!" he exclaimed. His smile lit up the room as he took her hand.

The following morning, he was up early, having promised to pick her up for breakfast and give her a tour.

Camden consists of a Main Street with some enchanting alleys leading down to the harbor and the docks, lined with small bakeries, bookstores, antique shops, gift shops, and clothing stores. A fragrant bakery tempted them to sit down for coffee and sugar donuts. Afterwards, hand in hand, they strolled down towards the waterfront. There, they spent a leisurely afternoon viewing the beautiful yachts anchored in the harbor, followed by an early dinner down on the pier.

As they strolled back to the Blue Fin Inn, where Pete had booked her a room, he decided not to press her into spending the night together. He had lost her once; he did not plan on losing her again. They kissed good night, held each other for an extended moment, and then he walked home happier than he had been in months.

Sunday evening, at his invitation, Pete's mother and father joined them for dinner. When Mrs. Watson discovered Shasa had never tasted a lobster, she insisted upon ordering one for her to try. When four arrived on large pewter platters, Shasa could only marvel that people actually ate these monsters. Then, watching the waitress tie a paper bib around Pete's neck, she couldn't help but smile.

"Just wait, your dress will never survive that lobster," he chuckled as she politely refused her bib.

It turned out to be a lovely evening with Shasa clearly the main focus of attention. Peppered with questions about life in Israel, Shasa happily answered them until asked about her family. Pete quickly stepped in to change the subject. The evening ended on a high note, however, as the owner brought a big chocolate cake over to the table with white letters saying, We Will Miss You Both, Love Mom and Dad.

As they walked back to the Inn, Shasa told Pete how lucky he was to have such a wonderful, loving family.

When they reached the hotel this time, she put her arms around his neck and whispered something in his ear.

On Monday morning when Pete did not come down for breakfast, his father asked if he had come home. His mother laughed, "I think not from the look in both their eyes. My guess is they spent a romantic night in the Inn, like we once did, remember?"

Shasa woke up first. Looking over to see if Pete was awake, she noticed the ugly raised scar where the second bullet had exited. My poor darling, she thought. Shatila seemed very remote to her at that moment.

Pete woke up to the touch of her finger tracing the scar on his chest. An hour later, they lay in bed exhausted, relishing the moment, neither wanting to contemplate what lay ahead.

CHAPTER 18

Abu's wound had finally healed enough to leave the hospital and return back home. Still weak from the loss of blood, he now ventured out only for short periods of time.

One day, he appeared for lunch at Nouri's café with the Iranian Colonel and another man who was a stranger. They took only one table, moving it over to a corner so they could be private. For the first time, Abu acknowledged Moussa's existence with a warm smile as he introduced the young boy to his new companions. "Meet my favorite waiter. He has the best looking red apron in all Shatila." The men laughed as they looked at Moussa but soon ignored him to continue their discussion.

The stranger sitting across from Abu had the face of a hawk. Fierce gray eyes dominated his dark visage. Clean-shaven, he radiated violence. Thinking they were finished, Moussa nervously started clearing their table. Annoyed at the interruption, the stranger grabbed him unexpectedly with a powerful grip, almost cracking his thin wrist. "Leave us alone and never remove a man's glass before it is empty." Moussa's eyes, filled with tears, glanced at the others but neither paid him the slightest attention.

"Are you coming or not?" demanded Colonel Mir.

Abu wiped his mouth with his napkin and sighed, "I am not sure. You still have not told me your plans."

The Colonel snarled, "I will tell you after you confirm your position. The world is changing, my friend. Your way is doomed, just look around you. Is this what you aspire to?"

Turning in his chair, he continued in his rasping voice, "Look, look at this filthy camp, is this your idea of a homeland?

Descent Into Paradise

Let me tell you what is going to happen here. Your soldiers are about to be killed or exiled to the four corners of the Arab world; your women and children are going to be murdered when you leave, and the Israelis, with their American friends turning a blind eye, are going to minimize you as an effective fighting force once and for all."

There was dead silence as Mir emptied his glass. Wiping his mouth with the back of his hand, he continued. "Right now, the Israelis are amassing their troops for their version of the Final Solution. This time, they will not be on the receiving end. You, my friend, are the ones destined to be exterminated."

Abu sat in stony silence as the Colonel went on unabashed, "They will kill you, believe me, and that bastard Sharon will keep labeling you as bloody terrorists so that he can justify the slaughter."

Leaning over the red and white-checkered tablecloth, Abu whispered, "Where do you get these notions from? Arafat told me his sources informed him they only plan to strike 60 miles into Lebanon; we are safe here, our families are safe here."

With a look of utter contempt, Colonel Mir, an Iranian by birth, leaned closer to Abu. Moussa, standing behind the counter, could barely make out the response. "Let me assure you, this lovely little camp of yours will be a mass gravesite before long."

Mir sat back in his chair and surveyed the other two, his eyes piercing into theirs. As his companion sat stone still, he continued. "Your days as a fighting force are over, your leadership in the terrorist world will follow suit." His voice was gradually getting louder. "Arafat is finished! The Israelis will never deal with him; the Americans want no part of him. Hell, he can't even count on the Arab world to back him anymore! We will unite the whole Islamic world against the infidels. It's your choice." Leaning over to be closer to Abu's face, he lowered his voice to a whisper. "Time... time is running out. I give you one week to decide." Mir silently rose to his feet, leaving a very sullen looking man staring at the glass in front of him.

Several minutes went by before Moussa got up enough courage to ask Abu if he would like anything else. Abu looked at the fragile child, wondering what would become of this poor little creature; what would become of all the children? What would become of his people as a whole? The pain in his shoulder flared up. The wound had healed; it was his heart that was still broken. Shaking his head, he wondered if Allah had truly forsaken them all.

That evening, a thin light filtered through the front door of Nouri's Café. An old woman passing by told her daughter, "I have lived in this hellhole for seven years and never once have I seen that old bag of wind work at night." She smiled to herself as she passed. "One thing I know for certain is that he is not doing any renovations."

They both pictured the interior of the only coffee house in their section of the camp. A cracked ceiling dropped a steady drip of dirty paint chips onto the old cement floor. They aged where they fell, eventually decomposing. The plastic tables were barely holding up under the constant use. The chairs were in even worse condition. The only decoration in the whole place was an old, faded picture of Brigitte Bardot.

"Old Nouri must still have a thing for that French whore," laughed the old woman. "At least he has feelings for somebody other than himself." They walked slowly past the Café towards their block and all the misery that awaited them.

Inside the Café, a half empty bottle of whiskey stood on a table flanked by two glasses and a plate of meat pies. The atmosphere in the room matched the décor.

Descent Into Paradise

"I fear we are nearing the end, my old friend," mourned Abu, taking his head in his hands. "I have been thinking about what that Iranian said, and I am beginning to believe him."

The old man reached for the bottle, pouring each another glass.

"One thing I will say, we are no match for those Israeli dogs. Look at us; we live in the squalor of this ghetto. Our children barely have enough food to eat while our young men sit idly by, complaining about what has been done to them."

Nouri began to cough. "What has happened to us? We have always been such a proud people. Where is our pride? I am just an old man, tired of life; tired of living in this hellhole we now call home. I am resigned to end my days because I have given up hope of ever going home. I am ready to die, for there is nothing left to live for."

Water was pooling in the corner of his eyes as he placed his shaking hands on the table. "You, my young friend, have your whole life ahead. You must decide what you believe in and how you will accomplish it. Your Iranian friend may not be to your liking, but he does have a vision for the future. We do not. All we do is complain about how unfair life is."

Taking another drink of whiskey, he put up his hand to stop Abu, who was about to interrupt him. "No, let me finish for I may not be able to do this again. Abu, your father was like a brother to me. He died fighting for what he believed in. You have a choice; fight for your beliefs and die for them, if necessary, or give up and become an old man like me. One way or another, we all perish. The only difference is some of us fulfilled our dreams, some of us did not, and some of us never even had the courage to dream in the first place."

Abu got up and came over to place his arms around the old man.

"Uncle Nouri, I have missed my father more than you will ever know. He was a beacon of hope and love to my mother and me. When that light was extinguished, it left us both in a darkness of hopelessness and despair. Maybe we are guilty of wallowing there, maybe we have just given up. I for one have given up hope of ever going home. Palestine is a beautiful dream, but that is all it will ever be."

Abu looked into Nouri's cloudy eyes. Then, in a low forceful voice, he added, "Having said that, I must continue to fight for that dream, because, at the end of the day, it's all we have left. The only question is how to wage that fight."

Both men sat there in stony silence. It was getting late for the old man, yet he sensed it was important for Abu to reach some conclusions. Nouri, fighting the desire for bed, leaned over to pour the remaining amber liquid into their empty glasses.

"Your father and I were best of friends growing up. Only when we were uprooted and my family moved here did we part ways. He was too proud to stand for the injustice wrought upon us. I was too timid to do anything but accept the fate that was dealt us. Your father is dead. I plan to join him soon. The fact of life for us, Abu, is that the Israelis will never accept us back into Palestine. We, as a people, are not strong enough to fight them, so we are destined to live a life of exile until we accept our fate and move on."

Nouri's chin, quivering slightly, said firmly, "You, Abu, have two choices, and I do not envy you either one. You can choose to give up this entire struggle, move to a different part of the world and begin again. Adopt a new country, adopt a new attitude, and let the past go. Or, you can choose to strike back to avenge the death of your father and the many others who have joined him. But, if you choose to fight, it will have to be on different terms than the ones which have failed us up to this point."

Descent Into Paradise

Both men realized the magnitude of this discussion. For one it was a major catharsis; for the other, a life choice.

"My son, for I see you as my son, to fight the Israelis effectively you will have to bring bloodshed to their soil, our homeland. You will have to wage a war of terror. You cannot hope to match them on the battlefield. The Americans will always back them, as they must politically. You can only hope to achieve vengeance through creating fear in their hearts and terror in their minds. Random acts of violence carried out on a consistent basis in their towns and cities with no warning. This is a terrible path, this will be a war in which there are no winners or losers, just terror."

Neither man moved. They both could picture the horror of what was being proffered. Finally, old Nouri spoke again. "Abu, it breaks my heart, but it is the only way. We must match violence with violence. They bomb our people, we bomb theirs. We may be forced to deliver ours in a bus, but we can wreak as much havoc as they can. Maybe, just maybe, the few sane members of the human race still left will then finally call for a halt to all this insanity. Only then can there be a just and lasting peace for all of us."

In a whisper, the drained old man finally finished. "I don't know if I even believe that will ever happen, Abu. I know I will never see that day. Nor do I think you will. But we must think of Moussa and his generation. For either we will all sink into this unholy world of escalating violence and revenge, or we will all finally come to our senses."

A foreboding stillness filled the bleak Café, only to be broken moments later by the faint movement of a tattered shirtsleeve wiping away tears of regret and sorrow.

Abu tried to help Nouri rise, but he was waved away by the broken old man who could not move at the moment. Abu knew

Descent Into Paradise

Nouri did not have far to go and honored his friend's wish to be alone to try to find some peace. Quietly he left the Café, trying to regain his own equilibrium.

The odor of unwashed bodies mixed with the rancid smell of open sewer lines filled the warm night air. Abu set off to find Moussa. He had no idea where the boy lived; he didn't even know why he wanted to see him. Empty beer bottles were strewn with empty plastic containers everywhere he looked. Empty cans were lined up across the wall behind him. Some with bullet holes, others just waiting for target practice. The narrow alleys were crowded with people going back and forth. The atmosphere was loud with angry voices raised in grating tones, everyone arguing, nobody listening. Maybe that was part of the problem.

After several blocks, he asked a young girl who was sitting on a large rock if she knew a young blond boy named Moussa. She looked up at the big stranger with his handsome face wreathed in a warm smile. His expression was warm so she tried not to be afraid. She had already learned enough not to give information to any stranger.

Abu clearly understood, so lying to her, he gently said. "I am his Uncle. I seem to be lost for I thought he lived near the Café where he works. Mr. Nouri said he was down this way."

Immediately the girl smiled. "Oh, you know Mr. Nouri then it's all right, Moussa lives around the corner." The girl pointed in the correct direction. Abu thanked her and started down the path, waving to her when he reached the corner. He continued until he reached a dead end. All that was in front of him was a dirt embankment covered with scrub grasses and old vines, which clung to the fence marking the end of the camp.

There were no lights, certainly no dwellings. I wonder what she meant by around the corner, he thought as he looked

Descent Into Paradise

around. On a whim, he walked over to the embankment to look more closely. There was nothing there other than several pigeons perched on the fence watching him as he watched them.

A small cough interrupted his thoughts as he turned to leave. Hesitating a moment, straining to identify the sound, he heard it again. He wondered where it could have come from. "Moussa," he whispered, "it is Abu. Is that you? I have come to see you."

A moment later, a very small head peeped over the hill amongst the vines. A trembling voice, barely audible, said, "What do you want with me? I have done nothing wrong."

Abu, realizing his sudden appearance had frightened his young friend, sought to put him at ease. "I'm sorry to bother you, my little waiter. I only came to apologize for the rough way my friend treated you at lunch. I hope your arm is OK."

Moussa wasn't sure how to reply. He'd never had anyone be concerned for his well-being, certainly not a big gruff stranger like this. "I'm fine," he finally offered.

Abu, searching for a place to sit, asked if he could talk for a moment. Moussa thought about the question, his face conveying all his trepidation. Reluctantly, he motioned for the big man to climb up to where he sat against the fence.

"Do you live here, Moussa?" No answer. So Abu tried again. "Do you sleep here on top of this pile of dirt?"

Moussa was not quite sure as to how to respond. He wanted this man to stay, to talk with him, but he was fearful of exposing his secret dwelling. Would the man tell anyone?

Abu could see the conflicting emotions play out on the boy's face. "If you don't want to share your secret place, don't. I only want to be your friend. You see, I no longer have any family. Sometimes a man needs to share his thoughts. Tonight, I thought we might just talk and share our thoughts."

Descent Into Paradise

Moussa's desperate loneliness overcame his fear as he stood up. "Here, follow me," he said as he slid down the other side into the clump of vines at the bottom.

Abu slid to a halt beside him. Moussa hesitated one more moment before pushing wide a branch, then gestured for Abu to crawl inside. Once there, Abu could only sit back against the concrete cylinder that formed the side of the sewerage pipe, unable to sit upright without banging his head. As his eyes became accustomed to the dark, he could just make out the mattress spread out on the ground, with the small boy sitting on it looking at him.

"So this is your home. I wish I had as nice a place as this," Abu said, smiling while looking around. "Nobody to bother you. It surely can't take long to clean up."

To Abu's delight, Moussa's sad face broke into a toothy grin. "It's small, but it's all mine. I don't have to share it with anyone." Abu sensed the pride with which that statement was made. He knew then why he had come. He had sensed something in this boy worth saving, and now he realized what it was. Pride. This skinny little fellow had guts. He clearly had neither family nor support of any kind, yet he had his own home and a job. But most of all he had pride.

"I'm very jealous," he told Moussa. "I didn't have nearly as much when I was your age. I'm not even sure I wouldn't trade places with you right now."

They talked for hours into the night. Finally, they both went to sleep. Moussa awoke during the night to find himself warm and happy. He went back to sleep dreaming of the father he never knew.

Abu stopped going to the Café for coffee or lunch, but on several nights he would come to little Moussa's dwelling. There they made their plans for the future. Abu told him that he would be leaving soon, but if Moussa wanted to join him, he could.

Descent Into Paradise

"Where exactly are we going?" Moussa asked in a very small voice.

"I am not sure yet."

Moussa, scared of the answer, asked anyway, "Will we stay together? You won't leave me alone if I go?"

Abu could sense the anguish in that pleading little voice. "No, Moussa, wherever we end up, we'll go together, stay together and fight together."

They talked so long that Moussa finally fell asleep dreaming of becoming a great warrior.

CHAPTER 19

General Argov left the Cabinet meeting with mixed emotions. He realized, while Israel had no other option other than to send troops into Lebanon, the mood in the room had bordered on fanatical. General Ariel Sharon had somehow convinced the politicians that this was their opportunity to finally eradicate the vermin infiltrating their northern border and be done with Arafat and his cronies once and for all. He had promised them a quick and decisive victory at a minimal cost of Israeli lives. They wanted to believe and they did. Argov knew, no matter how successful the invasion might be, it would merely give Israel a short reprieve from the inevitable. Once Arafat was gone, it would only be a matter of time before a new group would form, more militant and dangerous than the last. What Sharon was advocating was a very dangerous gambit, and he feared what the American reaction would be. He was not looking forward to alerting General Bradley to what the rest of the world would learn within the next 48 hours.

LEBANON

"Major, headquarters says keep going unless we run into heavy resistance."

"Keep going where?" exclaimed Zev. Tired and irritated, Zev and his men had been up for most of the past 48 hours. Having been tasked with advanced recon duty for the 7th Armored Brigade, they had left Camp Saar at dawn the previous day. Traveling through the Golan Heights from northern Israel, they had encountered only slight resistance. Now, having just secured their main objective, the town of Jazzin, they were apparently being ordered to keep heading north. Zev knew they had been lucky so far as the Syrian ground forces apparently did not possess the same zeal for combat as the Palestinians.

"I thought Jazzin was our final destination?"

"I don't know Major, rumor has it they're running into heavy resistance along the coast. I guess the General wants us to keep moving while we can."

Zev lit a cigarette and went to find his friend, Major David Ginsberg, the commander of the 7th Armored Brigade.

"David, what the hell is going on? We're already farther north than the original plan called for. Now I'm hearing we're to keep going."

Holding up his hand, he responded, "I have no idea what's going on. It makes no sense to me either. What I do know is we're going to spend the night right here. My men are exhausted, as I'm sure yours are as well. I will radio headquarters in the morning and see what they have to say."

Moussa awoke with a start. Something made him sit up. Then he heard it. A thump, which shook the earth under him so hard it took his breath away. A second later, the concussion from the explosion knocked him backwards. A moment later came another whooshing close overhead, followed by another loud explosion. He began to hear screaming and cries all around. Frozen with fear, Moussa pulled his thin cotton blanket over his head; shut his eyes tight, and prayed his concrete bunker would protect him.

For what seemed like hours, Moussa did not have the courage to leave his bunker. The high-pitched screams of incoming shells, together with the cries of their human counterparts, told him enough about the death and destruction taking place outside. Finally, the shelling stopped. Crawling out of his bunker to take a peek over the mound, he saw fires everywhere. Canvas tents, which comprised the majority of the housing, made ideal targets for the phosphorous shells being used by the Israelis. Apparently, so did the poor people who lived inside them. Pitiful moans and the smell of burning flesh filled his senses.

Abu had just completed his meeting with Colonel Mir when he heard the planes flying overhead. Waiting until dark to return back to camp, it took him over an hour to travel the three miles back to Shatila. There was virtually no traffic, but large bomb craters and various debris blocked several of the roads. Abu wondered how the civilized world could sit back and condone the Israeli bombing of a city full of innocent civilians with no official declaration of war.

When he finally reached the gates of Shatila, smoke enveloped the camp. Men, women, and children were scurrying about trying to put out fires and assist the wounded, whose anguished cries pierced the night air. Just as Abu recognized the familiar sign of Nouri's Café, the concussion from a shell exploding overhead knocked him to the ground. As he rose, he felt a sharp pain stabbing down his right leg; the culprit, a thin slice of hot shrapnel lodged in his thigh. Despite the pain, he limped on. Nouri's Café had been hit hard, its corrugated metal roof completely collapsed. As he peered inside, hoping beyond hope to find it deserted, he saw the old man slumped over a table, his head twisted at an impossible angle. Closing his eyes, he held his hands together and said a short prayer.

"May you go to a happier place, my friend, one which will honor you more than here." Passing by his own tent, which was now just a smoldering pile of ash, he knew to sit down was to die. Somehow, he managed to stumble towards the small dirt hiding place at the edge of the camp, which, to his great relief, remained unscathed.

"Moussa, are you there? Are you all right?"

A moment later, a little blond head appeared.

"Help me, I feel like old Nouri," said Abu as he put his arm around Moussa's shoulder.

"What's wrong?"

"It's nothing. Let's get inside before another shell decides to blow us both up."

Once inside, Abu sat down gratefully. The wound was still bleeding, but it didn't appear to be serious. Fortunately, he always carried a small medical kit in his shoulder pack, which contained all the essentials for minor battle wounds, including six morphine tablets, all courtesy of the Israeli Army. With the help of his young assistant, he pulled out the shrapnel, cleaned and bandaged the wound, then soon fell into a deep, drug induced sleep.

Abu woke up the next morning to the acrid smell of cordite mixed with the unpleasant odor of burning flesh, a grim reminder of what lay on the other side of the knoll.

Although the morphine had helped him get through the night, it left him feeling weak and a bit disoriented. He now realized that the Iranian Colonel had been right all along. After committing to join forces at last night's meeting, Mir had shared with him the Iranians' official notification to Arafat that henceforth Iran would no longer support the PLO either financially or militarily. Apparently, President Assad of Syria had sent a similar message, as he was now firmly entrenched in the Iranian camp. Arafat, having found himself completely isolated without any solid support, was now more or less a vagabond traveling among the Arab capitals, trying to drum up support which no longer existed.

Descent Into Paradise

A sudden explosion outside pierced through Abu's dulled brain and he instinctively rolled on top of Moussa in order to protect him from the blast. Fortunately, the knoll absorbed most of the shock, but the smell of burning sulfur lay heavy in the air. The heat was becoming unbearable, as the entire area around Moussa's bunker was suddenly ablaze. To his horror, Abu suddenly realized what munitions the Israelis had chosen to drop on the camp. Faced with a choice of death by asphyxiation if they didn't move out, or severe burns if they did, he gave Moussa his leather jacket, instructing the young boy to pull it over his head and keep his face as covered as possible.

"Moussa," he said with a forced smile, "I'm afraid we're going to have to abandon your little castle and make a run for it."

Moussa, hearing the crackle of fires and feeling the intense heat build up in the bunker, looked at Abu, fear written all over his face.

"We may suffer a few burns, but we'll survive. Don't worry, just tie up those sneakers real tight, and get over that hill as fast as you can! After you slide down, get up and run for anywhere that's not on fire! I will be right behind you."

With that, he gently pushed him out the entrance and watched as the nimble youth scrambled up the slope without a sound. Abu then followed at a much slower pace, the pain of burning flesh now competing with the searing pain in his thigh. Once over the top, he followed his own instructions sliding down on his backside through the burning grass, his eyes shut and his clothes on fire.

A piercing scream greeted him as he painfully got back on his feet. Not twenty feet in front of him stood Moussa, frozen still as flames inched up his pant leg. Abu, oblivious to his own burns, immediately grasped the situation. Moussa had inadvertently stepped on a shell fragment and the burning sulfur

Descent Into Paradise

had ignited the poor boy's pants. Rushing over, he picked up his leather jacket off the ground and wrapped it as tightly as he could around Moussa's burning leg, trying to deprive the fire of the oxygen it needed to continue. Moussa's screams gradually died down into agonized moans as the charred remains of his right leg began to give off a hideous odor. Everywhere people were running about like human torches, screaming for help that never came. Water did nothing to extinguish the fire; instead, it turned the flames to hissing steam until the burning phosphorous came back to life.

Abu did not recognize the two young women who came by and took Moussa to the Barbir Hospital nearby. With the aid of a walking stick, Abu arrived at the Pediatric ward shortly before noon. As he entered, he walked past the body of a small child still smoldering beneath a plastic body bag.

Abu visited two different floors of wounded, trying to get some information about Moussa. The nurses were so harassed and frantic he could not get any information. One station nurse, who clearly had seen sights no human should witness, suggested wearily that he look on the third floor. If the boy was still alive, he should be there.

Moussa lay staring up at the ceiling fan lazily turning its propellers in the foul air. The monotonous motion hypnotized his dulled brain, diverting his attention from the carnage below his waist. He had been given a shot of morphine earlier, which had blissfully given him some relief from the agonizing pain. Unfortunately, it could not shut out the screams of agony surrounding him. Thankfully, Moussa had fallen asleep before Abu found him. As he stood there, a young doctor stopped by Moussa's bed.

"Is this your boy?" he asked politely.

"Yes, yes it is," Abu, replied hesitantly.

"I thought we were going to have to take that leg off, but the joints are fine. He will have to live with the scars, but he should regain full use of his leg within weeks. We treated the burns as best we could and gave him a shot of morphine. That's what knocked him out. You can leave him here tonight and pick him up in the morning. I will take another look at him before he goes, but truthfully, there is not much more we can do."

"What about the bandages? How often will they need to be changed?"

"Twice a week should be fine. Other than the scar tissue, the leg should heal with no complications. Just beware; it will be quite painful for some time. He has suffered third degree burns over most of his lower leg." Reaching into his pocket, the doctor proffered a large tube of ointment. "Here, put this ointment over the affected area when you change his bandage. It will help the healing as well as the pain."

"Thank you Doctor, that's very kind of you."

Next morning, Abu walked past the charred remains of the café and couldn't stop thinking of poor Mr. Nouri buried under the roof of his beloved café. In a way, he envied those who were now in Paradise. There, at least they could exist in peace. Here, not only were his people forced to live in squalid refugee camps, but they were eradicated like vermin, burned like lepers so they would not spread their disease. His intense hatred of the Jews threatened to overwhelm him as he walked towards the place his mother was buried.

He knelt down to pray, asking for her forgiveness.

"Mother, I am leaving, for there is nothing more I can do. I will keep my oath to avenge father's death as I promised. I miss you both. May Allah keep you well."

He picked up his army duffle bag and headed towards the entrance gates. This place, as wretched as it was, had been the only home he had known since leaving his village as a young boy. Abu Dis was only a distant memory, as were the birthplaces for thousands of his fellow countrymen. Recognizing many of the faces he passed, he wondered if they guessed he was leaving for good. He could not tell; their expressions were as lifeless as their comrades buried beneath them. Beyond the gate, Colonel Mir stood waiting at the head of his convoy. His men were already on board the lead truck when he reached the gate. After stopping by the hospital to pick up Moussa, they headed northeast out of Beirut.

With Moussa sound asleep in the back seat, Mir explained to Abu what lay ahead. "Today, we will drive to Baleta, our newest training camp up in the Beqaa Valley. I have just been informed Israeli tanks are coming down the Hamieh Road into the city, we will be taking a slight detour. Since our meeting with the Director in Tehran is not scheduled until next week, I thought it mutually beneficial for us to visit. You can tell me what improvements, if any, you think may be needed, while it will afford you and the boy a chance to heal. The rest of the convoy will keep going on to Murat, where we will join them after our meeting in Tehran."

"When you say 'a training camp', do you mean a Syrian Army base?"

"No, I mean a camp for training our soldiers."

"And who exactly are these trainees, Syrians?"

"Actually, they come from all over the Arab world. Saudi Arabia, Iraq, Libya, Yemen, Egypt, and, naturally there are quite a few Iranian and Syrian volunteers as well."

"And Assad is funding this camp? I didn't think that miser funded anything other than his own entourage."

"As a matter of fact, Iran is the one funding the construction and the training as well as supplying all the arms."

Descent Into Paradise

Abu stared out the window as they wound their way up the steep mountain terrain to their destination. He was beginning to realize the magnitude of what the new government in Iran was setting up. Arafat had never dreamed of setting up a full scale training center, much less recruiting volunteers from all over the Arab world. He began to contemplate what could be accomplished now that a true power such as Iran was bankrolling the fight for Palestine.

CHAPTER 20

As Abu and his men were leaving the city behind, the forward elements of the Israeli Army received their orders to occupy it. The skies were quiet as the 36th Armored Division entered Beirut. The 7th Armored Brigade was given the assignment to secure the airport and surrounding areas, which included the Palestinian refugee camps of Shatila and Sabra.

As Israeli Centurion and Markava tanks made their way down the Hamieh Road into the outskirts of the Beirut, hundreds of civilians lined the road to observe their advance. No fanfare welcomed them, but luckily there were no outbreaks of violence either. That evening at dinner, David and Zev overheard some of the younger recruits' conversation concerning the refugee camps. Both commanders had an uneasy feeling as they were aware that the new Lebanese President, a Christian Phalangist, had recently been assassinated, the PLO apparently to blame. They were equally aware of the growing resentment of the Lebanese Christians towards the rising number of Muslim refugees coming up from Palestine. What added to their sense of discomfort was the fact that occupying Beirut had never been mentioned in any briefings, nor was securing the airport ever part of any plan either had seen. Now, an eerie quiet hung over the city. For the first time since they arrived, not a single Israeli aircraft flew over Beirut. After a brief discussion, Zev got up from the table and walked over to one of his men.

"Sergeant, get your Jeep and bring two men with you. We're going out on recon."

"Yes sir, give me a minute, and we'll meet you at the gate."

Descent Into Paradise

It was just after midnight when they pulled out of the airport, heading for Beirut. Ten minutes later, they heard the droning sound of aircraft.

"Props," Sergeant Brandeiss commented, "not jets." Suddenly, the sky was illuminated with flares dropping directly above them. They were nearing the refugee camps when they began to hear rifle fire accompanied by screaming and yelling.

"Sergeant, pull up to the entrance."

They almost made it when they encountered an Israeli tank blocking the road.

"Soldier, move that God damned tank out of our way, I'm Major Megrid of Shaldag Sayeret."

"Sorry sir, my orders are to remain here. No one, sir, is to be allowed through."

"Bullshit, soldier, we just watched someone run past here five minutes ago."

"Orders sir, directly from the General, please return to your base."

"What the hell are you thinking, soldier? There are innocent civilians being shot in there and you're here acting like nothing is happening."

"Major, with all due respect, I am just following direct orders from General Sharon. If you want to question those orders, that is your choice. Now, please go back to wherever you came from."

"Let's go men, this poor excuse for a soldier is too scared to get off his fucking tank."

The Jeep backed up and turned around, heading back towards the airport. Just around the first corner, Zev shouted to his driver, "Stop the Jeep, pull over here. Let's find out what the hell is going on in there."

"Major," Brandeiss responded, "are you sure this is a good idea?"

Descent Into Paradise

Zev, who had fought many a bloody encounter with his favorite Sergeant, knew his old friend was just trying to protect him.

"No, I think it's a rotten idea Sarge, but I'm not built to let innocent women and children get murdered while we sit around and have a cup of coffee. There are certain moral codes that should not be brooked, even in war. Now, I'm going in there, you all can decide for yourselves what you wish to do."

All four Israeli commandos climbed the fence, vaulting themselves into hell. Around them, women and children ran screaming for mercy as men chased after them, laughing and cursing. The lucky ones were just shot where they lay. The unlucky ones were stripped and ravaged by their pursuers, then knifed or shot. Some women were lying naked in pools of their own blood, their stomachs cut open, unborn children lying in a pool of blood beside them.

Zev could not comprehend what he saw. This was not a massacre, this was an atrocity. Anger welled up inside him as he drew his revolver, his men following his lead. They then set off in search of the perpetrators. The irony of defending Palestinians, instead of killing them, not lost on any of them.

By the time the sun began to shine in the pre-dawn sky, their ammunition belts were empty and their killing knives covered with blood. Zev wearily looked for any more intruders, but whoever had been responsible for this cowardly raid, and was still alive, had since left under the cover of darkness.

Sergeant Brandeiss was the only one who had been injured. He had suffered a minor knife wound, which he had chosen to ignore. The rest of them just suffered from emotional and physical exhaustion. Zev, satisfied that there was nothing further they could do, and wary of the fact they were wearing Israeli military uniforms in a Palestinian refugee camp, ordered his men back to their Jeep. So absorbed in what he had just witnessed, Zev never paid attention to the sounds of sirens as they became louder and louder.

They had just reached their parked Jeep when the police cars came into sight. Before they could get in, three Lebanese police vehicles pulled up beside the Jeep, guns pointing directly at them.

"Put your hands up, you miserable bastards. I should shoot you as you stand like the dogs you are."

Zev suddenly realized through the haze of his exhaustion what these men must think, catching Israeli soldiers leaving the scene of a night massacre inside the camp of their sworn enemy.

"Hold on, it's not what you think. We did not shoot these poor people, we came to help them."

"Sure you did soldier, just as you Jews have always helped the poor Palestinians. Well, this time you've gone too far. You bastards will pay for this, that I promise you." With that, he whipped Zev across his face with his gun knocking him to the ground. As the others made a move to help, the officer said calmly, "Lay one hand on me or any of my men, and I will gladly shoot you all right here."

CHAPTER 21

Having arrived late the previous evening, Abu accepted Mir's invitation to tour the Camp facilities the following morning. As they reached the northern perimeter, Abu queried Mir about the enclave of three large tents separated from the rest and surrounded by barbed wire.

"Officers' quarters?" laughed Abu.

"No, this is for some important guests we anticipate hosting shortly. They will have their own private facilities." Mir responded with his best imitation of a smile.

"Very charming. I particularly like the barbed wire touch. It adds a certain intimacy." Abu smiled back

"You are not interested in knowing a bit more about our guests?" The Colonel looked quizzically at Abu.

"I assume you will divulge that information when you are ready. But since you ask, yes I am curious who is going to be entertained in such splendor."

"An American woman should be arriving here in Baleta shortly."

"Not for a romantic rendezvous, I assume?"

"Oh no, strictly business, but quite a VIP for our first guest. You see, her husband is currently the United States Ambassador to Lebanon." Mir looked even more pleased with himself.

"Colonel, you better hope the Americans do not discover her whereabouts, or this little paradise of yours will exist no more."

"You give the Americans too much respect, my friend. First, they will never think to look here. They will be scouring Beirut, most likely blaming the PLO," he smiled.

Descent Into Paradise

"What exactly are you planning to do with her?"

"I am going to have the good Ambassador arrange her release for a small fee. We've discovered he's actually quite wealthy. I'm confident he can be persuaded to make a small donation to our worthy cause."

"And if he can't be persuaded?"

"I will have his wife raped and then raped again by the filthiest swine in this camp until he comes to his senses!"

Looking at the pure hatred written across his face, Abu realized the Colonel was fully capable of imposing upon others exactly what had been done to his own wife and daughter back in Tehran by the hated SAVAK. He felt an odd twinge of sympathy for the American woman.

The men walked back towards Abu's tent in silence. As they approached, the Colonel asked if he would like to join him on a social call to the Master of the big estate that adjoined their camp.

"He happens to be the richest man in the entire valley. They say he grows the best crop of hashish in all the Middle East."

"Thank you, but I need to attend to Moussa."

Just then, they were interrupted by a high-pitched wailing sound. Looking towards his tent, Abu noticed the sound was coming from a small figure kneeling in prayer.

"An angel of death," explained Mir as he saw the look of curiosity on Abu's face.

Abu looked from the wailing figure back to the Colonel, it suddenly occurred to him he was witnessing his first suicide bomber; his white robes signified death.

"Colonel, he is only a boy, he has his whole life in front of him."

"Abu, that young man, with four colleagues, has been entrusted with an upcoming mission of the highest importance."

"Is this the way your soldiers prepare for a mission, Colonel?" came the biting reply from Abu.

"It is up to of each individual as to how they wish to prepare to meet their maker," Mir replied.

Abu stared into Colonel Mir's dark gray eyes. There was nothing there, no feeling, no compassion. Nothing but a dark abyss stared back at him.

CHAPTER 22

"Major, you have a visitor."

Zev and his men barely survived that first night in jail. Had it been left up to several of their Muslim jailers, they would never have left Beirut alive. Thankfully, the officer in charge, concerned about his own wellbeing, not theirs, sent one of his men to alert the Israelis. Safely back in Israel, Zev had spent the next four days in the hospital recuperating from the severe beating he had received during their one night in Beirut.

"Major Megrid, allow me to introduce myself, I'm the Director of the Israeli Intelligence Service, and I am interested in learning what happened the night you and your men went into Shatila."

Zev then proceeded to give his visitor the details of why he went in and what he discovered.

"Thank you, Major. Yours is a noble tale and one which in normal circumstances would be praised by all. What you witnessed that night is entirely consistent with the other intelligence I have been able to piece together. It would appear that our illustrious General Sharon had his own ideas as to how to deal with the Palestinians, which I regret went way beyond his official orders. He apparently made some arrangement with the Christian Phalangists in Beirut whereby Israeli troops, as you experienced, cut off outside access to those refugee camps and allowed these thugs to go in and settle some old scores without being subjected to any official interference. What you and others observed was the result."

"You mean we knew what was going to happen and allowed it?"

"Actually, I fear the rest of the world believes we didn't just 'allow it', to use your words, but actually condoned it."

"My God. Whoever is responsible for this atrocity needs to be held fully accountable."

"On that, you and I are in total agreement. The entire world is becoming more outraged the more they learn of the horrifying details you experienced firsthand. The problem is this. Our leadership, to whom the General is closely associated, could not survive politically if the truth were to ever come out. Therefore, the truth will not be told. And that is why I am making this unofficial visit."

Confined to his hospital bed, Zev looked at this strange little man in bewilderment.

The Director, seeing the extent of the severe bruising on the Major's face and arms, realized the poor man had no idea what was about to transpire.

"Major, I hate to be the bearer of bad news, but allow me to inform you of what is about to happen. In speaking with several high ranking members of the government, it is apparent to me that they are unwilling to place the total blame on Sharon, presumably more out of self-preservation than any other reason. It is my understanding that you and your men are going to be held responsible for what happened in Shatila, and Sharon will bear the responsibility for allowing it to happen, even though he will not admit to having any prior knowledge."

"Sir, I have no idea what you are talking about; responsible for what? We did nothing wrong, unless saving innocent women and children from being massacred is now considered a crime."

"Right and wrong is sometimes not as clear cut as we might wish, Major. I know this must be difficult for you to absorb, especially in your current condition. Please believe me when I tell you the information I have shared with you is highly confidential and accurate. A man in my position lives and dies on the quality of information he gathers. I would go so far as to say the very survival of Israel depends upon the quality of that information. You and your brave men are now being held in a military prison, because the army intends to try you for war crimes."

As he sat there trying to absorb what he had just been told, he began to question why the director of Mossad would be the one sharing all this with him.

"Assuming what you say is true, why would you come here to divulge what must be highly confidential information, when I could use it to defend myself?"

"Now, Major, that is a very astute question. I am here because I would like to make you a proposal which just might help both of us." The Director then explained to Zev what he had in mind.

Two days later, Shasa arrived to visit Zev.

"Shasa, what are you doing here?"

"The Director called and asked that I come talk to you."

"Of course."

"Are you all right?"

"For a prisoner, I guess they're treating me fine. Some of these jailers look at me as a hero for my supposed crimes. It is bizarre. What have we come to when people admire you for killing innocent women and children? Incredible."

"Zev, we need to talk."

Then in a low whisper, Shasa related the whole story of how Mossad discovered what had really transpired that night.

She then shared how the Director, when he got word of what happened, had secretly sent several of his local agents into the camp; they soon discovered the truth from some of the women who witnessed what Zev and his men did. They even extracted a bullet from one of the dead perpetrators and matched it to Israeli issued ammunition.

"The Director went straight to the Prime Minister with the evidence, but the army needs a scapegoat."

"And I am it, eh?"

"I am afraid it looks that way."

"I only feel sorry for my men. They came with me because I shamed them into it. I just wish I could do something to help them."

The Director is truly upset with the way this whole affair has been handled. Not that he cares a whit about the refugees. He just thinks Sharon is a public relations nightmare for Israel's image around the world. An image, which, as you might have guessed, is not faring very well at this moment."

She then went on to explain the proposed deal struck between the army and Mossad.

"Sharon has admitted to allowing the Christian Phalangists to settle some old scores, as he put it, but that's all. They want you to plead guilty to insubordination and unlawful use of arms."

Seeing Zev's face, she held up her arms. "Let me finish. Conditioned upon your acceptance of our proposal, they will then agree to a two-year probation, as long as you are out of the country working with us. They are also willing to forego any prosecution of the three soldiers who went in with you."

"But I'm not guilty! Your own agency proved that!"

"You and I both understand that, but all they care about is the State of Israel."

"What about my name, Shasa? My honor?"

"Zev, your name will be associated with this evil, one way or another. The army is prepared to prosecute both you and your men. They know you're innocent, but they can't afford to admit it. Otherwise, Sharon would have to take the full brunt of this, and neither he, nor the powers that be, is willing to risk that. This is the only way out for you and your men. You can live with yourself, because you know you are innocent. You know, they know, and most importantly, your men know."

Those bastards, she thought. Is there anything they wouldn't sacrifice for their beloved State of Israel?

Finally, Zev looked up, "I really don't see another option at this point. Tell the Director I will accept his offer, on the condition my men are completely exonerated with nothing put on their record."

As Zev ate his final breakfast as a prisoner, Sergeant Brandeiss came over to pay his respects. "Major, I just wanted to wish you the best of luck and thank you for getting us off the hook. For what it's worth, there's not a man in the whole outfit who wouldn't follow you to hell if you asked."

"Thanks, Sarge. I'm sorry I ever got you boys involved in any of this, but I'm glad it worked out for you. Please say goodbye to the men for me, and tell them that someday I may just take them up on that offer." With that, they saluted, and Zev walked out of prison and the Israeli Defense Force.

CHAPTER 23

THE PORT OF HAIFA

Pablo Ramos, Captain of the Chilean freighter, lay on his cot listening to the whining of the cranes as they hoisted the heavy containers aboard his ship. All night, the sounds had been boisterous. Between the roar of the huge trucks coming and going and the high-pitched sound of the cranes, sleep was out of the question.

Despite the very generous bonus Ramos had been paid, he did not enjoy the fact that he was required to stay in his cabin during the loading of his ship. The cargo was obviously contraband, which was part of the bargain. But having someone else dictate to his crew was not.

As dawn approached, the noise abruptly ceased. A knock on the door interrupted Ramos's thoughts, as a stranger asked permission to enter. Ramos opened the door, and a tall, rather handsome man entered.

"Please, come in, I assume you are the one in charge of my ship's loading," said Ramos, gruffly.

Pulling out a bottle of rum, he offered the man a glass.

"No, thank you. My name is Megrid, and, until we reach our destination, you will report to me."

Ramos, choking on the rum, angrily replied, "Like hell I will! This is my ship, and when we leave this God forsaken port, the crew will report to me... Period."

At that moment, a pistol appeared in Zev's palm.

"Suit yourself, Captain. You will obey my orders, or you leave the ship now and return the very generous fee you apparently accepted. Your choice."

Sensing this man was no stranger to death, Ramos reluctantly nodded his acceptance. After the Israeli left, he proceeded to finish his bottle of rum.

My God, he thought, what have I done? The extra cash had been a godsend, as his young daughter desperately needed surgery. He had accepted the bribe as a gift for her, but now he was not sure if it was God's work or the devil's. Whatever cargo was stored in the hull of his ship was most assuredly not the shipment of medical supplies described on his manifold.

At dawn, the Chilean registered freighter slowly backed away from the dock, then made its way through the crowded harbor into the main channel. As Zev leaned against the railing watching the harbor and the hillsides of Israel fade into the distance, his thoughts turned to what lay ahead.

CHAPTER 24

BEIRUT

Alia Khadra listened politely as she trimmed her client's hair.

"I adore you, Alia, but I can't imagine how you can live here. Everyone is crazy. How can you live in a country where people go around blowing themselves up?

Alia's only comment was. "We live in very difficult times, Mrs. Holden. You just be careful, please."

"Don't you worry about me! I won't even get in a car driven by an Arab. If I have to go out, I've told my husband either I'm driven by one of the Marines or he takes me, period."

"I cannot imagine my husband driving me anywhere," Alia sighed.

"Well, mine doesn't like it much either, but he better get used to it." Looking up with a conspiratorial grin she added, "I told him either he agrees or I go straight home to Philadelphia."

Alia could only pity the poor American Ambassador for his ill fortune living with this spoiled child, but she kept her tongue. Having the Ambassador's wife as a client was very good for business. In fact, the salon owner had recently given her a big raise, and she badly needed the money.

Before settling her under the dryer, Alia asked what time she needed to leave.

"My husband is picking me up at five. Make sure I'm ready, as he doesn't wait well."

Alia turned the dial to 40 minutes, which would give her enough time to take out the curlers and style her hair. Then she went to call her husband.

Colonel Mir listened attentively to Salidi's excited voice at the other end of the line.

"Colonel, it would appear that the Ambassador himself is picking up his wife."

"When?"

"My wife tells me in one hour. What are your instructions?"

"Call me back in ten minutes," said Mir as he hung up the phone.

The original plan had been simply to kidnap the Ambassador's wife, but this opportunity was too good to pass up. Mir, flush with the success of the Marine barracks bombing, felt that these high profile kidnappings would secure Hezbollah's position as the new leader of the terrorist networks in Lebanon. The void created by Arafat's misfortunes must be filled, and Mir was not one to miss such an opportunity.

He also knew the kidnapping of both the American Ambassador and his wife would thrill the Arab masses. Arafat would never take on the Americans directly; nor would Syria, for that matter. The Iranians were not so bashful. His orders were to select his targets as they came, regardless of nationality.

The phone rang, interrupting his thought. He let it ring three times before answering.

"Pick them both up and bring them to me." Having made the decision, he went to find Abu.

Salidi hung up the phone, then looked across the table at his four associates. "The Colonel wishes us to take them both out to Beqaa Valley tonight. The only real change in the plan is we will have two passengers to subdue. Yussef, you will have to come with us to handle the Ambassador. Hussan, you will handle the wife. We will keep the Ambassador in the front seat until we leave the city. Just make sure that neither starts yelling or screaming. If they do, use whatever force necessary to silence them."

Turning to the other two, he went on, "You two will man the coffee trolleys. Your job is to cut off any incoming traffic on

Yafet Street. If anyone tries to interfere, shoot them. Once we leave, abandon the trolleys and meet us at the camp."

Looking at his watch, he announced they had fifteen minutes to get ready.

Ambassador Holden was fuming. He had an important call scheduled, and here he was playing chauffeur to his feeble wife at the hairdresser's. Maybe I should let her go back to the US, he muttered angrily, as he rushed out to get the car.

"I am going to pick up Diane, I will be back in 30 minutes," he called to his secretary. "If the Pentagon phones, tell them I had an emergency and will call back within the hour."

At 16h45, the American Ambassador rounded the corner onto Yafet Street. Rolling down his window, he ordered a coffee from the trolley on the corner. The vendor seemed rather inept, but he finally handed him a cup. As he couldn't see any parking places down the street, he just sat in the car with his coffee and waited for his wife to appear.

"Hurry, Alia, it's time for me to go," said Diane impatiently.

Alia finished combing out her client's hair, telling her how beautiful she looked.

"Little good it does me," was all she heard as her client ran out the door.

Salidi watched Mrs. Holden exit the salon as both trolleys maneuvered into the street, effectively blocking off any oncoming traffic. He then crossed the street as Hussan positioned himself behind the wife. Yussef walked directly behind, ready to move as soon as the woman reached the car.

On the other side of the street, Salidi approached the car on the driver's side. The Ambassador, leaning over to open the passenger door for his wife, was completely caught off guard when a man suddenly opened the rear passenger door, shoving

Descent Into Paradise

Diane into the back seat. As she screamed, he hit her across the mouth with his pistol. Before the Ambassador could react, Yussef climbed in the open front passenger door, grabbing the Ambassador with one giant paw, and shoved him head first onto the floor between his feet. Salidi then jumped into the driver's seat, threw the car into gear and drove off. With Yafet Street effectively blocked off, nobody had noticed the little scuffle outside the salon, allowing Salidi, now outfitted in a chauffeur's uniform, to drive off without incident.

Due to the car's diplomatic tags, they were waved through the usual roadblocks without stopping. One hour later, the car headed due east out of town along the very same route the Israeli tanks had utilized to enter Beirut earlier. Two hours later, they arrived outside Baleta Camp.

A delighted Colonel Mir came out to greet them. "Salidi, well done my friend! Any problems?"

"No Colonel, we were waved through all the usual roadblocks without a problem.

"Good. We will see how our American friends react now. Hopefully, they will all decide to return home where they belong."

CHAPTER 25

CHILE

The huge yellow ball slowly rose over the mountains of Valparaiso, illuminating a colorful hillside rising above a peaceful harbor. Zev stared at his new South American home with a mixture of sadness and anticipation. His life was in shambles, as was his military career. The thought of suicide crossed his mind more than once over the previous weeks, but Zev had finally come to the realization that, if he wanted to survive, he needed to leave the past in the past and start anew.

His orders were explicit. He was to bring this shipment of arms to Chile, turn over control of the ship to a man named Juan Rios, then assist Mr. Rios in training his private security force.

The most interesting aspect about this whole affair was that soldiers with his experience and training were rarely allowed to assist any foreign military forces. In fact, to do so was usually considered an act of treason punishable by execution. Nevertheless, Shasa's boss had confirmed his orders in person. Apparently, the Director of Israel's Intelligence Agency could operate above the law when justified by the circumstances. With the current state of events, Zev didn't feel like arguing the point. He was out of jail, out of the army, out of Israel, and on his own. During the days alone on the forward deck, he would look over the horizon and review all that had happened in his young but tumultuous life. The main conclusion he reached was that, from this point forward, he would look after Zev Megrid, and to hell with the rest of the world.

The ship's blaring horn shook him from his reflective mood. He could see men scurrying about the docks in anticipation of their imminent landing. He noticed a small knot of men, some obviously armed, standing in front of a long white limousine, as the ship was being secured. Two men got out of the car. As they approached the ship, he could see one was obviously the harbormaster. The other was a good-looking young man who carried himself with the easy air of someone used to commanding the world around him. Zev suspected this might well be his new employer.

Once onboard, with the introductions concluded, the Captain and the harbormaster excused themselves to inspect the ship's manifest. Alone in the Captain's office, Zev liked what he saw. "Mr. Rios, it is a pleasure making your acquaintance."

"Thank you Mr. Megrid, or shall I call you Major Megrid?"

With a slight smile, Zev responded, "Well, as I am now a member of your army, sir, I will leave my rank entirely up to you."

"Well then, let's maintain your current rank for now. Allow me to invite you to be my guest this evening, as we have much to discuss."

"I would be honored to accept your invitation."

That night at dinner, they had barely sat down before the waiter immediately brought over a large pitcher of sangria, after which the conversation soon turned to business.

"Major, I have read your full dossier given to me by our friends at Mossad, and I must say, I am really quite impressed. You are clearly a very accomplished soldier."

"Mr. Rios, please call me Zev. I am certainly well trained in combat. I don't like losing and I don't suffer fools very well."

A smile crossed Juan's face as he replied, "In which case, you and I should get along splendidly. Allow me to come straight to the point. I am a simple businessman who supplies what my customers, primarily Americans, desire. The US Government, in its infinite wisdom and archaic moral attitudes, wishes to deem our activities illegal and against their national interest. As it was in the Prohibition days of the 1920s, the US Government only succeeds in making a few daring entrepreneurs extremely wealthy, since one cannot deny the consumer a product he or she is determined to purchase. So it is with our business. Today's youth crave a greater high than alcohol and that is what we deliver. The problem is, like all such ventures, the high level of profitability attracts all types of people into the arena. For that reason, I am desirous of limiting the suppliers to a nominal amount."

Zev, having already deduced where he would fit in, smugly asked, "And I assume, Mr. Rios, that, by nominal, you mean one?"

"I believe we understand one another. The question I would like to pose is would you be willing to effectuate that plan?"

"Mr. Rios, I do not care much for the Americans naive idealism, nor do I care if the American government condones or forbids the importation of drugs. What I do care about is working for someone whom I can respect and trust. As to achieving your personal goals, I am a soldier. Your enemies are now mine."

"Splendid. With regard to respect and loyalty, I can assure you I only work with people whom I trust, and I value loyalty above all else. There is one final item I would like to discuss. A close associate of mine, Señor Estoban, currently serves as head of my personal security. As he is one of very few people whom I trust with my life, I will need you both to work closely together as we move forward. I hope that will not present a problem."

"As long as there are clear channels of command understood and agreed to by all parties concerned, it should not be an issue. Speaking of security, do you happen to know what is available in terms of military supplies?"

"I'm afraid to say I am rather ignorant about such details, but if you will be so kind as to make a list of what you will need, I will make sure they will be made available at once. As you are familiar with Israeli arms, I propose we use only Israeli weapons."

"Excellent. Señor Rios, I trust you will not be disappointed."

"I hope neither of us will. But before we go any further, don't you think we should discuss compensation?"

"It is my understanding that Mossad will continue to pay my Army salary and benefits, so there should be no additional costs to you for my services."

"That, I presume, is for whatever services you are rendering to the Israelis. I am talking about the services you will provide to me for my operations."

"Your offer is most appreciated, but I have no expectation of being paid anything."

"Well, I do. You speak of respect and loyalty. For me, that means taking care of my people. I would propose an annual salary of 100,000 US dollars, if that is acceptable?"

"I don't know what to say," Zev stammered. "That is most generous indeed."

"I am sure you will be worth that and more, my friend. Of course, we will also provide you with housing and transportation.

"Now, enough business for tonight. Let's finish this delicious dinner, then, if you will allow me, I would like to introduce you to some of the finer pleasures our beautiful country has to offer."

CHAPTER 26

CAMP BALETA

As his captors roughly removed their blindfolds, Ambassador Holden found himself in a Bedouin style tent. A central fireplace surrounded the heavy carpeting on the floor with the sleeping quarters off to one side. The aroma wafting through the tent was a combination of smoke, hashish, and unwashed bodies.

Looking over at his distraught wife, he tried to comfort her. "Don't worry honey. They will hold us for ransom, but they wouldn't dare harm us. The political consequences would be too severe."

"Tom, I'm terrified. Our children will never survive without us. What if these animals torture us?" The American Ambassador, a decorated soldier and successful businessman, had very little to offer in response.

"Diane, nothing is going to happen to us. We will be home with the children long before they even miss us."

Colonel Mir's entrance interrupted her response. "Please excuse the interruption, but I wanted to formally welcome you to our humble camp. My name is Colonel Mir, I am the camp commander. You have been brought here as prisoners of war to answer for the war crimes committed by your government." Tom Holden tried to rise but was restrained by the two guards, who had entered with Mir.

"Colonel, I must protest in the strongest terms. First, our two countries are not at war, and, second, I represent the United States of America as their Ambassador to Lebanon. I am therefore protected as such from any military action under the Geneva Convention."

Before he could go on, Colonel Mir simply replied, "Mr. Ambassador, I could care less about your Geneva Convention! You and your lovely wife are now here, and, if you wish to see those young children of yours again, you would be wise to cooperate fully!" With that, he turned around and abruptly left the tent.

The terms of that 'cooperation' arrived the next afternoon. The conditions of release demanded by the Iranian Commander amounted to one million US dollars being deposited into a numbered Swiss bank account.

"This is blackmail, plain and simple!" snorted the Ambassador to his wife as he read her the letter, to which she replied, "What choice do we have? We have the money, and our children need their parents!"

Obviously, he would get no support if he refused, but the thought of giving up the majority of his hard-earned savings to this Arab bastard upset him unduly. Fuck him, he thought as he reread the letter. What's he going to do if I say no? Kill us?

His thoughts were rudely interrupted by the return of the camp commander.

"Ambassador, please forgive me for my haste, but circumstances beyond my control necessitate that I get your response to my letter immediately."

Holden responded more emotionally than rationally. "My response, sir, is Fuck You!"

Colonel Mir, taken back by the hostage's response, replied, "By that, I assume my quite reasonable request is unacceptable?"

"An astute observation," was all he received in response. Mir's temper now began to rise. He had just received a summons to return immediately to Tehran for a meeting with the Director of Intelligence, a meeting he clearly could not postpone, and now this arrogant bastard was telling him to fuck off.

Descent Into Paradise

"Very well, sir. I really don't have a great deal of time to negotiate this matter with you. We will see how your lovely wife feels about my offer." With that, he turned around and left the tent.

"What does that mean?" asked Diane nervously.

"Maybe he thinks you are more reasonable than your husband."

They didn't have to wait very long for an answer, as four rather gruff men soon walked back into their tent. Without a word, two of them reached down and pulled Diane to her feet while the other two just stood facing the Ambassador as he rose. As his wife, kicking and screaming, was dragged outside, Tom slumped back on the ground as one of the guards slammed the butt of his rifle into his ribcage. Outside, there was quite a commotion as more men arrived. While he lay on the floor gasping for breath, he could hear his wife screaming for help. As her anguished cries were reduced to the whimpering of a child, the camp commander came back inside, facing the prostrate Ambassador.

"First, allow me to thank you for your intransigence. As it turns out, your beautiful wife has given great pleasure to some of my young soldiers! Lord knows, they were in need of some female companionship!"

"You filthy pig! You will pay for this with your miserable life, that I promise you."

"Ah, brave words from an old man who values his money over the wellbeing of his wife and children. Well, she has certainly earned a short break, although I must say it was getting a bit messy as well. Clearly, she is not accustomed to a having a real man penetrate her."

Tom had heard enough from this animal. His fists clenched, he leapt off the ground, lunging for the man's throat. The smug countenance of the Iranian colonel suddenly transformed into a look of shock as two large hands squeezed with all their strength around his throat. Struggling for air, the Colonel would have died right there had it not been for the swift reaction of his two guards. Even after the Ambassador blacked out, his grip held tight. His fingers had to be pried loose as he lay on the floor unconscious, bleeding profusely from his right temple.

Back in his tent, it took the Colonel several hours to regain his composure.

It was mid-morning the next day before Mir finished giving final instructions to his staff and was ready to leave. His final meeting was with his new ally.

"Salidi, my friend, regretfully I have a meeting in Tehran which unfortunately cannot be postponed. Yesterday, I proposed what I thought was a most reasonable offer to the Ambassador for his release and safe return back to Beirut. For reasons known only to him, he refused, thereby subjecting his wife to an afternoon of entertainment for some of my men. I now leave their future in your good hands to handle as you deem appropriate."

Salidi could only surmise that the Iranian had tried to extort a ransom from the rich American, a plan that obviously had not worked out to his satisfaction. How unfortunate for the Ambassador and his wife, he thought, as he had quite a different fate in store for them. That all can wait until tomorrow, he mused, as tonight, he had a rather large celebration planned back in Beirut.

As Colonel Mir relayed last minute instructions to his staff, Abu fetched Moussa, who quickly packed his bag. The three then boarded the Syrian army helicopter parked just outside the camp.

As Mir instructed the pilots to take off, Abu glanced out the window as Camp Baleta slowly disappeared below.

CHAPTER 27

MEDITERRANEAN SEA

The bridge of the carrier was relatively calm, in sharp contrast to the weather swirling above the majestic ship. Angry black clouds moved swiftly through the tinted sky. The weather desk reported a vast low-pressure system, which had formed over the Turkish peninsula, and was now moving directly towards them.

"Barometer dropping, Admiral. A nasty frontal system is heading our way."

Admiral William Brewster had been a sailor his entire life, having grown up on the rugged coast of Maine; and any Mainer worth his salt could feel a storm brewing. The Admiral nodded while staring at the weather map.

Taking another sweeping glance from the bridge, the Admiral turned to his adjutant. "What's the flight schedule look like today?"

"Other than the two Tomcats on Cover Air Patrol, the only other flights scheduled are the hellos bringing the Special Forces on board later this afternoon."

Taking one more glance at the weather map, Admiral Brewster shook his head, and ordered, "Call those special ops boys now. Tell them to get those choppers out here ASAP. I'm thinking this weather's going to be a real bitch real soon! Get the CAP on deck, then let the fleet know we will be sailing without air cover until the weather clears."

"Aye, aye sir," came the crisp response.

BEIRUT

Captain Harvey, senior pilot of the group, looked around the mess. Seeing most of his men already on their feet awaiting orders, he barked out, "Looks like the weather is deteriorating. Move it now."

Ten minutes later, all six birds were fully loaded and heading west. The two Cobras went out first, followed by two big Nighthawks each filled with a squadron of Rangers. They were followed by the two AH-6 bubble tops, carrying the Delta Boys sitting on their familiar side benches.

According to his latest update, the fleet was currently sailing on a northeasterly course straight towards them at approximately 22 knots. Captain Harvey estimated their flying time to be approximately twenty minutes, as the carrier was now some 25 miles off the coast and approximately fifteen miles south of Beirut. Major Pete Watson watched the coastline come up as the AH-6, affectionately known as the baby chopper, made its way due west out of Beirut.

Once out to sea, it was only a matter of minutes before the silhouette of the enormous carrier appeared on the horizon, its giant wake leaving a white foam trail behind. Once aboard, Pete was escorted to the Admiral's quarters, where he was introduced to Admiral Brewster.

Pete looked around the massive room, admiring the trappings of power conferred upon the commander of an aircraft carrier battle group. The Admiral, however, was the total opposite of what the Special Forces leader had expected. Contrary to his regal surroundings, Brewster appeared to be a humble man. While there was no questioning the confident and powerful aura he exuded, his welcome on board was nothing short of courteous and respectful. Having established their common backgrounds, both being from Maine, Pete found it refreshing that a man with the power to destroy any target within a 300 mile radius of wherever he sailed could be as humble and gracious as the gentleman who now acted as the perfect host. Three hundred miles from their present location lay the entire populations of Israel, Lebanon, Syria, and Jordan. It was a sobering thought for one man to have the power of life or death over so many people.

As the introductions ended, the Admiral motioned to the young Lieutenant next to him.

"One of my officers will show you to your quarters."

"Thank you, sir."

Pete was led down four decks to the main sleeping quarters of the ship. There, he found his squad lounging in a makeshift wardroom, along with several Army Rangers.

Pete invited his second in command, Colonel Dennis Smith, to join him in attending the early dinner cordially hosted by the Admiral and his top officers.

Polite conversation evolved quickly into the details of the night's mission as the Admiral was quite intrigued with the use of his carrier force in conjunction with special ops insertions.

"Major Watson, Colonel Smith, on behalf of myself and my officers, we appreciate you taking the time to brief us. Up to now, the only information I've received is a call from General Bradley yesterday informing me of the kidnapping of Ambassador Holden and his wife and requesting the use of my carrier in a rescue attempt."

Pete, as the Commanding Officer, then proceeded to give them a full briefing. "The Israelis confirmed yesterday what we have suspected for some time, namely that the Iranians, together with the Syrians, have set up a major new terrorist training facility in the Beqaa Valley. Given the fact that none of the Israeli agents in Beirut have heard a word of the Ambassador's whereabouts, Mossad suspects the whole operation is the brainchild of an Iranian operative, not the Palestinians. Actually, they suspect he is also the brains behind that suicide bombing of the marine barracks last week. Assuming they're right, it would be logical that they are holding the Ambassador and his wife in what they consider to be a secret location." Placing three grainy black and white photographs on the table, Pete continued, "These images, taken early this morning, show fifteen tents already constructed in the main compound. Assuming twelve men per tent, that would indicate the camp can house approximately 180 full-time occupants. Assume twenty of those are staff, that means there could be anywhere up to 160 trainees on site."

Using those same photos, Pete pointed out the smaller compound located on the northern perimeter of the camp. A grouping of three additional tents appeared to be separated from the main camp by several strands of barbed wire.

"Here is where we believe the hostages are being kept, as there would be no other logical explanation for why those tents are separated from the main camp. The plan calls for my squad to extract the prisoners, while Colonel Smith's Rangers deal with the main camp."

One of the Naval officers asked, "How many Rangers are going in?"

"Twenty-four Rangers in two groups of twelve," came the sharp reply from the Colonel.

Admiral Brewster then chimed in, "I mean no disrespect, Colonel, but 24 men against 180 seems a rather daunting task, even if you Special Ops boys are as advertised."

Colonel Smith smiled, and in his deep southern accent, replied, "Admiral, if those two little Cobras weren't going in ahead of us, I might agree with you. But, if you'd ever witnessed that little aircraft in action, you wouldn't be too concerned. By the time we hit the ground, I guarantee there won't be near that many Arabs left to fight."

Descent Into Paradise

Looking over at Pete for his OK, the Army Ranger Colonel continued, "The two Cobras will go in first. With luck, their Hellfire missiles should destroy most of the tents in the main camp. My Rangers will then come in onboard the Nighthawks to seal the camp off from the prison area and deal with any survivors still wanting a fight. Coming in right behind us, Major Watson and his Delta boys will fly that little water bug of a helicopter they are so proud of directly into the prison compound. Hopefully, they can take out those guards before they can harm the hostages. Quite frankly, that's one of the more delicate pieces of this whole operation."

Pete then finished, "Assuming we can manage all that, the plan is to put the two hostages aboard the second AH-6 and fly them back here to the carrier."

Admiral Brewster then offered one of his helicopters to assist in removing the hostages. Pete thanked him for the offer but said that his pilots were specially trained to go into very tight places and that he would be uncomfortable with anyone else involved. A discussion ensued, with the Admiral offering a compromise. "While I appreciate the special skills of your pilots, Major, our Naval pilots here are highly skilled in hot extractions as well. Since none of us know the physical condition of either hostage, it would seem prudent to have an extra chopper handy, just in case. Our hellos each accommodate up to six passengers, wounded or otherwise, in addition to a full medical crew, so, if either of your outfits suffer any serious casualties we could certainly accommodate up to four in addition to the two hostages. It is just a suggestion, but one I would ask you both to consider."

Then looking over at Pete, he finished with a chuckle.

"No offense, Major, but I think the Ambassador and his wife might just prefer our chopper to sitting on a bench outdoors in that little buggy of yours!"

Descent Into Paradise

As neither Special Forces officer could argue with that logic, it was agreed that a medical chopper from the carrier would join the mission, arriving only after the landing zone had been secured. Lift-off was scheduled in three hours, so Pete asked if they could be excused to make their final preparations.

Admiral Brewster, in the meantime, conferred with the SOAR pilots to determine the most advantageous location for the carrier to be positioned. Since flying a direct course over Beirut was not an option, the Admiral agreed to position the carrier some fifteen miles offshore and ten miles south of Beirut for both takeoff and landing.

"It's a bit close in for my comfort," admitted Brewster, "but that should help you a bit on fuel consumption if something goes wrong."

Most of the men had fully recovered from their all night flight from Fort Bragg to Beirut, but those who had taken a brief nap now joined the others to finish their final preparations. Weapons were oiled and cleaned, and knives were honed razor sharp.

"We will be traveling light tonight, gentlemen," Pete announced, as he put on his Kevlar vest. "I'm assuming, given the fact there are only two hostages, one of whom is a woman, that there shouldn't be more than five or six guards occupying the other two tents, so we'll leave the M-60s here on the carrier."

As the Rangers came out on to the flight deck, a burst of applause rose from the hundreds of curious sailors lined up on the observation deck. The big rotor blades of the Nighthawks began to whirl after the last Ranger climbed aboard. On the main runway, a Grumman F-14 Tomcat catapulted off the deck in a roar of flames. Immediately thereafter, the high-pitched whining of the two Cobras increased. Off they flew into the pitch-black sky, followed by the two Nighthawks.

Descent Into Paradise

Major Watson followed, leading out his squad dressed in black. The cheering was loudest for the Delta boys, the cream of the military. Not one of the crew questioned who occupied the top rung of the military ladder. These men, along with the famed Navy Seals, were the most lethal killers America ever produced.

Strapped in on the bench, Watson watched as the carrier deck sank below them. The carrier task force comprised the very core of America's sea power. The huge deck below was capable of launching supersonic jets in any kind of weather, day or night.

"Just look at that monster. That, gentlemen, is what protects America's interests all around the world," stated Pete proudly through his intercom.

With the coastline now in full view, he came back to the task at hand.

"Remember, just go in fast, take out the guards first, then get the hostages the hell out of there. No heroics. Tonight, we leave the heavy lifting to the Rangers."

The weather was ideal, with the thick cloud cover remaining from the recent storm effectively eliminating any moonlight. The tiny black hello quickly disappeared as it headed west towards the Beqaa Valley and its rendezvous with death.

"Three minutes to the target, Major," came the pilot's voice over the intercom.

Several miles ahead, the dark night sky suddenly lit up, with tracers and rockets slamming into the ground below, as the two Cobras unleashed their full arsenal of missiles straight into the main camp, creating their own version of hell on earth. Suddenly, as their tiny aircraft flew closer, they were rocked by the blast of a huge fireball engulfing the southern perimeter of the camp.

Descent Into Paradise

"God! That had to be their ammo dump," came the co-pilot's voice. "Hollywood would've loved that fucking explosion!"

Straight ahead, the lead Nighthawk immediately swooped down.

"Get ready! 50, 47, 45, drop… drop," the pilot shouted in his mike.

"OK boys, weapons ready, go… go… go," Colonel Smith yelled, as he went out.

They hit the ground in a cloud of dust temporarily obscuring their view. Fortunately, the machine gunners on board both big hellos could still pick out their targets; their 20mm cannons poured fire down into the smoldering ruins of the main camp. The yells and screams of the wounded mixed with the thumping sounds of the big rotors and the staccato firing of the machine guns to create a nerve-wracking pandemonium of sound. As the Nighthawks ceased firing, the Rangers headed towards the burning tents, firing their M-16s into anything resembling a human form, dead or alive.

Following just behind the two Nighthawks, the lead AH-6 flew straight for the three tents where they suspected the hostages were held. Hovering just above the barbed wire fence, six stun grenades immediately dropped to the ground, two in front of each tent. Like lightning, six bodies followed them, hitting the ground just after they exploded, the momentary white flash immediately blinding anyone not wearing protective goggles.

Abba Moussori, one of the five men assigned by Salidi to guard the hostages, thought there was a storm when he heard the first missiles hit. Only after the ammo dump exploded did he realize they were under attack. Neither Abba, nor his fellow guards, had ever experienced an American Special Forces operation. Therefore, nobody expected this kind of violence dropping out of the night sky straight into their camp. With

Descent Into Paradise

the American couple securely tied up, Abba had decided the posting of a guard in this isolated camp was completely unnecessary. He now gravely regretted that decision.

"Wake up you idiots! We're under attack," Abba yelled, as he pulled on his trousers and boots. There was a palpable odor of fear in the tent, as the five men rushed to get dressed and out of the tent before they were attacked.

Abba was the first to get out into the open. Most merciful Allah, he prayed as he glanced over at the main body of the camp. Dark creatures ran through the fiery remains, shooting at anything that moved. Flames and billowing clouds of smoke were rising into the air as the thump thump of the Nighthawks' huge rotors filled the night with their menacing sound. Abba stood there, virtually paralyzed with fear, trying to make sense of what was taking place around him. A second guard then came rushing out, literally knocking them both flat on the hard sandy ground. Finally coming to his senses, he got up, screaming, "Come on, let's get to the hostages before those demons head this way."

The two men grabbed their AK-47 semi-automatic rifles, leading the others towards the tent holding the two Americans. Abba put his weapon on full automatic as he reached the entrance.

Tom Holden immediately realized what was happening as soon as he heard the first missiles crash into the camp. In Vietnam, he had several Army Rangers friends, so he knew the basic tactics. The only difference now was the magnitude of firepower compared to twenty years ago.

Diane Holden lay curled up in the far corner of the tent. Oblivious to the fiery blasts outside, she was beyond caring if she lived or died. Her only concern was what would happen to her two young children back in Beirut. Head buried in her chest, she never saw Abba's rifle open the flap in front of their tent. Tom's worst fear was realized as a dark weathered face covered with a dirty black beard and mustache appeared in the opening. Hands and legs trussed tight, he lay there helplessly awaiting the inevitable slamming of bullets into his body. His last thoughts were of his two children as the night erupted in an excruciatingly painful white flash.

Abba's finger never pulled the trigger. The stun grenade exploded several feet behind him, paralyzing him instantly. Slumped in front of the tent opening, his body shielded the two Americans from the full force of the blast. Tom, despite the loud ringing in his ears, could hear his wife screaming incoherently. In utter panic, she struggled to get up. "Stay down," he yelled, knowing the fight was not over. Bullets were now tearing into the tent all around them, as men yelled and screamed in multiple languages just outside.

"Shit, we didn't get 'em all," was the last thing he heard before a bullet ripped into his left thigh. He felt no pain as the next one slammed into his shoulder.

Pete knew he couldn't waste another moment. There was clearly at least one guard still up, as the distinctive sound of an AK-47 discharged its magazine directly into the back of the tent in front of them. To fire at him meant firing into the tent he strongly suspected housed the two American hostages. Reaching down, he pulled out his last stun grenade and lobbed it up and over the tent hoping it would land close enough to at least knock down whoever was there, as his men encircled the tent from both sides.

Seconds later, the firing stopped. Twenty rounds of hollow core snub-nose bullets literally tore apart the two remaining guards, one's stomach now a mass of intestines hanging down his pants, the other's head staring blankly into space.

"Winder, get inside and take care of the hostages. Adams, make sure these bastards can't shoot anyone else." Pete ordered through his mic, as he and the rest of the squad checked that the other tents were empty. Harry Adams looked rather amused as he surveyed the scene. Shoot anyone else? he thought with some amusement. These poor bastards were already headed for whatever Allah had in store for them!

Pete soon realized there were no survivors. As he looked at the tangled mass of limbs sprawled over the ground, it was clear that none of these Arabs was ever going to kidnap anyone again.

Brent Winder, the only qualified medic on the squad, entered the tent to find both hostages lying crumpled on the ground. Fearing the worst, he raced over to check their pulses.

Outside, the sound of gunfire diminished. Watson could see the big Nighthawks beginning their descent, signaling the fight was over, as Colonel Smith would only allow them down once the target was subdued.

Brent's voice interrupted his thoughts.

"Major, the Ambassador is down with multiple bullet wounds. I had to put the woman under sedation, as she wouldn't let me touch her. She wasn't hit, but she is covered with blood around her vaginal area. I think those bastards may have raped her. We need to get them both to the carrier ASAP."

"Roger that." Pete then asked his pilot in the AH-6 to call down the medical chopper, explaining, "Both hostages require immediate evac."

"Roger, sir, will do."

"Brent, the chopper from the carrier is coming down. I am going to check to see if Colonel Smith has any casualties needing immediate evacuation. The rest of you boys get back on our bird and take off as soon as that medical chopper gets here. They can handle the hostages. I'll hitch a ride back with the Rangers."

"Yes sir, see you back on board."

Pete then made his way over to where Colonel Smith stood barking orders.

"Check those tents for any papers," Smith shouted to several of his men. "There's got to be a command post somewhere in this shit hole. I want it found."

Pete, having relayed to his pilot there were no serious Ranger casualties, began to observe what remained of this terrorist training facility. What struck him immediately, besides the total destruction of the camp itself, was the absence of any serious military hardware. Not really a fair fight, he mused, as he thought what it would have been like if he had been on the other side tonight. The Colonel then walked over to join his Delta counterpart and inquire about the hostages.

"Alive, but apparently in rough shape." They both then saw the Navy helicopter take off. "According to my medic, they both should make it."

Pete smiled as he surveyed the devastation all around him. "Well, it looks like you boys have everything under control."

One of the Rangers near him lamented, "Those damn Cobras took out everything before we even hit the ground. Not a god-damned towel head still breathing, Major. Why the hell do we do all this training, get all excited to go on a real mission, and there ain't nobody left alive to kill?"

Pete looked at Smith. Both men knew the young Ranger was overwrought and needed to talk to relieve his tension. Neither man bothered to reply, as the last Rangers came over to report.

"No papers, sir. If they were here, they're probably ashes now, along with the rest of this shit hole."

"OK men, get back on the choppers. There's nothing left to keep us here. You need a ride, Major? I'm afraid we don't have any outdoor picnic benches to offer you, but you may be able to pull rank and get one of the lounge chairs."

Smiling, Pete climbed on board. Seconds later, they were airborne, heading back to the safety of the carrier.

CHAPTER 28

MIAMI BEACH

Every major DEA office around the country had a budget for 'field operations' which was the term used for black ops. Miami was no exception. As the head of the office, La Bota controlled just how those funds were expended. Having just received her phone call from Chile, he decided to fly his new informant up for a visit. They met at his favorite restaurant where she described what her sister had told her. At a cost of $1,000 per month, Marianna was proving to be a bargain.

"Are you sure he's an Israeli?" asked La Bota after she described her evening with Mr. Rios and his friend.

"Oh yes," came the reply. "Mr. Rios doesn't know Madonna is my sister so he occasionally books me for an evening when he is in town. This time he said he had a friend joining him who had come all the way from Israel, and he wanted me to bring a pretty girl to make sure he had a good time. My girlfriend said he was very handsome and very polite. She thought he was in the military as Rios introduced him as Major something."

Thinking it over for a moment, La Bota remembered Pete asking him to keep him apprised of any unusual activity he related to these South American drug cartels. An Israeli Army Major showing up with Rios would certainly qualify. La Bota knew that Chile's President, Augusto Pinochet, used Israeli-trained troops in his palace guard, but he had never heard of any Israeli military involvement with the drug cartels. Mistaking his silence for disapproval, Marianne asked, "This is important, no? I thought you wanted to know about anything unusual happening with the Rios family."

Descent Into Paradise

La Bota just smiled at her concern. "No, you are right. This is very important information indeed. In fact, you have more than earned your fee for this; so much so that I am going to give you a little bonus for shopping. How's that?" As he handed her an extra $1,000, she accepted the envelope gratefully by asking if he would like to join her after dinner.

"No charge, of course, Señor."

CHAPTER 29

TEHRAN

"Good morning gentlemen, please come in. Allow me to introduce you to my good friend, Sheik Mohammed Bashir." With those words, Amin Rezvani, the Director of the Iranian Secret Service Agency, welcomed Abu and Colonel Mir into his spacious office.

"Before we begin, I'm afraid I have some rather unpleasant news to share. Last night, my communications officer received a short message from Camp Baleta stating that they were under attack. Immediately thereafter, all communication ceased. As of this moment, however, I am afraid we have no further details."

"Impossible!" Mir responded. "There is no way anyone could have discovered the camp's whereabouts."

"Again, we have no concrete intel as of yet, so my comments are strictly speculative. I will certainly keep you apprised as I receive more information. The Syrians have scheduled a fly-over this morning, so I expect we shall know more soon."

As Colonel Mir remained stoically in denial, Abu silently praised Allah, while the Sheik sat passively observing his two new potential allies.

The Director, allowing a moment for this unpleasant news to be digested, proceeded to the business at hand. "Abu, welcome. Your heroics against the Israelis are well documented, and you are to be congratulated for your bravery. I only wish we had more men of your stature."

"You are most generous, I only wish we had your backing several years ago. The sad truth is, we simply have never possessed adequate resources to fight the Jews effectively. Having visited Camp Baleta, however, I hope that may now change."

Descent Into Paradise

"Let's hope so. Clearly, at least up till now, the Israelis have had the upper hand. The fact is, they have the military prowess to enforce whatever policies their criminal government chooses to implement. In my humble opinion, that will only change once we can demonstrate the willingness and ability to mount strategic attacks on Jews wherever they may live or work in every corner of the globe."

Turning towards Bashir, the Director continued. "That, gentlemen, is the main reason I invited you here to join me today. The Sheik, having spent the past several years fighting the Russians in Afghanistan, is now ready to turn his attention west. A Saudi by birth, he has approached me to further align our mutual desire to have Islam reign supreme and rid ourselves of these corrupt puppets of the West who call themselves our leaders. What have they ever done for their people? Nothing! All they have done is enrich themselves and their friends at the expense of their populations, ignoring the Koran and all its teachings, all for a few million dollars in their secret Swiss bank accounts."

Bashir then entered the discussion. "I couldn't agree with you more, Director, it is time we put the teachings of the Koran above of the materialistic aspirations of our corrupt leaders who allow these western imperialists to desecrate our holy sites with their military bases.

"As to the Jews, thanks in part to the lack of any true leadership, the Arab world has sat idly by and allowed the Palestinians to fight on alone. Outmanned and outgunned, all they have been able to do is launch minor raids with, I dare say, rather meager results." Looking directly at Abu, the Sheik offered a slight apology. "I mean no offense, my friend. You alone have accounted for more Israeli deaths than most of us can take credit for, and for that I personally salute you. It is, however, as you just suggested, not enough. We need to work together in a more intelligent and coordinated approach. We simply can no longer allow the wanton aggression of these Jews to go unpunished. Only when they realize their blood will be spilled alongside ours will there be any chance of an equitable settlement."

Abu couldn't help but think of old man Nouri in his café suggesting the same formula. As he listened to what both these men were suggesting, he knew instantly where his future lay.

"Gentlemen, you have my full attention. What exactly do you have in mind?"

An hour later, the meeting ended with all in accord.

CHAPTER 30

The two Nighthawks departed earlier that morning, taking Colonel Smith and his Army Rangers back to Beirut, while Pete completed his debriefings with General Bradley. The Ambassador invited the entire Delta squad down to the infirmary, as well as the ship's Captain and, of course, the Admiral.

"Gentlemen, I apologize for greeting you all like this, but the damned doctor won't let me out of bed. I very much wanted an opportunity to thank all of you personally before you left. Admiral Brewster has given me the general outline of what happened, so I have some appreciation for the incredible job you did. All I can say is my wife and I will be eternally grateful for your efforts in rescuing us from what I fear was certain death. I can't begin to describe the joy and relief I felt when I heard those big rotors thumping, for I knew you special ops boys were coming to get us.

"I understand fully why you men operate without any publicity or public recognition, as I would want the same if I were in your shoes, so let me just say that last night you not only rescued an American Ambassador and his wife, but more importantly, the mother and father of two young children. These men would have killed both of us had you brave lads not had the courage, skill, and fortitude to come to our rescue. Words simply cannot express my sincere gratitude to all of you in this room, so, while I may not be allowed to recognize you officially, I can recognize all of you here unofficially and tell you sincerely if any of you ever need anything, you have only to call. If I can provide it, it will be yours for the asking. May God go with all of you, and keep you safe."

Descent Into Paradise

Pete then thanked the Ambassador on behalf of his squad. Up on deck, he also thanked the Admiral for all of his help throughout the mission.

"Major, allow me to add my own compliments to those of the Ambassador. You boys are special, and I'm sure glad we are on the same side! If you ever need anything the Ambassador can't provide, call me."

Having thanked the Admiral, Pete and his men then climbed aboard their little birds for the short flight back to Beirut, followed by a long flight home.

CHAPTER 31

The journey from Tehran to Murat by land took three days. Director Rezvani had been kind enough to arrange an appointment with his own personal doctor to treat Moussa's leg while Abu was busy setting up the logistics with Colonel Mir and the Sheik. Having agreed that Camp Murat would indeed be the logical place to base his Palestinian soldiers, Abu and Moussa left the following day in a convoy of military vehicles heading southwest for Murat. On the third day, Abu thought he saw a mountainous shape begin to rise as if floating on the distant horizon. The shape became clearer as they drove towards it until Abu realized their journey was coming to an end. He remembered Colonel Mir describing the camp as being at the foot of a large mountain range at the edge of a desert plain, a spot where nobody would ever find them.

In the deepening dusk, the convoy of headlights began to slow down and pulled off the main road towards the entrance to the camp. As the weary travelers took in the silhouette of the small valley, Abu stiffly walked towards several open fires glittering in the distance. He felt danger. He didn't need to see it; years of experience told him it was there. Carefully, he pulled Moussa near him as he checked for the dagger in the small of his back. It was a nervous habit of long custom. They reached the first fire ahead of the others. Several large tents surrounded a central square where sat a dozen men. These were men bred by the harshness of their surroundings. No quarter would be asked or given. A man's stature out here was in direct proportion to his ruthlessness and his willingness to demonstrate it.

Descent Into Paradise

"Mind if we sit? The boy and I are coming in from Beirut." Abu said in a low but clear voice.

"Which part of Beirut might that be?" asked a voice from the circle.

"Shatila," was all Abu replied.

"In that case, you may sit down. Welcome to Camp Murat. There happen to be several here who may share acquaintances."

Moussa sat down where he stood, crossed his legs in Bedouin style and waited. Abu looked over at the men seated around the big open hearth, noticing who looked at him directly and who kept their eyes averted. It was the latter that worried him, and he noted their positions for future reference.

"My name is Abu and my young friend is Moussa. We are grateful for your hospitality."

"My name is Abdul," said an elderly man with gray hair and goatee as he rose ponderously from his central position.

"Abu Nidal?" asked another without getting up.

"No, but he is a friend. In fact, I shared a meal with one of his lieutenants not long ago at the Yellow House," answered Abu, still cautious about their situation.

"With Arafat and his cronies," hissed the man called Kahil, a Saudi Bedouin who apparently had little regard for Palestinians in general.

"With Arafat yes, his cronies, well that depends upon your point of view," responded Abu quietly.

"My friend was only using a slang expression," said Abdul in a soothing voice. "We may all have different reference points, but we all serve the same cause here."

At that moment, several women appeared, carrying trays filled with food and steaming hot tea. The night air had cooled considerably. Moussa looked at the woman walking toward them with such an expression that she put the tray down

Descent Into Paradise

close enough to him so to make sure he got his share. Another tray appeared and yet another, until the men were all busily eating. Later in the evening, the dark muddy coffee began to arrive. This was the designated discussion time for topics of communal importance in the life of most Arabs and tonight was no exception.

As the evening wore on, Moussa moved closer to Abu, put his head on the older man's blanket and quickly fell asleep. Had he remained awake, he would have listened to a chilling outline of the upcoming mission being formulated. Abu remained for as long as he could stay awake, but the painkillers were taking effect. He excused himself and carried Moussa back to their designated tent, tucked him into a cot and fell into one himself. He slept soundly, despite the sense of foreboding which crept uneasily around the edges of his dreams.

The next morning, they woke to the sounds of a siren and men getting up for their early morning jog. Walking outside, Abu could now see the setting of this new camp was ideal. A seep ran through a rocky gully down the southern perimeter of the base, providing a steady flow of cold spring water to the inhabitants. Nestled against the mountains, the sheer vertical drop made any attacks from that side impossible. Commanding a clear field of fire in all other directions, the Camp was impregnable to a surprise attack. Abu and Moussa saw large supply depots spread around the base in such a way that no saboteur could blow more than one at a time. The whole operation was highly professional, even to the latrines dug deep and placed downwind.

Abu's professional eye missed nothing; tents were maintained, grounds meticulously clean, no trash or worn out equipment and the perimeter fencing was first class, as was the security patrol.

Descent Into Paradise

Morning began officially at 06h00, with a blast from the air raid siren. Men poured out of their tents to relieve themselves, then put on their light fatigues. There were twenty groups of fighters, each group consisting of 72 men. It was required that each one of these groups run a five-mile course before breakfast. The last five men to finish from each group drew latrine duty for the day.

Moussa watched, as the men got ready. He and Abu were both excused due to their leg injuries, so they walked over to the mess tent for breakfast.

"The desert has a way of making men adjust to her," commented Abu as he watched Moussa observe the men around them. "If you live out here for very long on this régime, you will also become very fit indeed."

"Abu, how long have these men been here?"

"I'm not certain, but I do remember Abdul telling me last night that the normal training program lasts four to six months."

"How long are we going to be here?" Moussa asked timidly.

"I don't know the answer yet but I think we should learn to like it here," Abu answered as they entered the canteen consisting of six long wooden picnic style tables, each seating twelve people, six to a side. Each table had bowls of various fruits, breads, pitchers of milk and fruit juices. The large room was virtually empty as most of the camp was out in the desert, still running. Apparently some of the men preferred eating here while others preferred the open fire outside, Bedouin style, as they had the previous evening. When they had finished eating, Abu took Moussa over to the small clinic nearby. As there were no patients in the small waiting room, they were ushered right in to a small examining room.

"Please tell me how the boy was hurt?" asked the young Syrian doctor politely as he began to undress the wound.

"He stepped on a shell fragment as we were trying to exit our camp."

"These burns came from a shell fragment?"

"Phosphorous shells, yes."

"Phosphorous shells were used against a civilian refugee camp? My God. And you sir, your leg was burned also?" the doctor asked.

"No, mine is a simple shrapnel wound."

The doctor quickly moved his body between Moussa's head and his lower torso so the young man could not see the damage.

"I was given this ointment by a doctor in Tehran. He said it would help the healing as well as the pain," said Abu, handing over the tube.

"Excellent, this leg will be better in no time. How does it feel, young man?"

Trying his best to be brave, he whispered he was fine.

"Good, good. First, I am going to cleanse your leg. Now, we are going to put on some lotion which may sting, but it will help your leg heal."

As they left the clinic, the heat was already oppressive. Out towards the desert, the landscape was a very flat brown. No planting could ever survive the arid soil or the intense desert heat. Everywhere they looked, there was only sand, rocks, and large tents whose bleached canvas blended into the drab background. Unlike the smaller camp in Beqaa Valley, this one had a ten-foot high barbed wired fence encircling the entire camp. As they walked on, they noticed multiple observation posts spaced evenly around the entire perimeter. Guards stood a 24-hour vigil armed with automatic rifles and machineguns mounted in place. Given this remote location, Abu wondered if this was really necessary, but it certainly did speak to the professionalism of Bashir. He could not imagine the PLO going to this trouble or expense.

Descent Into Paradise

Their walk brought them over to the training portion of the camp, where men were now heading after their breakfast. Here, demolition and explosion engineers apparently trained their recruits how to blow things apart. Realistic fights were beginning to take place in many parts of the camp, some becoming serious grudge matches, but seasoned instructors were able to keep control with no loss of life.

Moussa wanted to stay and see the fights but Abu assured him he would see lots of fights. "There'll be plenty of time to learn how to kill, Moussa, that is what this camp is built for, to teach stamina and how to end human life."

Later that morning, while Moussa went to lie down, Abu went to meet the Sheik and the Camp Commander. Abu took the opportunity to congratulate them both on the effective measures taken for the security of this new facility. Turning to the Sheik, Abu went on, "When you and the Director told me about Murat, I had no idea something like this existed."

"Commander, this is the gentleman I told you about last night. We met in Tehran last week at Director Rezvani's office. He has killed more Israelis than anyone we have trained here, and I am counting on him to help us kill many more! Now, I must take my leave as my flight to London leaves from Tehran this evening. It is time for the Saudis to declare if they are allies or enemies."

With that, Bashir left Abu and the Commander to carry on.

"Please, Abu, have a seat. Welcome to Camp Murat. Thanks to both Director Rezvani and the Sheik, we have built what I believe to be the premier training facility of its kind. Here, we not only train young men how to combat our enemies, but we train them spiritually as well. The Sheik mentioned you have brought your son with you, and I can assure you he will be well taken care of here. We have several young boys in residence, so he will have friends his own age."

LONDON

Sheik Bashir sat in the back seat of the hotel's Bentley, happy to be back in London. Having spent the past several days in Murat, he looked forward to the creature comforts of civilization, especially those of his favorite city.

A frequent and valued guest of the Berkeley Hotel in Knightsbridge, the Sheik was escorted directly to his suite on the sixth floor. The clerk then handed him the sealed envelope from the Saudi Arabian Embassy received earlier in the day.

CHAPTER 32

CHILE

Zev was ushered into the family library. Juan and Ricardo were the only two people in the room.

"Hello Zev, please come in. Thank you for coming. Pablo, please see that the Major gets a drink." Juan smiled at Zev and motioned him to the chair opposite his in front of the fireplace. Ricardo was seated on the sofa.

"The usual, Major?" asked Pablo.

"Yes, thank you Pablo."

Juan then went straight to the business at hand. "Zev, we've asked you here tonight to discuss your future employment with us. As we have all been aware from the very beginning, you are on loan to us from Mossad. Neither Ricardo nor I have any doubt that Israel's recent decision to distance itself from us has nothing to do with their public renunciation of the South Africans. It is our belief that your beloved Intelligence Agency is petrified that the Americans will learn of our mutual business dealings."

Ricardo then interrupted, "Which, if we are correct, places you in a very compromised position."

Zev laughed. "I would certainly agree with you both. One thing is for certain, the Director cannot afford the Americans discovering Mossad's involvement."

Juan had, over the year, become quite fond of this Israeli soldier, despite his obvious mixed loyalties. He now realized why he had hesitated putting this question to Zev. He was afraid of getting the wrong answer.

"Zev, although you have only been with us a short time, you have clearly become an integral part of our operation. Now that our arrangements with Mossad are likely to end, Ricardo and I would like to extend an invitation to join our family as a principal."

Before Zev could reply, Ricardo made it clear that this offer would require that he put his loyalty to the Family above all else and terminate his affiliation with Mossad. Zev did not respond until Pablo, who had just brought him his drink, left the room.

"First, let me thank you both. I am most flattered with your generous offer. In many ways, I have felt very much at home here as I have always been treated with respect for which I thank you both. However, strictly for personal reasons, I would ask your permission to return to Israel before I give you my answer."

Ricardo glanced at Juan who nodded. "Fine, when can we expect you back?"

"One week is all I need."

With that settled, Juan went to see Estoban. It was time to settle a matter he had too long ignored.

CHAPTER 33

TEL AVIV

"The Director will see you now, please follow me, Major."

"Welcome home, Zev. Please sit down. Shasa will be joining us for lunch, but I thought you and I could speak privately first."

Zev looked at the balding bespeckled figure across the room, wondering how many men he had sent to a premature death. It flashed across his mind: would his name soon be added?

The Director, cognizant of Zev's silence, went on, "My sources in Chile tell me you have put together a first rate fighting force for our former clients. A force so powerful, even our friend President Pinochet does not dare confront it."

"That's probably a wise decision on his part."

The Director, not one to waste time on pleasantries, came directly to the point. "To what do I owe the pleasure of this visit, Major?"

"I have been asked by Mr. Rios to swear an oath of loyalty to the Rios family and join them."

"And have you done so?" came the brusque reply.

"Not yet, sir. I thought I would have this meeting first, then decide."

"Very admirable, Major. I appreciate loyalty to one's country. Let me be frank, the Army treated you very poorly. Clearly that whole Beirut mess was the General's doing and, if it's any consolation to you, everyone now fully understands what happened. Having said that, I certainly would not blame you if you decide to join Rios. All I can say is that Israel can ill afford to lose her best soldiers." Receiving only a blank expression, he went on. "Before you decide anything, Major, let me explain what we are facing."

Descent Into Paradise

The Director then walked over to a large map of the Middle East, motioning Zev to follow. "Allow me to give you a capsulated version of Israel's current state of affairs. Since our withdrawal from Lebanon, the Syrians have kept their end of the bargain and continue to keep a tight lid on any terrorist activity near our border. Arafat has decided to go it alone, not joining any of the new Islamic groups. The old man is still delusional thinking he can persuade the Americans to force some peace deal down our throats. The trouble now lies here," he said, moving his pointer to Iran.

Zev looked perplexed.

The Director nodded. "The explanation has several distinct pieces. First, as I'm sure you know, the Mullahs in Iran achieved a great victory for Islam when they overthrew the Shah. The whole Islamic world looks up to them as the restorers of the faith. They, in turn, are ardent supporters of any group interested in restoring Islamic fundamentalism to the region."

He went over to a side table where a carafe of coffee and two cups awaited. He poured one for Zev and brought his over to the map.

"Then, we have the whole issue of American ground forces stationed in both Kuwait and Saudi Arabia to support their whole petro dollar regime. This has inflamed many of the fundamentalists who view this as an intrusion of Western corruption into some of the holiest places of Islam. As you well know, these are the same people who view the Saudi royal family as well as Kuwait's royal family as corrupt puppets of Western capitalism. Into this hotbed has stepped the most dangerous terrorist we have yet encountered. His name is Sheik Mohammed Bashir."

"Tell me about this Sheik."

"Well, to start with, he is a religious zealot. He was born in the deserts of Saudi Arabia, the son of a wealthy Bedouin

Descent Into Paradise

chieftain whose domain happened to lie on top of a large reservoir of oil. His father sent him off to England for his formal education, where he encountered a healthy dose of British disdain towards Arabs in general. He is very sophisticated, is well traveled, and considered very handsome by the ladies." This was said with a chuckle by the Director. "The combination is lethal, for this cultivated façade has enabled him to deal effectively with a number of very wealthy Arabs, many of whom now reside in England and have donated a sizable amount of money to his cause. This British façade, however, while appealing on the surface, masks a very smart and utterly ruthless fanatic.

"But, back to his story. He returned home from England in 1982, immediately joining the freedom fighters in Afghanistan to fight against the Russians. Recently, however, we are hearing rumors that he is focusing his attention on establishing a highly sophisticated international terrorist operation purporting to represent all Arabs who believe in Islam."

"Interesting. Where is he based now?"

"We're not sure. We suspect he is primarily operating out of Iran, but we have no direct confirmation of that. There are multiple reports of his being seen in Afghanistan, the Sudan, and even Somalia. We have tracked his operatives throughout the Middle East, including a good number in Saudi Arabia."

"I certainly appreciate the briefing, Director, but what's its relevance to our discussion?"

Sitting down, the Director responded in a rather icy tone. "I have not yet finished, Major. Please forgive me for being a bit longwinded for your taste. Do you happen to know where the bulk of the world's opium is produced?"

"Asia, more specifically the Golden Triangle in Burma, I believe."

Descent Into Paradise

"That figure is closer to 20%. The country which controls close to 70% of the world's supply of opium is, in fact, Afghanistan."

Zev let out a soft whistle. "I obviously had no idea. You said earlier that Afghanistan is now being taken over by a radical Islamic group called the Talisman."

"The Taliban. As the Russians begin to withdraw their forces, the power vacuum is slowly being filled by these nasty thugs. They won't even allow women to go to school; no pictures, no movies, no radio, no television; no entertainment of any sort. It appears they wish to return that society back to the Middle Ages."

"And they now control 70% of the world's opium?"

"Yes and no. They control the production. We suspect the man who is close to a deal to buy their entire production is our friend, Sheik Bashir. Now is the discussion becoming more relevant for you."

"My apologies, Director."

"The point, Major, is that we must find a way to infiltrate Bashir's operation to understand what he is planning. So far, we have been totally unsuccessful. I was rather hoping your South American friends might find a connection to the Sheik a most useful and rewarding one."

Zev immediately thought of the ramifications of controlling even a fraction of the Afghan crop. His thoughts were interrupted by a knock on the door. "Oh! That must be Shasa. Come in, the door's unlocked," called the Director.

Zev could not believe how beautiful she looked as a huge smile lit up her face. "Zev, you are here!" Ignoring the Director completely, she ran into his awaiting arms.

The Director allowed a thin smile to cross his lips as he paused for a second. "Shall we adjourn for lunch?"

Lunch entailed Zev filling both of them in on his activities and Shasa briefing him on the latest reports from the joint task

Descent Into Paradise

force that the Americans had organized to combat both terrorism and the major drug cartels. At one point during dessert, Zev looked at the Director, asking, "Do they really view us as terrorists?"

Shasa, quoting General Bradley, replied, "Those filthy drug dealers have caused more harm to this country than both World Wars combined."

The Director finished the luncheon concluding, "Major, you need to be aware that we have committed to helping Bradley eradicate the major drug dealers as well as these terrorist groups. He sees them as one and the same, meaning that we must as well."

The lunch meeting broke up with Zev promising Shasa he would meet her for dinner. She left first, leaving the two men to have a brief word.

"Let me take a day or two to think everything through, Director, then I will get back to you."

"Take your time, Major. I will be here all week. Just let my secretary know when you wish to meet. In the meantime, welcome home."

Shasa chose a small French bistro near Zev's hotel for their dinner date. The minute they sat down, she started bombarding Zev with questions about his new life in South America. It wasn't until their main course arrived that Zev finally got a chance to ask some of his own. Listening to her, it was clear she still had not fully recovered from her parents' death. He began to think of his own mother's death and what had become of his father. Having not spoken to him since his return to America many years ago, Zev asked if she had heard anything. She then looked at him. "You haven't communicated with him in all these years?"

"No. Ever since my mother died, I felt as if he had wished I had died as well."

Descent Into Paradise

Looking into those green eyes, he realized at that moment it was only his connection with this young girl, a woman now, that had made him return.

Reaching over to take her hand in his, he spoke in a soft voice. "You, my beautiful little sister, are the only family I have."

Shasa saw the raw emotion in his eyes and suddenly realized just how lonely and emotionally fragile this tough soldier really was. Her love for him only magnified as she responded. "We are the only family either of us has left. Please, Zev, I know how you feel about what happened here, but please, don't go back. I've lost both my families; you're all I have. Don't let them kill you too!"

Not quite sure which 'them' Shasa was referring to, he decided to change the subject.

"Now, tell me about you. How is my good friend Major Watson, you two are still seeing each other I hope?"

Her wide smile told him all he needed to know. "We still stay in touch, although it certainly is a long distance relationship. He always asks about you and what you're doing."

"I hope he's not involved in this crazy war on drugs?" She had never lied to him before, and she truly did not want to start now. After a moment of silence, Zev realized intuitively that of course Pete would be involved in it. He was, after all, one of their Special Forces aces, and they would certainly use their Special Forces in any covert action, which he presumed would be the way they would handle any illegal incursion into a sovereign country such as Chile.

"You don't have to answer that last question, I think I already know the answer," Zev told her gently.

"Zev, the truth is we are both very much involved." She then shared with him everything she had been involved with since Beirut, including helping negotiate the deal with the South Africans and his boss Juan Rios. Zev just sat there listening intently, his mind numb as he tried to absorb the full extent of what Shasa was saying. After she finished by describing her trip to America and her subsequent assignment in London, he ordered a stiff drink.

"I had no idea it had reached this stage. What do you think will happen next?"

"I really don't know. Pete usually tells me he will be out of touch when they go on a mission, but he never tells me where. There would be no way I could ever warn you. Zev, you can't go back, the Director is going to cooperate with the Americans; he has to. Politically, he has no choice."

"Do the Americans have any idea of Mossad's role in this?"

"No."

"So Pete has no idea of the double game you're playing?"

"No, he doesn't."

"Shasa, we both need to be very careful. Juan Rios's informants are telling him one day the Americans are going to come down to Chile."

"Zev, Israel cannot afford the Americans to find out what our involvement has been with Señor Rios or any of the other groups I have been dealing with, and we both know they'll not hesitate to kill either one of us to protect their interests."

"Let's talk tomorrow. Maybe with a good night's sleep, I can make some sense of this." The next morning, Zev phoned for an appointment with the Director, one that was granted that very afternoon. The Director looked up from his desk as he was ushered in.

"Director, I am leaving for Santiago in the morning. I have decided to join the Rios family upon my return."

"I see, well I cannot say I blame you. So where does that leave us?"

"I was hoping you and I could make an arrangement."

Descent Into Paradise

"What exactly did you have in mind?"

"I am willing to try to make a connection between Rios and Bashir. I obviously cannot guarantee anything will come of it, if I can make the connection at all. However, if Rios is interested, I will let you know, and you can take it from there."

"And what about you, Major, what do you want?"

"I am well aware of the predicament you are in with the Americans. If I play along with this, I trust I will not need to look over my shoulder for you, agreed?"

"Major, you and I have no quarrel unless you do something in the future to hurt us. As for the Americans, they may indeed come for Rios one day, and, if requested, we will come with them. If that were to ever happen, and, if I am informed of such an operation ahead of time, I would be amenable to giving you sufficient notice. You then must give me your word to remove yourself immediately without issuing any warning."

"I think we both understand each other. If I undertake to make the connection with Bashir, that will be my signal of acceptance. If not, then we both will need to look out for ourselves."

"I can find no fault in that. Be careful, and I hope we will meet again."

They shook hands and Zev left with a feeling he had seen the Director for the last time.

CHAPTER 34

Pete's heart skipped a beat when he saw two long arms waving from the back of the room. Driving straight to her apartment, they fell into each other's arms, both in need of the other. Their lovemaking had lost none of its enthusiasm over the years; if anything, it had become more passionate as they realized how little time they had together.

As they lay in bed exhausted, Shasa propped her head up on her elbow. "Pete, I have broken our cardinal rule and made a dinner reservation with a friend of ours."

"Really, you mean I have to share you on our first night? Not your General Argov, I hope."

"No, it's a surprise, and yes you have to share me, but just for dinner. After that, I am yours to do with as you please."

He chuckled. "Well, if that's the case, I trust you are in good shape, young lady."

They waited in the bar for 30 minutes before Zev arrived. Catching sight of each other, Zev and Pete embraced as long lost brothers.

"Zev Megrid, you sure look better than the last time I saw you. What a wonderful surprise."

They joked and slapped each other's backs as if at a college reunion.

As they sat in a cozy banquette, Zev started, "So tell me, Pete, what brings you all the way to Tel Aviv?"

"To be honest, I am now only a part time soldier. The balance of my time is spent playing spook, which means I get to travel here periodically to brief both Argov and Mossad on whatever we have learned and, in turn, gather up whatever little tidbits those two are willing to share."

He then reached over and took Shasa's hand while adding, "As an added bonus, I get to see this beautiful young lady."

"And what mischief are you up to? I've heard that you're involved in some clandestine work for our friends at Mossad, but nobody, including Miss Shasa, will tell me what it is you are doing."

Zev leaned back in his chair, unsure of how much he should say. He looked over at Shasa, who gave him a big smile but no guidance. "Let's just say I am living the good life playing double agent."

"Come on, you and I have been through too much for that explanation."

"Pete, all I can tell you is I have been down in South America. It is all top secret, I'm sorry my friend."

Pete hesitated for a brief moment before he held up his hand. "Zev, I apologize. If you can't say, don't. But, since you're now operating in my part of the world, I want you to keep this number." Handing him a card, Pete finished by saying, "This number is open 24 hours a day. If you need help or just want to say hello, I will alert the switchboard to find me whenever you call."

Taking his card, Zev looked across the table, realizing there really were only two people in the entire world he could count on for help, and they were both sitting across from him.

"Thanks. Who knows, I may just take you up on that offer. Now, I believe we should order a bottle of champagne to celebrate this occasion."

They toasted each other, their health and prosperity, and then Zev raised his glass for a final toast to both of them. "I love you both, and I want to wish you two all the happiness you so richly deserve."

Shasa got out of her chair, leaned over and gave Zev a big kiss. "You're a wonderful man, Zev Megrid, we both love you very much."

"I second that, though I won't give you a kiss. I think you need to stay over one more day. One night is not long enough to catch up."

"You're on if I can change my reservation."

The phone rang, waking up Shasa.

"Oh Zev, that's too bad. Pete will be devastated."

"Give him a hug for me, and Shasa…"

"Yes?"

"I do love you."

"I love you too."

"Good luck and please be careful!"

"You too, Zev, I will pray for you."

Pete came out of the bathroom. "Who was that?"

"That was Zev, calling from the airport. Apparently he could not get a later flight so he is flying out on this morning."

"That's too bad, I was really looking forward to spending some more time with him. I hope you said goodbye for me."

"I certainly did. He wanted me to tell you how wonderful it was to be with you last night. Now come over here before you get dressed. I want to tell you how wonderful you were last night as well."

Pete entered the Director's office slightly hung over from the night before. After greeting the Director, he sat in the chair opposite the desk.

"Good morning to you Major, I trust you had a pleasant flight."

"Yes, thank you."

"What have you for us today?"

"Sir, we are becoming very concerned about the Soviets selling some of their more sophisticated weaponry to the highest bidder, namely some unsavory characters who may decide to use them against both of us."

"Israel is equally concerned, I can assure you. It seems that the Iranians have been making some rather large arms deals lately. Are you getting similar data?"

"Yes, we are also hearing about a Saudi Sheik who is buying large quantities of arms but not through official channels."

"Really? We will keep our ear to the ground and let you know if we discover anything."

"One more thing, Director. Have you heard anything concerning the sale of large quantities of opium?"

"Out of Asia? I'm afraid our networks there are not completely reliable."

"No, we are talking about Iran or Afghanistan or even Pakistan."

"What exactly have you heard, Major?"

"Just some reference to a major new supplier of opium in the mountainous region around Iran."

"Very interesting. We tend to track arms more than drugs, but we will also keep our ears open to any information on that subject."

Pete, who always believed the Director gave him a fraction of what he really knew, then asked what Mossad could divulge to him.

"The only piece of new information we have for you is that we are getting wind of a plot to kidnap an American in Beirut. We don't know who, but our agents are telling us it is someone important."

Pete thanked him for that and asked to be kept up to speed if anything new came up.

"How did your meeting go today with the Director?"

"The usual. He tells me about one third of what he really knows, hoping that will appease me." Pete looked totally frustrated and annoyed.

"Pete, don't say that, I am sure that is not true."

"You're probably right, it's probably one eighth of what he really knows."

"OK, let's leave shop talk for tomorrow and tonight we will talk about us." Shasa smiled lovingly at Pete.

"What a great idea. Will you marry me?"

"Pete, you know I love you deeply. I am just not yet ready to move to Maine and become a housewife. Please try to understand!" Shasa looked beseechingly at Pete.

"If you are not ready, then so be it."

"Please, just give me a little more time."

"Take whatever time you need. Just remember, neither of us are getting any younger."

"We both seemed in good health last night," she smiled coyly back at him. "Shall we see if two nights in a row is too much for us elderly folks?"

"Are you flying back to London tomorrow?" asked Pete as they drove to the airport the next morning.

"Yes. The Director has someone he wants me to meet, so we are having dinner tomorrow night. Lord somebody or other. He's a friend of the Director's from way back and apparently is well connected in the business and social world there. The Director says he has recently been involved in financing several very large transactions for several prominent Saudis, so let's hope he can help."

"Well, keep your ears open. It would appear some Russian general made off with some very sophisticated weapons and is now willing to sell them to the highest bidder. My guess is there will be some willing buyers, and whoever they are probably will not be looking out for either of our best interests!"

The Director was questioning Shasa about Pete and she was patiently answering,

"The only shop talk we discussed was his interest in some general who apparently is trying to sell some rather sophisticated weapon systems. He thinks he is operating out of London."

"There was no discussion about Rios or Zev?"

"We actually had dinner with Zev the night before last. When asked by Pete, he declined to discuss what he was doing."

"You had dinner with Zev and Pete? What on earth were you thinking?"

"I was thinking that if Zev truly had plans to leave us entirely, he might have been a bit more forthcoming with his best friend about what he was doing. I thought you might want to know if he was crossing the line."

"My apologies. You were quite right to make him declare. We are going to have to be most careful how we handle our American friends. They must never find out anything of our involvement with Rios." Then, looking directly at her, he finished in a very flat tone, "Or it could put all of us in very grave danger."

Shasa could read between the lines and knew that the Director would not go down alone, her only response being, "I can assure you that information will never come from me."

"Good. Now to London, you are traveling there in the morning, correct?"

"Correct, I'm leaving in the morning."

"And you are still on for dinner with Lord Luxley?"

"I am."

"I want you to do your very best to ingratiate yourself with my old friend. He is a bit older, but very charming and quite debonair. He is, more importantly, a very good source of information for us about what is happening in London, especially in the Arab community. I believe the old goat has made a great deal of money legitimizing some of those desert rats with the old guard British establishment. I can't emphasize enough how critical it is we get a handle on this Sheik. Whatever you need, it will be provided for by our people in London. If you have any issues or problems, call me directly and they will be resolved immediately."

"I understand."

CHAPTER 35

Estoban couldn't help but smile as he left the library. Finally, he was going to get a chance to even the score with that little bitch who had treated him like a servant ever since she arrived. Now, he would show her who was in charge. That evening, Juan brought Madonna over to his little workshop. With a look of resignation, he turned her over. "Estoban, she is all yours."

Madonna, who up to this point had no idea what was happening, had a look of utter terror on her face as she turned on Rios. "What do you mean by that? He's a monster! You can't do this to me," she screamed as Juan turned to leave, oblivious to her cries for help. Estoban then carried her, kicking and screaming, downstairs.

"You see that table with the leather straps. That's not for fucking, although we may try that too. It's for getting people to talk who are too stupid to do it voluntarily. Now, before we go there, the boss wants to know who took out the contract on his parents?"

"What contract? I have no idea what you're talking about. You boys must have had too much tequila and pussy last night. It's muddled your brains. Or maybe the syphilis has finally spread out of your diseased crotch. You know it will kill you one day, if someone doesn't do it first."

Lifting her off the ground with one hand, he threw her on the metal table. Strapping her hands and feet to each corner, he went over to the medical cabinet on the wall. Opening it, he selected a rather small surgical knife. Madonna looked on in horror as he stood over her. A smile curled his lip as he started working on her with that glazed expression. Deliberately, he took a handful of her thick blonde hair, cut it off, and let it drift down onto the floor. He then slowly slid the knife under her tank top slicing it in two, exposing both breasts to the bright lights above. Her black mini skirt was next, then her panties.

Screaming hysterically, she pleaded with him to stop.

"Who took the contract?"

"I told you, I don't know what you're talking about."

Her tears made no impression on him whatsoever. Next, he took off her shoes one at a time. Holding her left foot first, he made a shallow incision the length of her sole. A piercing scream reverberated off the soundproofed walls.

"Stop! Please stop," she shrieked. "I'll tell you whatever you want."

Moving over to her right foot, he quietly repeated that long painful stroke. Madonna was sweating and shaking uncontrollably. "Please Estoban, you must believe me, I would tell you if I knew, you must believe me, dear God!"

"How much did it cost to have Juan's parents killed?"

She hesitated, knowing she was dead either way. He then shrugged as if it made no difference. He put his hands on her chest and began to play with her breasts. Since she was a young girl, she had always counted on her looks to get ahead. Now, looking into Estoban's crazed eyes, she instinctively knew her only chance of surviving.

"Lick them, honey, they're all yours."

Estoban had been with many women, most of them cheap whores in the surrounding villages. Occasionally Juan, as a reward, would give him one of the house girls, but he had never seen a body as perfectly sculptured as this. She knew she had only one chance to get off this table alive. She began moaning and moving her chest around his mouth.

"Yes, suck on me, feel me get hard." Her nipples responding to his tongue made him harder below the table. Lust began to take over. Dropping his knife, his hands began to move down her stomach.

"Unstrap me, and I'll take you places you've never been."

He released her, and she got off the table. Unable to stand on her bleeding feet, she knelt down in front of him and performed her best act. She took him on a ride he had never before experienced, draining him of his energy until he too collapsed beside her.

"Madonna," he said after a minute, "Tell me who killed his parents, and I will let you out of here alive."

"And if I don't?"

"I'll put you back on that table and kill you."

"You promise you'll let me go and won't hurt me anymore?"

"I promise you can leave with no more cuts on that beautiful body."

"Pinochet took out the hit on his parents. I was paid $20,000 for giving them up. I thought it would be good for Juan. He was always telling me his old man was in the way of his doing what he wanted."

Pointing at the door, Estoban told her to put on the robe hanging from a hook. "There's a car waiting for you in the garage. The driver will take you out of here."

"What about my clothes, my jewelry?"

"You will leave with what you are wearing. Be grateful you still have your looks. Now leave before I change my mind."

Despite the excruciating pain in her feet, she hobbled to the garage where the chauffeur helped her into the back seat. Madonna was so thankful to be alive she never bothered to ask where they were going. Somehow she felt safe lying down on the backseat, leaving that horrible man behind.

Descent Into Paradise

Thirty minutes later, the car came to a screeching halt. The door opened. As she sat up, two men reached in and dragged her over into a small tin hut. The room was filthy. Papers and open boxes full of junk littered the floor. The ceiling fan unsuccessfully fought to clear the room of cigar smoke. There was no air conditioning, and the huge ugly man facing her hadn't seen the inside of a bathtub in weeks. She felt like fainting when he looked at her.

"So you're Juan Rios's whore. Let's see the goods."

She just sat there, hoping she would wake up from this nightmare.

"I said stand and take off your robe."

"Fuck you, you pig."

With a slight nod, the two men who had dragged her in now came over to lift her off the chair, stripping the bathrobe off her shoulders. Yelling obscenities, she struggled in vain as her breasts bounced up and down. Nodding approvingly, a big dirty smile lit up his huge mustached face.

"Very tasty. Take her over to Juanita and get her cleaned up. I will try out the merchandise personally. Have her ready in an hour."

Madonna could not stop crying as Juanita put bandages on her swollen feet.

"You really should have a doctor look at these feet. I think they may require stitches."

"Then call one, you stupid bitch. Where am I anyway, and who are you people?"

"This is the Lazy Ranch, Miss. The gentleman you just met in the main office owns it. I work here as the laundress. My name is Juanita, what's yours?"

"Madonna. What is the Lazy Ranch? It looks more like a whorehouse than a ranch?"

Giggling, Juanita replied, "It is. Men come in from all the farms and villages for many miles. There are twenty fulltime girls who live here. I'm like their surrogate mother."

"Well, Juanita, or whatever your name is, thank you for bandaging my feet, but if you would call my driver, I think it's time I left you and your girls to their fun."

"Miss, if you don't mind my saying, you look a little old to be here, but my instructions are to get you properly dressed for business. You may not know this but you've been sold to Mr. Mendoza, the owner. Now you've got to work off your debt to him."

"What are you babbling about, you old crone? I have not been sold to anyone. I could buy this flea-bitten hovel with my weekly allowance."

At that moment, Mr. Mendoza opened the door. "I told you to have her ready, do you call this sexy?"

"Get out right now!" yelled Madonna. "I demand you call my driver immediately. Now vamoose before I call the police."

"That's rich," bellowed Mendoza. "Yeah, why don't you call the police, missy? Yell police loud enough, and I might come save you. I am the police in this village so what can I do for you?"

"Get me out of this two-bit flea-infested rat hole right now. Do you know who I am?"

"You're mine. Mr. Juan Rios just sold you to me for 25,000 US dollars. So I own you until you pay that off. The way you're going to pay that off is on your back. The house rules are very simple. Room and board cost you $400 a month. We are open for business six days a week. If you work hard, you should be able to book five customers a day. We charge $20 per customer. You get half, the house keeps half. That translates to $50 a day for you to pay your room and board and pay off the $25,000 you owe me."

Madonna just looked at him with a bewildered stare.

"Oh, there's one more thing. I don't pay for mine, and I'm on a tight schedule. Usually I like my girls all dressed up for me, but since you're new and just got here, I'll make an exception. Juanita, beat it."

"Yes Mr. Mendoza, good night."

"I'll say this about you. For your age, you're still a bundle of curves. You're going to do just fine here. Now let's see how you perform; Estoban just told me you give the best blow jobs in all of Chile."

After Madonna was driven away, Estoban went to see his boss.

"What did she say about my parents, did she confess to that?"

"Yes, she told me President Pinochet took out the contract on your parents. Apparently, he paid her $20,000 to set them up."

"As God is my witness, I will kill that fucking bastard with my own hands! What did you do with that whore? Kill her?"

"No Señor, I thought death too good for what she had done. I sold her to a brothel in a little village some twenty miles from here. This man I know is the chief of police there, Mendoza is his name, and he runs a local bordello with about twenty country girls working full time. It attracts the farm workers and transients from all over. A very rough place Señor, if you know what I mean."

"What did you sell her for?

"One US dollar Señor, and the promise that she would never leave there alive."

CHAPTER 36

As Abu finished packing his overnight kit, he thought about his upcoming meeting with Director Rezvani in Tehran. The air defense system Rezvani wanted to install around Murat would have to be carefully thought out. Abu had visited the ruins of Baleta and knew just how vulnerable these small camps were to a night attack by American and Israeli forces. As he said goodbye to Moussa, he admonished him to be careful and to stay clear of Kahil.

Moussa re-read the passage again. All six boys had recited it perfectly; only he had been unable to do so. The other boys exchanged little looks of disdain; this new boy obviously was not very bright. Moussa began to feel little beads of sweat form on his brow. He was not used to getting any attention, certainly not of this intensity. The teacher was an Islamic Mullah from Tehran whose patience matched Abu's, thought Moussa, somewhere between little and none.

Moussa was made to face the bare concrete wall and recite the passage over and over until he could do it from memory, then the class could proceed.

Abu had left the previous evening with Colonel Mir, leaving Moussa with strict instructions not to go around the camp alone. In the two weeks since his entrance into the school, only one of the boys had made an effort to be friends. His name was Ari; he was an Iranian whose parents had both been killed by the SAVAK before the Shah had been ousted. He was the same age as Moussa, both a year younger than the other four.

Ari thought Abu was Moussa's father, as did most everyone

at Murat, so Moussa had not told Ari he was also an orphan. With Abu gone, Ari was the only friend he had. He asked Ari if he wanted to spend the night in Abu's cot until he returned, an idea that had great appeal to the young boy.

Kahil waited patiently for the two youngsters to leave the mess area. His patience would now be rewarded. Since Abu's departure, Kahil had waited for a time when the new boy would be alone.

Looking to his comrade, he quietly told him, "You can have the Iranian, I want the other one." Both men grinned in anticipation.

Moussa had just reached the tent when he felt a hand grab his shoulder. Ari shuddered when he saw who it was.

The big Saudi, with the high-pitched voice, smiled down upon them both as he said to Moussa, "Abu should not have all the fun. Here at Murat, everyone learns to share, just like we are going to do."

Pulling Moussa over to his cot, he told him to pull his pants down. Ari was told to do the same. Moussa tried to cry out for help but a large brown hand wrapped around his mouth.

Ari pulled down his pants, then, bending over the cot, he closed his eyes, bracing for the pain. This time he promised he would not cry in front of Moussa.

Poor Moussa was petrified. Kahil was pulling his buttocks apart before he understood what was about to happen. He thought he would just get beaten until he saw what was happening to Ari. Moussa had never felt such pain as the next few minutes. When Kahil had finished, he just zipped up his fly, leaving Moussa in tears on the bed.

Ari waited a few minutes before coming over to help his new friend. Moussa was so ashamed; he could not even look up.

Descent Into Paradise

"Do not be ashamed," Ari gently told him. "Kahil has done this to all the boys at school. You are the last one."

Moussa looked up, trying to wipe away the tears. "You mean he has done this to you before?"

Ari looked down at his friend. "More than once."

"We should tell the Commander. He would stop this," Moussa told him as he tried to get up.

"Do not move, stay still until the pain goes away. You will be alright shortly." Putting his small hand on Moussa's shoulder, he told him that the Commander was well aware of what was going on and chose to do nothing about it.

"It is a part of our training, Moussa. We must learn to accept the pain and not let it bother us. It is part of being a soldier."

Moussa wondered who had given Ari that speech. Not Abu. He would kill Kahil when he returned and Moussa would be there to watch.

Abu returned several days later, but Moussa never told him what had happened. He had thought of nothing else but revenge during that first night. Then, the pain had gone away, and he began to have his doubts about telling Abu. What if Kahil killed Abu, then what would happen? He could not take that risk just to get revenge. No, he decided, Abu would never know.

Moussa never told Abu about what really went on in school. The constant beatings; the daily repetition of verses from the Koran added to the Mullah's daily lectures about the glory of dying in battle against the infidels. Moussa had learned to chant, the preferred method of communicating with Allah. He learned to hate the Jews. He learned to hate the Americans. He learned not to fear death but to welcome it in the service of his faith. He learned how not to learn anything but the Koran and to do exactly what he was told.

Descent Into Paradise

"Life is simple," lectured the Mullah. "Obey the Koran. Live your life according to the will of Allah and you shall have everlasting life. Defend the faith and He shall watch over you for eternity."

CHAPTER 37

The Maître d' at the Savoy walked Shasa over to a corner table where a very distinguished elderly gentleman awaited her arrival. Lord Archibald Luxley was not at all what she had envisioned. He was, in fact, quite handsome and not as stuffy as she had pictured.

"Shasa, please sit down. I trust your flight was not overly tiring?"

"No, in fact it was quite an easy trip, no problems at all. What a beautiful setting, thank you so very much for your thoughtful invitation!"

"Not at all, it is quite private, and, for my tastes presents some of the best food in London."

"Well, I haven't had the pleasure of sampling the cuisine, but the ambiance is charming."

"Will you join me in a glass of champagne? It's not Paris, but I think we can find something suitable."

When a bottle of Taittinger Blanc de Blanc accompanied two baccarat chilled champagne flutes, Shasa knew she was in for an elegant dinner. The evening could not have been more enjoyable as the conversation ranged from personal to business to the convoluted politics of the Middle East. Only after dessert did the topic arise that had brought them together.

"My dear, I have enjoyed our conversation so much that I have been remiss in not asking how I can be of assistance while you are here in London. My good friend, the Director, only said that you were here on official business and asked if I could lend a hand. While I assured him I would be more than pleased to help, we really didn't get into any specifics. I have great respect for what you and your organization do, so please tell me how I can be of assistance."

"I am here to gather whatever information I can about two subjects that are of vital interest to us. It has come to our attention that someone is offering some very sophisticated weapons systems to anyone willing to pay their asking price. We are also hearing some disturbing rumors concerning a rather large amount of raw opium being distributed into the market from somewhere in and around Pakistan, or possibly Afghanistan."

Lord Luxley, who had been listening intently as he sipped his brandy, asked if he could smoke a cigar. Upon her affirmation, he asked a simple question. "While I quite understand your concerns on both issues, why London? It would seem as if the answers you are seeking might better be discovered elsewhere."

"The answer to your question lies in the identification of the purchaser. It is our belief that the buyers for both the illicit arms and the opium are located here in London. What we are not sure of is exactly who those buyers are."

"And what, may I ask, makes you believe they are here in London? There would appear to me to be an ample number of potential candidates for both of those offerings, many of whom would be far more comfortable residing in the hot desert sands than the cold rainy climate of this din of western capitalism."

With a big smile, Shasa responded, "While I might agree generally, we are of the opinion that much of the money emanating from those hot desert sands is either resting in Switzerland undisturbed or has found its way here to enjoy your renowned British culture, despite the obvious drawbacks of the climate."

"Is there anyone here of particular interest, or are we operating on a general hunch?"

Descent Into Paradise

Not willing to divulge all she knew to this charming stranger, Shasa felt it prudent to keep the details of her mission private for now.

"Let's just say we are operating upon an educated guess at this stage. It would make sense to us that either the Saudis or the Iranians would be logical buyers of both. My assignment is to ascertain what both groups are up to here in London without, of course, anyone knowing my real identity or why I might be interested."

"I understand. I will endeavor to keep my ear to the ground, and, if I hear anything of interest, I will of course let you know."

Readily accepting his kind invitation to take her back to the hotel, they left the restaurant unaware of the man seated in the corner who watched them leave.

The Sheik did not have long to wait for his appointment with the Saudi Ambassador. Actually, he was quite surprised how quickly he was ushered in. He noticed that the Chief of Staff was hovering nearby, which did not surprise him. He walked in to the beautifully appointed room and gave a slight bow.

"Mr. Ambassador, this is most kind of you to see me."

"Sheik Bashir, your father was a good loyal servant to the Crown Prince as I know you are as well. We are always pleased to be of assistance."

Letting those cautionary remarks pass without comment, the Sheik could not help but send his own subtle message. "That is most gracious of you, Mr. Ambassador, as we are all of one Muslim brotherhood. I come today not for myself, but for our brothers in Afghanistan. They have suffered enormously fighting the Russians. Their country is in ruins. I would like to request the Saudi government to pledge aid to the Taliban to rebuild their schools, hospital, and their roads. In return,

Descent Into Paradise

I believe we could negotiate that the work be done by Saudi contractors."

"Could the aid be structured in loan guarantees or are you proposing that we give them the money for goodwill?"

"I would propose some combination. Afghanistan is a poor country; it cannot service a large debt. On the other hand, I cannot see the Royal Family contributing the entire amount needed."

"And what, Sheik Bashir, would you give as the reason we should contribute anything at all?"

"The reason is really quite straightforward, Mr. Ambassador. Either the Royal Family begins to curry favor with their Islamic neighbors to the north, or they risk offending their own very large, and may I add very poor, Islamic population at home."

"May I term it blood money then? Or would that be too strong a term?"

"You may term it anything you so desire. If you choose not to participate, I would simply term it foolish."

"And if we do decide in favor of granting an aid package, what assurance do we have that the Islamic militants will…"

"Behave themselves," the Sheik interrupted, with a cold smile crossing his face.

"Yes!" snapped the Ambassador, not liking the tone of this conversation.

"I believe the government's best chance of remaining in power is to make sure it does not give their Islamic population the impression it serves only its American allies. One way to accomplish that goal is to help the existing Islamic governments in the region. The Taliban are extremist, I admit, but they are an Islamic regime. I would counsel you to be very supportive of any Islamic fundamentalist who asks your assistance.

Descent Into Paradise

There will come a day of reckoning, Mr. Ambassador. Make no mistake. We all will need to make choices, you amongst us. Choose carefully, for the Arab world is watching."

"I will certainly pass on your thoughts to the appropriate persons. I am confident they will take all you have said under careful consideration. Where can I reach you?"

"I will be in touch with you but you can always leave a message at the Berkeley Hotel, I check in there regularly."

"Fine, I will leave a message with the concierge if need be."

"Thank you for your time, Mr. Ambassador."

"Thank you for coming by. I can assure you of a quick response to your request."

CHAPTER 38

Pablo came in with the obligatory pitcher of sangria and frosted glasses. Zev gladly took the offered glass. "Pablo, I have missed you! The gringos have no idea what they're missing."

The old man smiled warmly as he hobbled out of the room just as Juan appeared.

"Zev, there you are. Welcome home. We have all missed you."

"It's good to be back. Have you been able to operate without me?"

"Barely, my friend. I hear we almost had mass desertions when the troops thought you had left."

Laughing, Zev answered, "I'll bet! I can only imagine their forlorn looks when they see me tomorrow. God help them if they're not in shape."

Ricardo and Juan looked at each other and smiled knowingly. Zev was back, thank God.

"So tell me, how was your trip?" asked Juan.

"I sat down with the Director and took the opportunity to inform him of your generous offer."

"And his reaction?"

"He said he would not blame me whatever I decided, but asked if I would at least hear him out before I made any definite commitments. Having taken me through the current and dire state of affairs in the Middle East, he then appealed to my patriotism as an Israeli to stay and help. After thinking it through, I met with him yesterday morning and informed him that I would be returning here and terminating my involvement with Mossad."

Juan and Ricardo knew better than to push him on any further explanations. He had declared, and they accepted his declaration on the spot.

"We are delighted with your decision. Let Ricardo explain your compensation, and, if you agree, you can take the oath."

"Juan, before we discuss money, let me share with both of you something the Director shared with me. Apparently your informants are correct. The Americans have indeed set up a special task force to combat international terrorism, and, furthermore, the Israelis have agreed to join forces with them. According to the Director, all major drug cartels are now officially labeled as terrorists and will be treated accordingly."

"We are no more terrorists than those American bootleggers in the 1920s, for Christ's sake. What goddamned idiot dreamed this up?"

"According to the Director, I believe the goddamned idiot in question happens to be the President of the United States."

"Well, Major, if you told us that to get a better deal, you succeeded. It looks as if we may need to expand our little force."

"On the contrary, I shared this with you in case you wanted to rethink your future plans. It just so happens I know the man who would most likely lead any military incursion down here. He is one competent son of a bitch. A match for anyone, including me."

"That's high praise indeed; so does this mean you no longer want the job? I'm confused?"

"Juan, I am here to take my oath if and when you decide to let me take it. I accept whatever financial proposal Ricardo was going to make. You have always been more than generous. I just wanted you to know everything I know before we went any further."

"I appreciate your candor, Major. You're a man of honor and integrity. Ricardo, tell him his package."

"Zev, we would like to offer you your current salary of $100,000 per year plus housing plus expenses. Further, as a Principal in the family, you would qualify for an annual bonus of $500,000, which would be deposited into our special retirement account in Switzerland. You may withdraw it at any time you choose to retire, assuming of course you have been faithful to your oath."

"I accept. It is a very generous offer."

"Ricardo, give him his oath."

Ever since returning back to Santiago, Zev had gone back and forth regarding telling Juan about the Director's proposition on the opium trade. On one hand, it would be good business for all of them, and he would then have his own back covered, assuming the Director was good to his word. On the other hand, it would put everyone, including Shasa, directly at odds with the Americans. Zev was still struggling with how this was all going to end. If the Americans were serious about sending a strike force into Chile, things were going to get very dicey all around. His decision was made somewhat easier when Juan invited him over to his home one day for lunch.

"Zev, thanks for joining me. I would like your advice on something non-military for a change. As you are aware, we have been thinking of expanding our operations to Europe and the Middle East. The problem is we have no viable network of people to effectively operate in that part of the world. The fact is, we don't even know whom to approach. Furthermore, given what you have recently shared with us, we clearly don't want any partners who might be at odds with our friends in Tel Aviv. Any thoughts?"

Descent Into Paradise

"I agree on the Israeli front, but I clearly got the impression from the Director that he has no desire to get involved in any anti-drug campaign. In fact, it would not surprise me if our dear friend running Mossad isn't involved in several other similar partnerships to ours."

"And what makes you think that?"

"When we had our little discussion in Tel Aviv, the Director shared with me something I found a bit odd."

"No more Special Forces stories, please. I can barely sleep as it is."

"No. The topic was actually drugs. He was talking about the potential of a major new source of opium coming to the market. He suspected it was being harvested in Afghanistan, but whoever was buying and distributing it remained a mystery. The Director told me it could amount to a significant source of new revenue, and he was very fearful of that revenue being channeled into the wrong hands."

"How much opium are we talking about?"

"He said it could potentially double the world's current supply."

Juan dropped his fork. "My God, the Asians consume most of the opium produced in the Golden Triangle. If we could somehow get our hands on that, we would virtually control the supply for Europe and most of the United States. Do you know what happens, Zev, when you control the supply? No? Well let me tell you, you control the price."

"Juan, I'm sorry, I probably should have said something about this earlier, I was so caught up in the whole American issue I really didn't focus on this. As I'm thinking about it now, however, he may very well have brought this to my attention hoping that I would share it with you. If that's true, I can only assume he would like to make some arrangement with you, but what that is, I am not sure."

Descent Into Paradise

Ricardo and Juan flew to Israel later that same week and were met at Ben Gurion Airport by a young man who drove them directly to Mossad's headquarters. Fifteen minutes later, they were ushered into the Director's office.

"Mr. Rios, Mr. Menez, please come in. Despite the fact you have stolen one of my best soldiers, you are still welcome."

"From what he relayed to us about your conversation, we may need him more than you," answered Juan dryly.

"I assume you are referring to my comments concerning the Americans."

"Yes, although we hardly concur with their terminology, it would appear they are becoming more aggressive their little war on drugs."

"I believe that is a real possibility, Mr. Rios. Did Major Megrid also tell you that we, as part of this joint task force, could be part of any military strike against you gentlemen?"

"No, not specifically, although he did mention a Special Operations task force of which Israel was a partner."

"Obviously, if we shared the American viewpoint, we would not be having this meeting. I must warn you, however, that we need their support, and, if the price for that support is assisting them with their war on drugs, we have no choice but to pay that price."

"Director, while we appreciate your candor, it is my fervent hope you will not pit Israelis against Israelis. Obviously, that will be your decision, not ours. But we didn't travel all the way here to talk about the Americans. Despite all this nonsense, we would still like to find a way to work together. We understand there may be an opportunity to buy a large quantity of high-grade opium. Quite simply, we would like to get our hands on whatever supply of opium is available. Our issue is that we are a bit leery of getting involved with the wrong people. People that might justify the American point of view, if you follow. If you are still willing to work with us, we would be most amenable to some form of partnership."

"Just exactly what kind of partnership did you have in mind, Mr. Rios?"

"All we would require from your side is to understand where and from whom we could purchase the opium. In addition, we would not want to run afoul of any Israeli interference in the processing or distribution aspects of our business. If that suits you, we only need to understand your terms."

"As a matter of fact, I would indeed have an interest in such a venture. I happen to be aware that one of our agents is getting very close to the source of a significant quantity of pure opium. The reality is that since there is no way we can keep this transaction from taking place, all we can hope for is to infiltrate this organization at a high level so that we can know what it is planning. One way for us to do that would be to introduce you as a potential buyer. Our terms, as you call it, would be for the Rios family to use one of our people as the go-between. You want opium. We want to know who these people are and what mischief they are planning. Those are my terms."

"What about the Americans? If you know what we're doing, will they know?"

"We do not share 100% of our intelligence with them, as I am quite sure they do not share all of theirs with us. As part of this arrangement, we would agree not to disclose your name or your activities."

"Would you be willing to warn us of any impending military strike?"

"Only if I am aware of one, and only if my troops are not involved. Let me make it clear, however, that the Americans may not warn us if they are planning something in South

America. I think I would only be contacted if they need our assistance, which, quite frankly, I can't see why they would."

"But you would warn us, if you do know and if your troops are not actively involved. Are we agreed on that?"

"Yes, we are agreed."

"Who do you propose as the go-between and how do you see that working?"

"At this point, I have not yet decided, but I see us making the first contact on your behalf. Once the introduction is made, you will obviously make whatever financial arrangement is appropriate. Then you will use our agent as your representative in Europe and the Middle East. Your representative will then handle the logistics of how the opium is shipped and to whom."

"And the fees associated with such a service?"

"We simply want you to keep us informed. Your currency is money, mine is information."

"Sounds reasonable to me. Ricardo, any questions?"

"No, I believe the Director has stated his position quite clearly. I have no objections to his terms. We will leave the politics and espionage to those who understand its ramifications. Our only interest is a steady supply of opium."

"Director, you have a deal. We will wait for you to contact us. Suffice it to say, we will agree to purchase as much opium as becomes available as long as it is at a fair market price."

"I will leave those details to you and Mr. Menez, we will limit our role to the introduction. Before you leave, there is one additional bit of information I'm interested in."

"And that would be?"

"I'm hearing there is a former Russian general who apparently made off with some very sophisticated hardware and is willing to sell his goods to the highest bidder. When I hear that, I think of the Iranians first, but I also wonder if our friends selling the opium might be planning on using those proceeds to purchase some very expensive weaponry. If you were to run across that trail, I would be most grateful in hearing about that as well."

"Agreed."

CHAPTER 39

"Shasa, it's Archibald calling, I hope I didn't wake you?"

"No, no," lied a very sleepy voice. "I was just dozing, so nice to hear from you!"

"I wouldn't call this early except I'm at Heathrow on my way out of the country and wanted to get in touch before I left. I had dinner with my daughter Annabelle last night and took the liberty of bringing you into the conversation; the gist of which is that she plans on giving you a call to try to set up a luncheon for you both to meet. I believe you both are about the same age, so I am hopeful you might have some mutual interests. At the very least, my daughter is quite the social butterfly, so I am sure you will at least meet some interesting locals."

"How thoughtful of you. I would love to meet your daughter. If she's anything like her father, I'm sure we will get along famously!"

"That's most kind, I believe you both will find the other quite charming."

"How long will you be out of town?"

"I should be back in London sometime next week. It's a business trip with a few unknowns attached, so I'm not sure exactly when."

"I hope you have a profitable and safe trip. I quite enjoyed our dinner the other night and hope we can meet again when you get back."

"I would be honored to escort you anywhere, anytime. If it's all right with you, I will give you a call next week when I return. Will you be at this hotel till then?"

"My plan is to locate a flat to rent, but until then, yes, I will be right here. I will look forward to hearing from you!"

Descent Into Paradise

"Wonderful. Please let me give you my number just in case you are not there when I get back. And also, if it's acceptable with you, I think it might be prudent to keep your true identity a bit of a secret between us for the moment. I believe you will better understand after you get to know my daughter. I have told her that your family was killed in Palestine and that you were brought up by your aunt and uncle in Lebanon who happen to be good friends of mine. I mentioned they had sent you here to get away from all the violence. I told her I was prepared to help you find a job and a place to stay and that I thought you were a lovely girl and someone we should help. That's all I've shared at this point."

"Understood and agreed. In this line of work, it is preferable to limit the number of people who know what we do, so thank you."

Annabelle did indeed call, and asked if they could meet for lunch the following day. Much to Shasa's delight, she found herself back at the Savoy, this time to sample their lunch menu.

"You must be Shasa, terribly nice to meet you. My father has spoken most highly of you, evidently you made quite the impression."

Shasa sat down and took a good look at the beautiful girl seated across from her. It was quickly apparent that Lord Luxley's daughter was a very charming and a wonderful hostess.

"This is where your father took me the other night. I have been in London less than a week now, and, other than my hotel, this is the only restaurant I have been to. I'm afraid anywhere else is going to be quite a letdown!"

"I'm afraid you may be right! I absolutely love this place! Not only is it elegant and serves wonderful food, my father has an account here so anytime I come the bill is automatically taken care of!"

"Well, then I am feeling a bit less guilty."

Descent Into Paradise

They both shared a good laugh and luncheon proceeded to be a long, wonderful affair. Annabelle obviously adored her father, spending a good deal of lunch regaling Shasa with wonderful stories of his exploits and her upbringing. What became clear very quickly was that Lord Luxley, and his daughter, were both in a position to be quite helpful.

By the end of lunch, some two hours later, the two had become instant friends, with Annabelle promising to help on both the job front as well as securing a proper flat.

Shasa waited patiently in a small but beautifully appointed library, complete with newspapers in both Arabic and English. She still was unsure who had set this meeting up or why. All she knew is a young lady had called her the previous evening inviting her to the Saudi Arabian Embassy for a meeting with the Ambassador's Chief of Staff, and here she sat.

A knock on the door preceded the entrance of an elegantly dressed young man about her age. Although he possessed the dark complexion of his Arab ancestors, his dress and mannerisms were purely British. Even his accent, as he introduced himself, reminded her of Archibald. After offering her a cup of tea and exchanging polite small talk, the young man got to the purpose of their meeting.

"Miss Datre, a friend of the Ambassador has put forth your name to fill a very important vacancy here at the Embassy, so I wanted to invite you here for an informal interview."

"Why, that's wonderful. I have just been in London for a short time and would consider it a great honor to work here. If I may ask, what exactly are you looking for?"

"Sadly, our social coordinator has just been involved in a very serious car accident and may not be able to work for some time. We are, therefore, quite desperate for some immediate assistance as we are having a formal dinner party three days from tonight."

The discussion went on for some time as the duties of the social coordinator were explained and Shasa went through her background, mindful of her earlier conversation with the Director. It became clear to her as the conversation went on that the job was really more fluff than substantive, but, for her purposes, it was a gift from heaven. The young man seated opposite her, moreover, was clearly more interested in her appearance than her skillset as a glorified hostess. Apparently, she did not disappoint, as she was offered the position before she left.

CHAPTER 40

As Pete entered the restaurant, the hostess recognized him and brought him directly to a private booth in the corner. There sat not only La Bota, but also a very pretty Latina who gave him a sultry smile as he sat down to join them.

"Pete, thanks for coming down to Miami. I would like you to meet Marianna. She is the young lady I told you about in Boston." Getting a good look at La Bota's new informant, Pete understood immediately the attraction. As dinner went on, Pete was given the full story, including a copy of La Bota's full report.

"We gave some of this to the FBI and the local Miami Police Department, and everything they could confirm checked out. God only knows what else Madonna knows, but I'm guessing she's only given us a taste."

Then Marianna looked directly at Pete. "Señor, when we found out what had happened to my sister, I sent my brother out to see her with this message: 'give me something on Juan Rios and I will try to get you out of there'. Of course, nobody knew they were related so they thought he was just another client. He came back to me with her notes and this message: get her out of that hellhole and she will deliver both Estoban and Juan Rios to you on a silver platter."

"Seeing this, I don't think she has given us any choice, do you Bota?"

"No, and that's not all. Read the final paragraph."

"I'll be damned. That little bastard. Something told me they were involved. Has anyone seen this report other than you?"

"Only you, and as far as I'm concerned no one else need see it."

"That suits me fine. We'll just keep this between the two of us for now. Where is this little establishment, anyway?"

Marianne told them if they gave her a road map of that area, she could point it out.

"Any armed guards or other military personnel in that area that you are aware of?"

"No, my brother said the only security of any kind that he saw was the bartender, who was a rather large brute according to his description."

CHAPTER 41

Shasa had accepted Annabelle's dinner invitation with great pleasure. She was curious to meet Annabelle's beau and looking forward to seeing Annabelle again. Running a bit late, she rang the doorbell only to be met by a well-dressed gentleman who introduced himself as Hani Farouk. As she entered, Annabelle came running to the door. "Shasa, how wonderful to see you. Thank you so much for coming. I see you've just met Hani, and I would like to introduce you to his good friend, Sheik Mohammed Bashir."

After her initial shock of coming face to face with the elusive Sheik, Shasa soon discovered both men were actually very charming. When Hani asked about her new job at the Saudi Embassy, she realized who had spoken with the Saudi Ambassador. As they sat down to dinner, Shasa's interest was further piqued as Hani, in response to her innocent question as to how they met, began to talk freely about his younger friend.

"Sheik Bashir and I go way back, actually. His father was a dear friend of mine for many years. We regularly hunted together, although I must confess his father was a much better shot."

"That's not what he used to say, he would always come home complaining you got the best birds."

"Nonsense, but enough of that. Here we are with two beautiful young ladies, and I am babbling about hunting." Looking over at Annabelle with a loving smile, he subtly shifted the conversation back to the present.

"So my dear, please fill us in on what's been happening in the civilized world. I must confess, the two of us have been venturing into places no self-respecting camel would dare be seen!

I haven't had a decent meal, a good drink, or seen a newspaper in weeks!"

Annabelle told them of the bombing of the Victoria Cross subway station down the road. Everyone was blaming the Irish Republican Army, who readily acknowledged their involvement. She then told them about a suicide bombing in Jerusalem, killing eighteen people and wounding 65.

"Well, I can see the world is a lot safer place than when we left," smiled the Sheik innocently. "Maybe we should head back to the desert Hani, who needs this craziness?"

"I simply cannot make any sense out of these crazy people blowing everybody up, including themselves. But then, I don't need to. I just remember the world the way I want to. I'll leave all this for your generation to figure out. Now, if you will excuse me, I need to visit the loo."

The Sheik took this opportunity to thank Annabelle for her kind hospitality and to inform her that he had not seen his old friend so happy since his beloved wife had passed away several years ago.

"I have enjoyed Hani's company. He is a man of great class, which I happen to admire and enjoy."

"I couldn't agree more. Hani is a gentleman to the core."

CHAPTER 42

The parking lot was full of old pickup trucks and motorbikes, not a car in sight. Pete ambled into the Lazy Ranch reception area where an older woman, who apparently acted as the hostess, greeted him warmly. She took his $20 and ushered him into the bar, where the girls were dressed as waitresses.

"Take your pick Señor, they are all available except for the blonde woman in the corner. She costs $50 and if she won't have you, then you're out of luck. You get 45 minutes, then you'll have to leave or pay another $20. Enjoy yourself."

Pete spent several minutes at the bar ordering a beer. The bartender was a big surly brute who, as described, seemed to double as the bouncer if needed.

"What's the blonde's name?" he asked innocently when his beer arrived.

"Señor, don't waste your money on that old bitch. She's pretty, but there are nicer girls who will give you a better time for less money."

"Just tell me her name?"

Giving him a sour look, the bartender walked away, saying over his shoulder, "Madonna."

He had thought so. Sipping his beer, he watched her out of the corner of his eye. She was indeed very striking looking. Her long blonde hair was pulled back in a ponytail exposing fully her chest and shoulders. Her breasts stood out proudly through her black silk dress, her deep cleavage filled partially by a gold medallion on a chain. While he couldn't see her legs, the top half was certainly alluring enough.

Rios must miss not having this one to climb into bed with every night, he thought as he ordered a second beer.

Nobody had approached her during the time he had been there, so he left the bar, ambling over to where she sat.

"Mind if I sit down?"

"That depends," she eyed him with a neutral expression, "on what you're looking for."

"How about a little casual conversation for a start. Can I buy you a drink?"

"Sure, sit down. I'll have a shot of tequila."

The bartender brought over her drink as she asked him his name.

"Pete, what's yours?"

"Madonna. Where do you come from?"

"I'm from the US. I'm here on business."

"How the hell did you end up in this dive?"

"No offense, but I was about to ask you the same question."

Laughing, all she would say was, "That's a long story, so why don't you go first."

Leaning over, he whispered, "A young client of yours who saw you several weeks ago brought us a present from you. He suggested if we liked it, we should come down for a visit."

Becoming animated for the first time, her whole appearance changed as she gave him a warm smile. As she stood up, Pete got the full view. She was absolutely stunning.

"I cost $50, Señor Pete, so give the bartender another $30 and follow me."

Pete counted out the bills, dumping them on the top of the bar as Madonna walked down the corridor in her spike heels. Pete couldn't help but notice her lovely slender legs. She walked like a lioness on the prowl, her hips swaying back and forth.

Descent Into Paradise

Once inside her room, she turned to him pointing above the door. A small microphone protruded out above the sill. Putting her finger up to her mouth, she asked him if he liked Spanish music. He answered yes, that it put him in the mood for making love.

"Good, because that's what you just paid for. Take off your clothes, you've got 45 minutes."

Madonna watched as Pete reluctantly took off his clothes. Shy, she thought, but powerful and very handsome.

She turned up the radio, then went to light her candles before turning off the lights. As he stood there watching, dressed only in his boxers, she slowly walked over to him while she unzipped her dress. All she wore underneath were black silk panties. Pete could not help his physical reaction as she motioned to him to come to her bed.

"Look, I'm here to get you out, not screw you," he whispered.

"I'm sorry, but there's too many people around at this hour. I'm afraid we'll have to wait. In the meantime, it would look rather strange if you came here just to talk. That mic isn't going to pick up our whispering like this, but it will pick up louder noises. We have to let them know our clients are getting their money's worth."

"OK, let me tell you the plan, then we can fake whatever we need to."

Looking hurt, she whined, "You find me unattractive, Señor, I think part of you must like me, no?"

Embarrassed by what she was holding, he mumbled something about being inappropriate.

"Inappropriate? This is a whorehouse. You're the first attractive man I've seen in six months, so please don't deny me a little pleasure."

Pete looked into her beautiful blue eyes, then his body made the decision for him. It had been way too long. Reaching around her head, he pulled her to him. They kissed feverishly while their hands continued exploring. Her breasts were full and hardened under his caresses. He was rock hard under her expert sensual ministrations.

Their lovemaking was loud enough for the operators listening in to check them off their list.

Exhausted, Madonna rested her head on his shoulder, whispering to him, "No man has done that to me since I was a teenager. You took my breath away."

"It was mutual, I assure you. Now, we need to talk before our time is up. I have a driver out in the parking lot. What is the security procedure here?"

"The only security I know is the bartender, who keeps a 12-gauge shotgun behind the bar."

"No guards outside or alarms that you know about?"

"No, since I've been here there have only been two incidents, both of which have been handled by the barman."

"What if one of the girls decided to get up and walk out to the parking lot?"

"I don't know. Nobody has ever tried it, to my knowledge."

"OK, how late does this place stay busy?"

"On weekdays like this, usually one am."

"It's now just before midnight. Let's meet again at the bar at one am. I'll handle the bartender if necessary, but hopefully we can just walk quietly out to the car with no interference."

"You stay here. I'll be right back." Reaching for her purse, she went outside, closing the door behind her. A few minutes, later she returned, undressing and climbing back into bed beside him.

"Where did you go?" Pete asked, rather startled by her behavior.

"I sent one of the girls out to tell your driver to expect you around one am. Then I paid the old hag another 50 dollars for you to stay here until then."

"Who is that?" Mendoza asked as he listened to the microphone.

"Room number 4, Señor, Madonna and some gringo who has spent the last hour in there."

Carlos stood listening to Madonna say things to this American she had never said to him. His anger and jealousy threatened to explode inside him.

"Get Umberto, tell him to bring his bar."

"Si Señor," said the operator.

They lay panting in each other arms when a loud voice told them to open the door.

"Oh no! My God! That's Carlos, the owner. What in hell is he doing here? What do I do?"

Pete, rather perplexed by this unpleasant interruption, said quietly, "Act naturally, we have not done anything except what we're supposed to."

"We're busy, come back later," she yelled at the door.

"You open this door you little bitch, or I'll break it down," roared Carlos.

Now Pete went on alert; this was the kind of trouble he didn't want or expect. Letting Madonna move away from him, he softly said, "Tell him you'll be right there, you have to put some clothes on." That bought them a brief respite. She then walked over to the door and unlocked it. Mendoza and the bartender came crashing in the minute they heard the lock turn. The bartender was swinging a big iron bar in his massive hand. Pete was buttoning up his shirt, looking casually at his watch.

Descent Into Paradise

"I don't believe our time is up, gentleman. I paid until 1 am, that's another 30 minutes by my watch." He then calmly put on his shoes.

Carlos could barely control his rage as he roared at Pete, "Now get out and don't show your pretty white face in here again. Umberto, get him out of here. If he gives you any trouble, don't hesitate to teach him some manners."

Pete just stood there watching the two of them. Very quietly he said, "Now that you two have had your fun, why don't you both leave quietly like good little boys before someone gets hurt." Looking again at his watch, he said calmly, "I will be leaving this beautiful young lady in 30 minutes. If you want to discuss something with me then, I will be happy to oblige. Now, I'm busy so please go back to the bar and have a drink."

Carlos could not stand being summarily dismissed like a servant in front of his woman. "Fuck you, gringo. I'll teach you some manners myself."

Pete waited for the big man to come at him. Sidestepping at the last second, he aimed his right foot at his crotch. Carlos hit the floor with a terrifying scream of pain. Holding his balls, he lay on the floor whimpering like a baby.

Pete looked over at the giant bartender holding his iron crowbar, casually asking him, "Umberto, is it? Well, Umberto, do you want to leave quietly or would you like to end up like your friend here?"

Waving his crowbar in the air like a toy baton, Umberto replied, "I hate gringos, so it will be a pleasure to hear a few bones break. Come over here and show your woman how big and brave you are."

Stepping over Carlos, Pete put his hand up as Madonna told him to run for the door, screaming at him, "Don't, Pete, don't. He'll kill you, he's a monster."

"He looks like a big oaf to me. Without that crowbar he couldn't beat up the little goats he probably fucks every night. Am I right, Umberto? I bet you my little finger is bigger than your little prick. Tell Madonna why you have that iron bar." Looking at Madonna who thought he had gone berzerk, "It's because it's the only thing he can hold on to that's hard. Right, Umberto. Come on, drop it and let's see if you're a man or should we dress you up in skirts?"

Umberto realized everyone would know what happened here tonight. He had to destroy his tormentor, but he had to do it with his fists so everyone would know not to mess with him in the future. Dropping the crowbar he slowly advanced on Pete, who stood totally still.

Pete let him come. Instead of retreating, however, he moved in towards him and hit him in the solar plexus with a sharp right. The big man let out a surprised grunt as the air was knocked out of him. Pete then hit him in the chin with a sharp uppercut, followed by a knee into the crotch. As Umberto bent over in response to these rapid blows, Pete grabbed his hair, and brought his head down on his right knee, breaking his nose with a loud snap. As Umberto fell to the floor, Pete snapped a vicious karate chop to the back of his neck, rendering him unconscious.

"Come on, let's get out of here before someone else gets curious." He grabbed Madonna's hand and they walked out the front door as if she were escorting him to his car. Nobody paid them the slightest attention. Once in the parking lot, the driver started the engines and they headed north, away from Santiago.

Thirty minutes later, they stopped at the end of an abandoned airstrip. The driver said over his shoulder, "Should be here any minute, Major."

Descent Into Paradise

Madonna now spoke for the first time. "Where are we going?"

"A helicopter will pick us up in a few minutes and take us out to a US Navy ship sitting offshore. From there, we will make our way to Miami, Florida, where we will let you tell us all you know about a Mr. Juan Rios."

Once aboard the ship, Pete turned Madonna over to a young lieutenant, who looked star struck at this buxom blonde now in his charge. "This way, Ma'am," he stuttered.

The next morning, Pete knocked on her stateroom door. "Everything OK?" he asked as he came in.

"Fine, thanks. I was in such shock last night; I never thanked you properly for getting me out of that hellhole. You were magnificent," she smiled.

"Oh, they were just two big buffoons who had never seen a real fight."

"No, I meant in bed."

Blushing slightly, Pete responded, "You weren't so bad yourself. In fact, I woke up this morning dreaming of you naked in bed beside me."

"Well, I'm here now, soldier. Why don't you lock that door, and hopefully nobody will interrupt us this time."

CHAPTER 43

Shasa had just sat down at her desk as the phone message was brought to her. "I'm very sorry Miss Datre, but he wouldn't give me his name. He said you would know who it was." A big smile spread across her face as she read the short message. "Little One, I am in town unexpectedly. If you get this and are free, I will be in Trafalgar Square at noon."

She looked at her watch and called for a cab. She ordered him to leave her one block off Trafalgar Square. She then proceeded to walk slowly all around the Square, stopping occasionally to peer into a shop window. Vendors came walking through the growing crowd, hawking everything. Seeing no sign of Zev, she retraced her steps. Sitting down on one of the stone steps, she glanced again at her watch and waited.

Zev watched her arrive. He had been there since 11h00, carefully observing the crowd. He wondered if she would recognize him.

"Peanuts, hot peanuts!"

"Hey love, for you a mere ten pence." As she looked up, a man in baggy pants with a long greasy ponytail held out a bag of peanuts in front of her. A familiar smile then appeared beneath his mustache.

"Come on, little one, only ten pence."

She reached inside her purse and threw him a coin; he threw her the bag and moved on. Inside, she saw a small white sheet with one hand written word. She left it there, shelling several nuts as she looked around. Ten minutes later, she got up and left. Walking to a taxi stand, she rode back to the Embassy with the sheet of paper crumbled in her hand and a knot in her stomach.

Descent Into Paradise

Back at the Embassy, another message was being delivered. "Are you sure she didn't meet anyone?"

"I'm sure. She walked around the square, appeared to do some window shopping, had some peanuts, looked around occasionally, and then, walked over to the taxi stand and left."

"OK, I'll be in touch if I need you."

That evening, having heard nothing further from Zev, Shasa decided to get some take out Chinese food and go home. There, lounging on the front steps of her building, sat Zev, ponytail and all.

"My God, Zev is that really you?" she whispered.

Getting up, he turned and followed her to the door.

"Sorry for all the fuss, but someone with a pair of binoculars was either admiring those beautiful legs of yours or had some other agenda. I couldn't take a chance. Come on, let's get inside before someone sees us!"

Relieved to be with Zev and safely in her flat, she opened a bottle of wine to augment her rather simple meal. Zev seemed not to care as they caught each other up on what each had been doing.

"What are you doing in London? Who knows you're here?"

"Actually, no one knows I'm here except my employers, an old Russian general, and now you. All the Director knows is that I needed to get in touch with you. That's how I knew you were at the Embassy."

After Zev had described his meeting with a Russian general to purchase advanced surface-to-air missiles, her antenna suddenly went up.

"He said what?"

"He said, if I wanted to make a quick profit, he had just received a telephone call from an Arab buyer who apparently is willing to pay a great deal more for all 24 missiles. Shasa, let me tell you, these things are incredibly lethal weapons. They are Russia's latest model and can easily bring down any commercial airliner or even a top line military fighter for that matter. If these things get into the wrong hands, there will be hell to pay for someone!"

"Did he give you a name?"

"That's why I took the chance of contacting you. It cost me £5,000, but the bastard finally relented and gave me a number to call. It's a local number, but obviously unlisted. He told me to call only after dinner as the gentlemen wouldn't answer during the day. Some Arab kingpin from Saudi Arabia, he said."

"Do you have the phone number? I might be able to find out who it belongs to."

Reaching into his pants pocket, Zev pulled out the general's business card with the phone number scribbled on the back. She didn't recognize it.

"If you haven't got a place to stay, you're welcome to bunk here with me. It might be safer."

The following morning, Shasa was summoned to the Ambassador's office. The Ambassador, sitting by the fireplace, rose as she came in.

"Good morning Miss Datre, how nice to see you. Are you enjoying your time with us?"

"Yes, so far it has been a wonderful experience, Mr. Ambassador. I hope I am doing a good job?"

"From what I hear, you are doing admirable work, which is why I have asked you to stop in. I would like to ask you a personal favor, outside our normal Embassy relationship. You see, I am hosting a private party at my weekend home in Hampshire. There will be ten guests in residence, and I would very much appreciate your assistance. Because it's a personal affair, I am rather reluctant to use any of my staff here so I would prefer that nobody here even know about it. Would that bother you?"

"No, of course not. I would be delighted to help you any way I can. When is the event?"

"Not this weekend but the following one."

"I assume your staff in Hampshire will know about this."

"Yes, of course, you may wish to drive out there to meet with them and tell them what you'll require. I will make sure they understand you will be in charge."

"Should I coordinate through your wife or the Chief of Staff?"

"Neither. My wife will not be attending, and, as I just mentioned, I do not wish to bother any of the Embassy staff, including the Chief. Is that clear, Miss Datre?"

"Very clear sir, should I work on this during my normal work hours here, or only on my free time?"

"Why don't you ask for several days off next week without pay, I will compensate you personally for your time. You will not suffer financially for helping me."

"I am delighted to help, and I thank you for your trust."

Handing over his personal card, he informed her that if she needed him she should call him on his private line any evening after dinner, and he would answer.

That evening, after conferring with Zev, Shasa sent a message to the Director who agreed to fly to London immediately. Just in case the Israeli Embassy was being closely monitored, they decided to meet at the round pond in Hyde Park. All three came separately, each checking the other's tail in classic Mossad style. Shasa donned full Muslim attire, which carried the added benefit of obscuring her face from public view. Most of the Sunday crowd was heading home for dinner as the sun began to set over the horizon. Benches, which had accommodated numerous tired parents and grandparents, finally became available for the three Muslim tourists who had been walking, marveling at the beautiful gardens and lakes situated in the very heart of London. As the three Israelis finally sat down, the Director led off.

"What's your take on this fellow Bashir?"

"Cold, ruthless, cunning, highly educated. He could almost pass for an Englishman if his skin were a bit lighter."

"Handsome?" asked the Director with a bit of a smirk.

"Very," was all he got in return.

"Well, the Ambassador is certainly playing high stakes poker here. I can't believe he gave that Russian general his private number. Are you sure it's the same one?"

"One and the same."

"I would have to surmise the Ambassador is playing a private hand with whoever is after those missiles. Most likely to help fund his rather lavish lifestyle here in England. My hunch is we are very close to our prey so Zev, if it's alright with you, I have made arrangements with Shasa's new boyfriend to put you up at his daughter's house for the week. It will afford you privacy as well as a secure line of communication."

Zev looked quizzically over at Shasa.

"It's a private joke, I'll explain later."

Smiling, the Director continued, "Zev, I won't ask you how you found this Russian, but well done."

"It really wasn't that difficult. Juan put me in touch with a German who deals in illegal arms. Apparently, once you're vetted in that world, everyone knows everyone. Just one thing I should mention here. Juan also wants those missiles, so we will have to figure that all out when the time comes."

"I will make sure Zev's background is removed completely from our files along with any association with us, or Israel for that matter. Remember, it is imperative that nobody, including the Luxleys, discovers you two know each other, especially Miss Annabelle. She is as hardheaded as her mother and has somehow convinced herself that the Arabs are the poor victims of Israeli aggression. The last thing we need is for Bashir to become suspicious. Between the two of you, I am confident we can set up a meeting with whoever wants those missiles. Zev, you have my word that Israel will replace whatever missiles you end up selling for the same price you pay the Russian. If you can negotiate a better deal, you can pocket the difference, or give it back to Rios, or do whatever the hell you want to. But Shasa, until we find out who it is following you around, please use Archie or the Embassy if you need to contact me."

"I'm not sure Archie is safe either. The other night at dinner, Bashir asked me how I knew Annabelle's father. When I looked somewhat perplexed, he went on to say that he thought he saw the two of us at dinner the other night."

"And how did you respond?"

"I told him that we indeed had met the other night for dinner at the suggestion of my relatives in Lebanon, whom Archibald knew."

"Good. Now keep to that story, but I agree, let's leave Archie out of any future communications between us. Just the secure line at our Embassy from now on. Got it?"

"Yes."

With that agreement, they made their way slowly out of the park unobserved by any prying eyes.

The next day, Zev sat with Annabelle in her study while they discussed his stay in London. At first, she had been slightly annoyed with her father for offering this stranger a room in her house without asking, but, since his arrival, her temper had cooled down considerably. She suspected that this very handsome young man was being deliberately placed at her doorstep as a potential distraction to her present amorous interest. As she sat there observing her intriguing guest, she realized she really wasn't that upset and decided to make the best of it. With an engaging smile, she welcomed him accordingly.

"Mr. Megrid, I am delighted you will be my guest, please make yourself at home. Henry will show you to your room. If you need anything, laundry or whatever, just ask him and he will take care of it. I'm afraid my father told me very little about you, so I'm somewhat at a loss as to how I may be of assistance. But, if you don't have plans this evening, I would love for you join me here. Dinner will be served at eight o'clock, and I usually have a drink in the library around seven thirty."

CHAPTER 44

During the drive out of London, Hani caught up with Bashir about his recent visit to Murat.

"How was your trip?"

"Very productive. This Palestinian fellow is quite the warrior. I think I may have finally found my spear."

Hani then asked, "Are we still set for the Israeli Ambassador?"

Bashir nodded affirmatively.

"Good. I can't wait to hear the uproar in Tel Aviv. Those bloody bastards are now going to get a taste of their own medicine."

"This is just the beginning my friend, just the beginning."

The Ambassador from Saudi Arabia was seated at the head of the long mahogany table. After everyone was seated he raised his glass.

"Gentleman, let me officially welcome you all. I am most honored to host this weekend affair. Please treat my home as your own during your stay here. Many of you have already met our charming Miss Datre. Please stand my dear, thank you. Miss Datre is here to help with any requests you might have or special needs. She and my staff are here to assist you in any way they can. Now, please enjoy your dinner."

After dinner, the men retired to the library for cigars and brandy and the business at hand. Hani was the first to rise and address all present. "The Ambassador and I have invited you here this weekend to discuss something which could have a profound impact on all of us here, indeed on the entire Arab world. I know all of you are well aware of the political climate in which we find ourselves embroiled. I'm quite sure there is no one here who has not stockpiled a good bit of their financial assets in Switzerland or an equally safe haven. I know I have. The Royal Family currently is experiencing quite a dilemma. They are, in a way, the victims of their own greed. Oil, and the riches it has created, has made the ruling governments of the Gulf virtual partners of the western capitalists who consume that oil. Their economic fortunes have become so intertwined that each needs the other to prosper.

"What has been forgotten, unfortunately, are the millions of poor Arabs who live and work every day trying just to support their families. The gap between rich and poor is becoming a chasm and history will remind us that when the wealthy few leave the masses too far behind, social unrest is the inevitable consequence.

"I fear, gentleman, that, as we sit here today, we are fast approaching that boiling point. Believe me when I tell you the Americans will use their military might to prop up any regime that will continue to provide them oil at a fair price, regardless of their domestic policies. If you haven't noticed already, those who don't bow to 'The Great Satan's' wishes do so at their own risk.

"The Royal Family, and we along with them, must chart a delicate course. If we do not cater to the West, we may find Saudi Arabia the next Libya. If we cater to them too much, we may find ourselves the next Iran. This dilemma brings us to the reason for this gathering. By now, I hope you have all had a chance to speak with my honored guest Sheik Bashir. Many of you knew his father who died tragically eight years ago. I have, in my own way, adopted this brave young man and encouraged him to come speak with you tonight. Obviously, I fully support the views he will share with you now. Sheik Bashir."

Descent Into Paradise

"Good evening, thank you Mr. Ambassador for hosting us. Tonight, I would like to share with you my thoughts on the current state of affairs and what I propose we do about it.

"The Arab world, or more broadly, the Islamic world, has been in disarray since the noble days of the great Ottoman Empire. With the brief exception of Gammal Nasser in the 1950s, we have fought our battles sometimes with each other, sometimes against a common enemy, but never have we fought together as one. The results speak for themselves. Have you ever stopped to consider why in 1948, 40 million Arabs could not wipe out 200,000 Jews in Palestine? Or how one small Jewish state could, twenty years later, defeat the armies of the entire Gulf region in addition to Jordan, Egypt, Syria and Lebanon?

"The answer is simple. We do not think alike, we do not trust each other, and, quite frankly, our governments are entirely corrupt and put their own selfish interests ahead of those they are supposed to govern. Gentleman, we are an embarrassment, an embarrassment to our culture and, most of all, an embarrassment to ourselves. Yes, oil has made many of us wealthy men. And what do we do with this new wealth? If I heard Hani correctly, we put a great deal of it in Switzerland. I assure you those monies will never be used to help our fellow Arabs crawl out of their miserable economic conditions. Or will it? No, most of our people live in abject poverty while a few of us live in fabulous wealth. This is not a condition of stability; it is a pre-condition to social chaos. It is only a matter of time.

"The instrument that will ignite the unrest is already present. It is read daily in hundreds of million homes. It spells out how we should pray, how we should govern ourselves, even how we should live our daily lives. It is a book, gentlemen, that will ignite this social revolution. It is the Koran.

Descent Into Paradise

"The Islamic fundamentalists now rule in Iran and will soon in Afghanistan. I believe it is only a matter of time before Iraq, Kuwait and indeed Saudi Arabia will follow. Indonesia and Pakistan will be next. Think of what it could be like if managed properly. One Islamic nation controlling 300 million people and the entire oil reserves of the Middle East and Indonesia. How would the rest of the world look upon us then? Would we be ridiculed as we have been for centuries? Would western culture continue to treat Islam as a third world religion? Would American troops dare be stationed in and around our holiest sites any longer?

"It would be Arabs who decide the daily price of crude oil, not the Americans. It would be Arabs deciding for themselves the fate of the Persian Gulf, not American aircraft carriers. It would be Arabs who would decide the fate of the Suez Canal, not the US Navy, and who would decide the fate of the Israelis and the Palestinians? Believe me, not the Americans!

"They talk about globalization. What they mean is think like us, act like us, buy from us, and do what we tell you to do for your own good.

"Well, I, for one, do not care for American culture. I do not like their crass materialism; I do not like their promiscuity. I do not like their religion. I want to devote my life to Allah and the teachings of the Koran. I want to be proud of my rich heritage. I do not want to be globalized in the American tradition. I say to the Americans, get out, and leave the Gulf to those who live there. We will decide what's best for us, not you. The enemy is the Americans, my friends. The Israelis would never be able to exist without their unilateral support. Remove the American troops from the Gulf and make them rethink their stance towards Israel. Those are my goals. How will I accomplish those goals? Simple. I will first form a cohesive and powerful fighting force unlike anything the world has yet witnessed. It will not be made up of splinter groups armed with a few homemade bombs and some third generation rockets. We will arm ourselves with state-of-the-art modern weapons. The cash-starved Russians cannot wait to sell them to us. We will then declare a Holy War on the infidels and take this war directly to the Americans. When young American boys begin to die, then we will see what kind of stomach the United States has for leaving their troops in our lands.

"We will kill them where we find them. Then, we will take the Jihad directly to America. We will kill them on their own soil as they have been killing us for years. We will not just kill their soldiers; we will kill their women and children as they continue to kill ours. We may not use bombers and aircraft carriers to deliver those bombs, but deliver them we will. America is a very big target. We will find their soft spots. When we do, we will strike fear into the hearts of all 200 million people living there. They will know the price of continued involvement in our affairs will be death and destruction in their own great cities.

"Now, to carry out this war, I will need your help. We will have hundreds of thousands of young men ready to die for the glory of Allah. But we need to train them, to arm them, to transport them with the proper papers into America where they can carry out their missions. This will require money and political support. This I ask of all of you in the name of Allah."

Shasa stood outside the door, mesmerized by the cadence of the Sheik's voice and his heartfelt message. It was sincere and deadly in content. The spontaneous applause from his audience told how well he and his message would play in a society starved for heroes. That he would get their support was a foregone conclusion. That he would win over the popular support of the Arab people appeared almost as clear.

She quietly went upstairs to her room, wondering to herself if he would come.

Anticipation overwhelmed her fear when she heard a knock on her door and the Sheik's deep voice, whispering if she were still awake. Fleeting images of Abu raced through her head as she opened her bedroom door. Tonight, her stiletto was securely packed away, somehow neither needed nor desired. Anticipation quickly turned into raw lust for both as what had started as silent stalking amongst two predators swiftly reached a climax with few words being spoken. He departed as unexpectedly as he arrived, and it was only after breakfast when they were alone that he spoke to her.

"My dear Shasa, you've been the perfect hostess. On behalf of the Ambassador and Hani, I thank you."

"You performed admirably as well. It would appear you have achieved all your goals."

Looking at this young Palestinian, he marveled not only at her incredible beauty, but her absolute composure. Her role as an innocent hostess was incongruous at best, but her true identity still eluded him.

"If we have indeed succeeded in convincing these wealthy Saudis to align themselves with our concept of how the Arab world can better co-exist, then yes, we will have achieved something of significance."

"I applaud your efforts. I only hope you will bring peace and prosperity to all of our people, not just the privileged few."

"That is indeed our mission and our duty, not only for all Arab nationals, but for the Palestinians in particular."

Looking directly into those fierce eyes, she began to wonder just how much this man knew. She had a queasy feeling in the pit of her stomach as he smiled at her that it was more than she wished. Smiling back at him, all she could day was, "Someday, hopefully, this madness will end. Let's just pray we will both be alive to see it."

Later that morning, Shasa approached Hani, who was speaking casually to the Ambassador and Sheik, to ask if they could take a walk before lunch. He readily agreed and suggested a stroll through the beautiful gardens.

Hani put on his coat and, turning to both sheepishly, whispered, "She probably wants to talk about Annabelle."

The gardens were situated behind the main house, designed in such a way that one could meander down their gravel paths oblivious to all that was going on elsewhere.

Shasa had come to like Annabelle's beau and could understand his appeal despite the obvious age difference. As they chatted casually about the events of the past 24 hours, she became convinced that Hani had a true passion for what the Sheik was advocating. Whether he had any idea of the violence and bloodshed that would inevitably ensue was less clear. The serenity of their walk, however, dissipated rapidly after she began speaking of Zev and the Russian general. The warmth and gentleness she had felt before suddenly evaporated, his charm and appeal along with it. Shasa quickly realized that there was little difference between the elderly man she was strolling through the gardens with and the young virile one she had slept with the night before. The only difference was that this one had the advantage of a few more years to perfect his cover.

"I thank you for sharing this with me. When it comes to waging war, I usually defer to my young friend, but I will certainly pass this information on to him."

After all the guests, including Shasa, had departed, the Ambassador asked Hani and the Sheik to join him for lunch.

Descent Into Paradise

"Young man, you have succeeded in recruiting every single guest here. Congratulations! But, before we go any further, I want to also inform you both that despite my initial misgivings, my government has just agreed to your request for aid on behalf of the Taliban; ten million dollars per year for three years, and it will be in the form of an outright grant."

"That's wonderful news indeed," responded Bashir. "Thank you, and please thank the King. I believe it will prove to be a very wise investment for all concerned."

"I couldn't agree more," added Hani, "As for last night, I want to add my congratulations to that of our host. Last night you eloquently articulated a very powerful message, one our new partner in Yemen should help us spread across the airwaves. Now, before we leave, I have some rather interesting news to share with you both.

"My God you must be joking," replied Bashir when Hani related what Shasa had just told him.

"Not the ones that old Russian general was trying to sell us?" asked the Ambassador.

"Apparently the very same ones, Ambassador, all 24 of them."

"I'll be damned. How on earth did Shasa even know we were the other buyers?"

"That's where it gets both interesting and a bit bothersome. According to Shasa, she met this South American at our friend Annabelle's house at a dinner party. Then, when he learned for whom she worked, he took her aside and made her an offer."

Bashir then interjected, "The Russian must have given this gentleman your private phone number. Probably negotiated some sort of fee if we ended up buying them."

"Your supposition is absolutely correct. According to her story, he told her he would pay her ten thousand pounds if she could put a name to that phone number."

Descent Into Paradise

"And has she?"

"According to her, she has not yet responded. For some reason, maybe because of my relationship with Annabelle, she felt more comfortable approaching me to get my opinion as to what she should do. It sounds like our Latin friend may be willing to resell them before he returns to South America."

"Where is this gentleman staying? Do we know how to contact him?" inquired the Sheik. "Acquiring those missiles would be a godsend. I'm just surprised the Russians ever allowed them out of the country!"

"Before we do anything," responded Hani, "I first want to call Annabelle and find out what she knows about this fellow. As far as I'm concerned, we can then let the lovely Miss Shasa collect her money for the introduction. There is, however, another bit of news I should share with you, Mr. Ambassador. Apparently, your Chief of Staff has been asking Shasa a number of personal questions of late, which is making her very uncomfortable."

"He went to school with one of the King's nephews here in England, and they remain great pals. I brought him on for obvious political reasons, but I don't trust the young pup at all. I will deal with him my way."

Bashir nodded in agreement, although he had already reached a slightly different conclusion.

CHAPTER 45

Upon Bashir's return to London, he placed a call to Murat, requesting Abu to join him in London. Several days later, Abu met the Sheik at his hotel for breakfast. After exchanging the customary polite small talk, the Sheik got down to the business at hand.

"All is arranged, my friend. Your driver has been fully briefed and is intimately familiar with Kensington Gardens. He is British by birth, but don't let that fool you. He is Muslim to the core and one of the True Believers."

"Are we still on for tomorrow evening?"

"Yes. Your driver has everything packed in his trunk. He will then take you to the airport immediately after, as requested."

Ambassador Weinbaum attached the leash to his yellow Labrador and headed out for their evening walk. Lettie and her master had become inseparable over the past eight years. A gift from their only daughter, Lettie was now considered a second child. Without warning, Mrs. Weinbaum had been diagnosed with melanoma and within six months passed away, leaving her grief-stricken husband with a broken heart and a rambunctious Labrador to care for. Lettie had helped fill the void during those early years of widowhood, and a bond had formed between dog and master that had proven unbreakable over the ensuing years. Thus, despite several complaints from the Embassy security staff, the Ambassador and his dog seldom missed their ritual walks in the park across the street, one after lunch and one in the evening after dinner.

Having made a trial run the evening before, Moussa clearly understood his role as he sat quietly on the green park bench waiting for Abu to reach his designated location on the street, from where he could see the Ambassador enter the park.

"Lettie, slow down, for goodness sake!"

A particularly busy day meant the Ambassador had kept Lettie waiting fifteen minutes past their normal departure. She pulled him across the street to the park, as if she were late for an appointment. Meanwhile Moussa was becoming increasingly nervous. He kept looking down at his pager, willing it to vibrate. Glancing at his watch for the tenth time, it was now over ten minutes past the time Abu should have signaled. His imagination began to run wild as he pulled another peanut out of the brown bag to feed the pigeons. Had something gone wrong? Had Abu been picked up? Were they right now moving in on him? Slowly he looked up, glancing around casually as if he were looking for a friend's late arrival. What he saw made his heart pound. Fighting a rising tide of pure panic, Moussa sat still as two uniformed policemen came walking down the path, looking straight at him. Not knowing what else to do, he reached into his paper bag for another peanut. Unable to stop shaking, he prayed the two policemen could not detect his inability to crack open the shell. Then, just as they approached his bench, he felt a vibration on his hip.

"Good evening, lad," the younger constable said in a kind voice, "you wouldn't have a few extra of those to feed two hungry officers of the realm, would you?" Reaching into his bag, Moussa willed his hand to stop shaking. Unsuccessful, he was about to hand the man the bag so he could help himself when he suddenly remembered what else was inside.

Mistaking the fear on the boy's face for shyness, the policemen just laughed and continued down towards the pond. Looking back over his shoulder, the young one called back, "Just joking young man, don't you worry, we wouldn't want you or those poor pigeons to go hungry, now would we?"

Descent Into Paradise

Moussa just waved at them, not daring to say a word. Looking down at his paper bag, he now had to make a critical decision. Feeling the vibrator on his hip, he knew he only had three minutes. Fearful of doing anything while the two constables were there, he now had no idea how much time had elapsed. Realizing a decision must be made, he put his hand into the brown paper bag and set the timer on two minutes. Then, he slowly got up, walked over to the black metal trash bin and gently placed his paper bag inside. Remembering Abu's admonition not to leave too quickly, he slowly started up the path to where the van was waiting. At this pace, he realized two minutes would hardly give him time to reach the street. Looking once more at his watch, he wondered where the Ambassador was. He should have come into view by now. Then he heard loud barking just around the bend. He knew it would be a close call, indeed. Please, just keep walking, he whispered to himself. Then, the dog was upon him.

"Lettie, come here," yelled the Ambassador. "Leave that poor boy alone!"

Moussa used the dog's exuberance as an excuse to run towards the street. As he approached the van, Abu opened the rear door and literally pulled him inside. The driver had already left the curb before the door closed.

Ten seconds later, a deafening explosion sent a shock wave, which literally rocked them even as they exited the park. Abu turned around as the park bench erupted into flames. The driver never slowed down as he headed out of town.

The Bon Homme departed Plymouth on schedule, her hold full of British yarn destined for Europe. Captain Guillaume waved goodbye to the tug master, then gave the helmsman orders to increase speed to ten knots. The Captain was well pleased with himself, as his sturdy vessel headed out to sea.

Descent Into Paradise

Ten thousand francs cash will help us buy that little house in the country, he smiled. No more filthy apartments with rats crawling over all of us at night. The Mrs. will be happy. All that for giving two Arabs transport to Marseille. God is rewarding me for being a good husband, he thought.

Their departure could not have been more inauspicious. No police, no problems with the Captain. It was extraordinary, the harbormaster never even bothered to check the manifold, much less inspect the cargo aboard the vessel. They could have smuggled anything into or out of that port, thought Abu. Something to remember in the future.

Morning saw the Bon Homme heading southeast along the Normandy coast. Five days was the Captain's estimate for arrival in Marseille. From there, he had offered to contact a friend who was captain aboard a Greek freighter that frequented Beirut.

The Captain approached Abu on the deck, smiling as he said, "Good news! My friend is sailing for Beirut three days after we arrive. He is delighted to take you and your companion on the same terms as our arrangement."

"Thank you, Captain. That was most considerate of you. I trust your friend will compensate you for your trouble?"

"We are old friends who trade favors on a consistent basis. Don't worry about that. We are happy, you are happy. What else matters?"

Five days later, Abu and Moussa disembarked at Marseille and found a small hotel near the port. After check-in, Abu thought it best to keep out of sight, so he sent Moussa down to the docks to make inquiries about the Greek freighter. Moussa came back that evening with news that the freighter was due to load her goods the next afternoon.

The following evening they boarded the freighter, again without incident. Abu handed the Captain a rather thick

Descent Into Paradise

envelope and was shown to their quarters. Some unfortunate crewmember would now be doubling up with a shipmate, but the Captain was a most gracious host. The short voyage across the Mediterranean turned out to be quite pleasant. The weather was superb and the food much better than expected.

One evening after dinner, Moussa asked Abu why he had changed their escape route out of England.

"In this business, one can never be too careful, Moussa. Several people knew of our planned exit. That is several people too many. Remember that, if I am not around." He then went on to relay his consternation about the situation in Beirut. "If Mir is right, then I fear our friends in Shatila may be in great danger." The additional benefit of keeping Moussa away from that Mullah in Murat was a factor he decided not to share.

As the ship approached the harbor, Abu went to thank the Captain.

"You are most welcome, I have enjoyed your company and that of your son. I'm not sure what your business is here, but I would be remiss if I didn't share with you some information I just received."

Without responding, Abu waited for the Captain to finish.

"I have just been informed that an Israeli dock master will be in charge of our offloading. More than that, I cannot tell you. Just be careful, my friend."

CHAPTER 46

Within minutes of Shasa's arrival Monday morning, she was summoned to the Chief of Staff's office.

"Shasa, thank you for coming by, please sit down. So, how was your weekend?"

"I had a lovely weekend, thank you for asking. And how was yours?"

"Shasa, please, let's not play games here."

"Games? What I do or don't do with my private time should be no concern of yours. Now, if you will excuse me. I will get back to my work."

"Very well, but before you go, I have something here that might be of some interest to you."

Picking a red folder off his desk, he casually handed it to her.

Inside was a photocopy of the passport she used for her flight to London from Tel Aviv. Stapled to that was a copy of her boarding pass on El Al. Her cover completely blown, she now had to ascertain how he had obtained this information and who else knew of its existence.

"I assume you are the only one here who has seen this."

"A very astute observation indeed. The fact is, at this moment, I need you as much as you need me. You, my dear, as pretty as you may be, are simply a pawn in a much larger game. I merely want to know who attended your little weekend affair at the Ambassador's home, what was discussed, and what role our esteemed boss played. That is all. Your personal travel arrangements are of no particular interest to me, especially as you have just handed in your resignation."

Descent Into Paradise

With that, he handed her a typed sheet offering her resignation immediately for personal reasons. Having read it quickly, she pushed it back to him unsigned.

"Why don't you come over to my place tomorrow evening? You bring that little red folder and that letter with you, and I will make a list of all the interesting people I met over the weekend along with some notes as to what took place. Then, let's see if the two of us can reach some sort of private accommodation."

The expression on his young face confirmed her feminine instincts.

"Would eight o'clock be convenient?"

"Eight o'clock sounds fine. Shasa, one more thing, I don't believe anyone need know about this, agreed?"

"Agreed. Tomorrow night will be our little secret."

Zev and Shasa had agreed to meet at Salloos, a wonderful little Pakistani Restaurant on Wilton Court. Once there, they were ushered upstairs to a lovely table in the corner. The setting was absolutely perfect as there were no other tables immediately nearby, yet she could easily see if anyone was overly interested in their conversation.

After they ordered, Shasa took him through the events of the weekend, leaving out only her dalliance with Bashir. When she had finished, Zev asked the obvious question as to who this Hani fellow was.

"Up until your arrival, Hani was Annabelle's beau. Now, I'm not so sure, but he's the one I met at Annabelle's house with Bashir."

"I must say this is getting rather dicey, isn't it? Where do we think Miss Annabelle stands?"

"I'm not sure Zev, I know where her father stands, but I don't know her well enough to get a clear sense of her own politics."

Descent Into Paradise

"What do we know about her old man anyway? He is obviously working for your boss in some capacity."

"I really don't know very much other than he clearly has some longstanding relationship with the Director. He has been very helpful finding me a place to live, and either he or Annabelle helped me get this job, although they clearly used Hani's influence to do it. He apparently is also a partner with Hani and the Sheik on some big deal in Yemen, although he's made it clear to me that he is not a great fan of either one of them. For that matter, he is definitely not a fan of his daughter dating anyone from that region! I have to believe that's one reason he suggested you stay at their house."

"Am I really that irresistible?"

"Absolutely! I'm only surprised she hasn't already jumped in your bed."

"And what makes you so sure she hasn't?"

"Zev, are you falling for little Miss Annabelle? She certainly is a beauty, I'll give you that!"

It wasn't until they walked outside that Shasa brought up the meeting in the Embassy with her young boss. When Zev asked how she was going to deal with it, she told him and he agreed.

"Can I be of any assistance?"

"No, thanks anyway. I'll handle it."

"I'm sure you will, little one, I just hope, for poor Pete's sake, you two never get in a serious argument!"

Laughing, he got her a cab and walked off. Zev's comment about Pete still bothered her when she met Archie for dinner.

"What's wrong, my dear? You look upset."

Realizing she was letting her emotions become way too visible, she apologized, saying she was having a rather difficult day on top of which it was the wrong time of the month. She felt guilty deceiving him, but she couldn't handle sleeping with him tonight.

Descent Into Paradise

Sensing his obvious disappointment, she decided to use the events of this morning as the primary reason for her current condition. Guilt, she rationalized, really need not enter the picture.

"My God!" Archie boomed, "you poor girl."

Realizing there were diners all around them, he lowered his voice to ask several pertinent questions.

"When are you meeting this little bastard?"

"Tomorrow evening at my flat. I think he believes he's going to get me in bed as well as the information he so desires."

That was too much for poor Archie, who had fallen hopelessly in love.

"On that score, I can assure you you needn't worry. In fact, you needn't worry at all, I will handle this my way. You just avoid him until tomorrow night, and let me handle the dirty details. One thing I can assure you is that little pimp will never lay a finger on you, and that's a promise."

Shasa, looking across the table at this kindly old man assuring her of protection against her little schoolboy boss, made her smile. If he only knew, she thought. Mistaking her smile as an acceptance of his offer of protection, Archie went on boldly to proclaim that he would pass this information on to the higher ups and get back to her.

Remembering her conversation with the Director, she now regretted ever having told him anything.

"Archie, thank you for your kind offer, but I would rather just handle this myself. Believe me, I have dealt with much worse."

Both were so absorbed in their conversation that neither noticed the well-dressed elderly gentleman seated at the end of the bar nearby.

"Zev, I'm so sorry to be late. Give me a few moments, and I will be right down. Have you made reservations?"

Descent Into Paradise

"Nothing I can't move to later. Please take your time."

As he sat comfortably in Annabelle's library enjoying the fire, Zev, for the first time in his life, actually felt at home. Waiting for her to come down, he realized how extraordinarily comfortable their short relationship had been. His feeling of serenity, however, was short lived as his lovely hostess soon appeared looking elegant, but somewhat perturbed. "Zev darling, that was my father who just called. Would you mind terribly if we just stayed here tonight? Daddy said something about poor Shasa being in trouble. He first asked if you were still here, and when I replied yes, he asked if Shasa could come over and spend the night with us. Not exactly sure why, but I said fine. I'm terribly sorry, I know you wanted to go out."

Zev, who could guess the probable cause of her father's phone call, just smiled as he replied, "Sounds as if he may be a bit worried about his daughter and wants a chaperone to keep an eye on things."

Annabelle couldn't help but laugh as she came to sit on his lap. "He might be just a tad too late, don't you think? Maybe he thinks you can't handle two of us at once."

"Two of you? Hell, I can't handle either one of you."

With that, they headed upstairs before Shasa arrived.

Shasa, having spent the night at Annabelle's, took the next day off from work and went home. As she thought about how to handle her boss, it was obviously critical to ascertain just how this young man uncovered her past. Since he would never leave her flat alive, she also needed to find out if he had told anyone about their little rendezvous. That evening, having put on one of her sexiest short black dresses, she slipped into her black heels and put the finishing touches on her make up. Dimming the lights, she lit candles, put a bottle of champagne on ice, and made sure her stiletto was firmly in place.

Outside, an elderly man watched silently as the shiny black BMW convertible with diplomatic plates drove slowly up the street, clearly looking for somewhere to park. Having taken a moment to squeeze into the only available space, the driver, a young Arab man dressed in evening clothes, got out of the car. Opening the trunk, he proceeded to pull out a brown leather briefcase and a rather large bouquet of flowers. Locking the car, he then crossed the street, barely able to see over the 24 long stemmed yellow roses, which had been carefully wrapped in cellophane by the Embassy florist. After all, he thought smiling, even a Jewish girl deserved flowers before getting laid. Lost in thought as to how the actual seduction would take place, he never heard the footsteps approach from behind. All he felt was the razor sharp wire cut into his throat with agonizing pain. His anguished cry for help was drowned out by the torrent of red blood flowing down soaking his newly pressed white dress shirt.

Archibald, who was waiting patiently in the lobby pretending to look at his mail, heard the car door open and shut. As he carefully placed his mail in his own attaché case, he pulled out his Smith & Wesson handgun, complete with silencer, a gift from years past.

Shasa heard the commotion of people yelling for help outside her window. Reluctantly, she came down to see what had caused the uproar as police sirens pierced the night air. All she could see when she came out her front door was her date for the evening lying in a pool of blood, his throat sliced open, and his body covered by a bouquet of yellow roses. No briefcase or folder of any kind was visible. Whoever had gotten to him now knew who she was. She only hoped it was Archie, although she wished now she had kept her mouth shut and just dealt with this herself.

Shasa woke up early the following morning to call the Saudi Embassy, leaving a message that she was tendering her resignation and thanking them for the opportunity to work there. Her next call was to Hani, who agreed to meet Zev that afternoon at his hotel.

"Mr. Megrid, please forgive my poor manners, but I am operating on a very tight schedule, and, as I believe you have stayed over in London just to meet with me, I am sure you would like to get home."

Hani, who had been unable to reach Annabelle since he left Hampstead, left out the fact he was equally ready for this handsome stranger to go home as well.

"It would appear, from the little I know, you have purchased certain military hardware I had hoped to purchase. Therefore, if you would have any interest in making a slight profit on that purchase, I might be able to make that happen."

"Actually, while I am always interested in making a profit, I am even more interested in establishing a business relationship with someone who can assist my group in expanding our business into the Middle East."

"And what kind of business is your group involved in?"

"Drugs. In fact, we are currently the second largest producer of cocaine in South America, the largest outside of Colombia."

"That's very impressive, however, while I may know something about dealing in weapons, I'm afraid I'm not well acquainted with your line of work. Exactly what kind of assistance is your group seeking?"

"We are interested in three things: finding a suitable supplier of raw opium, which we are led to believe may be coming out of Iran or Afghanistan; setting up a network of dealers; and finding someone with the muscle and political connections to protect that network from the various local authorities."

"That is not exactly my definition of assistance. It sounds to me as if you're looking for a local partner. What makes you think we could assist in any one of those areas? I am simply interested in purchasing your missiles."

"I can deduce that anyone connected with the Saudi Arabian Embassy involved in purchasing sophisticated surface-to-air missiles on the black market has two attributes that would be of interest to us: one, they have access to lots of money; and two, they probably have no love for the United States or Israel."

"You will have to indulge me some time to respond, Mr. Megrid, I will call you tomorrow with an answer. Just a point of clarification before you go; assuming we are only interested in purchasing your missiles, would that still be an option?"

"Yes, that is still an option, although, I have no interest in selling those missiles for, in your vernacular, 'a slight profit.' If you only want the missiles, twelve missiles can be made available for the same price you offered the General for all 24."

That evening, Bashir went to see Hani. Having already briefed him about his trip to Afghanistan, and the full alliance offered by the Taliban upon learning of the Saudi's pledge of $10,000,000 per year for three years, both men contemplated this sudden turn of events. Hani wanted to be certain there was a firm deal on the table concerning the opium production.

"I already told you, Hani, the Taliban now forces the all crops to first be stored in government warehouses before it is shipped. It is their way of making sure their 10% mandatory tax is paid. They informed me the going price of pure high-grade opium into the warehouse is $300 per kilo. That is the amount subject to the tax. From there, most of it is purchased through intermediaries who take it across the border and sell it to the European and Russian middlemen. They then take their profit before it moves to the wholesalers. Hani, this stuff apparently sells on the streets of London and Moscow for $20,000 per kilo. Can you imagine the revenues we could generate if we controlled the entire crop once it made its way out of storage?!"

Hani laughed at the young revolutionary. "I am glad you are finally beginning to use your brain as well as that happy trigger finger of yours. Now listen, we are not in the drug business. We do not understand it, nor should we. Having said that, we certainly could put to good use the huge amount of revenue that opium could generate. This Rios fellow is in the business of selling drugs. He has certain commodities we desire. We have certain ones he desires. Therefore, I believe there are present enough ingredients to make a reasonable trade."

CHAPTER 47

"Ricardo, sit down. Zev just called. He has set up a meeting with the Arabs in London. He believes they are ready to deal."

"Juan, let's think this through very carefully. This is probably one of the most important decisions the two of us have had to consider. This is not only an enormous business decision, this has immense political ramifications as well. Let's be honest here, what we are about to do is declare war on the United States. Is this really what you want?"

"What I want is to get our hands on as much of that opium as possible. Then, let's help them set up in the States. God knows, we have enough cops on our payroll, we should be able to help somehow. Let them show these stupid Americans what real terrorists look like. Maybe then they'll leave us alone and focus on legitimate threats to their security!"

"Agreed, but please be careful. These characters make me very nervous."

Two days later, having heard back from Hani that there may be some mutual interest moving forward, Juan and Ricardo flew to London.

"Mr. Farouk, allow me to introduce Mr. Rios and his partner Mr. Menez." With introductions complete, the talks began. Everything went exceedingly smoothly, for both sides wanted what the other had to offer. The clincher came when Juan informed Hani that the Rios group controlled a major bank holding company in Miami, Florida. In the end, the Saudis got twelve missiles at the same price Zev had paid the Soviet general. Juan negotiated an annual fee of $10,000,000 in exchange for the right to purchase up to 100% of the Afghan opium production for $500 per kilo, payable in cash, exclusive of delivery costs. Finally, they reached an agreement whereby Bashir's network of operatives could utilize the Biscayne Federal Bank in Miami for wire transfers and credit cards without providing any form of ID as long as the recipient was registered on a pre-approved list. Rios also agreed to fund the account with his $10,000,000 annual stipend, effectively making it impossible for the US Government to trace any money being transferred into that account from abroad.

Juan, in turn, got everything he wanted. Exclusive control over the entire Afghan opium production; exclusive distribution rights in Europe and the Middle East, and a promise that the United States would experience terrorism first hand in the near future.

Everyone then drank a toast to the new partnership.

CHAPTER 48

Despite the Captain's warning concerning the Israeli dock master, Abu and Moussa were able to disembark without incident. Beirut, however, was clearly under martial law as they made their way towards Shatila. Several hours later, having been stopped and questioned by three different Israeli patrols, they walked through the main gate.

The familiar sign announcing the entrance to Shatila Camp greeted them in a strange silence. Instead of the teeming masses of people they were used to seeing, there were only a few people milling about. As they walked on in silence, they came across Mr. Nouri's daughter. She had aged beyond recognition and a look of contempt crossed her face as she looked up from her stool. Grey hair had replaced the black mane she had once worn so proudly, her eyes now lifeless as they met Abu's.

"What brings you back here?" she asked vacantly. Without waiting for an answer, she slowly rose while telling them she would give them a tour. Hunched over, she grabbed her walking stick. Abu thought she had aged 30 years in a few months.

"After you left, they came one night and went on a killing spree. Many of the women were raped; others were shot along with the children. Most everyone who survived left shortly thereafter. For those few of us who remained, it was like living in a nightmare for months, people woke up screaming in the middle of the night for no apparent reason."

They soon approached the orphanage where Moussa had spent his younger years. The two-story brick building was now deserted. Gaping holes, where the artillery shells had exploded, punctuated the bleak façade. Windows were mostly shattered, allowing unobstructed views into rooms littered with debris. Obviously, nobody had lived there in some time. Moussa walked ahead of them as he wished to be by himself; Abu looked down at the ground as he listened to his old friend go on.

"The only ones left are the old timers. Those of us just too tired to move anymore I suppose." She paused for a moment. "I suppose just tired of living."

Abu now asked her the questions he had been asking himself since he first saw her. "Who did this? The Israelis? Why did you stay? Why did you not leave with the rest? You are not old, you are younger than I am."

She never looked at him as she gave him her answer. "I don't know who they were. They didn't wear uniforms, and they all spoke Arabic, so maybe they were Lebanese, I don't know, and I really don't care. It doesn't matter now." Then, before she went on, she just started weeping openly. "Do you know what they did to me, Abu? They barged into our tent. We were just waking up to all the noise, and we were still in our nightclothes; three grown women and two teenage girls. There were at least ten of them, all drunk and bloodied when they stormed in. They argued between themselves as they made us sit down. They all wanted the young virgins, you see, and they could not decide who would go first."

Abu did not want to hear the rest, but that would not be his choice.

"They finally decided. We watched helplessly as they took turns raping the two young girls, who lay there screaming at us to make them stop."

She stopped for a long moment as if she were reliving that night again. "Then it was our turn. More men kept coming into the tent. There were lines of them going outside as they took their turn, five women, countless men. When they were finally finished they shot the two young ones. Laughing, they told us we could live because we would never have babies again. They told us they enjoyed themselves so much they might come back."

"Did they?" Abu asked.

"No, we never saw them again, thanks be to Allah. But, I am not sure if it really mattered. You see, we all died that night. Those two beautiful young girls were shot simply because they were Palestinians." Looking up at Abu, her voice was now down to a whisper. "Who wants to live in a world where innocent girls are raped and killed just because of where they were born?"

Her voice began to rise as she shook all over. "What was their crime, Abu? Forced out of their homes and made to grow up in the squalor of this rat infested refugee camp. Is that a sufficient reason to kill them? Because they can grow up and someday bring children into this world? Palestinian children? Is that reason enough to rape them, then shoot them in cold blood?"

She sat down, resting her head on her hands and just cried.

Abu decided to leave her there. Now, he realized why she looked so old. Like so many of their fellow countrymen, she had simply given up. The world could no longer affect her because she was already dead.

CHAPTER 49

MIAMI BEACH

"Boss, something interesting just happened down in Chile. Would you mind coming over to take a look?"

"Shit, when did this happen?"

"Yesterday, apparently. Major Watson just called from DC, he thought we would want to know."

"Has anyone determined the cause?"

"Nothing official. The pilot never opened his chute and the flight recorder is probably buried somewhere up in the Chilean mountains, but all indications are the plane blew up."

"A brand new F-16 fighter just blew up with no warning. No malfunctioning? No nothing?" The man known only as La Bota sat looking somewhat bewildered as he kept questioning his aide.

"That's right. There was no communication from the pilot indicating anything other than a normal flight."

"How far is the crash site from the Rios compound?"

"I'll have to check on that, boss. I don't know."

"I want that info ASAP, like yesterday!"

THE PENTAGON

"General, can I come over right now?"

"Sure Pete, give me fifteen, then come on by."

Pete did not believe in coincidences, but he wanted Bradley's opinion before he went any further.

"Good morning General. I need your thoughts on something."

"Shoot."

"You know that F-16 that went down yesterday outside Santiago?"

"I heard something about it. One of the planes we just sold them, wasn't it?"

"Exactly. The Chileans want us to replace it, saying it malfunctioned, and we said fine as long as they prove it was not pilot error. The pilot is dead and nobody has yet to find any debris from the crash much less the flight recorder, so everything is at an impasse." Pete leaned back in his chair.

The General looked bewildered. "While I'm sorry for the poor pilot and his family, I don't see where this concerns us."

"That plane was on a routine mission. No reports of any malfunction, nothing. All of a sudden it disappears off the radar, no parachute, no communications from the pilot."

"Does sound a bit strange, go on."

"I just got off the phone with our friends at the DEA in Miami. The crash site is only eight miles from the compound of Mr. Juan Rios."

"Coincidence?"

"Maybe. Or maybe our friends in Chile have finally gained access to some advanced Russian military hardware, and they wanted to see if it works."

"That's a bit of a stretch, Major, any proof to go along with that explanation?"

"Not yet, but I would like permission to go digging."

"Exactly what kind of digging did you have in mind?"

"A trip to Miami, for one. I don't think that F-16 just decided to blow up, General. We both know that Russian general is unloading some very advanced weaponry to anyone rich enough to buy it."

"Go. Let me know what you find out."

On the flight down, Pete felt a twinge of guilt for using the F-16 crash as an excuse to fly down to Miami. While he thought there might be a connection between Rios and the fact

Descent Into Paradise

a brand new fighter jet crashed without explanation near his compound, he was far more certain of his need to see a certain voluptuous blonde informer. While he would miss not eating Cuban food for dinner, he thought room service would definitely be more appetizing.

"Hello, Pete, is that you? You have some explaining to do!"

Despite her anger, Madonna ran to the bathroom to check her makeup. Slipping out of her pants and sweater, she pulled on a simple backless white cotton dress that was a size too small but seemed to suit her mood. By the time she had made a few necessary adjustments, there was a knock on her door.

Flowers in hand, Pete sheepishly offered them to her.

Pouting, she took the flowers, threw them on the table and put her arms around his neck. Standing on her toes to kiss him, she announced, "This is going to cost you a lot more than flowers."

Moments later, they were stark naked, the TV barely masking the ever increasing creaking of bedsprings. Exhausted but not yet satisfied, Madonna waved her fingers in Pete's face. "Don't you dare ever leave me for that long or you won't be invited into my bed ever again. Is that clear?"

"Yes, Ma'am, very." Reaching under her buttocks, he pulled her to him, asking her, "Am I forgiven?"

Breathing heavily, Madonna looked at him. "You're forgiven, but you are not allowed off this bed until you finish what you started."

The next morning, a tired Major appeared for his breakfast meeting with two concerned DEA agents.

"Good morning Major, I trust you had an enjoyable evening." Pete, feeling a bit guilty, wasn't sure how to take that so he just mumbled an affirmative.

"Allow me to introduce my partner, Arturo Sneider. Arturo and I have been through many a war together, and he is one of my closest friends. I asked him to join us as he's in charge of debriefing Madonna, who turns out to be a most intriguing lady."

While Pete would have a hard time arguing that last point, he found the whole topic a bit unsettling. Turning to Arturo, he said, "Very nice to meet you. What have you got for us?"

"La Bota has kept me abreast of your earlier conversations so I am aware of your concerns regarding the Israelis. It would appear, from what I have been able to piece together, there is indeed a direct connection between the Israelis and the Rios family. Madonna confirmed there was a high ranking Israeli military officer working directly for Rios." Before Pete could comment, Bota chimed in, "But that's not the best part, my friend. Wait till you hear the rest.

"According to her story, Juan brought her back a beautiful piece of jewelry from his trip to Tel Aviv, telling her he so admired it displayed on the neck of a beautiful Israeli girl that he had to buy one for her."

"Did she tell you what it was?"

Arturo, looking somewhat surprised by the question, answered, "If she did, I don't remember, sorry."

Pete's mind was now racing. The ramifications of what he had just heard were more than unsettling. He had trouble concentrating on what La Bota had to say next.

"Not only are our South American friends doing business with the Israelis, I'm beginning to suspect they have formed some sort of partnership with the Arabs as well."

"What makes you think that?"

"Major, you may not be aware of this, but most of the world's opium supply is harvested in Afghanistan. That opium is processed into heroin, then exported to Europe and the eastern half of the US. Now, we are seeing multiple numbers of young Arabs going in and out of Rios's bank, along with a flood of new heroin entering the market."

"Are you suggesting there is a connection between these Arabs using Biscayne Federal and Rios getting control over Afghanistan's opium?"

"I am suggesting that Rios would be willing to do just about anything to control that amount of opium. On the other end, if you were an Arab terrorist operating within the United States, what would it be worth to access bank accounts and credit cards without having to show any proper ID?"

"It would be worth its weight in gold," responded Pete. "There would be no way to trace them or keep tabs on them. Hell, we wouldn't even know they were here."

"Exactly. Now, we have the prospect of someone supplying these gangsters with advanced surface-to-air missiles and the whole picture becomes quite frightening."

"That it does," replied Pete. "If all of this is true, we have ourselves a worthy adversary."

"But help me with this, Major," asked Arturo. "How the hell is Rios able to deal with both the Israelis and the Arabs? If Rios is indeed employing a high ranking Israeli officer, you must assume they know what Rios is up to, they aren't that stupid."

All Pete could think of was the last time he saw Zev in Israel. Were they both involved? It was a thought too awful to contemplate so he just murmured back, "No, they're not."

It was almost noon by the time the three of them finished. Pete hurried back to his room to pack before meeting Madonna in the lobby. Realizing, after another round of early morning sex, their entire relationship so far had been conducted in bed, he had promised to take her out of the hotel for lunch before his flight back to Washington. As he watched her walking towards him at the Reception desk, he couldn't help but notice the bluish green stone resting elegantly around her neck.

The following morning, Pete made his report to the General. The only part omitted was the potential Israeli connection. Knowing how his boss felt about Israel, he had decided to keep that information between La Bota and himself.

"Here's my summary, General, pretty scary if you ask me."

Taking a few minutes to review the findings, General Bradley peered over his glasses.

"You're right about one thing, Pete. That F-16 didn't just decide to blow itself up. It looks to me like those bastards have set up their own air defense system using surface-to-air missiles. Could you confirm where the hell they got them?"

"No sir, but there are very few places where one can purchase arms like that, so I'm still thinking the Soviet Union."

"I guess it really doesn't matter where the hell they got them. They have them, and, more disturbing, they apparently are willing to use them. I'm going to kick this upstairs to see how they want to handle it. I'd suggest, Major, that you get down to Bragg and get your team ready."

CHAPTER 50

Juan and Ricardo were seated in the study when Zev arrived.

"Zev, when are those missiles scheduled to be delivered to New York?"

"They are due to arrive in approximately fifteen days. They have been confirmed onboard the cargo ship."

"Good. I want you to fly back to London." Juan then detailed what he had in mind.

"I will see if I can get a meeting set up quickly. If they're interested, they will need time to prepare."

Hani sat in the dining room of the Savoy waiting for Annabelle to arrive. He had to admit being somewhat nervous. What if she turned him down? Their relationship had certainly cooled off since that handsome South American had entered the picture. Of course, since neither of them had ever made any real demands on the other, it was difficult to gauge just how committed she felt. There had been some intimacy, especially in the beginning, but no sex. That had been fine with him, as his sexual appetite had diminished with age. He had heard the Brits, especially the upper class, were a bit prudish, so he thought nothing of the fact they had never slept together. Would she take the next step or not? He feared she would say no and their relationship would falter.

"Hani, sorry I'm late. The traffic was just awful. How are you? It's so good to see you! How long are you in town?"

"Never long enough since I've known you, my dear." They chatted on until their favorite dessert arrived on the table, at which time Hani finally summoned up the courage to pose his question.

"Annabelle, the Royal Family has just requested my attendance at the King's Court. While I'm not exactly sure why, I can guess, and it could mean I may not be back for some time."

What he didn't mention was that the Royal Family had insisted that he return and not travel outside Saudi Arabia without their express permission. Apparently, his ties to Sheik Bashir had become known, and this was their way of exerting some restraint on the Islamic Brotherhood.

"I was hoping you might consider traveling to Saudi Arabia to meet me there?"

An awkward silence ensued as Annabelle thought through the implications of his invitation. Their relationship, while still very cordial, had suffered an unspoken strain since Zev's arrival in London. While she still enjoyed his company, her heart clearly now belonged elsewhere.

"Hani dear, while I will truly miss you, I'm not sure Saudi Arabia is ready for a spoiled English lady whose idea of subservience is doing her own laundry."

While Hani smiled at her poor excuse for humor, he realized she was still her father's daughter and would never seriously consider marriage to someone like him. As much as the truth hurt, he was not shocked.

"Then, I'm afraid we may not see each other for some time."

The next morning, Hani, still depressed by the events of the previous evening, joined Bashir for coffee.

"Hani, what's wrong?"

Hani then shared the government's request for his return home and Annabelle's response to his offer to join him. Bashir, who had purposely not shared all he knew with his surrogate father, could only act surprised and give his old friend his heartfelt condolences.

Descent Into Paradise

"If they knew where to find me, I'm quite sure I would be joining you. In the meantime, I will sorely miss you and your sage advice. Just keep your television on, for there will be some interesting news shortly."

CHAPTER 51

Shasa arrived 30 minutes late to Salloos and was escorted upstairs immediately without her saying a word. Ever since receiving his phone call yesterday, she had debated the wisdom of accepting his somewhat curious invitation. Other than Annabelle, she had not alerted anyone where she would be tonight, or with whom. As she came up the stairs, she could see Bashir was already seated at the very same table she had reserved for her lunch with Annabelle and Zev. Standing up, he greeted her with the utmost courtesy.

"Shasa, good evening. I apologize for starting without you, but, quite frankly, I wasn't sure you were coming. Given the fact I had reserved this table, I felt obliged at least to order something."

The daughter of the owner stood politely by the table to see what she would like.

"Your usual, Miss?"

Shasa, a bit confused by the young lady first knowing who she was meeting and now hovering over her, just said, "Yes please," to dismiss her.

"I'm so glad you like this food as well. It's become my favorite restaurant in London, plus it's easy walking distance for both of us."

The game of cat and mouse continues, she thought. He obviously knows where I live. I wonder if he knows who owns it as well?

"That's right, the Berkeley is just down the street, isn't it How long are you in town for this time?"

"Actually, I am leaving tomorrow morning for Beirut; your part of the world. A beautiful city, don't you think?"

Descent Into Paradise

Shasa wasn't sure how to answer. Her carefully constructed background showed her being brought up by a Lebanese aunt. If he were aware of that, he would easily surmise she would have at least visited Beirut. On the other hand, she was not anxious for him to know she had ever visited there, as her face would still be well known to the people he was likely to visit.

"Yes, I remember it as very beautiful, but that was some time ago. Do you have friends there, or is this trip business?"

"Just business this time. I'm afraid the Israelis have managed to destroy what was once a beautiful city. Such a shame, really. The Lebanese are such a lovely peaceful people. It's their misfortune to be located north of such a pariah. Don't you agree?"

"Yes, I do. To say nothing of the ill luck of my own people, who had the misfortune of living just where that pariah wanted to be."

"That's right, please forgive me. I forgot, you are Palestinian, not Lebanese. Yet, you are working at our Embassy here in London. It is all a bit confusing." As she sat there waiting to find out where all this was leading, she sipped her wine, giving him her most beguiling smile. Realizing he was not going to get a response, he continued as more food arrived.

"Speaking of our esteemed Embassy, I heard about the Ambassador's poor Chief of Staff. How awful! And right there in front of your flat, I believe. What an odd coincidence. Were you home that night? I hear it was really quite gruesome. Blood everywhere, and apparently nobody has a clue as to who did it or why."

Shasa now saw where all this was heading, the whereabouts of her folder no longer a mystery. This probably also explained why Archibald had not been in touch.

"Yes, I happened to be home and unfortunately witnessed the aftermath. Quite awful, really. As to who did it or why, I assume my conversation with Hani may have played a role?"

Descent Into Paradise

Bashir sat there admiring this young girl's mettle. He was fairly certain she now realized who had possession of her folder and therefore her true identity. Yet, here she was, looking him straight in the eye without flinching. Maybe that's the reason he had let her live; or maybe he had just wanted one more taste of that exquisite body. Regardless, he had to decide what to do with her.

"As we both know, you played a central role, my dear. But was it your conversation with Hani that doomed that poor boy, or was it your recent dinner with that famous British secret agent, the Honorable Lord Luxley?"

Realizing the game of cat and mouse was finally coming to an end, all Shasa could do was smile and play on.

"Please enlighten me with your wisdom?"

Looking across the table, he couldn't help but appreciate just how exquisite was this feisty Palestinian beauty. He truly admired her chutzpah, yes, but what he really admired was her body. He wanted her as a woman, not a corpse.

"Another glass of wine? Good, yes I would be delighted to. To begin with, you will be happy to know your erstwhile savior was indeed there that night, but alas only as a spectator. After all, for Annabelle's sake, I didn't want her father to get himself into any unnecessary trouble. You see, at that point, I still hadn't realized the lovely Miss Annabelle had exchanged lovers. What I didn't understand is why you were so anxious to have the young man terminated. Then, after I read what the poor boy was bringing to you, it all became quite clear."

"And the purpose of dinner tonight? I would have thought, given what you now know, that we wouldn't be sharing this lovely evening together."

"Ah, that's an interesting question, one I have puzzled on myself. I suppose I wanted to hear directly from your lips why.

Why you would betray your own people, especially after what they did to you and your family."

Shasa now realized just how dangerous a position she had put herself in. She also knew the animal seated across from her. If he wanted her dead, she wouldn't be sitting here having dinner. She realized that, of course, before she accepted. This was a game for both of them. Two dangerous predators, each enthralled, each relishing the psychological and physical danger both had chosen as part of their very existence. Looking directly at him, she leaned across the table.

"I sincerely doubt you have any real interest in what I have done or not done in the past or why. The simple truth is you want to take me to bed, and that's the only reason I accepted your invitation."

Smiling back at her, he whispered back, "That may be the only reason you survive this evening."

"That may be the only reason either one of us does."

With that declaration, she suggested they finish their meal and go back to his hotel.

CHAPTER 52

WASHINGTON DC
THE STATE DEPARTMENT

Henry Cabot sat there simmering as General Bradley gave his presentation. He had never liked nor trusted that damned Mexican who ran his Miami office. La Bota or Bota, or whatever the hell he called himself. Damn flake, he thought. Now, having to listen to Bradley give out information that he, as head of the DEA, should have known beforehand was putting him in a foul mood. Finally, when asked his opinion by the Secretary of State, he was forced to accept what Bradley had said or look very incompetent by not being privy to what was being discussed. All he could muster to save face was to state he was going to Miami himself to interview the girl and make sure the information she was giving could be confirmed before he would sign off on any military actions.

Cabot had booked a suite at the Fountain Blue Hotel. A Miami landmark, it had the advantage of being situated right on the beach. Home to some of the best entertainment Miami had to offer, Cabot looked forward to getting away for a few days of sun and hopefully a little adult entertainment. Widowed for several years after a long, dull and lifeless marriage, he was still trying to make up for lost time. Still considered handsome by the ladies, he was often sought after by the socialites of Washington as a prime dinner partner. His tastes, however, favored the younger, more exotic types who were less interested in social standing and more interested in just having fun and wild sex. Having seen pictures of Madonna, he looked forward to his scheduled interview, regardless of what information she might have shared with his subordinates.

Descent Into Paradise

She certainly did not disappoint. Their initial meeting had taken place downtown with La Bota and Arturo present. Cabot then pulled rank and insisted upon doing a second interview himself. When he discovered Madonna was also staying at the Fountain Blue, he suggested they meet up for dinner, a plan which seemed to suit her as long as it was somewhere other than the hotel.

"Goddamned horny bastard just wants to fuck her," said an angry La Bota to Arturo after they had left. "I've never trusted that old fart from the day I met him. God only knows how many agents that rotten son of a bitch has sold out. He could care less about drugs. For him, it is all about prestige and money, period. And sex. But I guess they both go together, where he is from."

"Well, Bota, all I can say is they deserve each other."

That had been a week ago. Tonight, Cabot was landing at Miami International once again, having been driven to distraction all week. He had to see her again, so he had called Arturo to say he wanted to set up another interview. That interview was scheduled for noon tomorrow. Tonight, he had something a bit more intimate in mind.

Having left her a message about joining him for a drink, he hoped she would be available. To his delight, she was sitting at the bar alone when he came down after checking in. Her effusive welcome bolstered his wishful thinking.

"Henry, how wonderful to see you. I got your message and hoped you might buy me dinner – or do you have other plans?"

"No, I have no plans. Actually, I was rather hoping you might join me for the evening. I have a little proposition which I think you may find interesting."

As they walked out, the bartender, a slender young man known to his regular customers as Slim, went to make a call.

Descent Into Paradise

Estoban listened carefully and smiled. The damned head of the DEA, no less. Whatever one thought of the bitch, she still had the looks to lure any male into her intricate web of deceit. He had paid out a great deal of money to learn of her whereabouts since she had disappeared some months ago. Money which now proved to be well spent. Cursing his partner at the Lazy Ranch for ever allowing her to leave there alive, he planned to make sure that problem was put to rest once and for all. If it all went according to plan, Juan would never find out Madonna was still alive, and he would get the credit for setting up the hit. The final piece fell into place as he answered his phone.

"Hello Estoban, it's Zev. I am calling to tell you I am scheduled to see Bashir next week in London. If he agrees, I'm sure he will want to send a team over next week to set up. Who should they contact?"

"Me, I will stay here until they are ready to take over. When the Feds come looking around for culprits, let them look no further than our Arab friends."

Cabot escorted Madonna to their meeting the next morning, where she was much more forthcoming with information than in her previous meetings. La Bota and Arturo could only marvel at the sudden transformation.

Afterwards, Cabot escorted her back to the hotel.

"Are you sure you have to leave, Henry darling? We had so much fun last night."

"I wish I could stay. Believe me when I tell you I haven't enjoyed myself so much in years. I'll be back. I promise."

Pouting, she asked when.

Cabot quickly answered. "There is an international conference on drug interdiction being held here in two weeks. I am scheduled to be on one of the panels. Why don't I plan to stay over afterwards? We can spend a few days on the beach, then we will get you away from all this needless interrogation once and for all."

"Oh darling, I can hardly wait. Now, come upstairs and say a proper goodbye."

La Bota was on the phone to Pete shortly after Cabot left with Madonna. "The old fart is certainly enamored with our little informant. He insists upon only interviewing her alone so, in his words, he can double check what she has told us."

"Has he?" asked Pete, a bit annoyed.

"Hell, if you ask me, I doubt he's asked her a single question about drugs or Rios. A total waste of time and taxpayer money. But what else is new. Not to worry, he'll give you the green light, not because of anything he's learned, it's just the path of least resistance."

"OK. Thanks, man; the General and I are going to pay a visit to our good friends in Israel to see what they haven't been telling us. Let's touch base when I get back next week."

CHAPTER 53

Zev knocked on the door, flowers in hand.

"Oh, Zev, you darling. Come in! Aren't these beautiful roses? Thank you, love." Putting the roses in her favorite vase, she came out with a bottle of chilled champagne.

"A celebration due to having you home."

Somehow that thought touched him. He had never really had a home, a least not since his mother's death. Holding up his glass, he said, "To you, my dearest Annabelle, for the love and warmth that makes a home worth coming to."

They drank a small sip but quickly embraced, each happier than they had been since they parted.

"Darling, tell me everything," Annabelle said as they sat down. "What brings you back?"

"You."

"Flattery will get you in my bed, but it doesn't satisfy my curiosity. Now, tell me. What mischief are you plotting?"

"I'm here to meet Sheik Bashir. We are trying to get them to expand their supplies of opium so we can make more money," he lied.

"Well, I hope you're getting some as well so you can buy me a very expensive gift!"

Annabelle had gone out earlier, making a rare trip to the butcher. For some reason, she had wanted to cook Zev an old-fashioned English dinner featuring roast beef and Yorkshire pudding. Zev was delighted to discover his very beautiful British socialite girlfriend was an excellent chef as well. "To the most beautiful lady in the world," toasted Zev with his first glass of red wine, "and an excellent chef as well! I love you dearly." By the time dinner had ended, they were both caught up on all their news, at least that which each desired to share.

"Dessert tonight," she said, standing up from the dining room table, "is of an organic nature since I believe we have consumed enough calories for one evening. If you wish to partake, then please follow me."

Zev followed without hesitation. Climbing onto her bed, he reached out for her hand.

"That was a wonderful dinner. Thank you."

"That was a wonderful toast. I hope you meant it?"

"I meant all of it." He told her that until he met her, he had not felt at home since his mother died.

She pulled him towards her, knowing him to be a proud man who could not easily express his emotions. Tonight, she felt an urgent need to give him more than just her body. Tonight, lying together in her bed, she gave him her heart and soul. She spoke to him about subjects she had never discussed with anyone before, not even her aunt. She told him about her own mother, who had left her to go to Israel when she was six years old, never to return.

"My father only told me that my mother died there and is buried in Tel Aviv. To this day, he has never told me how she died, or why her grave is there and not here with us. I am ashamed to admit I have never even visited my mother's grave. Somehow, I can't forgive her for abandoning us. Isn't that awful?"

She then decided to tell him about her relationship with Hani and how she had declined his invitation to join him in Saudi Arabia. Finally, she told him that she had recently pressed her father on his affiliation with Mossad, to which he had finally admitted working for them for many years. The only piece she left out was the rather complicated family ties, which she was still trying to digest herself.

Descent Into Paradise

"I now see why he was so upset with my dating Hani! If I had only known!"

"Have you told him you're now dating a drug dealer and arms smuggler? He must be thrilled by your taste in men!"

"Actually, no, I haven't gone into any details on your background. He thinks you are somehow tied in with Mossad since the Director gave him your name and asked for his help. So, I think I'll just leave it at that for now. If you ever become his son in law, we will cross that bridge then."

"Well, while I may not relish that particular conversation, I certainly hope to get that opportunity one day."

"Me too!"

Their lovemaking reached a new dimension, transcending their physical lust, reaching down deep into their souls where few had been allowed before.

CHAPTER 54

The meeting with the Director and Argov took place in General Argov's office with General Bradley in a bellicose mood. Once the pleasantries were over, he launched right in.

"Yuri, as I told you on the phone, we believe this Rios group has recently acquired some very sophisticated weapons and are responsible for taking out a brand new F-16 fighter jet we were delivering to Chile. The White House just authorized a military operation down there to take out these bastards once and for all. Now, before I send my boys down there, I want to know everything you know about this gang of thugs, and I don't want any bullshit. Is that clear?"

The fact that the General's own son might be one of those going was not lost on the Israelis. General Argov, relieved that there had been no mention of any Israeli involvement, was the first to respond. "We understand perfectly, General. In preparation for this meeting, the Director and I have been comparing notes, all of which we would like to share with you and Major Watson."

Pete, waiting anxiously for Shasa to arrive, listened without comment as the Director proceeded to tell his half-truths, leaving out, of course, his own involvement.

"We have become aware of a meeting which took place in London some months ago between Sheik Bashir, his closest associate, another Saudi named Farouk, and Juan Rios. We know in that meeting, two major topics were discussed. First, the subject of opium was brought up. Then the subject of weapons from the Soviet Union was discussed. The net result of that meeting was that Rios agreed to sell the Arabs certain sophisticated Soviet-made arms in exchange for getting control over the Afghanistan opium production. In addition, Rios made a deal to agree to allow the Arabs to use his bank, the Biscayne Federal Savings and Loan, to fund anyone whose name appeared on a special list, regardless of ID or proof of citizenship. In other words, any Arab terrorist working for Bashir in the US now has a source of funds for their operations."

"My God, how did you get this information?"

"I am sorry, General. You know there are some things we cannot divulge, even to our best allies. Suffice it to say that this is 100 percent pure intelligence."

"I believe you. Both Major Watson and I want to thank you for sharing this with us. These bastards are about to get their just reward for fucking with the United States of America!"

"General, I know you are focused on the extermination of the Rios group, but please do not underestimate what these Islamic extremists are capable of. We are not talking about the PLO or Hamas anymore. This is an international consortium of well-organized, well-funded religious fanatics who have touched a chord within their own Islamic population. They hate you as much as they hate us. Please make no mistake, General. They fully intend to take this conflict across the Atlantic. American blood will be spilled alongside ours. That is their mission and their stated goal."

"Let the bastards come. They won't live long enough to cause any damage if I have anything to say about it!" General Bradley responded.

The Director then looked over to respond to Pete's question as to Shasa's absence. "The reason Shasa isn't here is that she is still out on assignment. If we learn anything new, we will keep you posted."

Descent Into Paradise

As they left, Pete knew intuitively that his long time love was absolutely involved, as was Zev. The fact he hadn't shared anything with his boss might save Argov and the Director some embarrassment, but it would not save anybody's life now that the Israelis knew what was about to come. Despite his mixed emotions, he had intended to warn Shasa and hopefully Zev, if she could reach him in time.

CHAPTER 55

Madonna decided to have her 'morning' coffee down in the bar as the rain continued to pour against her window. Her face buried in her daily newspaper, she never saw him walking over to her table. The look of shock on her face produced a gleeful chuckle as her uninvited guest then sat down. Speechless, she just stared at the scarred face looking back at her. His cold brown eyes yielded no indication of what was forthcoming.

"Did you really believe you could get away with this? That I would not find you?"

Madonna, for once in her life, had nothing to say. She knew she held no power over this demon. Even if he occupied a man's body, he had no feelings, nothing. He was as close to a monster as anyone she had ever met, and that included a number of close seconds. All she could manage in response was, "What do you want?"

After he explained his proposition, her relief was palpable.

"And you give me your word you won't come after me again?"

"I just gave you my terms; deliver what we just agreed to, then move to any city we don't do business in and I will leave you alone. If I ever see or hear from you again, I will kill you. Is that clear?"

The lobby of the Berkeley Hotel in London was very small for a major hotel. Zev could locate only one empty chair and immediately took it. He sat there watching the upper crust of British society walk through to the dining room. Soon the Sheik appeared.

"Zev, there you are, would you mind terribly if we ate lunch here? I am on a very tight schedule."

Descent Into Paradise

Walking into the formal dining room, they were escorted to a quiet table near the piano. Before turning to the business at hand, the conversation began by Bashir asking how he ended up staying at Annabelle's house.

Unsure of why the question was being asked, Zev gave him a roundabout answer. "To be honest, my boss made the arrangements so I'm not quite sure how it all came about. Why do you ask?"

"No particular reason. I was just curious as most of us traveling abroad stay at a hotel, yet you arrive and end up staying in a most attractive young lady's home."

Knowing that was not the reason for the question, Zev decided it was a good time to get down to the business at hand. "The reason I wanted to meet is that a certain situation has developed in Miami which Mr. Rios thought might interest you as well as serve our mutual purposes."

"Go on."

After Zev finished, Bashir thought in silence for a moment. It would certainly add to the drama he already planned, but would he have time to adequately set it up?

"And the missiles? Are they still on schedule?"

"They are on the open seas and scheduled to arrive in New York approximately twelve days from today."

"Good. Let me think about your proposal. I am inclined to accept your offer, but let me get back to you. How long will you be in London?"

"Only a few more days. As you know, the two of us have much to do."

"Isn't that the truth."

As they got up to leave, Bashir put his hand on Zev's shoulder. "And Zev, one more thing: don't involve Shasa in any of our future dealings. I don't trust her and neither should you, my friend, capiche?"

Zev felt that familiar nagging feeling in his gut as he pondered what the Sheik knew about Shasa. As Annabelle greeted him at the door, he asked if she had spoken to Shasa recently.

"She wasn't at the meeting?"

"No, I thought it somewhat strange as she has attended all our meetings. Hope she's OK."

With a conspiratorial grin, Annabelle responded, "Something tells me she and my father may be off somewhere. Those two have something going on which neither wants to admit."

In Zev's mind, that was a conversation that needed no further encouragement.

The whole thing about being off with Annabelle's father didn't make much sense, even if they had some amorous something going on. It was difficult imagining her with anyone other than Pete, but then he didn't understand this attraction for older men to start with. Fortunately, Annabelle was running late for an appointment, which precluded any further conversation. As soon as she left, he decided to walk over to Shasa's flat. No one answered her buzzer and her phone just went to the answering machine. Reluctantly, he placed a call to the Embassy and left a coded message for the Director. He then turned his attention to a more positive subject.

The old Jewish fellow was certainly a determined negotiator. It was only after Zev took out his Mossad identification card that the diamond merchant yielded.

His next stop was to rent a black tuxedo. Poor Annabelle didn't know what to think when he arrived back at the house with a tuxedo draped over his shoulder.

"Zev, what on earth are you planning?"

"Tonight, my dear, we are going out for a formal evening, just the two of us."

"Zev, that sounds lovely, but it's your last night here, darling. Can't we just stay in? We can eat an early dinner, and then spend more time in bed."

"We can stay up all night when we get back. Please, I want this to be a special evening."

Annabelle finally relented. Despite her protestations to the contrary, she enjoyed getting dressed in evening clothes. Zev looked very dashing in his tuxedo as he went to answer the door. "Who is that?" she called from her dressing room.

"I will get it."

Opening the door, he told the driver they would be right down.

"Who was that?"

"The driver."

"What driver?"

"Our driver for the evening."

"Zev Megrid, what on earth are you up to?"

The Maître d' at the restaurant recognized Zev from lunch and escorted them to a very private table for two.

A bottle of champagne appeared magically just after they were seated, with no instructions given.

"A toast," said Zev, raising his glass to her. "To the woman I can no longer imagine living without."

With a sly grin, he put a small black velvet box in her hand and asked, "Annabelle, will you marry me and take care of me forever?"

Annabelle almost dropped her glass. Opening the box, an exquisite diamond flanked by two beautiful sapphire stones sat sparkling in the candlelight. Her left hand trembled slightly as she handed him the ring to slip it on her finger.

"Zev, I hope you are serious because this ring is never coming off this finger."

"Does that mean yes?"

"That means I love you more than life itself, and I never want to be without you again."

CHAPTER 56

BEIRUT

Salidi Khadra read the letter one more time before responding. "I accept your terms, I am just not sure I can have everything in place in one week."

Colonel Mir had been hesitant to put forth such a short schedule, but events in London had forced the timing forward.

"I must apologize for insisting upon the date, I realize it does not give you much time, but I cannot stress how important it is to the larger picture. It must be scheduled for one week from today. Can you agree or not?"

Salidi had known ten years ago that their tactics against Israel must change, but could never convince his elders. Only Abu Nabile had agreed with him, although for slightly different reasons. After the disaster at Baleta Camp, Salidi had spent the ensuing years in charge of what Hamas termed the Journey to the Holy Land, or what the rest of the world knew as suicide missions. There had been no lack of volunteers after the successful mission at the Marine barracks back in 1983.

Salidi looked at a check made out to him for $20,000. All he had to do was blow up an Israeli commuter bus in downtown Tel Aviv one week from today. How can I refuse? he thought as he watched the Iranian enjoy the rest of his cigar.

"Alright," he said at last. "You have my commitment. You shall have your little fireworks show one week from today."

The Iranian helicopter, carrying the Sheik and Director Rezvani, landed at Camp Murat just after lunch. The war council convened shortly thereafter in the Commander's tent. Once the pleasantries were dispensed with, the Director was the first to speak giving everyone an update on his master plan.

"I want you all to picture the chaos this will create. Never before have the Israelis been attacked in such a systematic fashion. The Arab world will finally have reason to rejoice. Just think of the massive publicity we can create. I think it is time we showed the world who we are."

The Sheik had been so caught up dealing with the Rios issues; he had not focused upon this strategy of multiple attacks all launched in the same week. The PLO had never been able to pull off anything on this scale before. It would certainly serve notice that the war against Israel had now escalated. He then listened to the Commander's one concern.

"We need to broaden our base of support, on that I agree. These missions, if successful, will certainly bring us much prestige. My only question is, are we in a position to accept the response these multiple attacks are bound to cause?"

Rezvani had anticipated this question, for he had also pondered over this point. "I believe the risks of not moving forward outweigh those of acting now. We need to be credible with those who have agreed to follow us. Up to this point, all they have heard is talk. If we are truly to lead this Jihad, we must prove we are both capable of its planning and ruthless in its execution."

Abu then added his thoughts. "I agree with the Director; my men have been anxiously awaiting their turn to participate. They are ready to take this war to Israel and America. If you do not order these raids, I will."

Bashir, looking across the table, shook his head in agreement. "Commander, we have given you a state of the art air defense system. Murat is impregnable, so I would not be overly concerned about retaliation. Let them shoot their missiles at some poor factory somewhere so they can boast they have killed some poor civilians they'll label terrorists." Then, turning towards

Abu, he responded, "You have my blessing. I will leave you warriors to finalize the details while I lay down for a rest."

That evening, Bashir held another meeting. This time, only the Director of Iranian Intelligence was present.

"My congratulations, Director. I commend you for the audacity of your plan. It should indeed send shock waves throughout the Jewish community. Now, let me bring you up to date on what I have planned for the Great Satan. The surface-to-air missiles are now safely on the high seas heading for New York City. They should arrive in just under two weeks." He then put forth Zev's proposition.

There was no hesitation as Rezvani responded.

"I think we should go forward. The Israeli operations will definitely create uproar here, but the Americans will only react to blood spilled on their soil. I say we make it very clear; their continued military involvement in our affairs is going to cost American lives as well as Israelis."

CHAPTER 57

The Director and General Argov had a very serious conversation upon the Americans' departure. The Director, well aware of Argov's relationship with the American general, decided to use it to his advantage.

"General, we clearly have a problem here. The Americans are going to take out our friends in Santiago, that much is clear. If they ever find out we had any involvement, however innocent, I fear what the consequences would be."

Argov felt like telling the little bastard he had a problem, not we, but he realized they would both be held accountable if Israel's involvement with Rios were ever to come to light.

"What do you suggest? This whole affair was, if I recall correctly, your little brainchild."

The Director, clearly in need of the General's support, chose wisely to ignore the insult.

"I suggest we remove all traces of our ties to Mr. Rios before General Bradley sends in his troops."

"On that point, Director, we are in total agreement. I will leave it up to you as to how, but do it quickly and quietly. Neither of us can afford this ever seeing the light of day."

Zev left Heathrow having promised Annabelle he would wrap up his affairs in South America within the month. They had stayed up all night talking about where they would live and what he could do to earn a living. Zev lamented that if it were anything legal, he would just have to start over. Fortunately, he had saved enough money to be financially stable so they could laugh about his suggestion of becoming a security guard at Harrods.

Shasa, having decided it was too dangerous to return to her flat, had immediately left town. Their need for each other satiated, neither she nor Bashir suffered any illusion they might reunite. Her departure early that morning had been civil. No threats had been made, his only departing remark being, "Walk carefully, my dear, for there is danger all around you."

"You as well, my dear. Since I sincerely doubt you will be with us much longer, know I will remember you fondly just as you are."

With that, Shasa walked out leaving him naked in bed.

The Director, immediately upon leaving Argov's office, placed a call to London. Unaware of her indiscretion with Bashir and therefore her temporary absence from London, he sent her a coded message requesting an immediate meeting. Unable to respond on a secure line, she phoned the Embassy in London acknowledging she could attend a meeting the next evening.

Arriving back in town the following afternoon by train, she took a calculated risk returning home first. Having satisfied herself the flat was not under active surveillance, she went in, hurriedly packed her clothes, and checked her phone for messages. Annabelle had called three times, saying it was urgent, but there were no other messages.

Placing a quick call to a relieved Annabelle, they arranged to meet for tea at Harrods.

CHAPTER 58

Tiny sand particles tore through the air, temporarily blinding those whose goggles were not firmly in place. As the thumping sounds of the Iranian helicopter faded away to the east, the afternoon heat of the Jordanian desert took their breath away. Each man strapped on a 60-pound backpack loaded with explosives, extra ammunition clips, food, water and medical supplies. Their target was approximately 22 miles due west.

Kahil could feel the moisture being sucked out of his body. "We need to be well past those hills before sunrise, so keep the pace on me."

Single file they set out through the loose desert sand, each step an effort.

Twenty-two miles away, Rabbi Yuri Swartz took a mighty swing with his pickaxe. The blade broke in half as it hit a small rock. The Rabbi dropped the pick, uttering an uncharacteristic oath as he did so. They were constructing the fifteenth house of the settlement. His hands were hardened from the weeks of hard labor yet he still felt the pain of a blow like that. He looked at his watch; the dial announced it was 17h45. In fifteen minutes, it would be time for evening prayers. Rabbi Swartz gladly put his pick down for the day, grabbed the canteen and let the sweet well water glide down his parched throat.

Turning to his crew, he announced, "I am going to get ready."

There were a total of 50 Jewish pilgrims who had joined him in building this settlement. They had arrived some eight weeks ago amidst a storm of protest from the Palestinians as well as

Descent Into Paradise

a few liberal Jews. The official position of the Israeli Government was that no new Jewish settlements would be constructed in the lands allocated to the Palestinians. For Rabbi Swartz and his followers, this was blasphemy. The Palestinians were a curse upon the great crusade to reunite Jews from across the world in their own country, a birthright given to them by the Holy Bible. No left wing politician was going to overrule the word of God, not while Rabbi Yuri Swartz could still swing a pickaxe or stand in the pulpit of God to preach his sacred word. Today, like every other, God willing he would do both.

As the evening breeze began to howl through the open windows, he was well into his sermon. "I tell you, my friends, the Lord looks down upon us kindly, giving us his strength. We are his messengers. We are here to do his bidding. Not the politicians in Jerusalem or the protesters in Tel Aviv. They, God forgive them, have simply lost their way. They have lost sight of what God wants. They have forgotten that for centuries the people of Moses have wandered the world lost and alone. Now, through the grace of the Almighty, we have found our way home."

Pausing to let this point sink home, the Rabbi ended his daily sermon with the admonition, "We will carry on; we will continue to build homes and communities so that others may come and have a place to live safe from their oppressors."

The congregation began to clap as they stood to join in the singing of the Jewish National Anthem, a ritual performed every evening

Although they had marched throughout the night, Kahil only slept several hours the following morning. By 14h30, he was leading his five fellow Saudis towards their target, now less than eight miles away. He wanted to see it before it got dark.

Descent Into Paradise

Three hours later, they approached their target. Using their elbows as levers, they quietly crawled up to the ridge overlooking the new settlement below.

Kahil's men were all Bedouins, born and raised in the deserts of Saudi Arabia, all possessing the patience required of hunters. Like a pride of lions, they were content to wait and watch their quarry for hours without moving a muscle. All afternoon into the evening, they observed the routine of the settlement. That night, the six warriors held a war council, which was the custom of the Bedouin tribes. The men talked well into the night before the plan was approved.

At 18h00 the next evening, the six Arabs moved out. Once the barbed wire fence was cut, two of the men moved towards the houses already built. They would place their explosives and then join the others at the synagogue.

Kahil posted his men around the synagogue, the light machine gun aimed for the front entrance. Explosive charges had been placed on both sides of the building as well as the rear. The timers had been set for two minutes. As he checked his watch, the two men assigned to blow up the houses came running up behind him.

"All set for 30 minutes."

"Good, get ready, whoever survives the explosion will be coming out that door."

The men un-slung their AK-47s, selecting full automatic fire. At that very moment, he heard the rifle shots. A warning signal, he thought, as he checked his watch. The charges were scheduled to go off in ten seconds.

Kahil immediately ordered one of the Saudis to go take care of the guard, then knelt down beside the machine gun. With a wide grin, he told the rest of the men to get ready.

Descent Into Paradise

Rabbi Swartz stopped speaking immediately upon hearing the warning shots. Jumping from his podium, he ran for the entrance door. He had just stepped outside when he was thrown to the ground by the force of the explosion.

Had both his eardrums not been destroyed by the concussion, he would have heard the bullets screaming over his head. As it was, those bullets killed the people immediately following him.

For the men, women and children seated, their newly constructed temple of worship became their funeral pyre. The three simultaneous explosions collapsed the entire building down on those who were still alive, burying them in the rubble, while a steady stream of automatic fire killed the few who made it out. Only the Rabbi survived the massacre.

Yoshe, the young Russian student who had volunteered for guard duty, heard Kahil giving orders as they ran past the latrine. Furious with himself for allowing Arabs to infiltrate the settlement while in the bathroom, he now ran as fast as he could towards the synagogue, firing his gun into the air as he ran. Before he reached it, however, he felt the impact of the bullet strike his left leg. Rolling over behind one of the houses, he searched for the shooter. Despite the pain, he remained motionless, waiting for the man to make a move.

Minutes passed as the screams of the wounded died down, leaving an eerie silence. Suddenly, he saw a flash of light. The setting sun had reflected off something metallic 50 yards to his left. Then he saw the rifle barrel searching in his direction. Seconds went by before he finally got a glimpse of the man's head. Taking careful aim with his M-16, he drew a bead on the man's forehead then slowly pulled the trigger. Jacob saw through his sights the man's head explode as his body fell backwards.

Descent Into Paradise

Kahil, upon hearing the shots coming from behind him, assumed the last remaining guard was now dead. Walking over to the injured Rabbi, he hoisted him up on his shoulder. The Rabbi screamed whatever filthy oaths came to mind, but no matter how loud he yelled, he could not hear a word. Kahil dumped him onto the ground, beckoning two of his men to help hold the Rabbi down while he undid the man's belt, removed his boots, then his pants. Kahil unsheathed his own big hunting knife, flashing it across the Rabbi's face. Uttering some obscenities of his own, Kahil then reached down with his left hand to grab the Rabbi's testicles. With one swift stroke, he then cut them off, holding them in front of the Israeli's glazed eyes.

Pain seared through Rabbi Swartz's body as the big Arab cut him. Barely conscious and momentarily in shock, he felt something being stuffed into his mouth.

Kahil laughed with his men as they got up to leave. After one giant kick to the Rabbi's ribs, he wrote in the dirt. This is what happens to little Jew boys who build settlements on our land.

"Come on!" he yelled, "we need to get out of here before those houses blow."

Yoshe watched nervously as the terrorists knelt beside the body of their dead comrade. They looked around for the assailant, but, fortunately, it was getting dark with just a sliver of moon to light the evening sky. The young Russian watched them leave, happy to be alive but devastated by the fact he had allowed them to enter the settlement. Knowing from experience that a cloud of black smoke would instantly receive attention from the military patrols in the area, he decided to sit and just wait for help.

As he sat, he wondered what kind of demon would blow up innocent women and children as they sat in prayer? God should at least protect those who sit at his altar of worship. His mind began to wander as he thought of his own culpability. He had been the guard who had failed to warn his friends. Now those friends were all dead while he was still alive.

Poor Yoshe did not have long to dwell on those morbid thoughts, as the house just behind him was the first to explode. One by one, the painstaking efforts of the Rabbi and his followers went up in smoke.

CHAPTER 59

Bashir spent the morning finalizing travel plans for his trip to America. When his last call was finished, he finally turned his mind to the issue which had bothered him since she walked out that morning. It had to be done, he realized, there was no other option. Before taking a shower, he made the call.

Just after lunch, an elderly man walked through the hotel lobby into a small wood-paneled room where coffee and tea were served all day. There, in the corner, he found the Sheik reading a paper. Their meeting lasted only long enough for the elderly man to get his final instructions and to place a rather thick envelope into his jacket pocket.

"I think she plans to leave town shortly, and I want it done before we lose her, understood?"

The Sheik's guest rose to leave, assuring his host it would be handled immediately.

As she sat waiting at Harrods, Annabelle couldn't shake her premonition about her father. Apparently, he was not off with Shasa, as she had suspected, and normally he would call her if he were planning to be away any length of time. Thankfully, her morbid thoughts were interrupted by Shasa's arrival. Taking one look at her friend's face, however, told her something was amiss.

"My God, Shasa, what's wrong?"

Without answering, Shasa took a quick glance behind her, grabbing Annabelle by the hand.

"Quickly, come with me, I will explain everything when we are in the car."

Descent Into Paradise

The parked car had its engine running and rear door open as they jumped in. Without a word, Ehud, the Israeli security guard who had driven her to Harrods, headed straight towards the Embassy. Having already alerted the Embassy of their impending arrival, he drove them directly into the secure underground garage. On the short drive over to Kensington, Shasa told Annabelle she would explain everything once they were alone. Now, having been escorted by armed guards to that part of the building reserved for Mossad personnel only, they sat down to await the Director's arrival from Heathrow.

Poor Annabelle was bursting with questions when they finally sat down. "Shasa, what on Earth is going on here? I have been so worried about you."

"I will explain everything, but first I need to know if you've heard anything from your father?"

"No, I thought he might be with you. I was hoping that's why I hadn't heard anything from either of you this past week. I have been so worried about both of you. Please tell me what is happening? What are we doing here?"

"Just one more question before I answer yours. Where is Zev?"

"He left first thing this morning back to Santiago. That's one reason I wanted to reach you."

Forgetting her momentary shock, Annabelle could not resist showing off her left ring finger. Shasa, relieved Zev was safe and grateful for the short reprieve, now stared at a beautiful diamond and sapphire ring, immediately putting it all together.

"You and Zev are engaged? Oh Annabelle, how wonderful! Oh my God, I can't believe it. I am so happy for both of you! When did this happen?" Annabelle then launched into a detailed discussion of the past several days, her obvious joy supplanting her previous concerns about her father's wellbeing.

Descent Into Paradise

Before she could finish, however, the Director hustled in, apparently unaware of Annabelle's presence. Upon Shasa's introduction, the Director actually smiled as he greeted her.

"It is a pleasure finally meeting you. I have known your parents for many years and heard many wonderful things about you."

"Thank you, it is a pleasure meeting you as well."

The Director then asked if he could have a few moments alone with Shasa.

Omitting only her evening with Bashir, she gave him a full debriefing; her weekend in Hampshire, the Saudi Chief of Staff blowing her cover, his subsequent demise, and finally her encounter earlier that day.

"I just got a quick debriefing on the ride in. Apparently, you came within a few seconds of joining your young Saudi boss. A sniper had just killed one of our men and had you in his sights when Ehud shot him."

"How did you know I was in any danger?"

"You can thank your friend Major Megrid for that. Two days ago, he sent a message informing us your cover was blown and to send protection. Of course, I would have preferred hearing that from you, but apparently you did not see fit to inform anyone of such a minor issue."

Shasa, duly chastised, apologized. "When I got your message to meet, I assumed we could debrief then. Clearly, that was my mistake. In retrospect, I should have warned you earlier. Please forgive me."

"It is not a question of forgiveness, it is a question of survival. Fortunately for you, your good friend the Major covered for you. Just let it be a good lesson for the future. Shasa, I am pulling you out. You will fly back with me tomorrow. Now, I must get on a conference call. I want you to spend the night here. No calls, just tell the butler you will be sleeping over and to make a reservation for you on my flight to Israel in the morning."

Before she could reply, the phone rang. Judging by the look on his face, Shasa knew there was more bad news.

The coffin was brought to them by several of the security guards. It was addressed to Shasa but contained no return address. With a nod from the Director, the security guards cautiously opened the lid exposing the mutilated body of Lord Luxley, the Star of David burnt into his forehead.

"Do you know who is responsible for this?"

Shasa then explained her dinner with Luxley and his offer of help, which she had kindly refused. She went on to explain that she had been trying to reach him ever since that evening with no luck.

"So whoever killed the young Saudi probably killed Luxley as well. I assume, if they have possession of that folder, they also know your true identity. Given what you just told me about your alerting Farouk, I'm guessing the Sheik is involved. Would you agree?"

Somewhat taken back by this whole turn of events and her inevitable encounter with poor Annabelle, Shasa could only nod her head in agreement.

To the Director's credit, he took the responsibility of breaking the news to Annabelle, after which he took his leave.

"Oh Annabelle, I am so sorry."

In their mutual grief, Shasa decided to share with Annabelle everything: her adoption by Israeli parents after her own parents were killed, their subsequent deaths and her eventual recruitment by Mossad, her assignment here with the involvement of her father, and even her relationship with Zev. Through their tears of pain and loss, they bonded even closer.

"Without Zev," Shasa shared with her, "I doubt I would even be alive."

Annabelle chose to spend the night with Shasa at the Embassy. The next morning, they parted with the promise to all meet up as soon as possible to mourn the past and celebrate the future.

CHAPTER 60

JERUSALEM

Yani Weisberg woke up in a cold sweat. His alarm had not gone off. It was 07h30 and his job interview was in less than an hour. Panicked, he jumped out of bed and ran to the bathroom, condensing his morning routine in half. Running out the door, he glanced at his watch: 07h50. Yani ran for the bus stop, trying not to sweat. It would not do to appear disheveled in front of his prospective employer. Those thoughts were running through his head as he saw Bus Number 7, exhaust spewing out the tailpipe as it accelerated one block ahead of him.

"Please, light, turn red, please," he found himself yelling. Again he sprinted to try to catch up. "One red light, please, that's all I need," he kept repeating to himself as the sweat began to pour down his back while he kept pace with the bus, never quite catching it. Finally exhausted and drenched in sweat, he gave up. Sitting down on the curb with his head in his hands, he never saw the explosion. Knocked flat on the ground by the blast, bleeding from numerous cuts, Yani looked up half dazed to see debris scattered all over the sidewalk. Two blocks ahead of him stood a roaring inferno where Bus No. 7 had existed a moment before.

His driver, who was also to serve as his private bodyguard, escorted Yosef Meier from the hotel. Yosef, a career diplomat, had no use for such theatrics, but Israeli intelligence had picked up something about a potential kidnapping so, effective immediately, all Israeli diplomats traveling outside the country now had at least one security man detailed to them at all times.

Descent Into Paradise

Yosef didn't even like the looks of this man. Probably has a third grade education, more muscles than brains, he thought to himself as the driver shut his door behind him.

"We're going to the airport, I assume you have been told."

A grunt was his only response, but at least the car was heading in the right direction. Yosef pulled his briefcase onto his lap, pulling out the morning paper to read. He was halfway through it when the car stopped abruptly and the rear door flew open. Two men, masks covering their faces, reached in and pulled him bodily out of the car. While one pulled his arms behind him, the other, yelling something in Arabic, jammed a pistol in his mouth breaking his two front teeth.

"You scream, you die," he yelled in broken Hebrew.

Yosef was then dragged to a waiting taxi, thrown in the back seat, where a brute of a man, already seated, grabbed him with one giant paw. Smiling, he then threw his head against the back of the driver's seat, shattering his nose. Yosef lost consciousness, slumping to the floor.

Mossad Headquarters was in chaos. People were running in and out of the telex room to different offices while everyone was shouting.

"What the hell is going on?" yelled the Director as the latest telex was handed to him. Known for his cool demeanor under pressure, a string of curses emanated into the hallway outside his office, as his secretary headed for the ladies' room down the hall.

An hour later, an angry Prime Minister stared at his Defense Minister and the Director of Mossad, demanding an explanation.

"Mr. Prime Minister, we had no advance indications of anything unusual going on. We did receive one call from a secondary agent in Beirut saying he had heard some talk about a potential kidnapping but that was it. We even posted security personnel for our traveling diplomats."

"Very good work. It is comforting to see how well you train your security guards. I'm sure Yosef Meier would love to ring you personally right now. But he will not because your security guard drove him right into the hands of the PLO!"

"Our security guard was found an hour ago with a bullet hole in his forehead. That driver was one of the terrorists."

The Prime Minister, known for his sudden outbursts, apologized to his chief of intelligence. "I was out of line. I am sorry," was all he could muster in his defense.

"Gentlemen, we have a national crisis here. In the span of 48 hours, a security guard was shot dead in London, one of our senior diplomats has been abducted in broad daylight; a Rabbi has been castrated and his entire congregation killed, and now I have just received word that a dozen people are dead and 65 badly wounded in a suicide bombing in Jerusalem."

Shaking his head, the Prime Minister spoke in a somber voice, "We must not rest until we bring the perpetrators of these heinous crimes to justice." Looking across the table, he went on, "And I do not mean justice in a court of law. I mean the justice of Almighty God. We will send these men to their maker and let him decide their punishment. Understood?"

"Understood."

"Keep me apprised. I must attend an emergency cabinet meeting. Good day gentlemen."

CHAPTER 61

WASHINGTON DC
THE STATE DEPARTMENT

"Madame Secretary, the Israeli Ambassador and the Special Envoy for the PLO are both here, shall I send them in?"

"Please."

After the formalities were over, the Secretary of State wasted no time explaining the President's position.

"We will not tolerate this cycle of violence. This Administration wants a peace accord between the PLO and Israel, and we all know what it will take to accomplish that. A homeland for the Palestinians in exchange for a renunciation of violence by the PLO and full recognition of the State of Israel. At some point, gentlemen, you both are going to have to compromise if you want your children to stop dying. In the interim, we insist there be no further violence."

"Madame Secretary, I can assure you that no PLO members were involved in any of these incidents this past week."

"And I suppose you have no idea who could have perpetrated these criminal acts of violence against my countrymen?" asked the Ambassador from Israel.

"We have heard many rumors, Mr. Ambassador. The killers come from another country, possibly several other countries. They were not Palestinians, of that I can assure you."

"Madame Secretary, you cannot deny us the right to pursue and prosecute those responsible for these atrocities."

"On that point, Mr. Ambassador, you are correct. No civilized country in the world would deny you the right of justice. What I am saying, and please listen carefully, is that the United States will not tolerate any military reprisals against the Palestinians in response to the events of the past week. I reiterate that the only solution to this cycle of violence will be found around the negotiating table. Please convey my thoughts, and those of the President, to your respective leaders. Good day, gentlemen."

JERUSALEM

"That arrogant bitch couldn't locate Israel on a map. Who does she think she is, telling us what we can or cannot do? Are we, or are we not, a sovereign nation?"

"The Minister certainly makes a valid point," responded the Prime Minister. "But political realities being what they are, we cannot directly defy the express wishes of the United States. If we were to do so, it would be at our peril. This new President is very unpredictable, and I for one do not want to test him until we understand his thinking more clearly."

"Mr. Prime Minister, the way I interpret the text from our Ambassador, the American position clearly states that they will not tolerate any military reprisal against the Palestinians. I find no reference to their vetoing a military strike against another country."

Looking at both men, the Prime Minister responded, "Director, please give us the benefit of your latest analysis."

"Our best guess at this point is that all three incidents, the bombing in Jerusalem, the shooting in London, and the kidnapping of our envoy in Beirut, were ordered and carried out by one group."

"Does that mean the PLO was or was not involved in any of these incidents?"

"While we do not know for sure, it is my belief it was not the Palestinians. They simply have never demonstrated the ability to coordinate anything of this magnitude and none of our many agents heard anything about any of these incidents."

"Then who?"

"The Iranians are one possibility, as they actively support Hezbollah and others against us, but while they support these groups, they may have not participated directly."

"If not the Iranians, who?"

"I wish I knew. I have my hunches, but right now I am afraid to say that is all they are."

"Mr. Director, find those responsible and report back to me as soon as you have anything credible."

"I can assure you it is the Agency's top priority and we will find those responsible, that I promise you."

ARLINGTON, VIRGINIA
THE PENTAGON

"Major Watson, General Bradley would like to see you."

"Tell the General I will be right over."

"Yes sir."

Pete, having just read his latest telexes, could guess what the General wanted to discuss.

"Pete, my boy, sit down. Have you read the latest intelligence report?"

"Yes sir. It would appear someone would like to disrupt the Oslo peace initiative."

"Major, that probably is the understatement of the year. Did you read about that poor Rabbi? They stuck his testicles in his mouth while he was still alive. Then, the bastards just left him there to rot in the sun. Jesus, Pete, what the hell are we dealing with?"

"War, General, you've just been sitting behind a desk too long, if you don't mind my being blunt."

"Hell, Pete, you're probably right. Maybe I'm just getting too old for this game."

"No, General, you're just getting too civilized. It's funny, but the longer I'm in this position, the less I like it."

Sitting back in his chair, Bradley looked over at his young protégé. "Pete, most of us come into the military for the right reasons. We want to defend our country and prove to ourselves that we will be honorable soldiers worthy of other men's respect. The problem is, our job is to kill and eventually that eats away at you. Killing is not natural, that's why we train. Some of us get lucky and never have to experience death first hand. But men like you become victims of their own success.

"If you are cursed with a conscience, then you are in double jeopardy. All I can say, Pete, is your country needs men like you. And Generals like me need men like you, so don't be getting any ideas of running back to Maine with that pretty Israeli agent, at least not yet. Now, give me your thinking on this craziness."

"To begin with, I don't believe Arafat is behind this."

"Really. Why?"

"For one thing, it's too well planned. Second, none of the usual suspects are taking credit. Third, that stunt of blowing up the commuter bus in broad daylight was pure public relations. Whoever ordered that wanted to incense the Israeli public."

"In other words, whoever ordered these raids wanted Israel to retaliate. Why would Arafat want to jeopardize those talks when he finally has a sympathetic ear at the White House?"

"Exactly, General. No, I think we have a new player in the mix, and I'm afraid they may be a lot more competent than anyone we've seen to date."

"Not a pleasant thought. Have we heard anything from Mossad?"

"No, but I'm sure they are working late these days. If I'm right, they have a major unknown in their mix."

"While they sort things out, Major, let's get the men ready."

CHAPTER 62

Zev arrived back in Santiago the next morning, having flown all night. That very afternoon, he went to give Juan the news. Ricardo came out to greet him instead, as Juan was in Mexico on business. Having brought him up to date on his dealings with Bashir and the missiles, he waited to the very end to tell him of his decision.

"Ricardo, I am afraid I have upsetting news for you."

Ricardo, looking concerned, asked, "What might that be, Zev?"

"I have fallen in love with a woman in London, and I have just proposed to her."

Relieved, Ricardo asked, "Where is the bad news, Señor? This calls for a celebration. Congratulations, Major."

"I am afraid you do not understand. We have decided to live in England, which means I must ask you to release me from my obligations here."

A frown now replaced the smile on Ricardo's tan features. "I see. I would have thought a wife should follow her husband. This is upsetting news, then. When do you contemplate leaving, Major?"

"As soon as you deem it acceptable. The defense force is in excellent shape, but I will stay as long as it takes to satisfy you and Juan that everything is in order."

"That is most honorable, as well as most appreciated. I will alert Juan of this news and call you with his response."

The following afternoon, Ricardo came to visit. "I have just spoken with Juan who is understandably quite concerned about your departure, as am I. Having said that, we both understand and appreciate all you have done for the family since your arrival. Therefore, I am pleased to inform you of our acceptance of your departure and ask only that you make sure everything is in proper order regarding our proposed defenses against an American invasion. Juan is most concerned that your proposed departure could put us in jeopardy."

"Let me assure you, even without me, the safety of these grounds is in excellent hands. This compound is virtually impregnable to anything except an incoming missile. Allow me to show you exactly what I mean."

Having completed the tour, for the first time, Ricardo could well appreciate the job Zev had done training his men. Certain people, he knew, designed their job so as to make themselves indispensable. Some were excellent teachers, allowing others the responsibility of command. Zev was clearly one of the latter group.

"Major, you may proceed as you deem reasonable. We have appreciated your efforts, and I speak for Juan, as well as myself, when I tell you we will miss your company."

Shasa, back in Tel Aviv, sat on her couch watching television while enjoying a simple dinner. It was difficult to digest all that had transpired in the past several days. She pictured a professional sniper outside her flat in London, knowing full well Bashir ordered the hit. Then, she couldn't help thinking of poor Archie, who would still be alive if not for her foolishness. Now, as if that were not enough, she was being ordered to kill her closest friend. A man, she thought, who had done nothing but serve his country faithfully his entire career. She could never do it, she knew that much, but, as she finished her soup, she stared up at the ceiling in hopes of some divine intervention. Who was she? An angel of death? Lord knew, it followed her wherever she went.

Descent Into Paradise

Her thoughts were interrupted by a news flash showing the carnage from the suicide bombing in Jerusalem. Just then, the phone rang.

"Shasa, how are you feeling?" asked the Director.

"Dreadful, sir, I am just now watching the news of that bus being blown up.

"I'm afraid it gets even worse. Not only has one of our diplomats been abducted in Beirut, apparently the American CIA Station Chief in Beirut has just been kidnapped as well. Moments ago, I received a call from General Bradley. He and Major Watson are arriving here the day after tomorrow. I would like you to attend the meeting."

"I will be there, sir."

Pete was just finishing lunch in his office when La Bota returned his call.

"Bota, I wanted to share with you some news we heard in Tel Aviv. The Israelis have picked up some very interesting intelligence concerning our friends in Chile. It would appear your take on Biscayne Federal Savings and Loan is correct. According to what we just heard, certain Arabs are, in fact, receiving credit cards and lines of credit from that bank without the need to provide any formal identification. We need to keep a sharp eye on that bank for sure. I would suggest you to keep a photographic record of any Arabs going in or out of their banking lobby."

"Interesting. I will get right on it after we hang up. Just so you know, we are also getting copies of all residential leases executed with any Arabs near or around the Fountain Blue. We assume, since we know Rios owns a home nearby, that these same Arabs may be using that as their base."

They then spoke of Madonna and what fate lay in store for her.

"Pete, I know you have struck up a relationship with her, but please be careful."

"Thanks, I appreciate the friendly advice. As you know, she's most enticing, but not someone I plan on taking home to mother."

La Bota was relieved that Pete was not getting serious, as he and Arturo had learned a good bit about Madonna and her rather sordid history with men.

"Let's concentrate our efforts first on taking out Rios once and for all, then we can deal with your girlfriend. She is not going anywhere, that I can assure you."

General Bradley had asked Pete to join him at the Officer's Lounge for a drink before dinner. There he told Pete about Riordan.

"I hate to upset our evening before we've even ordered, but I have just been informed someone has kidnapped Bill Riordan in Beirut."

Pete looked stunned. "You don't mean Mary's husband, the CIA Station Chief over there?"

"Yep, one and the same."

"What's your thinking? We're getting ready to launch down south, are we going to go into Beirut also?"

"I don't know yet. It depends upon what the White House decides. They have some interesting choices to make. Will they continue to keep the Israelis at bay, or will they now allow Israel to retaliate for these latest raids? Or, do we retaliate for them? I don't pretend to know the answer."

CHAPTER 63

Colonel Mir walked into the room as they tied Riordan, still gagged to a metal chair.

"So Mr. Riordan, what's it to be, the easy way or the hard way? You can give us the information we desire, in which case you will soon be home with the lovely Mrs. Riordan, or you can play the hero. As we will get it out of you one way or the other, you choose. One thing I can assure you, if you do not tell me what I want to know, you will never see your wife again."

He undid the gag in Riordan's mouth to get his answer. Bill looked at him and spat out, "Fuck you, you little prick."

"I see. An interesting turn of phrase as little prick was the description your wife used to describe you when I slept with her in Shatila years ago. Or didn't she tell you about that? Oh yes, we had a wonderful time together until those two apes came to take her away. A shame really, she was quite good in bed."

Bill's expression gave him away. Mary had never slept with him after she returned. Now, he began to wonder.

"Leave my wife out of this. You want something from me, forget it. Torture me, do whatever you want but remember, harm me and you'll sign your own death warrant. The United States won't rest until you're dead or captured."

"Very macho, Mr. Riordan. Except you forget one thing. I blew up your vaunted Marines years ago and I'm still here. I am on Mossad's most wanted list, yet here I am with you. The fact is, Mr. Riordan, I am not that easy to kill. Now, I am short on time. I want to know what you know about Sheik Mohammed Bashir?"

"Nothing. I have never heard of him."

Looking very skeptical, he went on. "Very well, have you heard of a camp in Iran called Murat?"

"No."

Turning to the two men in the room, Mir simply told them they had twelve hours to change Mr. Riordan's mind about cooperating. Then he informed them privately to be sure that Riordan could still talk when he returned; he wanted answers.

CHAPTER 64

TEL AVIV

Shasa knew she shouldn't call Annabelle, but she had to see how she was holding up.

"Annabelle, it's Shasa, I am so sorry I haven't called sooner. How are you?"

"Not to worry, love. Having listened to the news, I understand completely. I am holding up just fine, thanks. I really had no idea what my father was involved in, but I am learning quickly. I must say, the old man was really quite a clever sod. He has actually left me quite a tidy sum of assets, God love him. I am so glad you rang me up as I had no idea how to reach you. I am coming down your way tomorrow for the funeral. In his will, he requested to be buried next to my mother. It is all being arranged for early next week. How can I reach you when I'm there?"

Shasa gave her the number and said if she were still in the country, she would gladly attend.

"Wonderful, thank you. Oh dear, I almost forgot to tell you, I will be leaving there to go to Miami to meet Zev. We are staying at the Fountain Blue Hotel right on the beach. I have reserved a room for you under our name, so please come if you can."

"Annabelle, I would love nothing more. Let me see what I can arrange at this end."

"Say no more. Take care of your business, and hopefully we'll see each other tomorrow. Please try to come to Miami if you can."

Pete went back to his quarters at Fort Bragg to find a note from the General instructing him to pack his gear ASAP. They had been ordered to get Riordan out fast.

Descent Into Paradise

Safely on board their flight, the General started to brief Pete.

"Sorry for the abbreviated note, things are moving rather quickly. Apparently, this Riordan fellow is a walking encyclopedia of intelligence. Unfortunately for us, and Mr. Riordan, the rumor is that an Iranian named Mir is involved. He's the one suspected of blowing up the Marine Corp's barracks back in '82. The Israelis would dearly love to get their hands on him._

"Mossad thinks they know where Riordan is being held, and they want Mir worse than we do."

"What's the plan?"

"We will meet up with the Israelis on the Coral Sea tomorrow morning. From there, we will insert you into Beirut once we can confirm the location. If you can nab this Mir alive, all the better, if not, so be it. One way or another, it's imperative we get to Riordan before he talks."

Pete closed his eyes, picturing his last visit to Beirut. He remembered Shasa putting her own life in jeopardy to save them. Somehow, he could picture every detail as though it were yesterday. Then his mind wandered back to Maine and their time together. What went wrong? We were so close, and then we slowly grew apart. Distance yes, but it was something more. God knows I wanted to marry her. She knew that, yet she never could commit. There must be something else there. He wondered if she would be on the carrier tonight, before falling into a deep sleep.

A call came from the Director's office ordering a change of plans. Shasa was now directed to pack her bags for a potential combat mission and ordered to get herself to Palmachim Air Force Base. There, a US Navy plane would transport her on board the USS Coral Sea.

Descent Into Paradise

Shasa hung up, thinking about Pete. Surely, he would be there if they were planning to go in after the hostage. Given his previous assignments, she assumed he would be the obvious choice. She had not seen him since their dinner with Zev. Why had she let it go this long? Why was she so afraid? She knew she was attractive to men, but why did she treat them so callously? Was that her karma, not to be able to have a lasting relationship? She was now in her thirties. If she ever wanted a family, time was beginning to run short. She began to wonder if Pete would still want her.

Just as they exited their aircraft, the Admiral appeared on deck. He had aged since Pete had last seen him but his greeting was effusive. "Major Watson," he smiled as he came up. "Son, I'm proud to have you back on board." Saluting General Bradley, he went on, "George, it's wonderful to see you again."

"Admiral, you've got to find a better way to bring your guests on board. I'm way too old for this."

"Oh come on George, we'll get you a hot bath and a stiff drink, that ought to fix you up."

Pete followed them up to the Admiral's quarters. He had forgotten about Shasa in all the excitement, but there she was sitting on the couch as they entered. For Pete, she was the only person in the room. He just stood there watching her get up, that radiant smile telling him everything was alright between them.

"Major Watson, are you alright?" Pete realized the Admiral was making introductions. He tore his gaze off her and went through the motions of shaking hands and saying the right things.

"The briefing is scheduled for 18h30 in the situation room. Until then, please feel free to use the main dining hall if you're hungry. My staff officer will show you to your quarters. Major, your team arrived this morning. I believe they are in the same quarters you used on your last visit."

Pete thanked the Admiral as he quietly followed Shasa out of the room. Just outside the door, he whispered, "Where are you staying?"

She handed him the card they had issued her. "Here, come when you can."

As a consequence of her being an agent of a foreign country, Shasa had her own private quarters, a rare luxury onboard a USS naval vessel, even one as large as the Coral Sea. She waited patiently for an hour before she realized Pete might not come. Finally, there was a knock on the door.

Pete took her into his arms, squeezing her so hard she thought her ribs were fractured. His first instinct was to carry her to bed, but then he realized she was not Madonna.

"Pete, sit down, we need to talk." Reluctantly he let her go and sat down.

Subconsciously, he found himself comparing the two. While one was light skinned with blonde hair and sparkling blue eyes, the dark skinned brown haired beauty now looking at him was clearly the only one who had captured his heart. What to do, he thought. As much as he wanted to trust and believe in her, the bluish green King Solomon stone he had given her as a present sat staring back at him, just as it had on another chest in Miami several weeks ago.

"Pete, what I am about to tell you could easily get me killed."

Seeing the stress written on her face, he realized he may finally hear whatever information Mossad had been deliberately keeping back. Only now, he may never be able to use it, for fear of compromising Shasa.

Descent Into Paradise

"Hold on, before you go any further. May I assume you are going to divulge secrets about your Agency which have been deliberately kept from us?"

She nodded in the affirmative.

Pete, looking straight into her eyes, gave her one big caveat. "Before you say anything, please understand this first. If this information puts my men in danger, I will not agree to withhold it."

Her love and respect for him only increased as he was clearly unwilling to compromise his integrity, even at the price of losing her.

"Agreed. I would never put you in that position."

"Let's hear it then." He leaned back in the chair and waited, his face expressionless. Shasa talked for over an hour nonstop. She began with what had happened to poor Zev in Beirut, his discharge from the Army and subsequent recruitment by Mossad, who forced him to transfer to Santiago. Then, she explained her first meeting with Juan Rios in Tel Aviv. It was after midnight when she finished by telling him about her assignment to kill Zev and her subsequent invitation from Annabelle to join them in Miami.

Pete, in utter disbelief at what he had just heard, sat still, silently consumed by rage at the incredible duplicity of his erstwhile friends and allies. His absolute disgust must have been evident as he just silently looked at her. It was only her mention of Zev which elicited a response. The mere thought of her being ordered to kill him, under any possible pretext, was literally beyond his comprehension. All he could mutter was, "How could they possibly expect you to kill someone who has been like a brother to you? Why not use one of their professionals? God knows you bastards have enough!"

Her silence slowly penetrated his tired mind. As much as he

had always wanted to picture her as an innocent young orphan, helplessly caught up in something she did not understand, he now had to remind himself of that day in Shatila. She wouldn't leave with them because she had gone there deliberately to kill Abu. For her own personal reasons yes, but she had gone on a specific assignment as a Mossad agent. Looking at this beautiful young woman lying on her bed, he wanted to ask how many men had she killed, and how many of those had been in her bed before they died?

Depressed, he got up slowly, his only response being, "Shasa, we have a briefing in four hours. I need to get some rest. Let's finish this tomorrow."

The sadness in his eyes told her more than mere words. As she listened to the door shut quietly, she knew a confession of all her sins was no longer necessary.

Riordan woke up barely able to see. The pain returned as he tried to sit. They had beaten him with rubber truncheons until he had mercifully passed out. His eyes were swollen almost shut, but he could still see he was lying in a pool of his own blood. He began to wonder if they would have the audacity to kill him. His answer then walked in the door.

"Clean him up, then put him back in the chair. I'll return in ten minutes."

Mir came back and handed him a cup of coffee, adding, "Good morning Mr. Riordan. I trust you enjoyed a comfortable night. Now, if you will kindly answer my questions, we can return you to the Embassy with no further inconvenience."

Riordan sipped the coffee, the hot liquid painful as it passed his cracked lips, but just holding a hot mug in his hands and smelling the rich aroma helped soothe his nerves. He looked at this nice looking, rather elegant Iranian, who was talking as if nothing had happened. It was then he began to question if he would ever leave this room alive.

CHAPTER 65

The Director had sent one of his top operatives to join Shasa on board the carrier. They laid out their intelligence concisely, ending with their belief that Riordan was being held in the basement of an apartment building near the airport.

"That building is under the direct control of Hezbollah, which leads us to conclude a certain Colonel Mir may be involved. He is Iranian by birth, but now believed to be associated with the Islamic Brotherhood."

Pete interjected, "So you now believe this is not a PLO kidnapping?"

"Correct, our agents inside the PLO are unaware of any abduction plans. Something this big would certainly have crossed their desks. We also have a well-placed mole inside the Hezbollah faction. That is where we are getting this information. Colonel Mir, gentleman, is a very nasty operative. He will not hesitate to torture or even kill your man. He is ruthless and clever enough to still be alive. My suggestion is that time is running out. Any chance of getting the hostage out alive will diminish the longer he's there."

Pete looked at Shasa. "Can you provide us transportation once we land?"

"Yes, we have two vans available with Arab drivers who know the city intimately."

"Tell them to stand by for tonight. We will go in by boat at midnight, then we will need those vans to get to the target. Once there, we will go in hard and fast, then retrace our steps back here. We will avoid using any of our normal channels, as they will be looking for us to come in from the air. Gentlemen, we will transfer over to the USS Forestall at 22h00. Have all your gear ready to go by then. Now I suggest you all get some rest."

Shasa followed Pete out of the room. "May we finish our discussion from last night?"

Nodding, he led her out to the observation deck. The breeze was clear and fresh as they watched the yellow-jacketed crews running across the flight deck.

"Reminds me of home, the smell of the ocean, the whitecaps rolling endlessly towards the horizon." Pete took a deep breath.

"Pete, I'm so sorry I never told you before. Maybe I was ashamed of my behavior; maybe I was just terrified you would not want me as a woman if you knew."

Pete thought of Madonna as he looked at her in silence. Deep in his heart, he knew where he belonged, he just couldn't say the words.

"Are you coming in with us tonight?"

She looked down at the deck, realizing she was not going to get a simple answer. "My orders are to help facilitate this hostage rescue in any way possible. If you wish me to join you, I am fully equipped to do so. It is your call, Major."

Pete didn't know why he was acting this way. Maybe he wanted to punish her. Maybe he needed her to feel as guilty as he did for not telling her about his little exploits. Whatever the reason, he left telling her to be ready by 22h00 for the transfer.

Riordan finished his coffee as Mir gave him one last chance to answer his questions. He thought about his marriage, his career, his own self-esteem. "Fuck you," was all he said.

Mir's eyes narrowed as he got up. Walking to the door, he whispered something to the guard then left.

Descent Into Paradise

Zev met with Estoban, who had flown down from Miami, before addressing the troops.

"I will miss you, old friend. Is it true you're getting married?" Estoban was genuinely upset over Zev's departure.

"Yes, I finally found a woman to settle down with, but I will miss you also. You have a first class fighting force here. I would hate to be opposing you. Just keep a sharp eye on the electronic perimeter and keep your men close. Let the machines warn you, then you can counter attack in force. Remember, they will come from the air in small fast helicopters. They can rain down bullets such as you've never seen. You must take out those birds before they get within range. Put your best men on those missiles. If you let them land, there will be hell to pay. I leave you with one piece of advice, do not let them hit the ground alive."

"Major, I only wish that you could be here to see those gringos fry. Do not fear, they will all leave here in small pieces."

Zev patted Estoban on the shoulder as he walked out to tell the troops of his imminent departure.

CHAPTER 66

Having taken on the new arrivals from the carrier, the Captain of the USS Forestall brought his destroyer closer inshore. His orders were to place his ship in a position to put Major Watson and his men ashore at 23h00 and be there for their return sometime after midnight.

Lieutenant Fred Fielding had night duty on the lower deck for the third time this month. Unable to keep his mouth shut when he had too much to drink, Fielding had mouthed off to one of his superiors on their last shore leave and this extra night duty had been the result. Half asleep at 23h00, Fielding almost fell overboard as he watched the gunnery officer lead a procession of five Palestinians to where the mail boat had been loading the ship's mail.

Twenty minutes later, the mail boat eased alongside its berth to begin unloading the mail pouches of the fleet into vans so that the mail could be delivered to the airport and flown stateside. All the vans were lined up at the dock. All but one went directly to the airport.

The driver of the last van carefully checked his rearview mirror for any tails. He drove cautiously from the harbor toward the outskirts of the city in the direction of the airport. At this hour, he was unlikely to run into any roadblocks, but, as added insurance, he carried several thousand dollars of cash. The trip took only 30 minutes. Knocking three times on the rear of the cab when they had reached their destination, he heard the van door open and his cargo depart. The five Palestinians walked slowly to the street corner, entering an all-night diner. At this hour, only a few drunks were trying to eat their way sober. They never noticed the men as they made their way to the restrooms.

Pete quickly disrobed, as did the others. Putting on their night goggles, they made their way over to the back entrance. Directly across the street, two men stood guard on the sidewalk. Pete motioned to his Sergeant to take them out. He did not need to say silently. A knife across the throat made no noise.

Once inside, they ran down the steps. Pete could smell the corpse before he saw it. The door off the hall was open. Two men were drinking and laughing when Lieutenant White pulled the trigger on his automatic pistol. The hollow core bullets exploded upon impact, knocking them both off their chairs. Their twitching bodies were then shoved in a corner.

Pete moved over to the corpse lying on the floor. He turned it over, almost retching from the smell. Riordan's mutilated face looked back at him.

"Let's get him out of here. Call those vans, we're heading back to the ship."

Back aboard the carrier, Pete gave his report to Bradley and Brewster.

"General, I will send the body to the Embassy for a proper funeral. Will you be needing any further assistance from us?" inquired the Admiral.

"No thank you, Admiral. Whatever comes next, it's not going to take place here. If you can arrange transportation back to a decent runway, we can take a proper plane home."

CHAPTER 67

Abu and Moussa moved through customs without incident. They took a cab directly to Biscayne Federal Bank. As instructed, they met with their contact. Having handed him their Saudi passports, they waited while he got up to fetch a package.

"Gentlemen, I'm sorry to keep you waiting. I believe this envelope contains everything you requested. Would you please take a minute to check it out in case something is missing? This way you won't have to make another trip."

Abu carefully examined the contents: two Visa credit cards, ten thousand dollars in crisp new bills, keys to the safe house, and finally a note of introduction from the bank addressed: To Whom it May Concern.

They got a cab to take them to the safe house, which turned out to be within walking distance of the target's hotel. Tucked in a secluded residential neighborhood, it was a perfect location for their mission. In the rear of the property; a small speedboat lay alongside the dock, the keys in the ignition. After the hit, they had been instructed to take the boat out the inland waterway through the cut to reach the ocean. There, one mile out, a cigarette boat would be waiting to bring them to Havana.

USS CORAL SEA

Pete went to Shasa's cabin shortly before their scheduled departure. She was at her desk when he knocked.

"Come in."

"Shasa, I came to finish our conversation."

"Sit down, Pete, you're making me nervous."

"Shasa, from the very beginning, you've been aware of my feelings towards you, and, while my feelings haven't changed, I just can't go on this way. I would have climbed mountains to marry you once. Now, I am tired of waiting, tired of being lied to, tired of being lonely. I want to share my life with someone special and hopefully one day have a real family."

Pete took a deep breath before he continued, "Shasa, for your own sanity, you need to decide who you are and what you really want in life. If it's revenge, then I'm confident your boss can provide you with multiple opportunities. Maybe enough deaths will somehow satisfy you. For me, revenge is about the past. Life is about the future. I am moving on, and I pray, for your sake, you will too. If I am still available, great. If not, then maybe it just wasn't meant to be."

Heading for the door, he looked wistfully over his shoulder. "Sometimes, I wonder why I love someone who doesn't even like herself?" He then walked out without waiting for a reply.

Zev arrived at Miami's International Airport just prior to the arrival of the British Airways flight from London. Annabelle was one of the first passengers to come through the Arrivals gate. Seeing Zev, she flew into his arms.

"Zev, oh, how I missed you," she cried.

He had just put her down when someone tapped him on the shoulder. A distinguished Arab gentleman stood behind him.

"Sheik Bashir, what are you doing in Miami?" Zev asked in total surprise.

"I was about to ask you the same question, but, having flown with your lovely lady all the way from London, I now know why."

"Are you here for pleasure or business?" Zev couldn't help asking.

Descent Into Paradise

"Unfortunately business. And you? Are you mixing the two or just pleasure?"

Looking at Annabelle, Zev responded quickly, "Pure pleasure. Annabelle and I are planning to get married very shortly."

"Congratulations are then in order. Where are you staying?"

"The Fountain Blue, we will be all there week."

"I will ring you up if I get a chance."

Annabelle almost spat as she pulled Zev towards the exit.

"I hate that man! What absolute gall! If he dares call, I absolutely refuse to see him, understood?"

Zev hadn't really spoken to her at length about her father's death as she had been very busy dealing with all his financial affairs and, of course, his burial. She had honored his wish to be buried next to his wife in Tel Aviv. It had been her one and only trip there and seeing her mother's grave for the first time had made it even more emotional. Zev never questioned her about what had happened, but he now had his first clue.

TEL AVIV

As exhausted as she was, Shasa couldn't fall asleep. Lying in bed, eyes wide open, her thoughts floated back to Ben Ami. She could hear her father's voice in her ear telling her lovingly, "Shasa, life is for the living, so either get busy living or get busy dying."

He now was dead, and she began to wonder if, somewhere along the way, she had died as well.

The next day, right after lunch, the Director called her into his office to give his final instructions.

Descent Into Paradise

MIAMI BEACH

Arturo Sneider instructed his detectives to follow the taxi leaving the bank. This was the third time they had a positive ID on Arabs going into Biscayne Federal. This time looked more promising, as the suspects had arrived by cab and now were leaving the same way.

"Report back to me when you get an address."

Zev and Annabelle had checked in to a lovely suite with an ocean view and a cozy balcony filled with pots of geraniums, a small table, and two deck chairs.

"Oh love, this sun feels so wonderful."

Zev just looked at her with a devilish grin, commenting that her beautiful white skin would get burnt very quickly if they went down to the pool at this time of the day. When asked if he had any other suitable suggestions, they both laughed as he quickly pulled back the bedspread.

"Well then, I guess the sun will just have to wait."

"Bota, I'm coming down to see you. What's your schedule tomorrow?"

"For you, Pete, it's wide open. In fact, I was planning on calling you. It seems two Arabs came into Biscayne Federal yesterday, arriving in a taxi from the airport. They left minutes later carrying a large envelope. We tracked them to a very posh house just across the inland waterway from the Fountain Blue."

"My! My! Interesting. Let's discuss it when I see you. How about lunch tomorrow?"

"You're on. Give me your flight number and someone will pick you up."

Descent Into Paradise

Shasa landed in Miami very late that same night, and by the time she reached the hotel, it was well after midnight so she just unpacked and went to bed. Still on Israeli time, she woke up very early, deciding to take a run on the deserted beach before breakfast. Lost in thought, she didn't notice the dark handsome man running up behind her.

"I would recognize that good looking bottom anywhere in the world," said an amused voice.

"Zev," she laughed, stopping for a moment, "is this how you picked up girls in Haifa? Trailing them on the beach until they were too tired to run away?"

"Absolutely. But, I must admit not one of them could match you from the rear, or the front for that matter. When did you get in?"

"Very late last night, I was going to call you after breakfast."

"Come on, let's finish our run, then we'll go surprise Annabelle."

They talked and laughed all the way back to the hotel. Annabelle was thrilled to hear Shasa had come. She promised to hurry to meet them at the pool for breakfast. Once she arrived, Zev remained about an hour, by which time he realized he was totally superfluous to the conversation so he excused himself to go read the paper.

After breakfast, the girls announced that they were going shopping. He graciously declined an offer to join them, agreeing to meet for lunch back at the hotel. Zev couldn't remember the last time he had done nothing all day so he decided to buy a book and sit by the pool until the girls came back.

Bota picked up Pete at the airport, which gave him the excuse to eat at his favorite restaurant on Henry Cabot's dime. They discussed in depth Rios and his seemingly new strategic alliance with the Arabs. They were in total agreement that the recent string of events would culminate in something much grander, and they were both of the opinion that something would take place on American soil.

"Speaking of which, I got a call from one of my people at the Fountain Blue the other day. He told me Estoban was in the hotel bar last week."

"You're joking?"

"I wish I were. He even took a picture for me."

Pulling a Polaroid out of his jacket pocket, he handed it over.

"Interesting. Was he meeting someone there?"

"As a matter of fact, he was. According to my source, he had a drink with none other than our beautiful informant."

"No. How could that be? Are you sure they know who Estoban is? Maybe it was someone else."

"Hold on, Pete. Allow me to play detective for a moment. Assuming my friend is right, we now have Estoban in town meeting with Madonna at the very same time two suspicious Arabs arrive in town who happen to be staying at a home belonging to a corporation which we highly suspect is controlled by Juan Rios. Then, we hear these two Arabs are scouting out the hotel where Madonna is staying. Since I am not a big believer in coincidence, I would suggest these are not random events, but rather part of a larger picture; one which, quite frankly, has not yet come into focus, at least for me."

"I can't argue with your logic, Bota, something is going down, and I suggest one of us best figure out what it is before it blows up in our face."

"Agreed. Why don't you see if your girlfriend is willing to shed any light on this, and I will get back to my source to see if they know anything else which may prove useful. By the way, how long are you staying?"

"I go back the day after tomorrow. Then, confidentially, we're heading south of the border for a little cookout."

Annabelle came out to the pool all excited, running over to where Zev was reading under an umbrella. With a great smile, she gave him her news. "We've found the perfect wedding dress."

Zev untangled himself from his fiancée to mutter, "Is it low cut and very short?"

"Men, they have the mental capacity for one subject only and even that becomes hazy after orgasm."

Zev pulled her down beside him. "Darling, you should listen to yourself, then picture our early days at your flat in London. Then, we'll see who has the mental capacity for what."

Annabelle snuggled beside him, remembering fondly those nights of wild abandon. "Zev, I think you're getting burned. Let's get you out of the sun."

"Where's Shasa?"

"She went up to her room for a rest. She said she would come down and meet us here later."

Madonna awoke with a roaring hangover. She was getting too old to go out with these youngsters, too much tequila on top of too much sex. That Cuban was like a machine, she smiled, how many times had they made love? She was sore thinking about it.

Reluctantly, she got out of bed, took two aspirin then put on her bikini. She longed for a hot cup of coffee. Today, I am going to look for a man, she decided. Boys were fun but not very intriguing. She needed a challenge and lifeguards did not fit that bill.

Pete, having already checked in, came straight down to the pool looking for her. He didn't have to wait very long for her arrival. Immediately, the waiters were vying for her attention as they delivered her coffee and pastry. He had to admire her. She was no longer a young woman, but she could have any male she desired. He waited out of her view until she had settled down to read the morning paper. Obviously, she was just starting her day, although it was now 14h00. She must be keeping some late hours, he thought.

Finally, he couldn't wait any longer.

"Pete darling, when did you get in? Here, sit down and kiss me before I think you are just a dream."

"I'm just happy to find you alone for once."

She smiled as he leaned over to give her a kiss. "I have all the waiters and lifeguards totally mesmerized, it's the men I'm missing. The strong silent types whom never call to let me know they still love me. I crave their attention, yet they don't give me any."

"I think you're looking in the wrong places."

"Really, where should I be looking?"

Pete held out his room key. "I would suggest room number 524 for a start. I hear you may find someone who will give you all you can handle."

"Well then, maybe I shouldn't keep him waiting, he might disappear on me."

They walked away from the pool hand in hand, oblivious to the unhappy glares from Madonna's entourage.

Pete let Madonna undress him as she stood in her high-heels wearing only her tiny string bikini. He gently put his arms under her, carrying her to bed. Her body was well oiled, filling his senses with the aroma of coconuts. He laid her on the bed and began to massage her. Madonna groaned with pleasure, arching her back towards him, begging him to take her.

Trying to restrain himself, her urgings proved too much. Afterwards, they lay silently until their breathing came back to normal. Madonna reached up to kiss him. "I can't remember the last time I had multiple orgasms. Pete, will you take me with you when you leave. I can't stand being here without you."

"I wish I could, but I seriously doubt you would be very happy joining me. When I leave here, I will go to an Army barracks. No pool, no young lifeguards to rub suntan oil into your parched skin, no room service. No my dear, you are far better off right here."

"Pete, I'm being serious. Please take me with you!"

Pete propped his head up on his elbow as he gazed into her beautiful blue eyes. Would he take this woman with him to settle down? God knows he had become sexually addicted to her, but what did they have in common beyond a bed and a good orgasm? Pete's thoughts then floated back to the carrier. He had left Shasa without so much as a goodbye. What was he thinking? The fact was, he really didn't know. Now, this whole issue of a meeting Estoban thoroughly confused him. Why ruin a good night of sex, he thought. That conversation could wait until morning.

"Do I take your silence as a no, or I'm thinking?" Madonna asked.

"I'm thinking of what you would do as I travel the world killing bad guys and rescuing beautiful women from country brothels. Would you really be happy attached to a soldier on soldier's pay?"

"Pete, I need to be with a man, and quite frankly there are precious few left." As they talked, her hands began to massage him back to life. "And what would he do without his Madonna to take care of him?" she whimpered.

It was an hour later when they made it back to the pool.

Shasa was busy talking to Zev when she saw them walking past hand in hand. Pete had not seen them, as his head was turned in the other direction. Pete looked happy and relaxed, but all she thought of was her stiletto as she watched Madonna.

Descent Into Paradise

Zev followed her eyes, exclaiming, "Jesus Christ, I don't believe what I am seeing." When questioned by Shasa, he explained. Now, it was Shasa who couldn't believe what she was being told.

"How does he even know her?"

"I have no idea. I didn't think she was even alive."

"I am putting a stop to this right now," Shasa spat as she began to get up.

Zev grabbed her, pulling her back down.

"No, little one, you are going to stay right here until I talk to him. I need to understand this as much as you. Why don't you go up to your room before he sees you? Let me find out what's going on, then I'll fill you in. There is obviously some explanation to all this, but, for the life of me, I have no idea what it could be!"

Abu finished his melon in silence. Moussa had put on his new headphones, effectively ending their conversation. The plan was simple. The conference was scheduled to end at 17h00. From there, it would take Cabot a minimum of 30 minutes to reach the Fountain Blue. At 16h30, Moussa would leave the safe house and walk the five blocks over to the hotel carrying his weapon in the backpack they had purchased. The woman had given them her room number and was expecting Moussa.

Once the hit was made, Moussa would call Abu at the safe house to confirm everything had gone as planned, then he would exit the hotel by taking the fire stairs on the beach side which opened onto the pool deck. From there, he would proceed to walk north on the beach, where Abu would pick him up.

Abu's only concern was the unknown. If something went wrong, Moussa spoke a minimal amount of English and understood only a few words. The woman, while certainly attractive, had not struck Abu as very bright during their one meeting.

Descent Into Paradise

Watching Moussa lying on the couch, he realized they had been in America less than a week, yet Moussa was beginning to act like a typical American teenager. The only difference, Abu thought, was most American teenagers were not asked to kill people in cold blood. Abu wanted to go over everything one last time, but Moussa had raised his hand saying all was understood. Now he wanted to prepare himself. At least he's not dressed in white chanting to Allah, Abu thought, his fury over the Angels of Death un-diminished. Finally he got up, deciding he would go over to the hotel bar to confer one last time with their contact at the hotel. Removing Moussa's earphones, he wished him good luck and reminded him of the time.

Slim had arrived early today, going through his usual routine of cutting lemons and limes and getting the ice chest full. He enjoyed this work far better than running drugs. Here, the job was simple: make drinks, talk to the customers, most of whom were lonely and needy of someone to listen to all their woes. Occasionally, a pretty girl would come in looking for some action. If they were still there at closing time, he would gladly accommodate them. La Bota chipped in an extra hundred a month just to keep him informed about one broad who seemed to live at the hotel. He kept waiting for her to end up at his bar at closing time, but that had not yet happened.

The bar was quiet when Abu arrived. Slim recognized trouble when he saw it, but this man just quietly ordered a cup of tea and drank it without a word.

Shasa was so upset over seeing Pete with an attractive woman that the last place she wanted to go was up to her room. She paced around the lobby until she saw the bar. Why not, she thought, a good stiff drink is just what I need. As she walked in, the bar was empty except for one man sitting quietly, nursing his tea. She was almost up to the bar when he asked to pay the bill. Stopping abruptly, she quickly turned around and saw Zev and Annabelle walking towards the pool.

"Zev," she whispered, "please come with me." Looking at Annabelle, she said, "Sorry, we will only be a minute."

"What's wrong?"

She quickly told him about her aborted assassination attempt after he left Shatila. "That's Abu sitting at the bar."

Zev guided her out onto the terrace where they could be private.

"Zev, Abu is not here on vacation, he does not even speak English very well. I think we should take him out."

"Wait, little one, I am not in that game anymore. I have just retired to take up residence in London with Annabelle. No more killing, no more drugs, I am going straight. If you want to take him out, call Tel Aviv. I am sure they will give you the green light."

For a brief moment, Shasa forgot all about Pete and Abu. "Zev, did you say you are moving to London? You mean you're not going back to Santiago?"

"That's right. As of this moment, I am currently unemployed. From here, Annabelle and I fly straight to London, where I will strive to become a proper British gentleman. So, please don't be getting any notions about my returning to Israel. I long for a normal life with a wife and kids."

Shasa put her finger up to her lips as she saw Abu walking out. "I am going to tail him."

She instinctively checked the small of her back before standing up, her eyes never leaving her intended target. She watched silently as he paused, looked at his watch, then went outside.

Descent Into Paradise

Pete finally got up to take a swim. He had fallen asleep shortly after lying down on a chaise. Now he could feel the burn on his back despite the lotion Madonna had put on. He noticed the lifeguard giving him a dirty look, as if he should not be swimming here. Ignoring him, he swam several laps until someone bumped into him in the water. He was about to apologize when he recognized who it was.

"Zev Megrid, my God! What are you doing here?"

"I was going to ask you the same question, I didn't know there were any terrorists operating in Miami Beach?"

It wasn't until after he had insisted upon Zev joining him for dinner that Pete remembered what Shasa had shared with him aboard the carrier.

"I would love to Pete, I'm here with my fiancée and we already have dinner plans, but let's you and I meet for a drink, we need to talk, just the two of us."

"You're engaged? Congratulations. Who is the lucky lady?"

"Come, let me introduce you," Zev said as he brought Pete over to where Annabelle was reading. Zev made the introductions, after which Pete responded politely, "I tell you what, if you already have dinner plans, let's meet for a drink afterwards in the bar. I'm off tomorrow, and I'm not leaving until we've had a proper toast."

"You're on, Pete. But first we need to talk."

"Give me 30 minutes, and I'll meet you in the bar." As he looked over at Madonna, the whole picture began to crystalize. If Zev truly did work for Rios, that would certainly explain their military prowess. It would also mean he and Madonna would know each other, which would explain his quick departure and his request to meet. Reluctantly, he went to ask a question to which he really did not want an answer. As he approached, Madonna looked up from her book, her eyes blazing. It turned out he didn't need to ask.

"What in God's name is this all about? How on earth do you two even know each other? You're now best friends with Rios's military advisor? Hell, whose side are you on anyway?"

As the verbal tirade began to subside, Pete responded seriously, "Does that mean you won't join us for dinner?"

Not understanding the humor, the tirade continued. "Join you for dinner? Are you fucking crazy? Do you want to get me killed? Maybe I should tell those idiots who always question me that you are the real enemy!" Calming down slightly, she then launched another attack. "Anyway, I already have dinner plans."

"What do you mean, you already have plans? Just reschedule it. I'm leaving tomorrow. I was just kidding about joining Zev for dinner. He already has plans so you and I will have a nice dinner, just the two of us."

"I can't."

"You can't or won't?" Pete was still standing looking down at her sprawled on the chaise, naked except for three tiny triangles of pink cloth. He could feel himself getting close to a genuine rage.

"Both." She languidly shrugged. "I'm sure we'll see each other tomorrow before you go."

"You can't do this to me. I came all this way to see you."

Madonna rose slowly, and with fury in her eyes, fired right back.

"When you are ready to take full responsibility for me, then you may have exclusive rights. Until then, I do whatever I please, whenever I please."

Pete watched as she turned and left him just standing there, her swaying hips in full motion, her spike heels angrily tapping her exit. He was surprised by the level of her anger, but realized she had a point. He reminded himself of who she was, a tough hooker who had led a very rough life. After all, what did he expect?

Descent Into Paradise

An elderly lady with purple hair interrupted his thoughts by asking if his chaise was available. He decided it was time to brief the hotel security about his conversation at lunch. Then he and Zev were going to have an interesting conversation.

Zev walked in to the bar, took a table near the back, and ordered a pitcher of sangria from Slim. Pete arrived just as he was taking his first sip. Pete asked Slim for an extra glass and sat down, deciding to break the ice with a bit of humor.

"Now please tell me, what does that beautiful English lady see in a worn out retired Israeli major?"

"Charm, my friend, pure old world charm that somehow passed you poor Americans by."

"Must be something intangible." Pete laughed, "Seriously, congratulations Zev. I could not be happier for you. Where are you going to live?"

"From here, we fly to London, where Annabelle lives, and I guess we will just take it from there. The one place it won't be is Israel, of that I am certain."

"What about South America? Aren't you still stationed down there?"

Pete then got the answer he had prayed for.

"Not anymore. As of this trip, I'm officially retired; time for me to settle down and go straight. How about you, Pete? Tell me what is happening in your world. You can start with that sexy broad you were with at the pool."

"She's a long story. Let's just say she's a government witness whom I rescued in South America. She thinks I'm her savior, and I think she's great in bed. That's about it."

"Is this serious or just playful?"

Shaking his head, Pete responded, "I'm lonely, Zev, so I am probably mistaking serious for playful, but we'll see."

"And how is Shasa, have you heard from her lately?"

Descent Into Paradise

Pete then related the Riordan fiasco and some of their conversations onboard the Coral Sea, leaving out, for the moment, her confession about Zev. Pete looked so pained that Zev felt obligated to say, "She is a complicated lady, Pete. Think what she has endured. I can remember a very frightened little girl whose family had just been violently killed, who found herself in a strange country with people who did not speak her language and who treated her very badly. That experience alone will leave permanent scars, believe me."

"I get all that. I just wish she could confront those demons who seem to haunt her."

"Slay her dragons so she can ride off into the sunset with her American prince charming?"

"Something like that, yes. Although I must say it sounds rather naïve when I hear you say it." Pete looked sheepishly across the table at the only man who knew her better than he.

Zev reached over and placed his hand on Pete's shoulder, saying quietly, "I hope for both of you she can do that. Maybe with a little active participation from the prince, that ride may still happen."

Zev took a long swallow of his drink while he let that thought sink in. "But enough about women. Tell me, what are you planning on the battlefield?"

Pete casually shared with him what he knew about Rios and the Sheik, the missiles and opium. Zev was taken aback that the Americans apparently knew so much. Seeing Zev's reaction, Pete decided to get to the point and offer him the deal he had been contemplating since he sat down.

"Zev, I know you're getting married, but I need your help one last time. Word has just come down from the top to take out this Rios crowd and soon. I need you to guide me."

"Guide you, how would I know where to go?"

Pete put up his hand. "Let's not play games. If I know as much as I have just told you, what else do you think I know? What else do you think my blonde companion knows?"

A look of dejection crossed Zev's dark eyes as he spat out, "Madonna, of course!"

"Zev, while I certainly don't condone what you've done, who am I to judge? God knows neither of us have been choirboys, so let's look forward shall we. You want to move to London, get married and put all this behind you, right? Well, let's be realistic! You think Mossad is going to just let you ride off and risk us discovering their involvement in this little triangle?"

Zev took a long look at Pete's face before responding, "Is this conjecture, or a warning?"

"Both."

Zev looked puzzled as he quickly asked, "Shasa? How did you know she was here?"

Pete looked Zev right in the eye as he responded. "I didn't realize Shasa was here, but the fact she is does not surprise me, nor should it you. Now, unless you wish to put your relationship with her to the ultimate test, I would suggest you listen to me very carefully. While I could easily be court-martialed for this, I am willing to bury your dirty little secret down south if you will agree to help me take them out. I'm even willing to place a call to our mutual friend and ally, the Director, and offer him the same deal. Your life for one mission, think about it. And while you're at it, think about Shasa and Annabelle as well."

Both men sat a moment longer, each watching the other in silence. Finally, Pete got up to leave. "I'll see you after dinner. Whatever you decide, I owe you and Annabelle a toast. I'll take care of the drinks. Think hard, Zev, we have both been through some rough scrapes together. I would truly miss you, my friend, to say nothing of making poor Annabelle a widow before you two are even married."

"Pete, sit down. It would appear I have some explaining to do."

Zev then took Pete through the whole Beirut debacle and subsequent aftermath. Pete knew he was being truthful because his story matched up to Shasa's rendition of the same events.

"Pete, I appreciate your offer, especially knowing the jeopardy you're placing yourself in. I will go in with you, my friend, not for any quid pro quo, but because I need a best man, and, judging from our joint exercises together, you may need my help!"

Both men got up, shaking hands, before Pete went over to the bar, left a $20 bill for Slim, and walked out. Zev sat stone still at the table for a few more minutes, trying to digest all that he had just heard. Finally, he too got up and left, heading straight to Shasa's room. To his great consternation, she wasn't in. Pete could have easily learned about his role with Rios through that tramp Madonna, or had Shasa said something to him? Apparently, she had shared other vital secrets with him, but would she really betray him? He stood outside her door, unable to move. What if roles were reversed, could he kill her? It was a choice neither of them should ever have to make. The thought of it, and who had potentially ordered it, made him seethe inside.

Shasa followed Abu without incident, as he never once bothered to check his back trail. She watched from a distance as he took out his keys to open a rather formidable wooden door built into a ten-foot high concrete wall hiding the house from the street. As she watched him enter, two men in a nearby car watched her. Quickly deducing there was no way to access the house from the street, at least in broad daylight, she just kept walking. Turning the corner just past the residence, she soon realized Abu's safe house backed up to a small canal. There, tied to its dock, sat a sleek blue Chris-Craft speedboat. Surveying the area, she soon realized there was no way to access the property from the canal side, other than by water. Removing her shoes, she looked both ways until there were no cars approaching in either direction and then dove into the green still waters below.

Swimming easily to the boat, she used the small ladder hanging over its stern to access the dock. From there, she crawled through the thick ivy hedge, which served as a useful screen to anyone's prying eyes from passing boats. As she emerged into the back yard, she crawled towards the back of the pool house. From there, she made her way to the rear of the main residence, using the outdoor air conditioning system as cover. As she crouched down to peer around the corner, she heard the refrigerator door close; then the television came on. Crawling on her elbows to the house, she peeked through the side window. There, not ten feet from where she stood, was the back of Abu's head as he sat watching TV. She tried the screen door. It was unlocked.

The TV screen was full of images of people yelling and screaming. Apparently, someone had just blown up a school bus in Jerusalem. The images only increased her fury. Reaching behind her, she slowly pulled the thin dagger out of its holster. Silently, she crossed the kitchen to the edge of the far wall. Abu now sat only four feet away in an oversized armchair, glass in one hand, a handful of chips in the other. There was no other sound in the house. She had missed once, she would not do so again. Thinking of her beloved parents, Mary Riordan, the Ambassador in London, and God only knew how many others, she took two quick steps, rose behind his chair, and grabbed a handful of hair. Yanking his head back with her left hand; she drew her razor-sharp dagger deep across his throat.

His look of complete bewilderment changed to a thin smile as he recognized her. Slumping down onto the floor, he reached out to her, unable to speak through the gurgling blood flowing down his neck. His eyes continued to stare into hers even as his heart stopped pumping. Without a word, she watched him die. Wiping her blade with a towel, she removed her own bloody shirt, throwing it in the trash. Now, dressed only in blood-stained shorts and a bikini top, she grabbed a beach towel to wrap around her waist. Having ascertained there was no one else in the house, she calmly let herself out the front door.

"Now that's one piece of ass."

"Just make sure you get her face in the picture," smiled his partner behind the wheel.

"Fucking Arabs. I wonder what she costs?"

Walking on the grass, as the pavement was quite hot, Shasa walked past the same white Ford sedan she had seen earlier. Cops, she thought. I wonder if they know who's inside? As the two Latinos just smiled at her as she walked past, she let out a deep breath and continued on back to the hotel.

Henry Cabot had just finished checking in as Shasa walked past him in the lobby. Looking at his watch, he had 30 minutes before meeting Madonna at 18h00. Cabot, always on the lookout for a pretty girl, couldn't help but stare as they both entered the elevator together.

Moussa had arrived right on schedule, making his way up to Madonna's room without incident. Unable to speak more than a few words of English, the two coexisted in silence as he explored the best place to remain hidden. It wasn't long before the phone rang.

"Henry darling, is that you?"

"Yes darling, I just checked in and thought I would see if I could come up a bit early."

"Of course you can, but I'm not quite dressed. You can wait a bit or just come now to assist me."

"Always happy to assist a beautiful woman. I will be up shortly."

Hanging up, Madonna looked over at the young blond-haired assassin, pointing over to the curtains and nodding her head in agreement. She then went to the bathroom to check her makeup and slip into her favorite pale blue negligee, which left precious little to the imagination. She had barely finished putting her lipstick on when she heard a knock on the door. That was fast, she thought as she went to welcome him. "Henry darling," she greeted him as she wrapped her arms around his neck, pressing her chest into his. "That was fast. I know it doesn't look like it, but I will be ready in two minutes." She started to glide to the bathroom when she turned, as if she had a new thought. "Unless, of course, you might enjoy a little appetizer before we go?"

Cabot moved faster than he had in years. Moussa watched from behind the curtain as the old man could barely get his clothes off before she pulled him onto the bed. As she was laughing and coaxing him on, it wasn't long before he heard grunting like a dog in heat. Moussa, feeling neither fear nor emotion of any kind, continued to watch as he tightened the silencer on his pistol. Quietly stepping out from his hiding place, he calmly aimed his gun. Pulling the trigger slowly, the man's head exploded as the soft-nosed bullet ripped through brain tissue before exiting out of his left eye socket.

Madonna screamed as blood and brain tissue splattered over her upturned face. "You stupid clod, you were supposed to wait until I went to the bathroom." She never stopped screaming as Moussa just stood there silently admiring her naked chest, blood oozing down her crevice. As he admired those big breasts, he aimed his pistol at the one on her right. Smiling, he once again pulled the trigger, killing her instantly. He then walked over to the phone to call Abu. The phone rang and rang with no answer. Moussa hung up and tried again, thinking he may have dialed the wrong number. Again there was no answer.

Placing his gun back into his backpack, he exited the room leaving both bodies as they lay. Using the emergency staircase, he walked slowly through the lobby back out to the back terrace as planned. Nobody even looked his way. He was just another blond teenager with a ubiquitous backpack. Once outside, he walked quickly back to the house.

When Shasa opened her door, she found a handwritten note on the carpet. It was from Zev, asking her to call as soon as she could. As she went to the phone, she noticed the message light blinking. Having retrieved her message, she decided first to take a much-needed shower, placing her clothes and borrowed towel in the laundry bag to throw out. Feeling somewhat cleansed, she called Zev.

"Shasa we need to talk, where have you been?"

"Taking care of some long unfinished business. Give me twenty minutes, then come on over." She hung up and dialed another number.

Pete tried Madonna's room again; still no answer. He wanted to apologize for his behavior that afternoon. The phone interrupted his thoughts.

"Pete, it's Bota. I hate to have to tell you this but there's just been a double homicide in your hotel, Madonna and Cabot have both been shot dead."

"Madonna and Cabot? Where were they, was anyone else hurt?"

"No, they were in her bedroom, naked in bed. He got hit in the back of the head; she took a bullet through the heart. No sign of forced entry. My boys are there now, I'm on my way."

Descent Into Paradise

"I'll meet you there." Pete hung up, cupping his face in his hands. My God! He now realized Cabot was the reason she couldn't join him tonight. In bed... naked... at 18h00? He began to wonder if Cabot had offered her the security he wouldn't. Jesus Christ, what a mess this is going to be. Putting on his jacket, he took the elevator up to the seventh floor.

The hotel corridor was swarming with police, hotel security, and DEA agents. Fortunately, he recognized one of the men as he came out of the elevator.

"Major Watson, you're cleared to enter, just please don't touch anything."

The scene pained him more than he would have suspected. He had seen more than his share of dead bodies, but seeing her naked in bed with another man truly upset him. He turned to leave when one of the agents stopped him to ask when he had last talked to her or seen her.

"This afternoon, a bit after 15h00. We were at the pool together. I tried calling her a few minutes ago but obviously there was no answer. Do you have any idea who did this?"

"No, Major, although it looks like someone she knew. There appears to be no forced entry, nor any sign of a struggle. We've only recovered two bullets. Whoever did it must have used a silencer and been in the room when they got here. The couple next door never heard any shots or anyone forcibly trying to enter. The only thing they heard was some groaning on the bed, which they took as pleasure, not pain, then they heard a woman screaming 'you stupid clod, you were supposed to wait' or something to that effect. They just assumed it was some sort of lover's quarrel."

One of the security staff then told Pete a young Arab boy with a backpack was seen exiting the hotel lobby, shortly before a maid called to report the shooting.

Pete began to put it all together, her meeting with Estoban now self-evident. Poor Madonna obviously didn't realize he would use this opportunity to tie up a major loose end, namely her. They probably used the Arabs as the executioners. He decided it was time to see Zev.

He rang Zev's room but got Annabelle. "Hi Pete, I am not sure where he is, but I thought I heard him say he was going to visit Shasa."

Turning to the DEA agent, Pete told him he would be in Miss Datre's room if anyone needed him.

From the passenger seat of the white sedan, still on stake out, Officer Saldana spotted the teenager walking hurriedly towards the front door. He immediately radioed headquarters. "Here he comes."

Moussa heard the television as he opened the front door. "Abu, Abu where are you? Are you alright?" he shouted as he ran into the kitchen. There, he saw Abu lying on the floor, his throat slit open, blood still oozing out onto his chest. With eyes still open, he stared vacantly up at the ceiling. Moussa knelt down tearfully pleading, "Abu, talk to me, please don't die, you can't leave me."

There was no response as Moussa cradled Abu's head in his arms. He was so absorbed in his grief he didn't hear the doorbell ringing.

"Police, open up immediately," came a voice over a loud-speaker. Moussa, not understanding what was being said, sensed trouble. Yet he refused to leave Abu's side.

"Break it down!" yelled the sergeant.

Moussa heard the commotion outside. Looking down at Abu, he whispered softly, "I could never go back without you, Kahil would just make me his bum boy; I have nowhere else to go."

Descent Into Paradise

The door broke down and men in blue uniforms came rushing in, their guns pointing straight at him. "Hands up, right now, or we'll shoot."

Moussa looked up at them blankly, then down again at Abu. Reaching under his windbreaker with his right hand, he chanted a final prayer to Allah. The explosion shook the foundations of houses three blocks away.

-

Pete found Zev in Shasa's room. She was in her bathrobe wearing no makeup when she opened the door.

"Pete, are you alright?" She had seen that same look on his face that fateful night in Shatila, hurt and bewildered.

"Zev, Madonna and the Director of the Drug Enforcement Agency have just been murdered in her room."

Looking straight at him, he knew immediately Zev knew something. "Who did it, Zev?"

"I'm guessing Juan Rios's chief henchman, a guy named Estoban, ordered it, but I don't know who carried it out."

"Why didn't you tell me, you bastard?" Pete moved toward Zev, who defensively put his hands up.

"Hold on, Pete. I didn't know who was getting hit, but, before I left Chile, Estoban warned me to be careful while I was here. What I do know is Rios wanted Cabot dead, and we all thought Madonna was terminated months ago. Since Estoban has been up here for several weeks, it would make sense he somehow discovered Madonna was here and came up with this neat little plan. Not only does he get the credit for the Cabot hit, he eliminates the possibility of Juan Rios ever finding out Madonna was not only alive, but feeding the DEA vital information."

Since Pete had come to a similar conclusion, he decided Zev was shooting it straight. Then, turning to Shasa, he asked if she knew anything about it.

"Of course not. I just arrived myself yesterday evening. I didn't even know who this Madonna was until I saw you two holding hands this afternoon."

Pete, not wanting that conversation to continue, looked back at Zev. "It looks like the hit was carried out by some teenager, at least that's the thinking as of now. Do you know if Bashir is tied up in this?"

"I don't, Pete, but he certainly could be. I saw him at the airport the day I arrived. He said he was here on business. As to what specifically, he did not elaborate."

The phone rang. Shasa picked it up and handed it to Pete. Listening intently, all he responded was, "Got it, thanks."

"Zev, turn on the TV, channel 4." They all stared at the screen. Sirens were howling, red lights flashing, and smoke was billowing out of what was once a house.

"We don't need to guess anymore, that Arab boy they saw in the lobby was staying in that house you now see in flames. Apparently, the local police were on a stake out when the boy returned. After they got a call about the shooting, they knocked on the door. When nobody answered, they broke in. A minute later, they were all blown to pieces."

Shasa thought of Abu lying there on the floor looking up at her. She thought if she had only waited a day, he would have died on his own. Death just seemed to follow her wherever she went. She looked at Pete, his face still distraught, but not over her. She needed to sit down.

"Would you both please leave?" she asked as she curled up on her bed.

Pete stood in the elevator lobby, thinking. He knew he should go back upstairs to deal with Bota but, instead, he turned around and walked back to Shasa's room. For once in his life, his feelings won out. When she opened the door, he just stood there and announced, "Shasa, I have loved you since the moment we met." With that pronouncement, he took her in his arms.

"Pete, come sit down, I have more to tell you." Looking up into his face, she said calmly, "Then we shall see if you still love me."

For what seemed an eternity, she proceeded to tell him everything, including her lovemaking with Annabelle's father and even her lustful affair with Bashir. She finished by sharing with him where she had been earlier that afternoon, and finally her assignment to kill Zev here in Miami. She left out nothing that could ever stand between them.

Speechless, Pete just sat there, suddenly overwhelmed by an awful sense of guilt. Her confession onboard the carrier had hurt him, and, instead of offering comfort and understanding, he had chosen to judge her instead. She was the one exhibiting great courage, not him. By exposing her deepest secrets to the light of day, she had chosen to risk everything to bring honesty and integrity to their relationship. Now, it was his turn to respond.

"Shasa, I'm not sure I am worthy of your trust, but I will let you decide that."

He went on to explain his relationship with Madonna, knowing full well she had been Rios's mistress and only wanted him for protection. "I felt needed. You wouldn't have me, and I just needed someone to need me."

Shasa could barely hear Pete's soft voice as he finished. No longer listening, her attention was riveted on the hurt etched across those sad blue eyes. Words were no longer necessary, for this was one of those rare moments when the truth allows itself to be seen, not heard.

Both of them had spent a lifetime building up barriers, his for fear of rejection, hers for fear of losing everyone who became too close. Tonight, under the weight of their mutual longing, those walls of isolation, so meticulously constructed, began to come crumbling down.

Like an early morning mist yielding to the rising sun, their deep-seated fears and self-doubts gradually succumbed to the onslaught of disclosure and honesty. Recognizing this might be her only chance to extricate herself from the web of deception she had so meticulously woven around her, Shasa made her decision.

She got up and took Pete by the hand across the room to her bed.

"Peter Watson, kiss me and tell me you'll never leave me."

Before he could reply, her wet lips covered his and they fell back onto her bed, holding each other with such passion no one could have pried them apart.

Down in the dining room, a bottle of champagne arrived at Zev's table.

"Annabelle, my darling, a toast to the most beautiful woman our Creator has ever produced."

"Good lord, are you trying to get me to bed before dinner? If so, you are doing wonderfully, keep it up."

"To the most charming and lovable lady England has to offer." Zev raised his glass again.

"I've just lost my appetite, let's go," she laughed, holding out her hand.

"Let's eat first, then we will take a trip to the stars, just the two of us."

"Zev, I love you so much, how could I be so lucky."

Taking a large swallow of his bubbly for additional courage, he said, "Darling, I need to ask your advice on something very important."

A look of concern crossed her face. "What's wrong?"

"As you know, Pete and I had drinks this afternoon. He told me that he is leading a covert mission into Chile to wipe out the entire Rios organization."

"Good! In my opinion, that's exactly what they deserve! That is, as long as you are here with me."

"He also told me he was aware of my involvement with Rios."

"How on earth would he know that?"

"That sexy little creature he was with at the pool this afternoon was formerly Mr. Rios's lady friend. It's a long story, the gist of which is Pete apparently rescued her and brought her here. She, in return, apparently told the Americans all she knows about Rios's operation, including my role."

"My God, Zev, what is he going to do? I thought you two were like brothers? And aren't he and Shasa an item?"

"Wait, it gets even worse. Pete believes Mossad has issued a hit on me so that the Americans will never learn of their involvement."

"They can't do that," she snarled. "Why would they want to kill you if you were working for them?"

"Because they would have to admit they've been lying to the Americans for years."

"Jesus, Zev," Annabelle exhaled. "Do you really think Pete knows all this, or do you think he's just guessing?"

"No, I don't think he's guessing."

"Let's think this through, how could he possibly know what Mossad plans to do or not?"

"On that piece, I would have to agree. Unless," he then hesitated to say what he was thinking.

"Unless what?"

"Unless someone told him," he muttered.

"And who could that possibly be?"

"We both know there's only one answer to that question."

Indignation replaced concern as Annabelle withdrew her hand. "Don't be ridiculous. Shasa would never tell him anything that would hurt you. She loves you almost as much as I do!"

"Please Annabelle, listen to me. Pete offered to call the Director and make a deal. My life in exchange for my agreement to guide Pete and his troops through Rios's defenses."

"Zev, let's be realistic here. Why would the Israelis agree to that deal? Who's going to guarantee them that your involvement will never come to light? You? Pete? Do you really believe they are going to trust the both of you to remain silent when neither of you even works for them? Come on, they are not that trusting, and you know it! If they have, in fact, ordered you terminated, then your American friend isn't going to change their mind, even if they were to tell him otherwise. From what you've just told me, there is too much at stake."

Zev sat there in silence as he absorbed her logic. She was right, of course. And, if they found out Pete knew of his involvement, his life would be in equal jeopardy.

"Annabelle my dear, as much as I hate to admit it, you may be right."

"Darling, if that offer is still open, I may take you up on that trip to the stars. This world has become a bit depressing."

"Pete, are you awake?"

Her head lay on his chest. She never looked up as he acknowledged her by grunting.

"Pete, are you leaving today?"

"Yes, Zev and I are flying up to an Army base to get ready."

"Will it be dangerous?"

"I guess that depends. Hopefully, they haven't changed much since Zev left." Pete left it at that.

Descent Into Paradise

Shasa sat up as the sun appeared over the distant horizon. She watched it rise slowly out of the ocean's depths until its light filled the room.

Quietly she said, "Pete, would it be alright if I stayed with your parents until you get back?"

They stared at each other in silence until Pete, still sensitive to her multiple rejections over the years, responded obliquely, "It's cold in Maine this time of the year. There's not that much to do."

"Well, then I think I better get used to it. Just make sure you don't leave me up there alone too long soldier!"

"Shasa." He hesitated.

"Yes?"

"Will you marry me?"

"Yes, yes I will. Tomorrow, if you want."

After Pete went downstairs to meet Zev, she picked up the phone to place one final call to Tel Aviv. Having finally made up her mind to marry Pete and leave the past in the past, she wondered if they would let her live long enough to enjoy it.

CHAPTER 68

TEL AVIV

"Please hold one moment, General Argov, the Director is just finishing up a long distance call and asked if you could hold for just a moment. He very much wants to speak with you. Here you are."

"General, good evening. Sorry to keep you waiting, I just was on a call from America."

"Shasa?"

"No, actually my niece, who also happens to be in Miami. She has just become engaged and wants me to attend their wedding."

"Oh, wonderful. Sorry to bother you with this, but I actually just received a rather disturbing call from Shasa and thought we should discuss."

"Yes, we should indeed. This has all become rather confusing and personal. For both of us I believe."

"Really?"

"We both know of your long standing relationship with Shasa, but what you don't know is that my niece is now engaged to Major Megrid."

"My God, man, how did that happen?"

"It's too long a story to go into over the phone, but suffice it to say I have suffered the misfortune of burying both her parents. Years ago, it was her mother, who also happens to be my younger sister, and most recently, her father, both of whom died in the service of Israel."

"I'm so sorry, I had no idea."

"Well, as you can appreciate, I never mix personal matters with my duties here. I'm afraid, however, in this particular case, I may be forced to make an exception."

Descent Into Paradise

Argov thought, as he listened politely, that the devil himself almost sounded human.

"General, I need your professional opinion here. We both know the Americans have decided to go in after Rios, but are you aware exactly how they plan to do it?"

"As a matter of fact, it would appear they are sending in troops to target Rios's compound, but they are going to use a naval aircraft to deliver the blow. From what I hear, Pinochet has agreed to the strike and has promised to use local forces to clean up whatever remains."

"If that's accurate, then the chances of the Americans ever discovering Zev's presence is rather nil, would you agree?"

So the rascal is going to call off the dogs, I would have never believed it, thought Argov as he almost chuckled over the phone.

Knowing Shasa as he did, it didn't surprise him she had refused to fulfill her assignment. In many ways, he could well understand. The two of them had been like brother and sister as long as he could remember. That's why he had left it in the Director's hands as to the details. He could never have ordered her to make the hit, no matter the circumstances. That's certainly one reason the Director was good at his job, he thought.

"General, you there?"

"Yes, sorry, I was just thinking. I agree, given the current scenario, I cannot see any way the Americans would ever discover our involvement down there, and we both know President Pinochet could care less."

"Good, then as I see it we can call off the hit, which Shasa has refused to execute anyway. Did she tell you that over the phone? And did she tell you she was submitting her resignation?"

"As a matter of fact, yes she did. She also told me she and that American major are engaged, which is the main reason she is leaving us. Hopefully, I may be invited to a wedding as well."

"Well, then it would appear both of us have gone somewhat soft in our old age. If you are in agreement, General, I am going to call Shasa and relieve her both of her assignment and her position with us, both without further prejudice."

Now, there would be no retaliation for her actions. Hearing that, he answered, "Director, you have my agreement and thanks."

"Officially, all I need is your agreement, but, between us, I appreciate the thanks. As long as Israel remains safe, I see no reason to needlessly execute one of our own, especially given the current circumstances. I will place the official call to Shasa after we hang up."

An hour later, both girls arrived downstairs smiling and laughing. Shasa put her arm around Pete and broke their news. Annabelle burst into tears of joy as Zev and Pete hugged each other like the brother neither of them ever had. At the end of a raucous breakfast, Shasa informed the men that she and Annabelle were going shopping while they played soldier.

"When you both return, you will be poorer by the price of two very expensive wedding dresses, which would have been white if you two had not already ravaged us," Annabelle announced.

"We will be ready, gentlemen, just make sure you are!" With that, the two beautiful brides in waiting marched out the door.

CHAPTER 69

General Bradley was in a thundering rage as he entered the final briefing at Fort Bragg.

"Circumstances have changed, gentlemen," he announced upon taking his seat at the head of the table. "Last night, someone shot a missile at a chartered 747 leaving Kennedy for Israel. The plane went to the bottom of the Atlantic Ocean with all 275 passengers and crew aboard."

Looking around the table, the General paused. "We don't know who's responsible, but what we do know is both Juan Rios and Sheik Bashir had dinner together last night in New York City. Both were observed toasting each other in a triumphant manner."

Pete had heard something earlier in the day about a chartered plane going down from a ruptured fuel tank. He asked the General, "Is this another incident or are you telling us the story of the fuel tank explosion is false?"

"We have satellite photos of a missile being launched from a boat in Long Island Sound. That missile can be seen exploding the under-belly of that jet, breaking the aircraft into a thousand pieces. Judging from the angle that missile struck, I'm sure the fuel tank did indeed explode. It just didn't happen on its own."

"Jesus, does the press have any idea?" asked La Bota.

"No, and they never will. The White House doesn't want this known. They believe it only plays into the terrorists' hands."

"Who knows this, General? Was it a military satellite?"

"Yes, only the people who saw those photographs in the Pentagon have actual knowledge. That satellite was not even supposed to be there, so it's in everyone's best interest to let it be."

"How does this affect us?" asked Pete.

"The President just got off the phone with the President of Chile. He informed him of what happened to that F-16 that went down, and requested permission to launch cruise missiles to take out the Rios compound. It would appear, gentlemen, that the government of Chile has endured quite enough of Mr. Rios's arrogance over the past several years and agreed to our request."

"Jesus, you mean we're not going in?" asked Pete.

"It looks like we'll let the Navy handle this. They'll probably use a nuclear submarine they have stationed near there.

Pete started to get up, but the General motioned for him to sit. "I'm not finished," he snarled. "The President apparently has taken the execution of his good friend Mr. Cabot very hard. He wants blood and Rios is not enough. He wants to go after the Arabs as well. Our friends at Mossad think this is Bashir's doing. What do you say, Major Megrid?"

Zev, unsure exactly what information Pete had relayed to his General, described what he surmised had gone down. Bradley then nodded in agreement.

"I will pass this all upstairs, but sit tight. I figure you boys will get in your fighting; although it may be in the desert instead of the mountains."

The President came directly back to his office from the burial service. The Cabot family had held up well, but his heart was heavy for the loss of one of his best friends. He had promised the Cabot family revenge would be swift and deadly. He now meant to convert that promise into action. After the briefing, he announced his decision.

"Move the Coral Sea into the Gulf. Wipe out that damn camp and bring back as much intelligence as you can. Use whatever force you deem necessary, including the Israelis if you

Descent Into Paradise

think it helpful, but it must be done covertly. I'm not going to alert the Iranians, they'll just tip those bastards we're coming."

Pete was summoned into General Bradley's office right after breakfast.

"Well, Major, it looks like that damn pacifist has finally woken up. Too bad it took the death of a good friend to shake him into action. At any rate, we finally got the green light to take out Murat."

Pete, looking somewhat concerned, asked, "Where are we going to launch from?"

"The President has ordered Admiral Brewster to sail immediately into the Gulf. This time, I'm going to let you go aboard without me. The President, I assume to throw a bone to the Israelis, has also approved their participation. While I haven't spoken to Argov, I'm assuming they'll send Zev's old unit since they're the ones we trained with."

"Who will be in command?"

"You will. That's non-negotiable with me."

They sat and discussed logistics for most of the morning before finally breaking for lunch. Pete immediately went to find Zev. He found him at the range, getting some target practice.

"I'm glad to see you can still shoot straight," Pete joked as he saw six holes puncturing the target's head some 50 meters away.

"Where I come from, you don't live very long if you can't," smiled Zev. "Next stop, Miami Beach?"

"Afraid not, at least not me. The President has ordered us over to the Gulf. We've been ordered to take out a major terrorist facility in Iran where Mossad thinks most of these recent raids have emanated from."

"You mean Murat?"

Pete just nodded in agreement.

Descent Into Paradise

"Jesus, Pete, don't think that's going to be easy. Several years ago, we were asked to look at taking out that camp. After reviewing all the satellite photos, I recommended against it. It's too big for a small force, and, unlike your little foray into the Beqaa valley, this one is very well defended."

"To say nothing about its location," Pete added. "From what I just learned, it's way the hell inland. It's one thing to fly in undetected; it's quite another to fly 100 miles out, after the Iranians know what we've just done."

"Same conclusion we reached. I'm sure that's one reason it's located there. Why in God's name don't they use cruise missiles like you're planning for Rios? You could wipe that camp off the planet without risking any casualties."

"I asked the same question. The answer is both Mossad and the CIA want to get their hands on whatever files are there so we can figure out who's behind this latest wave of violence."

"Shit, Pete, you don't need to be a genius to figure that out. I can tell you that without leaving here."

"They want proof, Zev, you're just guessing, although I think we would both agree. No, we're going in, that's been decided. And guess who's going with us?"

"My boys?"

"Yep, none other than your former Army rejects."

"A joint mission?"

"Yep, just like Palmachim, where we whipped your ass, remember?" Pete laughed.

Zev snorted. "You were so love sick with Miss Shasa you couldn't hit the side of a barn with a bazooka."

Pete was still chuckling as he thought of how jealous he had been of Zev. "You're probably right, but at least we'll get one last chance to shoot real terrorists. I have just told Bradley I am retiring after this one."

Descent Into Paradise

"Hold on, you're not going over there by yourself, lover boy. If it's a joint mission with my boys, I'll not be left out. After all, somebody's got to watch over you."

Admiral Brewster strode into his Command Center, a concerned look etched across his face.

"Gentlemen, please sit down. Captain, we have a bit of planning ahead of us. I just got off the phone with the Joint Chiefs, who have ordered the task force into the Persian Gulf. We have been designated, once again, as the launch platform for our friends in the Special Forces. This time, however, we will be operating within Iranian airspace. The mission also entails us hosting Israeli Special Forces, who are scheduled to come on board this evening. Therefore, before we get under weigh, we will need to disembark some of our Marines to make room for our guests. Also, we will be taking on board nine extra helicopters so we will need to make the necessary arrangements below deck before they arrive. If we need to offload some, they can transfer the Marines into Beirut and stay there until we return. Captain, please chart a course for the Suez Canal and alert the rest of the Task Force."

Shasa looked at Annabelle with a pained expression. "When did this happen? I thought they were going down to Chile?"

Annabelle shared her long conversation with Zev.

"Apparently, Pete is tied up in meetings all day and will call you later tonight when he can."

"What did you tell Zev, aren't you upset?"

"Of course I'm upset, but he was adamant he could not let Pete go over there while he was safe here with us. You know, the two of them have become very close. They act more like brothers."

Shasa could only smile at the thought.

Descent Into Paradise

Pete had spent the last four hours going over intelligence reports on Iran in general, and Murat in particular. Satellite photos had been blown up revealing both anti-aircraft batteries and advanced Russian surface-to-air missile launchers protecting the camp on the desert side. Even more disturbing was the discovery of five tiny concrete bunkers located some twenty miles out from the camp. Intelligence believed they formed an early warning radar system capable of detecting even low flying aircraft. The camp, furthermore, was situated in a perfect defensive location, tucked in against the mountains so there was only one way to approach it, across flat open desert. As he studied the photos, it became clear the only part of the perimeter not heavily fortified were the sheer cliffs which provided a natural barrier to the camp's northeastern quadrant.

Murat itself was massive. Split into three separate groupings, it would be impossible to take them all out at once without utilizing a very large force. While Pete had the utmost respect not only for his soldiers but the Israelis as well, how could 120 men be expected to effectively deal with over 1,000 armed militia spread out over such a large expanse. The fact they were protected by an advanced air defense system fully capable of eliminating any element of surprise just added to his unease. As if that weren't enough, they would also have to deal with breaching a ten-foot barbed wired fence surrounding the entire perimeter, with guard towers spaced every hundred yards. Those towers, upon careful inspection, were each manned by two guards and a 60-caliber machine gun mounted on a protruding platform. Any attacking force would be subjected to withering fire from multiple directions without the benefit of any cover whatsoever.

As he sat there, Pete saw no possible way to survive a frontal assault. Assuming the choppers could get them in close, which he doubted, those machine guns would tear them apart before they could hope to reach the main camp.

To effectively mount an attack against 1,000 trained terrorists spread out like they were would require at least two to three times the number of men under his command. The logistics just were not there. He would have to find another solution and quickly. They were scheduled to leave Bragg in the morning.

The men of Sayeret Matkin were now seated in the main briefing room at Palmachim. Their Commander, General Arial Bragman, stood alongside General Argov at the podium. The Israeli Defense Minister addressed them first.

"Gentlemen, our Intelligence Service has recently concluded the terrorist attacks conducted against Israel over the past several weeks have all emanated from one terrorist facility. Yesterday, the Prime Minister informed me he wants justice, Biblical justice, instructing me to destroy that facility and secure whatever documents are to be found. I suffer no illusions as to the difficulty of this assignment, which is why I came here today. I once described Sayeret Matkin as the tip of the Israeli spear. Our enemies have attacked us ruthlessly over the past several weeks, now it is time for them to pay the ultimate price for their wanton violence against innocent women and children. As it has so many times before, your country is depending upon you, and I am depending upon you, to exact that retribution. Good luck, gentlemen."

With that, the Israeli Defense Minister left, leaving General Bragman to give the actual briefing.

Zev joined Pete and his men, most of who remembered the Israeli major from their joint exercises at Palmachim. All were glad to have the Israeli major on board, and all were excited to finally go into actual combat side by side. The flight to the carrier required several planes and several stops before they finally climbed onboard a small naval transport prop to their final destination. As their small plane began its approach to the carrier deck, Pete warned his fellow passengers to buckle up. "It feels like a miniature crash landing, so just be prepared," he shouted.

Then, leaning over so only Zev could hear, Pete went on, "Look, I have a feeling things may be a bit hectic for both of us from here on out, so I just want you to know how much it means to me to have you here. It's funny, we've been through a lot together, and you've become like family to me. Be careful out there, we've got two beautiful women waiting for us and a great life ahead."

"Hell, I only came to take care of you, remember? Hey, seriously, I feel the same way about you little brother."

Once onboard, Pete was met by the ship's captain, who immediately ushered him up to the Admiral's quarters. Zev went to have an unexpected reunion with his old squad.

General Bragman, who had been informed of Zev's imminent arrival, was the first to greet him with a big smile and a bear hug. "Major, welcome back, what a nice surprise."

"Thank you, General. It's great to see you as well. It's been too long. How have you been? You look well."

"I'm fine, thanks. We've all missed you, especially your gang."

"I've missed you all as well; who's on board?"

"The best unit we've got, of course. The very same ones you attempted to reconstruct, remember?"

"You mean my boys?"

"They're all here, most of them anyway. Some have retired and several unfortunately are no longer with us."

"Do they know I'm here?"

Descent Into Paradise

"No, I haven't told them. I wanted a chance to speak privately first. Look Zev, this is a bit tricky. I only learned you were coming several days ago myself when one of the Americans informed me what room you were assigned to. My first thought was you were coming on behalf of Intelligence, but when I mentioned it to the representative from Mossad, he knew nothing about it."

"So, the Director sent one of his own to keep an eye on us? Who?"

"I didn't know him. All I know is he goes by the name of Simon, no last name given."

"He's one of the Director's top people. I guess everyone is taking this mission seriously."

"Let's not kid ourselves Zev, this is going to be a bitch. I was one of those you persuaded not to go last time, remember?"

"God, that's right General. Sorry, that was a while back."

"Look, Zev, even the men are a bit skeptical, which we both know is no way to go into combat. Here's what I'm thinking. If you agree, I would be willing to turn the overall command of this mission to you. Not officially, of course, as I obviously outrank you, but for all practical purposes. Let's face it, you were the best counter terrorist leader in the Special Forces, everyone would acknowledge that. The men, once they know you're here, wouldn't want anyone else, including me. What do you say?"

"General, that's quite a gesture on your part, and one not many in your position would normally make. I appreciate it, and, given what I know of the subject, I agree with you. This is going to be an absolute nightmare, if not done properly. Since I have a good working relationship with the American major who will be in overall command, I think it would be best for all of us if I could have some serious input."

"Agreed, Major. Why don't we let the men in on our little agreement, I know they'll be thrilled to have you back."

Descent Into Paradise

After his meeting with the Admiral, Pete made his way down to the officers' cafeteria. Having barely eaten over the past several days, his stomach was in full rebellion.

"Major Watson, how nice to see you again. May I join you?"

Pete had not seen Simon since their last brief encounter in Boston. "Simon, please sit down. I didn't expect to see you here, how are things in the devious underworld of espionage?"

"Well, I guess that depends upon who you ask. For me, all is well thank you."

"So, I trust you are here to give us the blueprint for taking down this bloody camp."

"Bloody's not an inappropriate word, I'm afraid. I wish I had such a blueprint, but while we all would like to get a look at whatever records they keep there, none of us think taking down this place is going to be easy."

"No, none of us do either. I just hope whatever is there proves worthy of the lives that will inevitably be lost obtaining it."

"We do as well, Major, believe me. We certainly wish to help in any way possible as we happen to know some useful bits about the place, which is why the Director asked me to come."

"That the only reason?"

"What other reason might there be?"

"Look Simon, I don't have time to play your little cat and mouse games so I'll get to the point if you won't. Zev and I are both retiring after this. We're both engaged and equally desirous to leave this soldier's life to those younger and more capable."

"Well, congratulations to you both then. I had no idea. I assume and hope your fiancée is someone I know."

"Yes, Shasa and I are getting married when I return home, and Zev is engaged to a lovely English lady who happens to be a friend of Shasa."

"Personally, I couldn't be happier for all of you. Please send her my congratulations and best wishes, but I'm not sure what is it you wish to point out."

"Please ask the Director to let the past stay in the past. Tell him I, for one, have no interest in who did what to whom, nor do I wish to pursue the matter further. I trust he will do the same."

"I understand. I will certainly inform him of what you just shared with me. I believe he is of like thinking."

"Good. I wish you both well."

"Thanks, and likewise to you and your new bride."

That evening, Admiral Brewster called an official meeting of all the officers involved, including the representative from Mossad. He began the meeting by introducing himself and his top naval officers before turning the meeting over to Pete.

"Good evening gentlemen. It is my privilege and honor to be the commanding officer of this mission."

Pete then asked everyone to introduce himself around the table. After the introductions, a long discussion ensued concerning the best way to approach the camp to minimize casualties.

Zev was one of the last to speak. "They will expect us to come in by helicopter, which is the basis for their entire defensive framework. Just look at these photos." Then, picking up the pointer, Zev illustrated what he meant. "As you can see, they have set up a series of early warning radar stations to alert them of our approach. Their intent is to take down our choppers before we ever hit the ground, and I am confident they are fully capable of doing just that."

General Bragman, who took a moment to share with all those in attendance the fact Major Megrid had been tasked by the IDF several years earlier to formulate a plan to take out this particular camp, then asked Zev for a feasible alternative.

"General, I can see only one way to do this. First, we will need to land a force near these mountains, far enough from the camp so as not to alert them. Unless Intelligence knows something different, I do not see any radar up on that crest. I must assume they believe any attack will come from the desert side. If we get to this point unobserved," he then moved the long wooden pointer to the crest of the cliff just northeast of the camp, "we can neutralize whoever is in those caves.

"As to the desert side, we will first need to take out the early warning radar sites strung along this line here. Immediately thereafter, before the camp is fully cognizant of that occurrence, we will need to take out those SAM missile sites just prior to the Cobras coming within range."

Zev reached for a glass of water, then returned to the photos. "Whatever they miss, the Black Hawks will have to deal with. It would be wonderful to keep the Cobras up there the entire time, but I'm guessing we're dealing with fuel constraints."

Bob Gough, the senior SOAR pilot, responded by saying he felt the Cobras could stay over the target approximately six minutes, assuming they could fly straight in. "If we get held up anywhere along the approach, every minute we're delayed is a minute less over the target."

"Understood," said Pete, "Thank you for those thoughts, their validity is self-evident. I fully agree with Major Megrid's suggestion of landing a force on the other side of the mountains to deal with the caves, but I'm not convinced that will be enough. We really don't have a good handle on how many men are up there, do we?"

Simon then stood, picking up the pointer to explain. "Our sources indicate many of the residents actually reside in those caves, not in the tents as one might surmise. It is our belief that many of those tents are there simply to draw fire from the Cobras."

"Are you telling us they're empty? Why would they build tents in the middle of nowhere to intentionally leave them empty? And no disrespect, sir, but how on earth would you know that?" questioned the Admiral.

"That is exactly what I'm saying, Admiral. It is our belief that those tents were constructed solely for the purpose of drawing fire in case of an attack. You see, Admiral, they have learned from past raids how devastating those little helicopters can be. As to how we know this to be the case, all I will say is it cost one of our agents his life to get us that information."

"My apologies, sir. I did not mean to demean your input."

Pete then interjected, saving the Admiral any further discomfort. "Bob, while we're on the subject of targets, these towers you see strung along the perimeter need to come down or those machine guns will wreak havoc as we land. Also, those cave entrances, as we just learned, could be full of soldiers. You must be careful not to expend all your ammunition, or precious time over the target, solely on those tents. Somewhere in your attack plan, you need to focus on those cave entrances and those towers."

"I hear you Major, I will need to think it through, but we will come up with something, I assure you. It is a large area, as you know, and we may just have to prioritize what we go after."

"Anti-aircraft batteries first, towers second, tents and caves last."

"Yes sir, but, as I said, it's a big camp and we might not have enough ammo or time to get it all done."

"Bob, you and I have been doing this together for as long as I can remember. I trust you'll do the best you can."

"Thanks, Major. We'll do the very best we can for you."

Pete then turned to where the Israeli officers sat as a group, "General Bragman, I would like you to formulate a plan for removing those early warning radars and missile sites. We can't risk the Cobras, or the Black Hawks, near the target until we know those missile sites are down. Major Megrid is correct to point out without the Cobras, there is no way we can take that camp. It is simply too big and spread out for the number of men we have on board."

"Major, allow us some time on that. I have some ideas, but let's reconvene in the morning."

Pete nodded his head and said, "If the Admiral will allow us, we will reconvene here tomorrow morning at 08h30. Let me just remind everyone, we leave here tomorrow night so we don't have much time to get this right."

CHAPTER 70

MURAT

The Sheik stepped off his helicopter just as the air raid siren sounded. He dashed for cover as his pilot hit the throttle and was airborne instantly. It turned out to be another false alarm, the third of the day.

"Everyone is a bit on edge after the President's speech the other night," said an embarrassed Commander. "Sorry to inconvenience you."

Bashir had to smile openly. "Not to worry. It was unfortunate that it ended up costing us two brave soldiers, but I believe it was worth it. Even that coward in the White House cannot ignore such an insult."

Then the commander asked, "Do you think he was serious when he implied they knew who did it and they would hunt them down?"

"Who cares, let them come. The important point is that there can be no peace talks now. We're at war and the Americans cannot ignore us any longer."

Colonel Mir, who had just arrived back in camp, then joined them. "I'm sorry to be late. As we flew in, we discovered one of the early warning radar stations is malfunctioning. Given the high level of security we are now under, Kahil and his men decided to escort the technician in case there was any sabotage involved. He sent his regrets he couldn't be here. As it's the one on the end of the line, I doubt he will be back before you are scheduled to leave."

Bashir turned to Mir. "While I would like to give him his reward personally, I must leave within the hour."

Handing the Iranian a rather large leather bag full of gold sovereigns, Bashir congratulated him profusely on the excellent job he had done. Turning to the commander, he handed him two others of similar size, explaining, "One is for Kahil with our personal thanks for the splendid job he did with those illegal settlers, and the other was for Abu and Moussa. I don't know if they have any relatives. If so, please see that they receive this. If not, then please distribute it as you see fit. I'm sure there are lots of worthy recipients."

Before he left, Bashir gave his hosts effusive praise. "Murat should stand tall, Commander. You and your brave men have dealt four major blows to our enemies these past months. The Arab world salutes you, we salute you, and Allah smiles down upon you."

In response, the commander raised his cup of tea in salute. "On behalf of everyone here, I thank you and salute you for what you have accomplished. May Allah watch over you, for you have earned the wrath of powerful adversaries."

Mir then added, "The American in Beirut gave me a similar admonition before he met his God. I told him I do not kill easily."

Bashir raised his cup to add, "I hope not, we have many battles left to fight, and we will need all of our best men to achieve victory. Praise Allah."

CHAPTER 71

Admiral Brewster was drinking his ritual pot of morning coffee as he pondered the ramifications of what he was about to offer. He had asked Pete to join him in his private quarters, once the final briefing was finished.

"Major, thanks for stopping by, I know you're busy. I just wanted to ask you for an honest off-the-record assessment of this mission."

Pete noticed there was no one else present, so he assumed the Admiral to be sincere in his request.

"Admiral, off the record, I fear we're going into a giant hornets' nest, one whose eradication may well cost many good men their lives."

After a moment's silence, the Admiral put down his coffee. "I appreciate your candor, Major. I'm sorry to say I happen to agree with that assessment. Have you considered aborting?"

Pete looked at the Admiral to see if he could read anything in his face before answering that unusual question. A kindly smile was all he saw.

"Yes," he nodded. "As a matter of fact, once we're finished here, I plan on calling General Bradley to suggest this mission is better suited for cruise missiles than Special Forces."

"If it would help, please convey that I agree with you fully, and it so happens I carry the necessary ordinance on board my fleet to do the trick."

Pete thanked him before leaving to make his call. Having gone over the plan in its entirety, Pete finished by telling his boss it was his personal opinion that the mission's risks far surpassed normal tolerance and they should abort. Bradley's only response was he would get back to him shortly.

That afternoon, the Admiral sent word to Pete he had received the General's reply. As Pete walked in, he could guess the answer from the Admiral's expression.

"Major, General Bradley just sent this to my attention. He asked that I read it to you.

"'Admiral, after a full review, the Commander In Chief has ordered the mission to proceed as scheduled. He has every confidence in your ability to achieve the objective of destroying the terrorist camp at Murat and bringing back proof of who is responsible for these heinous acts against the United States and Israel.' Signed General George Bradley."

It was obvious from the tone of the response that General Bradley had been overruled. Clearly, direct orders from the Commander in Chief would have to be carried out. However, the Admiral was well within his rights to offer operational assistance.

"Major, as of this moment, I am placing the fleet on full alert. What that means is we will be prepared to launch air support at a moment's notice, if called upon."

"Thank you, Admiral, I appreciate the predicament that would put you in."

Standing up, the Admiral walked Pete out.

"That's why I'm making this very clear, Major. You and your men may count upon the full resources of this battle group. As your senior officer, I am hereby ordering you to contact me immediately if circumstances dictate. Between my cruisers and destroyers, this battle group carries 35 Tomahawk cruise missiles, all of which now carry the coordinates of Murat in their guidance systems. Do I make myself clear, Major Watson?"

Pete stopped at the door and looked straight at the Admiral.

"Perfectly clear, sir. You are a man of honor as well as a topflight commander. I salute you for both, in that order."

Kahil watched the balding man with spectacles get down on his hands and knees to inspect the satellite. He now presented Kahil with a full view of his buttocks as he peered underneath the control panel. A deep aching permeated Kahil's loins. He could feel himself begin to enlarge as he pictured this man naked and helpless. He turned away while he could.

"Do you see anything suspicious?" he yelled at his searching troops.

"There's nothing around here but sand," came the response. "No footprints, nothing. Nobody's been out here except us."

Kahil then went over to the technician. Kneeling down beside him, he asked, "What's wrong with the damned thing, do you know?"

The balding man sat up, looking right at Kahil and told him, "We will need to pull this dish off, then look at the connections. I think there is a short in the wiring."

"How long to fix it?"

The man leaned closer to Kahil as he said in a low voice, "Well, that depends on how long you want?"

"What does that mean?"

"It means that maybe you should send all those men back to camp." Putting his hand on Kahil's thigh, he whispered, "Then you and I could take our time making sure these connections are all nice and tight, with everything plugged into the right hole."

Kahil gave him a big toothy grin. He got up and gave his orders to check the other stations before heading back to camp, yelling out, "I'll stay here to help lift off the dish. I'll meet you back at camp tonight."

When his men had left, Kahil came back to sit down. "You're new in camp, I haven't seen you."

"Yes, my name is Mohammed, and you are Kahil, right?"

"Yeah, how did you know my name?"

Descent Into Paradise

"Everyone knows your name, you are the man who killed the rabbi and stuffed his testicles into his mouth, right?"

Kahil laughed at the thought of it. "Yes, I confess."

"I wish I had been there to see it!"

Putting his hand back on Kahil's thigh, he purred, "I bet he wasn't as big as you are. I bet nobody is."

Kahil now was feeling that familiar current of excitement as he grew bigger and bigger. Mohammed's excitement also began to grow as his eyes began to cloud over with anticipation. His own member began to throb as he pictured what was growing under his hand. Mohammed wanted this man more than anything and he was determined to make it so good that this big Saudi would keep him forever.

Rubbing up against him, Mohammed crawled over to get his blanket and lubricants, leaving Kahil to see his inviting buttocks sway back and forth in invitation.

The sun had begun to set as Mohammed felt the massive intrusion enter him for the third time. He and his new mate renewed their grunting in ecstasy.

The first two Israeli helicopters lifted off the carrier deck at 18h30. Flight time to touchdown was estimated at 40 minutes. Just prior to takeoff, General Bragman had unofficially turned over command of his Scout force to Major Megrid, much to his troops' delight.

At the last minute, he and General Bragman had decided against trying to land near the crest of the mountains. It was simply too risky trying to find a suitable place for the Scouts to land. Instead, Zev decided to bring his entire force with him, putting down in the desert some eight miles short of the expected radar picket screen. Once the picket line and missile sites were taken out, Zev and his Scouts would join Bragman and the rest of the Matkin unit in the camp.

Descent Into Paradise

The flight plan called for them to fly into Iran well west of the Iranian Air Force base, due south of Tehran. Despite the increased fuel consumption, they had chosen to fly in at 'tree top' level all the way to the drop zone. This would allow them to get closer to the early warning radars without risk of detection. Both Black Hawks would remain on the ground until given the all clear signal, at which point, having refueled, they would pick up the Scouts, bringing them directly into camp.

Due to the uncertainty surrounding the exact number and locations of the early warning radar stations, the Admiral had agreed to send in an F-14 Tomcat to 'light up the radar sites'. The supersonic fighter would not close in on the camp itself but merely fly the perimeter zone before heading back to the carrier. Hopefully, the radar control room within Murat would put off the incident to an Iranian aircraft on routine patrol.

An EWAC from the battle group would be dispatched to circle above at high altitude. Its state of the art EMS tracking system should then be able get a fix on all the missile sites and radars as they locked on to the Tomcat. Those locations would then be radioed down to the helicopters on the ground. Having first dismantled the early warning radar sites, Zev's Scouts would then proceed east to take out the missile locations. Only then would the Cobras be released to go in.

The success of their plan hinged upon those SAM-6 missile sites being lightly defended and far enough from the camp itself to render immediate help impossible. The decision to launch the Cobras would be made by Zev, once he could ascertain the situation on the ground. If he waited too long, the camp would be on full alert before they arrived. If he ordered them off too early, they would be forced to circle in a holding pattern, lessening their time over the target. These were the most crucial decisions of the entire mission.

All this was going through his mind as the pilot radioed, "Five minutes to touch down."

"Get your gear ready boys, we're down in five," Zev ordered briskly.

The landing was uneventful. Zev told the pilot to begin refueling and be ready for his signal.

Upon touch down, they headed off at a fast trot, using their GPS system to track the southernmost radar site as given to them by the EWAC. At 21h40, they came across the first satellite dish. The size of a home television system, it hung suspended several feet off the desert floor by a stout metal pole. Underneath the dish was its metal-encased control panel, capable of detecting any encroaching aircraft and directing the SAM missiles to their target. There was no cover for anyone to hide so the Scouts knew immediately the area was clear. After a small explosive device was attached to the dish itself with the timer set for 70 minutes, they moved on.

Both the Admiral and Pete were waiting in anticipation aboard the carrier when General Bragman announced, "They have just set the first device. According to the AWAC, there are three more stations in the picket line. Each one is approximately 500 yards apart. He anticipates blowing them all within the next 70 minutes."

Pete asked, "I thought there were five altogether. At least, that's what those satellite photos showed."

"I think you're right, Major, but only four locked onto that Tomcat. Maybe the fifth one is down."

Missing one of those radar sites could prove disastrous, but Pete let it go for the moment.

Descent Into Paradise

"How far from there to the missile sites?"

"Looks to be a bit under three miles. They should be able to cover that distance easily in under 30 minutes. Zev wants the Cobras leaving as soon as he has set the final charge."

Looking at his watch, Pete made his own mental calculations.

"The Cobras should be within range of those missiles some 45 minutes after takeoff. That gives Zev's Scouts less than fifteen minutes to take out those missiles, isn't that cutting it a bit close?"

"It's all a bit close, Major. Once those early warning radars go down, Murat will be alert for trouble. Those Cobras need to arrive before they have time to prepare. The whole operation depends upon my Scouts taking out those missile launchers just prior to the Cobras coming within range."

Pete felt his stomach tighten. There was absolutely no margin for error. Experience had taught him nothing ever goes perfectly, especially when your whole plan depends upon it.

"OK, let's load the birds. We'll take off six minutes behind the Cobras. Remember those caves, General. We're still not sure how many men are in them."

"Will do. Good luck to you, Major, I will buy you a nightcap when we get back onboard."

Smiling more out of politeness than confidence, Pete gave his counterpart a stiff salute, then went to join his men.

To avoid the anti-aircraft sites, the three remaining Israeli helicopters would fly in over the mountains, disembarking their troops in the northern quadrant near the entrance to the caves. Once Zev's Scouts were ready, they would fly in directly from the desert side. This, of course, presumed the Cobras had taken down the anti-aircraft batteries in their initial assault.

The Rangers, alongside his Delta Force, would land further to the south. The Cobras would first launch their Hellfire

Descent Into Paradise

rockets at the anti-aircraft sites situated along the southern perimeter then proceed to rake the camp with their deadly Gatling guns. Six minutes of those murderous machines should render all but the caves inoperable. The five American Black Hawks, each carrying twelve commandos, would follow them in, using their twin 20mm machine guns to provide immediate air support. The little bubbletops would be left on the carrier as the big Black Hawks' vastly superior firepower outweighed any advantage of stealth for this particular mission. The Israelis would use the same strategy in the north. Hopefully, the Cobras would not leave much standing before they needed to head back to the carrier.

Pete led his troops out to the choppers, the cheers from the observation deck reminding him of his last mission from this same massive flight deck. It inspired his men to have such thunderous support. Within minutes, the rotor blades picked up speed, sending them straight up as they headed for shore. The lights from the carrier soon faded into the distance as the sun departed the western sky.

The atmosphere in the chopper was sober. The men had picked up their commander's somber attitude, knowing the task before them would be formidable. American Special Forces were taught to believe they were the best troops in the world. Armed with the best equipment, trained to a sharp edge, that confidence still permeated the small cabin of the Nighthawk.

"Eight minutes to the target," came the voice of the SOAR pilot. "They're lighting it up for us dead ahead."

The men crouched forward to get a glimpse of the fireworks.

After the charge had been set on the third radar station, Zev realized the sites were completely isolated with no guards posted. Knowing his schedule was tight, he made the first major decision of the night. Turning to Sergeant Brandeiss, he barked, "Sarge, take two men with you and set the charges on that last site. Just make sure you signal the carrier as soon as the charge is set. Then, join us as fast as you can." Zev led his remaining force of twenty Scouts towards the missile sites. Checking his watch once again, he had just under an hour before the Cobras would come into range.

Kahil lay sound asleep with Mohammed cuddled up beside him, an arm draped over Kahil's shoulder in a possessive manner. The night air was cold so he had pushed his body up against the big Saudi for warmth.

Neither stirred until the first explosive went off some half a mile away, quickly followed by three more in rapid succession, the final one a mere 500 yards from where they lay. Jumping up half naked, the big Saudi searched the night sky for aircraft. Nothing. Just the stillness of the night air and the smell of burning cordite. He rushed to put on his pants and boots as Mohammed asked what was wrong.

"Is this thing working?" was the response.

"You know it's not working, we got a bit distracted, remember?" Kahil just growled something as he picked up his AK-47 and headed back towards camp. It wasn't long before he felt the dreaded throb of those big rotors. "Shit! Don't let them find the missiles," he yelled as he began to run harder. Just then, he thought he heard rocket fire. Next, he saw flames shooting into the air in front of him, as explosions pierced the night air. As he continued to run, a premonition of death began to seep into his consciousness, his animal instincts screaming danger into his every pore.

Zev checked his watch for the hundredth time. He had to take out these missiles just before the radar went down. "One minute," he whispered into his mic. "Get ready."

Descent Into Paradise

Ten commandos, two per site, rechecked their RPGs as the rest of the Scouts put their Uzis on full automatic. "Ten seconds… six, five, four, three, two, one, FIRE!"

The men lounging next to their launchers never got to their feet. Without warning, the night suddenly lit up with a hail of bullets ripping their bodies to shreds. From point blank range, the RPGs had blown the missiles off their launchers, most exploding into the remains of the men assigned to use them.

Two men from the guard towers, some seventeen miles away, thought they saw a flash. One called down to the radar control room to see if they had picked up anything on their screen.

"No, but we do seem to have a malfunction on the early warning radar control. It looks like a short in the transmission system. All of them suddenly went down."

"Call the Commander, two of my men thought they saw something suspicious out there. I don't like it."

"Alright, I'll let him know." Putting down the phone, he picked up the red command phone.

Kahil soon saw the deadly black helicopters overhead heading directly for Murat. He knew from experience what would follow.

The Cobra pilots, alerted that the radar stations were out and the missile batteries no longer a threat, pulled up on their sticks for altitude and headed directly north towards Murat. At three miles out, they locked in their control systems on the anti-aircraft batteries and launched their Hellfire rockets. Minutes later, the last remaining layer of a once formidable air defense system was effectively destroyed.

The pilots then radioed the all clear to the American Black Hawks approaching some six minutes behind. Pete saw the missile streaks as they hit their targets. So far so good, he thought, as tracers lit up the night sky ahead heading towards the myriad of tents known as Murat. Pete removed his helmet, placing it under his seat. The chopper was beginning to take a real pounding on its final descent. While the antiaircraft installations were now effectively removed, several of the heavy machine guns located in the towers were still operational. Those guns were now taking a heavy toll on men and machinery. Of his five Black Hawks, one was billowing smoke and another had lost both its gunners.

As the defenders scrambled for cover below, 60 elite American troops dropped 40 feet in a matter of seconds. Hitting the ground, they ran towards a concrete water tower nearby. Fortunately for them, the nearest guard tower had been demolished. Despite that good fortune, they had immediately run into heavy automatic rifle fire. Far from being suppressed, the camp was still alive with defenders.

The six Bedouins who had gone out with Kahil had arrived back in camp just as the initial attack began. Immediately taking shelter in one of the concrete bunkers, they were impervious to the attack launched by the Cobras. All the bunkers had been designed to withstand direct hits from the air. All six were still alive and itching for a fight when the first US troops arrived.

There were fires everywhere as Pete watched a Black Hawk go down in flames. Only three of his birds were still flying, their twin 20mm guns pouring out death at 1100 rounds per minute. It wasn't enough, however, as more men kept pouring out of their caves screaming like wild banshees. He could hear the familiar sounds of the CAR-15s and M-249s, the two weapons the Delta boys favored; interspersed were the standard M-16s all on full automatic. Unlike his last raid, this time he also heard the distinctive and deadly sounds of AK-47s, also on full automatic. It was becoming increasingly clear the Cobras had not been able to finish what they started before having to withdraw.

Descent Into Paradise

Colonel Mir awoke to the crashing sounds of missiles taking out the antiaircraft batteries. His small cave remained unscathed as the Cobras directed the bulk of their deadly fire on the myriad of tents below. He grabbed his AK-47 and headed towards the firefight enveloping the camp. Yelling to his comrades to follow, he ran screaming obscenities at the infidels attacking his home.

To the Arabs waking up to this onslaught, the attackers looked like demons from another planet. They wore strange helmets with even stranger looking goggles. Their aim was uncannily accurate even in the dark.

Zev watched as the tiny black Cobras pummeled the camp. He then watched as the Nighthawks flew over, bringing Pete and the Americans into Murat.

"Where are those damn choppers?" he screamed into the night air. Neither bird had come down to pick them up, and the fight was about to be fully on. Finally, he heard the welcome thumping herald their arrival.

"Where the hell have you been!?" Zev yelled in his headphone.

"Mechanical trouble sir, the other bird just took off. The pilot just radioed he should be here in five minutes."

The twelve Scouts nearest the chopper hopped on board, anxious to join the fight. Zev and his remaining men stood watching the fireworks in the distance.

"Never would have believed it," Sargent Brandeiss shouted to him over the din. "I can't believe anyone in there could still be alive."

"Let's hope they leave one or two for us," Zev shouted back as they waited impatiently for the second chopper.

The camp commander headed for his tent the moment he heard the dreaded thumping sound of those big rotor blades.

Descent Into Paradise

"Where are those damned missiles?" he shouted to the night sky. Something had gone terribly wrong. No one had warned him of any approaching aircraft, no aircraft had been shot down, and men were pouring in all over the perimeter. None of this was supposed to be possible. The millions of dollars they had spent to defend against this type of attack had proven totally useless. Now he had to get to his office to destroy his files. It was pitch black when he arrived. The generator had been blown up along with most of his beloved camp. He sensed, rather than saw, the apparition who stormed in right behind him. The only thing he could see was the flash from a gun barrel. Then his stomach seemed to explode.

Colonel Mir led a valiant effort to rally his men around the concrete water tower. There were a growing number of dead and wounded attackers littered on the ground, but the steady stream of fire from the men around him began to diminish. With everyone's weapons on full automatic, their ammunition was running low.

"Bayonets, men," he shouted. "Let them feel the cold steel of Islam!"

The Israeli Scouts, seeing the carnage below, landed near the water tower just as Mir and his band came out screaming. Sergeant Zimmerman was the first to hit the ground. Putting his Uzi on full automatic, he leveled the first four men before he took a bayonet between his ribs. The other Scouts opened up on the remaining terrorists, killing all of them in a hail of fire. But, as quickly as the Israelis could kill them, more appeared.

On the southern end of the camp, the tide was beginning to turn against the Americans. The whole plan was predicated upon the Cobras and Nighthawks reducing the opposing force down to a manageable size. Clearly, that had not been accomplished. Two of the big Nighthawks now lay on the ground in flames and the others had been forced to land nearby to refuel for the flight home. Now, without air cover, Pete could sense the inevitable conclusion. "Medic, medic," came a constant chorus of cries as his remaining troops fought bravely on. Pete took a deep breath, then pulled out the black satellite phone handed to him by the Admiral before they took off. He then made a call he swore earlier he would never make.

"Brewster here."

"Admiral, we're taking heavy casualties. I'm afraid we just don't have enough men or firepower to finish this. This is going to end very badly if we don't get some immediate help!"

"OK, Watson, where are your men?"

"On the southern perimeter. The Israelis are on the north. It looks as if the heaviest resistance is coming from the main water tower in the middle of the camp, and at the base of the mountain."

"Give me your coordinates, Major, then start digging. As soon as I get a fix on the Israelis, I am launching the Tomahawks."

"Roger, and Admiral, thanks. I would never ask if I had any other option."

"I know that, son."

After Pete read off the position of his teams, he instructed them to retrench and bury their heads. "The cavalry is on its way, boys," he yelled into his headset. "Get down!"

For the Arabs facing the Americans, they felt victory at hand. The rate of incoming fire had diminished substantially in the past few moments, leading most of them to think the attackers were either dead or too badly wounded to fire. Slowly, they advanced, meeting no resistance.

The cruiser USS Melville's forward turret carried four Tomahawk cruise missiles. Activated by an automatic fire control system, the first missile was set to launch in 30 seconds.

Their guidance systems had been reprogrammed, using Pete's data. Accurate to within a radius of 50 feet, they would cover the distance to Murat in slightly less than six minutes.

"Fire," came the captain's voice.

"Fire one, fire two, fire three, fire four."

Four separate blasts lit up the cruiser as the Tomahawks each made their way skyward towards the coast. The resulting devastation was enormous. Four direct hits on the Arab positions left hundreds dead and wounded. Taking full advantage of the resulting chaos, the Americans and Israelis now came out of their foxholes. The stunned defenders, still in shock from the cruise missile strike, threw their weapons down and began running back towards the safety of their caves.

Seventeen miles away, Kahil pulled up completely out of breath as he watched the black helicopter landing a hundred yards to his right. He could not comprehend why the pilot was putting down, but then he saw some soldiers getting up in front of him ready to board. Illuminated in the tail was the blue and white Star of David. Something inside of him just burst. His hatred of the Israelis combined with the frustration of watching helplessly the total annihilation of his home was too much. Pushing his lever to automatic, he began running for the helicopter firing from his hip as he went. The gunner just behind the pilot saw him first.

"Get down! Enemy fire coming in," he yelled. The gunner then took aim on the flashes coming off the barrel. He slowly pulled the trigger on the big machine gun. Twenty rounds of 20mm projectiles ripped through the air literally disintegrating the big Arab into hundreds of flying bits of flesh and bones.

"Medic," screamed one of the Scouts, "The Major has been hit. Get over here."

They dragged Zev on board, his uniform riddled with bullets.

The medic jumped over several bodies to reach him. One look told him it was serious. Over his mic, he yelled to the pilot, "If we don't get him to the carrier now, we'll lose him for sure."

The pilot looked east as they gained altitude. After the cruise missiles hit, the firefight around the camp had diminished to sporadic and isolated cases of resistance. He put it to a vote.

"I'm heading back, anyone object? This fight is over."

"Get the Major back to the ship," was all that came back.

The pilot came around to the southwest, heading straight for the carrier force, pushing the Black Hawk to its maximum speed of 180 knots. Zev lay on a stretcher, both medics working feverishly trying to cauterize his exposed arteries.

Zev, having already received a full syringe of morphine, lay staring at the co-pilot who had come back to check on him. Unable to view the carnage, Zev asked plaintively, "Will I make it? How bad am I?"

"Don't worry, Major, we are heading straight back to the carrier. You know the Americans; they have a full hospital on board that big ship of theirs. They will fix you up like new. Just hang on for a few more minutes."

His optimism was short lived as he exchanged a silent glance with one of the medics. It was a look that said if you do not get us there very soon, he won't make it. Moving back into the right seat, he hooked on his headset, the pilot questioning Zev's status.

"Not good. He is losing too much blood. How much longer?"

"ETA is twenty-eight minutes. I've radioed ahead to let them know we have one critical on board. They are standing by for him."

"Let's pray he will still be with us."

The Black Hawk soon passed the coast, quickly catching sight of the massive carrier.

Descent Into Paradise

Zev was slowly losing consciousness. Sergeant Brandeiss, who had been holding his hand the entire flight, bent over to whisper in his ear. "Please hang in there, Major, we have the carrier in sight."

Zev smiled as he squeezed his friend's hand. "I can't die, Mort. I promised Annabelle I would marry her," he whispered. "I promised!"

"And you will keep that promise, sir. Hell, you are too tough to die, we all know that." But, as he spoke, the pressure on his hand began to lessen.

The pilots brought the chopper down hard and fast; a medical team was right there to take the wounded Major. None of the Israelis spoke as they disembarked. It was considered bad luck to make predictions.

The emergency room on board the Coral Sea was as well-equipped as any stateside. Two Navy surgeons were standing by when they brought Zev in. The chief nurse immediately inserted an IV into his left arm, pouring antibiotics and anesthesia through the needle. As she quickly removed his bloodstained uniform, the two surgeons went to work. Two bullets had torn a gaping hole in his abdominal cavity, while another had punctured his right lung.

Despite their frantic efforts, Zev never regained consciousness. He died on the operating table, 23 minutes after landing.

At Murat, the camp was eerily quiet, the last resistance finally overcome. Pete, blood oozing out of his wounded left thigh, limped over to his lieutenant.

"What's the body count?" he asked, his lips compressed with pain.

"Nothing definite, Major, it's heavy, I can tell you that."

"Get me a number and call in the birds."

Descent Into Paradise

Once the Iranian Air Force Base south of Tehran had picked up the four incoming cruise missiles, the Iranian commander had immediately called his superior to ask permission to launch his aircraft against the US Fleet.

"You have permission to launch your fighters, but do not initiate a direct attack without my express authority, understood?"

"Yes, sir."

The AWAC hovering over the fleet immediately picked up the Iranian fighters taking off.

"This is Scout One to leader, enemy fighters coming up."

"How many, Scout One?"

"Still counting." A few seconds later, the AWAC confirmed eight fighters airborne, but none heading directly for the fleet.

"Launch Hazard and Fireball. Get Lightning and Falcon up on deck."

The pilots of the two active F-18 fighter jets, already on the flight deck loaded and ready to go, now lit their afterburners and were catapulted skyward to join the four fighters already aloft.

Armed with an entire squadron of F18s, the Navy's newest and deadliest jet fighters, the Admiral was prepared to fight if necessary. "Track those choppers coming home. If those bogies get within missile range of our birds, or this fleet, my orders are to take them out."

Brewster had already committed himself by launching the Tomahawks. Hopefully, the Iranians would leave it alone and stand down.

Pete collected the last batch of papers out of the command bunker. He and his men had discovered an entire filing cabinet full of operational plans. Those plans, plus what looked like a personal diary found on the body of the commander himself, would prove an intelligence bonanza.

Descent Into Paradise

There was nothing they could do about the two downed choppers. The Iranians knew by now what had happened anyway, so they headed out to the waiting birds.

The wounded were flown out first, the body bags next, followed by those still able to walk.

"Choppers are heading our way, Admiral. One hundred kilometers out, doing 160 knots."

"Get that AWAC on the line."

"Scout One to leader. We have seven birds heading your way. Speed 160 knots, altitude 7500 feet. No enemy aircraft on intercept."

The Admiral took a deep breath. He now had six F-18 Hornets aloft, with two more ready to launch if needed. Those Iranians were dead if they made the wrong move.

The flight back to the Coral Sea went without incident, although the pilots were on constant lookout for any hostile fighters. All five landed safely, discharging their wounded into the already crowded medical facilities on board. Once he had been sewn together, Pete went to debrief the Admiral. In attendance were General Bragman and another Israeli major.

"Major," came the Admiral's booming voice from the back of the room. "Glad to have you back on board, son. Please make your report."

Pulling out his tally sheets, Pete gave his senior officer the grim news.

"As of 30 minutes ago, we have a total of fifteen dead. Seven more are seriously wounded, two critically, and another eighteen in sickbay for various injuries." Noticing the Major's heavily bandaged left leg, the Admiral inquired whether Major Watson had also checked in with the ship's medical staff?

"Yes, sir, I am counted amongst those mentioned."

"Go on, please."

Pete then detailed his part of the operation, giving particular credit to the impact of the Tomahawk strike. "Without that, I seriously doubt any of us would have survived." He then finished with an accounting of the intelligence files gathered. For the first time, a hint of a smile appeared on the Admiral's face.

"Let's hope we can nail these filthy bastards before we are all relieved of duty."

Motioning for Pete to sit, he apologized for keeping him standing. The relief was obvious by his worn expression.

Brewster then went on to recap the Israelis' report. "Twelve dead and 21 wounded, six severely. Quite a heavy toll for one night's fighting. Well done, gentlemen. I know I speak for every one of my sailors when I commend all of you for your bravery and courage under extreme duress. I'm sure you wish to rejoin your men, so please feel free to do so."

All three Special Forces officers limped down the metal stairs to rejoin their men. Before they parted ways, however, the Israeli General put his hand on Pete's shoulder. "I dislike being the bearer of bad news, Major, but I was informed shortly before entering the Admiral's quarters that Major Megrid was badly wounded during the attack. Although he made it back on board, his wounds were such that he died on the operating table."

"What did you say, General?"

"I said Major Megrid is dead. He died on board this ship just over an hour ago. I know you both were close. I am so very sorry. We will all miss him dearly."

Pete slumped down on the stairs, his wounded leg unable to carry him further. The Israeli general, respectful of his American counterpart, continued down the stairs, leaving him to grieve in private.

They left him alone for a period of time. Then several of his men gently helped him up and brought him into sickbay. The nurse left him in bed, sedated.

TEL AVIV

The television channels all carried the state funeral live. Blue and white flags were draped over the wooden coffins as the Prime Minister himself gave the eulogy.

"Today, we welcome home these brave sons of Israel. Fourteen young men who willingly gave up their lives so we could live ours in peace."

Pete and General Bragman, both in full dress uniform, stood at attention on either side of Zev's coffin. Every surviving member of Sayeret Matkin, including four men on crutches and one soldier in a wheelchair, were lined up directly behind. In the first row of the raised bleachers, both dressed in black, sat Shasa and Annabelle, neither able to hold back their tears. Shasa tried listening to the Prime Minister, but the only thought that crossed her dulled mind was poor Zev had to die to finally be accepted by the country of his birth. She looked up at the cloudless sky, silently asking Eileen and Papa to look after him.

Beside her, poor Annabelle could not stop sobbing. The great love of her life had somehow been taken away at its very birth. How cruel were the Gods of this wretched land. Placing a trembling hand upon her upset stomach, she softly prayed her beloved Zev had managed to leave a small piece of himself behind. Absorbed with this thought, she never heard the Prime Minister's closing remarks.

"May those who had the good fortune to know you now salute you. May those who follow know they do so in the footsteps of men whose courage and bravery will set an example for generations to come. The forces of evil will never cease to exist, as much as we wish it were so. But, this great Jewish nation will never succumb, for, as long as we breed such men willing to make the ultimate sacrifice to preserve this, the land of our forefathers, we shall prevail."

CHAPTER 72

Summer had come to Camden. The village was a visual garden. Hanging baskets adorned the top of every lamppost and virtually every shop had window boxes full of petunias, geraniums and cascading ivies. The lawns and trees were richly green with new growth. As Shasa walked towards the Community Hall of the orphanage, she was grateful that all their guests could experience a special Maine day, so clear you could see as far up the coast as Bar Harbor. The islands, out in Penobscot Bay, were shimmering in the sun as it reflected off the huge, granite boulders that formed the shorelines.

Annabelle and young Zev Jr. had flown in from England the previous week. Annabelle served as the matron of honor at Pete and Shasa's wedding, while Shasa had gone to England to be with Annabelle when her son was born. Most of the trustees of the orphanage had also come to attend this special occasion. Mary Riordan, who volunteered to assist with the fund raising, General Bradley, and Ambassador Holden had all arrived yesterday. Admiral Brewster had come all the way from San Diego to be with them as well as to visit his own grandchildren in Rockland, which was right down the road. The Admiral was always fun to have visit as he was a great favorite of all the children. The only board member missing was General Argov, who had assumed the role, upon his retirement, of locating young orphans in both Israel and Palestine. Despite his desire to attend, his doctor had forbidden his flying. His heart condition was now too advanced. La Bota, down in Miami, had volunteered to do

Descent Into Paradise

the same for South American children orphaned from drug related incidents. He flew up early, as he loved these trips to Maine.

When everyone was seated, Pete walked up to the stage banked in wild flowers and branches. All 50 children, scrubbed and neatly garbed for today's ceremony, watched in wonder as, for the first time since his marriage, he wore his full dress uniform.

Shasa couldn't help but admire her handsome husband as he began.

"Good morning everyone."

"Good morning Mr. Watson," came the happy chorus of children.

"Today, we are all here to celebrate the birthday of a very special man. Now I would like to share his story with you.

"This man, like all of you, grew up without parents. As a young boy, he was forced to watch as his mother was brutally murdered just yards from where he and his father were standing. She was killed because she came from a different country and believed in a different God. Afterwards, his father, unable to cope with raising a young boy by himself, moved away to a different country. My friend, now alone and unwanted, grew up in a small village, disliked by many who lived there. When he turned seventeen, he was asked to leave. Having nowhere to go, he left the only home he had ever known and joined the Army. He desperately wanted to be accepted, but alas, that would not be his fate. Instead, he died on the battlefield fighting for his country. Upon his death, he was awarded his nation's highest military honors.

"He died fighting for the right to live in a free society, free of terror, free of fear, and free of religious persecution."

He stopped to look down at the rapt young faces looking up at him. He then asked, "But do people die, or do they live

Descent Into Paradise

on? Christians are taught that Jesus lives on in all our hearts. I believe that. I also believe my friend lives on through all of us assembled here today. He asked that all of you be given a chance to succeed in life so that his life would not be in vain.

"Today, I would like to thank him. I thank him for his friendship, for guiding me when I was lost, and most of all for reminding me what matters most in life." Shasa could see the tears forming in his blue eyes as he looked straight at her.

"Thanks to his wisdom, I can stand here before you and tell you all what is most important to me. My wife." Then reaching out as if to embrace the whole congregation, he smiled, "And all my children. So today, on the day we remember Major Megrid for all he has done, let's say a prayer and thank him for bringing us together."

Shasa knelt down, her stomach protruding up against the next row of chairs. She put her hands together and silently prayed her unborn child, along with all these children, would be able to live in a world where they could go to sleep each night without fear, knowing the next morning they would still have a roof over their head. Most of all, she prayed they would have someone to tell them how important they were and how much they were loved. As she felt a tiny kick in her stomach, she heard all the children repeat after Pete, "Thank you Major Megrid, we love you."

Then, still kneeling, she prayed for both her families. Finally, she said a short prayer for those who had died by her own hand. She ended with a special thanks to her Papa, who had once reminded her, "Life is for living."

She slowly got up, took Pete's hand as they walked out of the hall, followed by the trustees and the children. From the youngest to the oldest they walked out into the beautiful morning, the sound of feet crunching down the white clamshell path to the dining room for lunch. As Shasa approached the main building, her eyes went up to the plaque above the entrance door.

The Megrid Orphanage
In Loving Memory of Zev Megrid
May He Rest in Peace

EPILOGUE

The raid produced a host of documents linking Murat directly to the terrorist bombings in Jerusalem, the kidnappings in Beirut, the death of the Israeli Ambassador in London, as well as the castration of the rabbi and wholesale slaughter of his congregation.

Iran issued a sharply worded protest to the United Nations condemning the flagrant violation of its air space, but it never took any direct military action against the US fleet or Israel.

Admiral Brewster retired shortly after returning to San Diego, thereby eliminating the need for any formal censure for his controversial actions during the Murat raid.

In sympathy, General Bradley also retired. Unhappy with the laissez-faire attitude of the new White House, he preferred doing battle with his rose garden in Roanoke, Virginia.

Juan Rios, whose compound had miraculously escaped any damage from an errant US cruise missile attack, continued his international expansion, eventually overtaking the Colombians as the largest drug dealer in terms of pure volume. The fact he now controlled most of the non-Asian opium supply certainly had played a major role.

His ongoing ties with to the Islamic extremists, both in the Middle East and in North Africa, became a well-documented fact at Mossad, if not the CIA.

Sheik Bashir used his initial successes to garner support throughout the Muslim world. With the aid of Yemen's new worldwide broadcasting abilities, they were able to recruit scores of young men, eager to throw away their lives for the greater glory of Islam. Financed by powerful factions within the Arab world,

Bashir's forces soon became the predominant terrorist network in the Middle East region. Given the effective retirement of both Major Watson and General Bradley, combined with questionable leadership from the White House, the American anti-terrorist efforts never fully recovered.

La Bota, operating without ongoing support from General Bradley's former task force, launched his own campaign against the Rios group in his beloved Mexico. He, however, along with two of his top lieutenants, were killed in Acapulco when their car mysteriously blew up.

Annabelle, with her son Zev Jr., moved to a small village outside of Oxford, England, where young Zev now attends an English public school. Every summer, Annabelle travels with her son to visit Israel. There, high up on a hill overlooking the Mediterranean, exists a small plot of land where, marked by a grove of magnificent olive trees, lies the resting spot for both her parents. Right behind them, a beautiful polished granite tombstone carries the inscription

HERE LIES ONE OF ISRAEL'S GREAT HEROES
MAJOR ZEV MEGRID

A small patch of grass just adjacent awaits the day Annabelle will be able to join them and reunite with the great love of her life.